Praise for Irene Hannon and her novels

"Irene Hannon's *The Way Home*
is such a delightful read with some great
scenes. Both the conflict and pacing are right
on, while the realism and tenderness draws
you into their story."
—*Romantic Times BOOKreviews*

"*The Unexpected Gift*…is absolutely stellar.
Unique characters exude warmth, and the
ending will leave readers with tears of joy."
—*Romantic Times BOOKreviews*

"Irene Hannon's *Gift from the Heart*
is a beautifully written love story filled
with faith and blessings for both
the characters and the reader."
—*Romantic Times BOOKreviews*

IRENE HANNON

A Groom of Her Own

The Way Home

Steeple
Hill®

Published by Steeple Hill Books™

STEEPLE HILL BOOKS

Steeple Hill®

ISBN-13: 978-0-373-65270-9
ISBN-10:   0-373-65270-4

A GROOM OF HER OWN AND THE WAY HOME

A GROOM OF HER OWN
Copyright © 1998 by Irene Hannon

THE WAY HOME
Copyright © 2000 by Irene Hannon

www.SteepleHill.com

Printed in U.S.A.

CONTENTS

Books by Irene Hannon

Love Inspired

†Vows
* Sisters & Brides

IRENE HANNON

is an award-winning author who has been a writer for as long as she can remember. She "officially" launched her career at the age of ten, when she was one of the winners in a "complete-the-story" contest conducted by a national children's magazine. More recently, Irene won the coveted RITA® Award for her 2002 Love Inspired book, *Never Say Goodbye*. Irene, who spent many years in an executive corporate communications position with a Fortune 500 company, now devotes herself full-time to her writing career. In her "spare" time, she enjoys performing in community musical theater productions, singing in the church choir, gardening, cooking and spending time with family and friends. She and her husband, Tom—whom she describes as "my own romantic hero"—make their home in Missouri.

A GROOM OF HER OWN

Ask, and it shall be given you; seek, and ye shall find; knock, and it shall be opened unto you.

—*Matthew* 7:7

To Tom
My Perfect Valentine

Chapter One

ᗕ

"Well, kiddo, this is it." Sam Reynolds gently edged the door closed behind Laura Taylor's mother and turned to face her best friend.

"Oh, Sam, I can't believe it's really happening!" Laura's eyes glistened suspiciously in her radiant face, and Sam felt her own throat contract. If anyone deserved a happy ending, it was the woman standing across from her. Sam wouldn't have laid odds on it, though. After trying mightily—but unsuccessfully—for years to find a man for Laura, she'd practically given up hope of ever seeing her best friend walk down the aisle. But in the end Laura surprised her by finding Nick Sinclair on her own—with a little help from fate.

"Well, I'm your witness. Literally," Sam said with a grin. "It's real, all right. And you look absolutely beautiful. I don't think I've ever seen a more radiant bride."

"Do you really think so?"

"See for yourself." She put her hands on Laura's shoulders and turned her to face the full-length mirror on the far wall.

Laura gazed at the woman in the reflection, hardly recognizing the image as her own. Her peach-colored tealength gown highlighted her slender curves and accentuated her femininity. The satin underslip softly hugged her body, and the lace gown overlay, with short, slightly gathered sleeves and a sweetheart neckline, had a quaint old-fashioned air that suited Laura. She wore her strawberry blond hair loose and full, the way Nick liked it, pulled back on one side with a small cluster of flowers and ribbon. Her bouquet was simple, a trailing arrangement of ivory and peach roses intertwined with ivy and wispy fern. It was a lovely ensemble, perfect for a second wedding, and she was grateful to Sam for helping her find it. But what she noticed most as she gazed in the mirror was her face, glowing and content and happy.

"Oh, Sam, is that really me?" she whispered. "I look...well...pretty."

Sam moved beside her and placed an arm around her shoulders. "Honey, *pretty* is a gross understatement. Try *ravishing, drop-dead gorgeous* and *fantastic*, and you might come a little closer." She shook her head and chuckled. "Wait'll Nick gets an eyeful!"

Laura reached for her purse and fished out a tissue. "I'm so happy it's almost scary," she admitted, dabbing at her eyes.

"Hey, hey, hey, no tears!" Sam said. "Your mascara will run and you'll look like a racoon. Not a pretty picture, let me tell you. You can cry after the reception—although by then I think you'll have better things to do," she said with a knowing wink that brought a blush to the bride's face.

A discreet knock sounded on the door, and Laura's brother, John, stuck his head inside. "Ladies, it's your cue."

Sam gave Laura's hand one more squeeze. "You'll knock their socks off, kiddo," she whispered. "And if you don't believe me, just watch Nick when you walk down that aisle."

She moved toward the door, pausing in front of the mirror to cast a quick, discerning glance at her own reflection. The pencil-slim skirt and short-sleeved peplum jacket of her pale sea green brocade suit showed off her fashionably slender figure to perfection, and the color complemented her shoulder-length red hair. She adjusted the peplum, smoothed down a few stray strands of hair and gave her expertly applied makeup one final inspection. Then she turned and winked at Laura encouragingly. "Okay, here we go."

Sam stepped into the vestibule and took her place behind the double doors that led to the church. She heard the organ music pause, then change melodies, and a moment later two of the ushers pulled back the heavy doors.

As Sam made her way past the sea of smiling faces in the small church, she was struck by the romantic ambiance. The deeply fragrant scent of rubrum lilies filled the air, and wispy greenery anchored with white bows trailed from the ends of the pews. Late afternoon light illuminated the stained glass windows, which in turn cast a mosaic of warm, muted colors on the rich wood floor. It was a beautiful and appropriate setting, Sam thought appreciatively.

The icing on the cake, of course, was Nick Sinclair. She

looked at him as she moved down the aisle, and he smiled at her. Tall, handsome, charming—those words accurately described him. But he was also a patient, caring, decent man. In other words, exactly what Laura deserved. She smiled back with a small, approving nod, which he acknowledged with a wink.

Nick's best man and business partner, Jack, met her at the altar and offered his arm. As they took their places, the organ music faded and an expectant rustle filled the church as the guests turned for their first glimpse of the bride.

When the doors opened and Laura and her brother stepped forward to the majestic strains of "Trumpet Tune," Sam glanced again at Nick. The tenderness and love she saw in his eyes made her throat constrict. What must it be like to be loved like that? she wondered, turning to look back at Laura, whose gaze was locked on Nick's. Clearly they had eyes only for each other. For the eleven years she and Laura had been friends, Sam had never seen such peace and joy and confidence on Laura's face. Little wonder, considering the trauma she'd had to overcome. But with Nick's help, Laura had found the courage to put her past behind her and look with hope to the future. Sam was happy for her.

What surprised Sam was the tangle of other emotions that suddenly overwhelmed her. Sadness, for one. In the excitement of the last few weeks she'd had little time to reflect on exactly what this marriage meant to *her*. Now, as she watched Laura walk down the aisle and take her place beside Nick, she realized that while their friendship was solid and would endure, change was inevitable now that Laura was becoming Nick's wife. Laura wouldn't need Sam as much anymore, and that knowledge brought with it an unexpected sense of emptiness.

She also discovered that she was jealous, and that jolted her. She certainly didn't begrudge Laura her happiness. It was just that she longed for her own happy ending, futile as that wish was. She wondered if Laura ever stopped to think how odd it was that Sam, the vivacious partyer with more dates than she could keep track of, had never re-married. What Laura didn't know, of course, was that Sam's life-style was a sham, a pretense, a way to keep the loneliness at bay—not an attempt to find the right man, as she always claimed. Because there was no right man for her.

Sam glanced around at the small group clustered in the chancel. Nick and Laura now had a lifetime to look for-ward to as a married couple. Jack, the best man, was hap-pily married, with a lovely wife and children. Her gaze moved to the minister, an attractive man with sandy brown hair touched with silver, who looked to be in his late thirties or early forties. Even he had a ring on.

Suddenly Sam felt more alone than she had in years. Alone and lonely and empty. Laura would find that hard to believe, she knew. Through the years Sam had made no secret of the fact that she led a very active social life. By entertaining Laura with tales of her various dates and drag-ging her into the singles scene, Sam had hoped to convince Laura that *she* needed a social life. But Laura never bought it. With her faith providing a solid foundation, she'd found her own quiet way to deal with loneliness.

And maybe her way was better, Sam thought dispirit-edly. Because while Sam's frenzied social life kept her busy, it didn't ease the deeper loneliness. If anything, it left her feeling lonelier than before. The men she dated were out for a *good* time, not a *life* time. Which was fine, of course. It was safer to avoid dating the kind of man she might want to settle down with—stable, not afraid of commitment, caring. Because she might fall in love, and she didn't deserve someone like that. At the same time, she wasn't willing to settle for anything less. Which meant, bottom line, that she would spend her life alone.

Unaccustomed tears of self-pity welled up in Sam's eyes, taking her off guard. She usually kept her emotions in check, hidden beneath the brassy, irreverent veneer that had been her protection for more years than she cared to remember. She closed her eyes, willing the tears to evaporate, then blinked rapidly, struggling for control.

Suddenly Sam realized that the minister was looking at her.

"The ring," he prompted softly, in a tone that indicated he'd made the request more than once.

Sam blinked again and removed the ring from her right pinkie, where it was hidden by her bouquet. As she moved forward and handed it to him, he looked at her questioningly.

"Are you all right?" he asked in an undertone.

She felt Laura's concerned eyes on her and somehow managed a shaky smile. "I'm fine."

Sam stepped back, her face flushed, embarrassed to have caused even a slight glitch in what was otherwise a perfect ceremony. She forced herself to focus on the moment, listening intently as the minister spoke.

"On behalf of Laura and Nick, I want to welcome you here today to witness their declaration of love and their pledge to spend the rest of their earthly days together," he said. He had a pleasant voice, mellow and soothing, and Sam felt calmer just listening to it. "I know it means a great deal to them to have so many friends and family members here to share this very special day. Their marriage is indeed a joyful event that we all celebrate.

"Witnessing a wedding is always an honor. It is an event marked with hope and love and commitment, and there are too few of those in today's world. But witnessing this wedding is a special honor for me. As many of you know, Laura and I share the same hometown. Her brother, John, and I are good friends, and through him I became acquainted with the whole family. So while I've been Laura's minister ever since she came to St. Louis, some fifteen years ago, I was her friend long before that.

"Through the years my respect for Laura as a woman and as a Christian has continued to grow. For all of us who are fortunate enough to know her, she is an inspiring example of what it means to lead a Christian life. I know that she will also be an inspiring example of what it means to be a Christian wife.

"I've known Nick for only a few months, but I have come to realize that he is a fine and caring man. I know he will love and honor Laura with a commitment and a steadfastness that will add richness and dimension to both of their lives.

"I think it's appropriate that Laura and Nick chose today—the first day of spring—as their wedding day. For both of them it marks a new beginning, a new life, a season of beauty and growth and hope, a new direction in their earthly journey. And that journey will hold challenges. Because as all of us know, the road of life isn't always easy or straight. We make wrong turns, we take detours, we hit roadblocks, we have flat tires. But as long as we keep our eyes focused on the destination, and as long as we are willing to listen to the Lord's direction, we can find our way home.

"Laura and Nick know their ultimate destination. They know the Lord will always be there to guide them. They've known that, individually, all of their lives. But now, as man and wife, they will have an earthly partner to help when the journey gets rough, as well as a friend with whom to share all the moments of joy and beauty that the Lord blesses us with along the way. I know that all of you join with me today in wishing Nick and Laura Godspeed on their journey as a married couple. And now let us pray...."

Sam stared at the minister, mesmerized by his rich, well-modulated voice and the words he'd spoken. His remarks were the most insightful, moving and comforting she'd ever heard in a church—a far cry from the "fire and brimstone" sermons she remembered as a child. For the first time Sam looked—really looked—at his face. He was actually quite handsome, she realized. And appealing in a way she couldn't exactly pinpoint. He seemed to radiate an innate character and kindness that spoke of trust and integrity. She frowned as she tried to recall his name. Laura had introduced them at the rehearsal the night before, but Sam hadn't been paying that much attention. It wasn't a "religious" name, she remembered that. Bill? Brent? Brad! That was it. Brad Matthews. Before the day was over she would find an opportunity to compliment him on his talk.

As it turned out, Sam didn't have a minute to herself until hours later. After the ceremony there'd been pictures, then the drive to the reception, then more pictures, a receiving line and finally dinner. All of this was followed by the bride and groom's first dance, the wedding party dance and the cake cutting. But finally the ceremonies and rituals were over. Maybe now she could find a quiet spot for a moment and take a deep breath, she thought hopefully.

Except that Laura's cousin intercepted her as she was searching for just such a spot. Sam tried to be polite, tried to focus on what the woman was saying, but she was suddenly bone weary, tired of smiling and plagued once again with the feeling of emptiness that had overwhelmed her during the ceremony. The melodic strains of Gershwin's "Our Love Is Here to Stay" drifted through the room, and she glanced at the dance floor to find Laura and Nick in each other's arms, moving as one to the music. The tenderness in Nick's eyes as he gazed at Laura was suddenly too much for her, and with a mumbled apology to Laura's cousin, Sam fled toward the terrace. Maybe some fresh air would help chase away the blues. At least it was worth a try.

Brad Matthews jammed his hands into the pockets of his slacks and leaned against the wall, breathing deeply of the chilly air. It had been a nice wedding, and he was happy for Laura and Nick. They made a wonderful couple, and he knew that their life together would be full and rich. He prayed that they would be blessed with the children they both wanted and that the Lord would give them a long and happy life together. They deserved it.

But so had he and Rachel, he thought sadly. They would have made good parents, he was sure of it. And their love would have endured, standing as an example for others in this day of quickly forgotten commitments. But the Lord had other plans for them.

For the first time in a long while Brad allowed himself to remember his own wedding day. Rachel had made a beautiful bride, he recalled with a tender smile. She had been absolutely radiant as she'd walked down the aisle to meet him. Theirs had been a union of kindred spirits, firmly based on a strong Christian faith and the ability to find joy in the simple pleasures of life. They had eagerly looked forward to starting a family and creating a legacy of love for their children.

Brad's smile faded. Even after six years, the pain of Rachel's untimely death still made him feel physically ill. Not a day went by that he didn't miss her lovely smile or her musical laugh. His work usually kept him too busy to allow time for self-pity, but occasionally something would trigger memories that made him feel his loss as keenly as if it had happened yesterday. Laura's wedding had done that.

But it had done something else as well. For the first time since Rachel's death, Brad acknowledged that although his work was fulfilling, something was missing. No, he corrected himself, make that "someone." Because Brad had enjoyed such a wonderful marriage, he knew what it was like to share the day-to-day joys and sorrows with another person. And he missed that.

Would it be possible, he wondered, to find love again? Could there be someone else like Rachel somewhere out there? And what would Rachel say about it? Would she be hurt? Would she think he was being disloyal if he remarried?

Brad had never asked those questions before. Even when Rachel was alive, they'd been so young that they'd never discussed the subject. Death had seemed like such a remote possibility. But how would he feel were the situation reversed? he asked himself. Would he want Rachel to live the rest of her life alone? The answer was simple: Of course not. To deny her the chance to give expression to her bountiful love, to condemn her to living a solitary life just because he didn't want to share her with someone else, would be selfish. And he suddenly knew with absolute certainty that if she could speak to him, she would tell him that she felt the same way, that it was time for him to move on.

Yet Rachel still felt like such a part of his life. How did a person let go? As a minister, Brad knew he was supposed to have those kinds of answers. But suddenly he didn't feel at all like a minister. He just felt like a very lonely man.

As Sam stepped onto the dimly lit terrace, she realized that the late-March air had cooled considerably with the setting of the sun. Unfortunately, the short sleeves and sweetheart neckline of her suit didn't offer much protection from the chill. She shivered and wrapped her arms around her body for warmth. It was silly to stand out here and freeze, but she couldn't plunge back into the festivities just yet. For someone who was usually in control, the unexpected whirlwind of emotions she'd been experiencing all day was disconcerting, leaving her feeling off balance and confused, and she needed to regain her equilibrium. She sniffed, struggling once more to hold back the tears, and groped in the pocket of her jacket for a tissue.

"Excuse me...is everything all right?"

Startled, Sam gasped and spun around. Brad Matthews stood in the shadows, a few feet away, watching her intently. She had no idea how long he'd been there, but it was apparently long enough for him to realize that she was upset. Embarrassed for the second time that day, Sam turned away, struggling to compose her face, grateful for the dim light on the terrace.

The voice moved closer. "I'm sorry if I startled you."

Sam took a deep breath. "It's okay. I just didn't expect anyone else to be out here. It's pretty chilly."

Sam heard fabric sliding over fabric, then felt a jacket being draped over her shoulders. It still radiated body warmth, and she gratefully drew it around her even as she protested. "I shouldn't take this. You'll freeze."

"I'll be fine," he assured her. "You seem to need it more than I do."

This time Sam successfully retrieved the tissue and dabbed at her eyes. She was struck by the man's insight. When he'd realized she was cold, he hadn't suggested going back inside, as many people would have done. He seemed to understand that she needed some distance from the festivities, and had instead offered her his coat. She found that touching, and once again her eyes blurred with tears.

Brad frowned as he stared at the back of the woman in front of him. Laura often talked of Sam, and Brad had formed what he'd assumed was a fairly accurate picture of the bride's best friend. Physically, he was pretty much on target. Sophisticated makeup, svelte figure, striking hair. Not quite as tall as he'd expected, though. She was a good four inches shorter than he, with heels, and he was just under six feet. He thought she'd be statuesque. But it was the demeanor and personality that really surprised him. Laura always talked admiringly of Sam's composure and self-confidence, described her as the strong, invincible type who was never thrown by anything and never at a loss for words. But the woman who had nearly gone to pieces at the wedding and who now stood silent and shaky an arm's length away didn't fit that image at all.

Brad debated his next move. Should he discreetly disappear or, as was his nature when people were in trouble, offer his help? The decision was easier than he thought, because when she sniffed again he spoke automatically.

"I'm sorry if I'm intruding, but…is there anything I can do?" he asked gently.

She shook her head. "I'm fine, really," she assured him, but she knew her shaky voice belied her words. Desperately she tried to think of a reasonable explanation for her teary state. "I'm just a sucker for happy endings," she offered, grasping at the first idea that came to her.

Brad didn't quite buy that. The Sam he'd heard about from Laura might be moved, but she'd hide it behind a flippant remark. She wouldn't cry. There was something else going on here, but he was a stranger to her, and the best he could do was empathize.

"I know what you mean. You know, I think we witnessed a real miracle today. I honestly wasn't sure if Laura would ever risk that kind of commitment again."

"Me, neither," Sam agreed with a sniff. "But I knew if she met the right man she might, and I sure tried to get her into circulation."

The minister chuckled. "So I heard."

Sam wiped her nose and turned to stare at him suspiciously. "What exactly did you hear?"

"She told me about a few of the singles dances you dragged her to. I just can't picture Laura at one of those things."

"She never did feel comfortable," Sam agreed, and he saw the ghost of a smile flicker across her face.

"You know, I realize we were introduced last night at the rehearsal, but it was all pretty rushed. So how about if we start over?" He held out his hand. "I'm Brad Matthews. And you're Sam Reynolds. It's very nice to meet you."

Sam took his hand. It was firm and strong, yet there was a warmth and tenderness in his touch that she found appealing.

"It's nice to meet you, too." She paused, and he sensed that she was searching for words, an experience that was obviously foreign to the usually glib Sam. "You know, ever since the ceremony this afternoon I've been wanting to tell you how wonderful I thought your talk was," she said slowly. "I've never heard anything quite that moving in church before."

"Thank you."

"I really mean it," she said earnestly, reaching out to touch his arm, wanting him to know that her words weren't just an empty compliment. For some reason, that was important to her. "I've never been much of a churchgoer, Reverend, but if there were more ministers like you I might have been."

Brad took her hand between his, engulfing it in a warm clasp. She had small, delicate fingers, and again he was struck by this woman's unexpected and touching vulnerability. "I appreciate that, Sam," he said with quiet sincerity.

For a moment there was silence, and the strains of "Till There Was You" drifted through the slightly ajar door. For some reason, Sam felt less lonely now. Maybe it was the way this man was holding her hand, his touch conveying caring and warmth and compassion. It had been a long time since a man had touched her like this with something other than sex on his mind. And it felt good. Very good. Too good. It was going to make her teary eyed again.

Reluctantly she withdrew her hand and slipped his coat from her shoulders. She'd monopolized enough of his time, anyway.

"Thank you for the loan," she said, holding the coat out to him. "It certainly came in handy. But I really should let you get back inside. Your wife is probably looking for you by now."

There was a moment of silence, and she could see even through the dimness that he was frowning. "My wife?"

Now it was Sam's turn to frown. "I noticed in church that you were wearing a ring and…well, it looked like a wedding ring," she said uncertainly.

"Oh." He glanced down and touched the gold band. Then he sighed. "Yes, it is. But my wife died six years ago."

Sam stared at him, her eyes growing wide. "I'm so sorry," she said softly.

"Thank you." He looked down again at the ring, and his face was deeply shadowed when he spoke. "The ring confuses a lot of people. I suppose I should take it off, but I've never seen a reason to. Rachel is still part of my life, even though she's gone."

"It sounds like you have wonderful memories," Sam said wistfully. Then she turned away, and when she spoke again there was a trace of bitterness in her voice. "I couldn't get my ring off fast enough."

"Laura mentioned you were married, once," he said carefully.

"Yeah." She gave a mirthless laugh. "I always used to tell her we married two losers. Randy was a rat, plain and simple. He just walked out on me one day after only five months and never came back, even though…" She cut herself off sharply, shocked that she'd almost revealed a secret she'd never shared with anyone, not even Laura! What was wrong with her today?

Brad waited a moment, and when it became apparent that Sam wasn't going to continue, he spoke. "Weddings can be an emotional time—for the guests as well as the bride and groom. They stir up lots of memories, good and bad," he remarked quietly.

Sam looked at him again, struck once more by his insightfulness and empathy. But unlike her memories, she was sure his were happy.

"Well, life goes on," he said. "Laura should be an example to us. She finally found the courage to stop letting the past control her future, and look at the happiness she's found."

"Not everyone is that lucky, Reverend," Sam replied sadly, turning away once more to stare into the darkness.

Brad knew that Sam was close to tears again. He also sensed that whatever troubled her was a deeper issue than could be dealt with tonight. But at least he could try to cheer her up. "I'll tell you what," he said. "Suppose you stop calling me Reverend and start calling me Brad. Then maybe I can ask you to dance.''

Sam's head snapped around and she stared at him. ''Dance?''

''Ministers can dance. It's allowed,'' he teased.

Sam found herself smiling. ''I appreciate the offer. But you don't have to do that. I'm fine.''

''Don't you like to dance?''

''Well, yes, but…'' Her voice trailed off.

He grinned. ''But not with ministers?''

''It's not that,'' she said quickly. ''Actually, I've never danced with a minister.''

''Well, if I promise not to preach while we polka, will you give it a try? Because, to be honest, I've been wanting to ask you all night but I just didn't have the nerve.''

''Are you serious?'' she asked incredulously.

''Would a preacher lie?'' he asked solemnly. Okay, so he'd stretched the truth a little. He *had* hoped to have the opportunity to speak with her, though, considering how upset she'd been in church earlier in the day. But the invitation to dance was a spur-of-the-moment idea.

''Well…if you really want to, sure, that would be great.''

''I wouldn't have asked if I hadn't wanted to. Let's catch the next number. Maybe it will be a nice fox-trot.''

Brad pushed the door open and guided her inside, his hand at the small of her back. Sam liked the nonthreatening and protective feel of it. It was…nice.

As they reached the dance floor, the band swung into ''In the Mood,'' and Sam turned to Brad with a grin. ''So much for your fox-trot. That's okay. We can skip. But I appreciate the offer.'' She started to turn away, but he grabbed her hand and she looked around in surprise.

"You're not getting off that easy. Is this number too much for you?'' he challenged with a smile, his eyes twinkling.

"No, of course not,'' she stammered. "It's just... well...fast. It's a swing number,'' she pointed out.

"I know. I'm game if you are.''

Sam grinned and shrugged. She was beginning to really like this preacher. "Okay.''

By the time the number ended, Sam was gasping and laughing all at once. "You are really good!'' she said. "Where did you learn to dance like that?''

"I haven't always been a minister,'' he reminded her. He looked around and then dropped his voice conspiratorially. "Can I tell you a secret, Sam?

She leaned closer. "Sure.''

"Ministers are really just regular people. For example, even though you may think I dance divinely—no pun intended—I can't carry a tune in a bucket. My sister inherited the voice in the family. But I love to sing, and it drives Rose, our choir director, crazy. She just hasn't figured out a way to diplomatically tell me to shut up. She thinks ministers are specially blessed or something and she'll incur the wrath of heaven if she insults me. So if you ever meet her, don't let on that I'm just an ordinary guy.''

Sam giggled and shook her head. "I've never met a minister like you.''

"I'll take that as a compliment.'' He paused as the band struck up the opening notes of "As Time Goes By,'' and then he smiled. "Now there's our fox-trot. And that song is too good to pass up. How about one more dance before I call it a night?''

"Are you leaving already?" Sam asked, suddenly disappointed.

"I'm afraid so," he replied regretfully. "I've got an early service tomorrow. Shall we?"

He held out his arms, and Sam moved into them. The last dance had been exhilarating and loud and fast. This one was slow and…different. Brad held her close—closer than she expected for a minister—as they moved to the romantic melody. She could smell the scent of his aftershave, feel the slight stubble on his chin against her temple. She felt…strange. But good. He was a nice man. And it was nice to be with a nice man, even if only for a little while.

Brad hadn't danced in a long time. A very long time. He was surprised the steps came back so easily. But then, he and Rachel had liked to dance. She had been a good dancer. Tall, with the build of a ballerina, she had been almost eye level with him when they danced. Sam was smaller, the top of her head barely brushing his mouth. And she was soft. She smelled good, too, and instinctively he tightened his hold.

Brad grinned ruefully as he considered the situation. If someone had told him a few hours ago that he'd end the evening on the dance floor with Sam Reynolds, Laura's flamboyant, uninhibited and—he hated to think it, but the term came unbidden—hot-to-trot friend, he would have stared at them in surprise. But then, he'd been surprised by a number of things about Sam tonight. He'd seen a vulnerable, insecure side of the woman in his arms that he had a feeling even Laura had never seen, and he'd had to revise his image of her. He didn't know exactly who Sam really was, but he suddenly suspected that she wasn't quite what she seemed to be to the world.

When the music ended, he stepped back and glanced down. Her green eyes looked soft and appealing and suddenly bereft, and he was surprised by the sudden rush of tenderness that swept over him. He took her hand once more, cradling it between his. "Thank you, Sam. I enjoyed the dance."

"So did I," she said, her voice unusually husky and tinged with regret now that it was over. It had felt good in this man's arms. Protected, somehow, and safe.

"Is someone taking you home?"

"Yes. Laura's brother, John."

"Then I guess I'll say—"

"Sam, I've been looking for you! Brad, are you still here? I thought you left half an hour ago," Laura's surprised voice interrupted them.

Brad transferred his gaze to Laura and grinned. "I got sidetracked."

"Well, don't sleep through your own sermon tomorrow," Laura warned with a laugh before turning her attention to Sam. "I wanted to say goodbye, and I was afraid I'd miss you. Nick's getting anxious to leave."

"*Anxious* isn't exactly the word I'd use, and leaving isn't the reason for it...but it'll do," Nick said with a chuckle as he came up behind Laura and wrapped his arms around her waist. When he pulled her back against him, she blushed becomingly.

Sam laughed. "Laura, the man has been patient beyond belief. Why don't you put him out of his misery?"

Laura's face went an even deeper shade of pink. "Will you two stop? There's a minister present."

Nick looked at Brad, and the two men smiled at each other. "I think Brad understands," Nick assured her, and then he leaned down and nuzzled her neck. "But just so I don't look too…anxious…how about one more dance?" he murmured huskily.

Laura turned to look up at him, her eyes shining. "I'd like that," she said softly. With an effort, she tore her gaze away from Nick and stepped toward Sam, drawing her friend into a warm embrace. "Thank you," she whispered, knowing that Sam would understand the wealth of meaning in those simple words.

Sam hugged her tightly, blinking rapidly to keep the tears at bay. She would not cry, she told herself fiercely. Not now. Not in front of everyone. The cool, composed, wisecracking Sam Reynolds wouldn't cry, she reminded herself. It would ruin her reputation.

With a superhuman effort, she steadied her emotions and stepped back. "Have a wonderful honeymoon, you two. And try to get at least a little sleep," she added, forcing her lips to turn up into a smile.

"Now *that* I can't guarantee," Nick replied with a grin, taking Laura's hand and urging her gently toward the dance floor. "Come on, Mrs. Sinclair. Let's have that dance so we can get started on the honeymoon."

Sam watched them move naturally into each other's arms, as if they belonged there, and she sighed. "They look so right together, don't they?" she remarked wistfully.

"Yes, they do," Brad agreed, aware that Sam's emotions were once more on precarious ground. Again he was surprised at the contradiction between the woman across from him and his preconceived image of her.

Suddenly Sam frowned and turned to him. "Laura said you were planning to leave earlier. I must be the one to blame for keeping you here. I'm sorry."

"Don't be," he assured her. "As a rule I do try to get home at a reasonable hour on Saturday nights so I'm coherent for the early service. But after hearing about you all these years I'm glad we finally had the chance to get better acquainted."

"I've heard about you, too. But…can I tell you something?" she said impulsively. "You're not what I expected. Even though Laura said you were nice, my only experience with preachers is the fire and brimstone variety. Sort of intimidating and 'holier than thou,' you know?"

Brad smiled. "I think so. I've met a few of those myself. But hopefully they're a vanishing breed. And as long as we're playing true confessions, I'll admit that you're not what I expected, either. So we're even."

Sam looked at him thoughtfully. He didn't elaborate, and she was tempted to ask what he had expected. But she could imagine. For years she'd cultivated the image of a swinger. She purposely let Laura believe that she shared more than her time with the many men she dated. So it was reasonable to assume that while Laura may have talked to her minister in a positive light about their friendship, somewhere along the way the "swinger" image had been conveyed as well. For the first time, and for reasons she didn't quite understand, it bothered her that someone thought she wasn't exactly the girl-next-door type.

Brad, watching her face, accurately assessed her train of thought and decided to make a hasty exit before the blunt, outspoken Sam that Laura admired resurfaced and asked the question he knew was on her mind—and which he wasn't prepared to answer. He reached for her hand and cradled it between his. "Good night, Sam. And thank you for the dances. I enjoyed them."

Sam swallowed, her emotions once more close to the surface. "Thanks. I did, too." She tried to think of a typical "Sam" remark, something witty and lighthearted, but her gift for repartee seemed to desert her when she was around this man.

"Take care, okay?" he said, his warm, insightful brown eyes locked on hers.

"Sure."

He let go of her hand then, and Sam immediately missed the warmth of his caring touch. With one more smile, he turned and disappeared into the crowd.

Sam watched him leave. Now she understood why Laura always spoke so highly of her minister and why she turned to him in times of trouble for comfort and guidance. He had a gift for making a person feel that everything was going to be all right, that he really cared. Too bad Sam hadn't known someone like him seventeen years ago, she thought with a sigh. Maybe things would have turned out differently. Maybe...but it was too late for maybes, she reminded herself sharply. At thirty-five, seventeen years was almost a whole lifetime ago. She couldn't change what had happened. It was too late for amends, for regrets, for...a lot of things.

She looked at Nick and Laura on the dance floor, and once more she found herself envying her best friend's happiness. Which was wrong. Because Laura deserved a happy ending. Sam didn't. It was as simple as that. And as final.

Chapter Two

Sam deposited two bags of groceries on the breakfast room table with a thud, pushed her damp hair out of her eyes and shrugged off her dripping raincoat. Too bad the April showers had decided to arrive a few days early, she thought ruefully, although the gloomy weather suited her mood. She shivered and moved the thermostat up, hoping the heat would kick in quickly and take the chill out of her condo. It felt more like February than the end of March, she concluded in disgust as she fished in one of the bags for the mail she'd picked up on her way in.

As she flipped disinterestedly through the stack, a colorful postcard with a picture of a white sand beach and blue skies, framed by brilliantly colored flowers, caught her eye. She paused with a smile. Laura. Eagerly she flipped it over and scanned the contents, coming to the obvious conclusion: Nick and Laura's Hawaiian honeymoon was a resounding success.

Sam propped the card on the windowsill and gazed out at the gray, sodden landscape, her smile fading. She could use a little tropical sun herself about now, she thought wistfully. The idea of spending the afternoon stretched out on a beach, caressed by warm solar rays, instead of traipsing from one house to another with a hard-to-please client, was very appealing. And also totally unrealistic, she reminded herself. Not that she couldn't afford a trip to Hawaii. That was within her reach. Sharing it with a new husband who had pledged to love her for the rest of her life was not.

Wearily Sam put the kettle on the stove, hoping a soothing cup of tea would improve her mood. Ever since the wedding, she'd been on an emotional roller coaster, up one minute, down the next. But mostly down. It wasn't like her. Even a few of her colleagues had noticed her uncharacteristic melancholy, asking her if she was feeling okay. She had to get a grip, she told herself sternly. It wasn't the end of the world. She had been alone before the wedding. She was alone now. Nothing had changed in her life. Her situation was exactly the same as before.

And that, she realized with a sudden pang, was precisely the problem. That, and the fact that it would *never* change. Laura had found her happy ending. She had a wonderful husband and, unless Sam missed her guess, the newlyweds would start working very soon on the family they both wanted.

The sudden whistling of the kettle momentarily interrupted her reverie, and she absently selected an herbal tea bag and filled a mug with water. Distractedly she stared out the window, mindlessly dunking the tea bag, her thoughts far removed from the mundane action. Laura would be surprised at Sam's melancholy, she knew. Around her best friend, Sam was perennially upbeat and optimistic about finding a husband. She always told Laura that the right men for them were out there somewhere. And Laura had found hers. But Sam had always known that her own happy ending was an impossible dream. Her optimism had been for Laura's sake, not her own.

She sat down at the table and propped her chin in her hand. Sam knew she could get married. She was attractive enough, had a good personality, was reasonably intelligent. And there were plenty of available guys. Not too many like Nick, true, but she could find someone. There were probably a lot of men who could overlook the painful past that still haunted her.

The trouble was, *she* couldn't overlook it. She'd carried the guilt with her for years, would always carry it, because there was no way to right the wrong. All she could do was atone for it by denying herself the kind of happiness Laura had found. And by her weekly volunteer work at the counseling center.

Sam knew that most people would think her self-imposed punishment too severe. That what had happened hadn't been her fault. That she needed to get over the tragic event and move on with her life. And sometimes, when the nights got especially long and lonely, she almost began to believe that herself. Time had a way of softening the horror.

But then the nightmare would return with vivid intensity, bringing back the harsh reality of what she'd done, and she would wake up shaking, the sights and sounds so real that it always took her a moment to realize that it was, in fact, only a dream. Yet what it represented was real enough. She had *lived* that nightmare. It wasn't just a figment of her imagination. And for days afterward she would feel haunted. Because she knew that what had happened that fateful night *was* her fault.

Sam rose slowly and walked back to the stove to refill her cup. As she lifted the brass teapot, it suddenly reminded her of Aladdin's magic lamp, and she paused. She didn't allow herself many forays into fantasy. That was a waste of time. But just for a moment she broke her rule. If she had one wish, she thought wistfully as she gazed at the teapot, it would be to erase that night from her life. But it was too late, and no amount of wishing could change that.

Suddenly Sam felt a tear trailing down her cheek and realized that she was crying—again. It had been happening with alarming frequency since the wedding, and it had to stop, she told herself firmly, heading for the bathroom to get a tissue.

The sudden ringing of the phone startled her as she passed, and she stopped in midstride, reaching for it automatically. "Hello," she sniffed.

There was a moment's hesitation. "Sam?"

"Speaking."

"This is Brad Matthews."

Brad Matthews...the minister? "You mean Reverend Matthews?" she asked cautiously, swiping at her eyes.

"The same. Although I thought we'd gotten past that to 'Brad.'"

"Oh. Right. I was just...surprised."

It was obvious to Brad that Sam was either crying or had been recently, and he hesitated. "Listen, is this a bad time? I could call back."

"No. It's fine. Really." For some reason she felt better listening to his voice. It helped even more than the hot tea.

"Are you sure? You sound…well…is everything all right?"

"Everything's fine," she lied, touched by the concern in his voice, struggling to get her emotions under control. Good grief, every time she had any contact with this man she was crying! He must think she was a nutcase! She searched for some plausible excuse for her emotional state, and her gaze fell on Laura's note. "I just got a postcard from Laura, and like I told you at the wedding…I'm a sap for happy endings."

Her explanation didn't ring quite true, but Brad let it pass. "So are they having a good time?"

"It sounds like it."

"Well, I guess we won't know for sure until they get back. If they look sleep deprived, we can assume they enjoyed themselves," he said with a smile.

Sam's eyes widened. "Isn't that a rather…racy…remark for a minister?" she asked in surprise.

"Why?"

"Well…I don't know. It just seems like maybe sex would be a taboo topic for a preacher."

He chuckled. "Oh, you might be surprised at some of the subjects ministers tackle these days. Besides, Laura and Nick are married, and sex is a natural and good part of marriage. No reason not to hope they're enjoying it."

Sam found herself smiling. "I must say, Reverend, you continue to surprise me."

"Pleasantly, I hope."

"Definitely."

"Well, then here's another surprise. I'm actually calling for professional reasons."

Sam frowned. "Professional reasons?" she repeated, puzzled.

"Yes. Believe it or not, I'm in the market for a house, and I know from Laura that you sell real estate. So I thought maybe you could offer me some advice."

"Well, sure, I'd be glad to. But I thought houses were usually provided for ministers."

"That was true in the old days. But things are changing. The parsonage I live in is more or less falling down around me, and the congregation just doesn't want to sink any more money into it. Besides, we need to expand our parking lot. So…*voilà*…the parsonage is coming down. I've known about it for a couple of months, and I still have ten months before I have to move, but I figured I'd better start looking."

Sam reached for a pad and pen and sat down at the kitchen table. "Okay, why don't you tell me what you have in mind, and I'll take a few notes."

"Now?" Brad hadn't expected to actually do anything today, just sort of get the wheels in motion. But Sam had other ideas.

"Why not? That way I can line up a few things for you to look at and get a better idea of what you're after. Ten months may seem like a long time, but it's really not when you're buying a house."

Brad couldn't argue with Sam's expertise, so he did his best, with her prompting, to describe his "ideal" house. Within minutes she had the information she needed to line up some prospects.

"How about if we get together Wednesday to look at a few houses?" she suggested. "Would nine o'clock work for you?"

Brad flipped through his calendar, not at all sure how things had moved this quickly. He wasn't quite ready to let go of the parsonage. It was too filled with memories of his happy years with Rachel. But the day had to come sooner or later, and it looked like it was going to be sooner, if Sam was in charge. Which she seemed to be, he thought with amusement. "That would be fine."

"Great. I'll call to confirm on Tuesday night and let you know how many houses I've come up with. But don't get your hopes up," she warned. "This first trip will be more fact finding than anything else. It takes one hunting trip before I get a good feel for a client's tastes."

"I'm in no great rush."

"Good. You can't imagine how many people expect to walk into their dream house first time out. I can't promise that, but we'll find it eventually."

"I'm sure we will."

Sam heard a hint of laughter in his voice and frowned. "What's so funny?" she demanded.

"Not a thing," he assured her, but she could still hear amusement in his tone. "It's just that you don't waste any time, do you?"

"Oh." The light dawned. "I came on a little strong, huh? Sorry about that," she apologized. "I sort of get carried away when I have a prospective client. In my business we really live by that old saying, 'He who hesitates is lost.' Or, in this case, she."

"Well, I'm impressed."

"Don't be impressed until you see the results," she warned again, but this time there was a smile in *her* voice.

"I have a feeling my house search is in good hands. So I'll talk to you Tuesday?"

"You can count on it, Reverend. Goodbye."

Sam replaced the receiver and glanced out the window. The day was just as gray and rainy as ever, but for some reason she felt a whole lot better. It was illogical, of course. But for once she didn't try to analyze her emotions. She just enjoyed the sudden sense of well-being that her conversation with the preacher had produced.

Brad slowly hung up the phone and leaned back thoughtfully in his desk chair, swiveling to stare out at the soggy landscape. For the first time he'd gotten a glimpse of the Sam Laura had described all these years. Professionally, it was clear that she had her act together. She knew her stuff, had initiative—and then some, he thought with a smile—and seemed very efficient. She was confident, articulate, knowledgeable and clearly a go-getter. No wonder she was so successful at her job. He had no doubt that she would be a great help to him in his house search, and he was glad he'd contacted her.

But Brad was honest enough to admit that while he'd justified the call on the basis of needing her professional services, there had been more to it than that. For some reason she'd been on his mind ever since he'd found her in tears at the wedding reception. And while she'd quickly pulled herself together on the phone just now, it was obvious that she had been in tears just prior to his call, as well.

Brad frowned. Sam seemed like such a troubled soul, alone and adrift, almost as if she'd just lost her best friend. Which, in some ways, was true, he realized. Laura's first loyalty was now to Nick, as it should be. He was sure Laura and Sam would remain staunch friends, but it would be different. Sam's days of dragging a protesting Laura to singles events to spice up her nonexistent social life were over.

Brad smiled at that picture, shaking his head. He couldn't even imagine Laura in the singles scene. The fact that Sam had managed to get her to go spoke eloquently of the woman's considerable persuasive powers and the strength of their friendship.

Brad stood up and strolled over to the window, his hands in his pockets. Sam and Laura's friendship was still an enigma to him. From what he'd gathered during his conversations with Laura, the two women were as different as night and day. Laura's deep faith had provided a firm foundation for her, during her rocky years. Despite her hardships, she'd never wavered in her beliefs, and she led an exemplary Christian life. She had sound morals, a gentle and sensitive nature, and lived simply.

Sam, on the other hand, was apparently just the opposite—fashion conscious, outgoing, flamboyant, blunt, assertive and definitely not the "religious" type. At least that was the impression he'd formed based on Laura's comments. What had drawn the two women together initially he had no clue. But something had clicked, and they'd become the best of friends. Even though Laura admitted that they didn't necessarily share the same values, she admired Sam's strength and self-confidence and spoke with affection of her sharp wit and frank manner.

Until their phone conversation, however, Brad had seen little evidence of those qualities in Sam. Rather than the confident, outspoken, unsentimental, no-nonsense businesswoman he'd expected, he'd found a lost soul. For some reason Laura's wedding seemed to have thrown her off balance. She said it was because she was a sap for happy endings. He was convinced it was more than that.

But what? And, even more relevant, why should he care? Sure, as a minister his job often involved dealing with troubled souls. So he could say he had called her for professional reasons—*his* profession—wanting to help. And there was some truth to that. But it wasn't the whole truth, and he knew it. The simple fact was that for the first time since Rachel's death, Brad found himself actually noticing an attractive woman. And, even more surprising, Sam brought out a protective instinct in him that had long lain dormant—the last thing he had expected. Laura always described Sam as self-sufficient, able to take care of herself. But she didn't strike Brad that way. Not even close. She seemed like someone desperately in need of just being held.

Which was silly, of course. Based on what Laura said, Sam led a *very* active social life that probably included a whole lot more than just being held. So then why did she seem so lonely? And if she led such an active social life, and really wanted to get married, as Laura said, why was she still single?

Brad raked his fingers through his hair in frustration. He ought to be working on his sermon for tomorrow, not worrying about one very attractive—if troubled—redhead. He walked back to his desk and sat down in front of the word processor, determined to finish his sermon. And even though he eventually found the words, he also found himself spending an inordinate amount of time staring at the screen and looking forward to his next encounter with Sam Reynolds.

* * *

The rain had stopped by Wednesday, but it was still unseasonably cold for April, and by the time Sam and Brad inspected the three houses she'd lined up she was chilled to the bone. She shivered as she slid behind the wheel of her car and reached over to unlock the passenger door, and when Brad climbed in beside her a moment later, he was rubbing his hands together.

"I don't know about you, but I'm freezing. How about a cup of coffee before we call it a day?" he suggested.

Sam nodded as she put the car in gear. "Great idea. Can you believe this is April? I think somebody upstairs turned the calendar *back* a month instead of forward."

Brad chuckled. "It sure seems that way."

"Besides, this will give us a chance to talk about the houses a little more," she said over her shoulder as she pulled out of the driveway. "Have you ever been to Michele's?"

"No."

"It's a little European tearoom not far from here. Great pastries!" She glanced at her watch. "In fact, it's almost noon. Would you like to grab a quick lunch while we're there?"

"Sure."

Within minutes they were being shown to a cozy booth, and as Sam started to shrug out of her coat, Brad moved behind her and smoothly lifted it off her shoulders.

She turned her head at the courtesy and smiled. "Thanks. You're quite a gentleman, Reverend."

Brad gave her an exasperated look as he placed her coat on a nearby hook. "Are we still hung up on that 'Reverend' bit? What's wrong with 'Brad'?"

Sam watched him slip off his leather bomber jacket. He

was dressed casually today, in a cotton shirt with sleeves rolled up to the elbows and a pair of fitted, well-worn jeans that highlighted his athletic physique. He certainly looked different when he wasn't in clerical garb, Sam mused. Not at all like a minister. More like an ad for aftershave—one that featured a rugged outdoorsman or athlete. *Handsome* didn't even do him justice, she realized. Sam glanced around the room. Judging by the discreet looks being directed his way from women at nearby tables, she wasn't alone in her appreciation. However, he seemed totally oblivious to the admiring glances as he slid into the booth across from her and smiled.

"Well?"

Sam reined in her wayward thoughts and stared at him. "Well what?"

"What's wrong with 'Brad'?" he prompted.

"Oh." She reached for her napkin and looked down on the pretense of adjusting it on her lap, embarrassed at the inappropriate direction of her thoughts. Although he didn't look it today, the man *was* a minister, for heaven's sake—and definitely out of her league, even if she was in the market for romance. Which she wasn't, she reminded herself sharply. "Sorry. I guess I just think of you as a minister, that's all. I'm so used to hearing Laura refer to you that way. And at the wedding you were *dressed* like a minister. But you do look…different…out of uniform."

He grinned. "Well, I'm off duty today. So I can dress like a real person."

She smiled at his down-to-earth sense of humor. "I noticed."

"Actually, I think I underdressed," he admitted a bit

sheepishly. "You look great. I sort of feel like a poor relation."

Sam dismissed his comment with a wave. "I'm *on* duty, remember. This is *my* 'uniform.' Always look professional with clients, that's my motto. It helps build confidence." Nevertheless, his compliment left her with a warm glow. The black skirt and green jacquard silk blouse, embellished with a long gold and pearl necklace and a matching bracelet, was her favorite outfit, and for some reason she was pleased he'd noticed it.

Brad propped his chin in his hand and smiled. "Oh, you already have my confidence. After that third degree on the phone, I was convinced you knew your stuff."

She smiled ruefully. "I can come on a little strong, I guess. Laura should have warned you. Anyway, as for what you're wearing, you look fine. To be honest, it makes me forget you're a minister."

"Well, I won't complain if that makes it easier for you to call me Brad."

"It might." She didn't tell him that his attire today not only made her forget he was a minister, but sent her thoughts in a physical rather than spiritual direction.

He grinned engagingly. "Well, we can hope."

The waitress arrived, and after they placed their order Sam pulled out her notebook. "Why don't we finish up the business stuff before the food arrives? That way, I won't have to eat and take notes at the same time."

Brad was agreeable, and by the time their food was served they'd moved on to other topics.

"So how long have you been in the real estate business, Sam?" Brad asked as he buttered a roll.

"About fifteen years. It's the only thing I've ever done."

"You seem to be very successful."

She shrugged. "I do okay. And I enjoy it. That's the important thing. Plus, I get to meet lots of interesting people. I imagine you could say the same about your work."

"Actually, in many ways we're in the same business," he remarked.

Sam tilted her head quizzically. "How do you figure?"

He shrugged. "Well, you devote yourself to helping people find *earthly* homes. I spend my time helping them find their *eternal* home," he said matter-of-factly.

Sam smiled. "Has anyone ever told you that you have a way with words, Rever— Brad?" she corrected herself, and was rewarded with a warm smile. "I enjoyed your talk at the wedding, too."

"Thanks. You know, that was the hardest part for me about becoming a minister."

"What?"

"Having to get up in front of people and speak. I do better one-on-one. It's pretty intimidating to stand up there every week and see all those faces looking at you expectantly for words of wisdom."

"You could have fooled me. You seemed totally at ease at the wedding."

"Well, it's nice to know that at least I *look* calm. But I'm really kind of a stay-in-the-background kind of guy. I was pretty shy growing up."

"Yeah, I know what you mean. So was I."

Brad looked at her with a skeptical smile. "Now *that* I find hard to believe."

Sam grinned wryly. "Most people would, I guess," she

admitted. "*Shy* isn't exactly the word my friends use to describe me. But believe it or not, it's true. Or used to be," she said, correcting herself. "I was overweight as a child, and you know how kids can be. I was the butt of a lot of jokes, which made me even more self-conscious. But I finally figured out that the way to be accepted was to be sort of outrageous and funny. So I became the class clown, and I ended up being pretty popular. The only thing was, when I got to be about sixteen I realized that even though the guys thought I was a lot of fun, they never asked me out. So in my senior year I decided to lose weight, and by the time I graduated I was in pretty good shape. My weight's never varied more than a few pounds in all these years." Suddenly Sam frowned and looked down. "You know, I've never told that to anyone. Not even Laura," she said slowly.

"Why not?"

She shrugged. "I don't know. It's just part of a different life, I guess. And even though I'm glad I lost all that weight, it's sort of what led to my disastrous encounter with matrimony, so I don't think about it very often."

"I did get the impression at the wedding that your experience with marriage wasn't the best," he admitted.

Sam gave a mirthless laugh. "You could say that."

"Can I ask why, or would you rather not talk about it?"

Sam looked down and creased her napkin. There was something about this man's understanding manner that inspired confidences. Which probably came in handy in his job, she supposed. His job, she thought with a frown, the words echoing in her mind. Was this conversation part of his job? she wondered suddenly. Was his interest professional—as a minister lending a willing ear to someone who needed to talk—or personal? It shouldn't matter, but for some reason it did. And she needed to know. "Do you have your collar on now, figuratively speaking?" she asked, striving for a light tone.

Brad's gaze was direct and warm. "No. I'm not being a minister right now. I'm just trying to be a friend."

Sam stared at him, and her heart felt lighter. It was also beating just a little too fast. "Why do you want to be my friend?" she asked, finding it surprisingly difficult to keep her voice steady.

Because you seem to need one, he thought. But his spoken words were different. "Why not? A person can never have too many friends."

Sam stared at him a moment longer, still a little taken aback by the suggestion. "I think ours would be an odd friendship, Brad," she said slowly at last. "We're…really different…in a lot of ways."

"So are you and Laura," he pointed out. "And you two are the best of friends."

"Yeah, I know." He had a point. And it might be nice to have a male friend. It would be a welcome change of pace from the guys she usually met, who were out for a good time—and whatever else she was willing to offer. "Well, I guess it wouldn't hurt to give it a try."

"Good," he said with a smile. "So do you want to tell me what happened with your marriage? Or am I being too nosy?"

"No. But there really isn't much to tell. Randy played bass guitar in a rock band that came to town the summer after I graduated. He noticed me, and not having a lot of dating experience, I was flattered by the attention. We ended up falling in love, and he asked me to marry him.

My parents were very strict fundamentalist Christians, and they were appalled that I was even *interested* in someone in show business, let alone that I would consider marrying him. But we got married anyway, and that caused a rift with my parents that never really healed.''

She paused and looked down at her plate, tracing the edge with a red-polished nail. ''They're both dead now,'' she continued more softly. ''I was a late-in-life only child, and I think they expected great things of me. The day Randy and I eloped and got married at the courthouse in a civil ceremony was sort of the last straw.'' She took a deep breath and looked up at Brad. ''To make a long story short, we were only married about five months when he just walked out one day, leaving me five hundred dollars and a note saying he wasn't ready to settle down and that getting married had been a mistake. So I got on a bus and came to St. Louis, which I'd visited once and liked, and started over. Now you have my life story.''

Brad looked at her silently for a moment. She'd said the words matter-of-factly, but he knew there was a wealth of pain and disillusionment, as well as courage, behind them. ''I'm sorry, Sam,'' he said finally, and the compassion in his brown eyes made her throat tighten.

She tried to laugh. ''Yeah, so am I. But Randy was right about one thing. Getting married was a mistake.'' Unfortunately, it hadn't been the only one, she thought sadly.

''What ever happened to him?'' Brad asked.

Sam toyed with her water glass. ''I never saw him again. But about six years after he left me I ran into one of the guys from the band. They were in town for a gig, and it was just one of those chance encounters. Anyway, he told me that Randy had died of a drug overdose a couple of years before.''

Again there was a moment of silence before Brad spoke. ''I'm sorry you had to go through all that, Sam,'' he said quietly at last.

She shrugged. ''Well, it's history now.'' She glanced down, and with a start she realized that he was holding her hand. She stared down at their entwined fingers, unable to recall when they'd joined hands, knowing only that it felt good. Too good. Suddenly self-conscious, she gently eased her hand out of his grasp, but she missed the connection immediately.

Brad took a sip of coffee, and Sam used the moment to compose herself. She was surprised that recounting the story had upset her. It was ancient history, and she rarely thought about the failed relationship anymore. Sometimes she could hardly even remember what Randy looked like. But there was one part of the story that she couldn't forget, and she'd very deliberately left it out. She was too ashamed. Besides, she'd already told Brad far more than she'd intended.

''Can I ask you something else?'' he said slowly.

She looked at him hesitantly. There was something in his voice that put her on alert. ''Sure. I guess so.''

''Well, you're a very attractive woman, Sam,'' he said frankly. ''And you have a great personality. From what Laura says, you lead a very…active…social life.''

Sam's lips quirked wryly. ''Is that how she described it?''

Brad felt his neck redden. ''Well, not exactly. But that was the general idea.''

''I do…go out a lot, Brad,'' she admitted cautiously.

"So your bad experience with Randy didn't turn you off men in general?"

She looked surprised. "Good grief, no! He was just a bad apple. That's what I used to tell Laura. We just happened to marry two losers. But there are lots of nice guys out there."

"So then how come you've never remarried?"

Sam stared at him. She should have seen that question coming. She'd set herself up for it, and now she had to find a way to avoid answering it. Because she couldn't tell him the truth. "I guess I'm just too picky," she said at last, forcing her lips up into a smile.

Brad looked at her with his perceptive eyes, and she knew he didn't buy that explanation. But before he had a chance to pursue the subject, she changed the focus of the conversation. "So tell me about your marriage, Brad. I have a feeling your story is much nicer."

He smiled. Sam had clearly revealed as much about herself as she intended to—for today, at least—and he respected that. He was actually surprised she'd been so open. And turnabout was fair play. So he took her cue.

"Yes, it is. Rachel and I had a wonderful marriage."

"How did you two meet?"

"Well, as I told you, I was pretty much a quiet, stay-in-the-background kind of guy. I didn't date much during high school, and hardly at all when I was in the seminary. Then, when I got my church, I was too busy. It was a plum call, but there were also high expectations, so I didn't have much time to rustle up dates. Rachel was an organist at another church nearby, and when our organist was on vacation she filled in. That's how we met, and it just seemed like a good match right from the start. We had so much in common. We liked the same things, we both had a strong faith, we laughed at the same jokes—you know, that kind of thing. We both loved kids, too, and we planned to have a big family.''

Brad's eyes clouded, and he glanced down, stirring his coffee. ''We only had four years together, but they were good years,'' he said quietly. ''Rachel helped me see the world in a whole new way. For instance, one of her most enduring legacies to me was an appreciation for classical music.'' He smiled, his eyes distant and tender, and Sam knew that he was lost in remembrance. ''Her uncle always gave us season tickets to the symphony. We couldn't afford it on our salaries, so that was a real luxury. We enjoyed it so much.'' Suddenly his smile faded and he cleared his throat. ''I haven't been back since she died,'' he said softly. ''I've missed it. I've missed everything I did with Rachel. She filled my life with music in many ways,'' he finished simply.

Sam gazed at him, deeply touched by what had obviously been a devoted relationship and an enduring love. Impulsively she reached over and placed her hand on top of his. ''It sounds like she was a wonderful woman,'' she said, her voice catching.

Brad looked at her, and though he smiled, Sam saw the pain in his eyes. ''Yes. She was.''

''What happened to her?'' Sam asked gently.

''A ruptured brain aneurysm. No warning. She was here one minute, gone the next.''

''Oh, Brad, how awful!'' Sam exclaimed in a shocked whisper.

''It was a very hard time for me,'' he admitted. ''For a long time I was bitter, and I was angry at God. I even took a leave from the ministry for six months. But I eventually came to terms with Rachel's death. Ultimately I had to learn to live what I'd always preached—that sometimes we have to accept God's will even if we don't understand it.''

Sam shook her head. ''You're a better person than me, then. I don't know if I could ever accept something like that.''

''That's where faith helps.''

''Well, mine obviously isn't as strong as yours.''

''So you do still believe at least?''

She shrugged. She hadn't thought about it in a long time. ''Yes, I suppose so,'' she said slowly. ''I guess some of my Christian upbringing stuck. Deep inside I still believe the basics. I'm just not into the external trappings. No offense intended.''

''None taken,'' he assured her easily. ''After all, everyone is at a different place on the faith journey.''

''Well, I think maybe I've taken a few too many detours.''

He smiled. ''So I assume you haven't been to church for a while?''

''Except for Laura's wedding, I haven't been in a church in eighteen years. I don't think I'm church material.''

''Why not?''

She toyed with her water glass. ''Like I said, I think I've taken a few too many detours.''

''Sam, churches aren't for saints. They're for sinners. Perfect people wouldn't need churches. If everyone in my congregation was perfect, I'd be out of a job. I like to think of a church as a kind of spiritual travel bureau that provides people with the maps they need to stay on course.''

Now it was Sam's turn to smile. "That's a nice analogy."

"Only if it's convincing."

"You do have a point," she acknowledged. "But we got off the subject. You were telling me about your marriage."

Brad's face sobered. "There's really no more to tell. Rachel's been gone for six years now, and I still think of her every day. It's hard to let go of someone who's become so much a part of you."

"But don't you ever get lonely?" Sam asked.

"Only lately. For some reason I've suddenly started to notice the empty place in my life," he said, surprising himself by his admission.

"Loneliness is the pits," Sam agreed.

Brad looked at her in surprise. "Don't tell me *you're* lonely. I thought—" He stopped abruptly, embarrassed by his indiscretion, and his neck took on a ruddy color.

Sam smiled ruefully. "You thought I had plenty of male friends who were more than willing to warm my lonely bed on a cold night?" she said bluntly.

Brad's face flushed and he started to speak, but Sam held up her hand. "It's okay. I have no one to blame but myself for creating that image. It's what most people think, I suppose. Even Laura. But can I tell you something? Reports of my promiscuity have, to borrow a phrase from Mark Twain, been greatly exaggerated. I do go out a lot. We have a few drinks, dance a little, maybe go to dinner or a show, and then…well, I'm not saying that I haven't been…physically close…to some of the men I dated, but I know when to pull back. And that's long before we get to the bedroom door," she said frankly.

Brad stared at the woman across from him, taken aback by her blunt honesty. But he was also curious. "Why are you telling me this?" he asked.

She frowned. "I don't know," she admitted slowly, as surprised as he was by the confession. "I usually try to create a 'swinging single' image, and now I've just blown it."

"But why do you want people to think you live that kind of life-style?" he asked, puzzled.

Sam looked down, still frowning, and stirred her coffee. She'd never really analyzed it before. "I guess maybe because I don't want anyone to know I'm lonely," she said slowly. "I hate it when people feel sorry for me. It must be pride or something."

"But you told me the truth," he pointed out.

"Yeah, I did," she conceded. "And that was probably a mistake. Listen, do me a favor, will you?"

"What."

"Don't spread it around. I wouldn't want to ruin my reputation."

Brad chuckled. "Okay. I promise. But Sam…can I tell you something? I don't think it was a mistake. I'm glad you told me."

She looked at him, and the warmth and sincerity in his brown eyes filled her with a strange sense of optimism and hope. Those were feelings she hadn't experienced for a long time, and impulsively she leaned forward and smiled.

"Can I tell *you* something?"

"Sure."

"So am I."

Chapter Three

"Sam, there's a Don Williams on 7335. Do you want to pick up?"

Sam looked over at Kelly, seated at the next desk, and nodded distractedly. Don Williams was a corporate customer who sent a lot of relocations her way, and she couldn't afford to put him off, even if she was knee-deep in details on an especially tricky contract.

Sam propped the receiver on her shoulder so she could continue working on the contract wh... she
punched the appropriate butt...

"Hi... ...h... ...or me?" ...g?" "Hi, Don."

...r let it be said that Sam Reynolds

Sorry. Not this time."

...to ask, you know," she said with a

"can I do for you today?," ...it could always be better. Have

...e two corporate tickets to the symphony for

and

tomorrow night that my wife and I aren't going to be able to use, and I wondered if you'd be interested in them.''

''The symphony?'' she repeated, her mind clicking into gear. Might be fun. She hadn't been in a long time, and Powell Hall was such a beautiful place. But who in the world could she ask? Laura would enjoy it, but she was still on her honeymoon. Besides, she had Nick now, and Sam suspected her free time would be otherwise occupied for the immediate future. Sam mentally ran through her ''black book,'' which she had pared down considerably since Laura's engagement, but came up blank. The few men she currently dated were more into sports than Schubert.

She opened her mouth to refuse, and then suddenly it hit her. Brad liked the symphony. She could ask him. It had been over a week since their house-hunting expedition and lunch, and this would give her a good excuse to call him. He'd been on her mind a lot these past few days. She liked being with him, and after all, he was the one who had suggested that they be friends. So a call wouldn't be ~~out of~~ line. Would it?

~~...~~ you still there?''

~~...~~ trying to think who I could ask. ~~...~~ might really enjoy that. So

~~...~~ courier later today.

~~...~~ might not

~~...~~ uldn't

''Sam? Are y~~...~~
''Yes. Sorry. I was t~~...~~
Actually, I have a friend wh~~...~~
yes, thanks, I'd love them.''
''Great! I'll have them sen~~...~~
Have fun.''
Sam hung up the phone on such sh~~...~~
even be available on such sh~~...~~ she tho~~...~~
know until she asked, she~~...~~
through her client address bo~~...~~
dialed his number.

* * *

Brad reached for the phone to call Sam, then dropped his hand. It was the third time he'd gone through this routine while his neglected paperwork stared at him accusingly. This is ridiculous, he told himself in frustration. It was only a phone call. What was so hard about that? After all, *he* was the one who had suggested to Sam that they be friends.

He rose restlessly and walked over to the bookcase, pausing in front of Rachel's picture. And there he found his answer. He felt guilty. For the first time since his wife's death he was actually thinking about another woman. Okay, so it was just a friendship thing. In fact, he was the one who had set those parameters. Because, despite Sam's revelation that she wasn't quite as loose and free as he'd assumed, they were still very different. Too different for anything serious to develop. But this was nevertheless a first, safe step back into the social world.

Brad reached over and picked up Rachel's picture. He knew she wouldn't want him to be alone. And yet he felt somehow disloyal even thinking about another woman. As if in doing so he was negating the beauty of the relationship they'd shared. Which was foolish. He knew that intellectually. But how could he convince his heart that it was okay to move on?

And how could he let go? He had so many wonderful memories of his time with Rachel. Those memories had helped keep his loneliness at bay during the six difficult years since her death. The thought of letting go of them was frightening. Because maybe there wouldn't be anything to take their place. And he had a depressing feeling that as difficult as it was to face loss, emotional emptiness would be even worse. But if he clung to those memories, to the past, he knew he was denying himself a future with someone new. As long as his heart was focused on memories, there would be no room for anything—or anyone—else.

Brad sighed and replaced the picture, leaving one hand resting on it lightly. There were no easy answers. Certainly none that he could come up with on his own. So he did what he often did in such situations—he closed his eyes and turned to the One he relied on for guidance.

Lord, he prayed silently, I need to find the courage to move on with my life. Help me to overcome the fear of risking a new relationship, to understand with my heart as well as my mind that without risk there is no growth. I don't know what the future holds, but I do know that I'd like an earthly partner to share it with, if that's Your will. I'm trying to take a first step by opening the door to friendship with Sam. She seems so in need of a friend, and I need to relearn how to relate to a woman socially. I think a friendship would benefit us both. But I can't seem to let go of the past and move on. Please help me.

Brad opened his eyes and once more looked into Rachel's face. I love you, he said in the silence of his heart. I always will. But I can't live on memories anymore. What you and I had was special and unique and will always be ours. A new love won't diminish what we shared. It, too, will be unique, just as ours was. No one can ever take your place, but I think there's room in my life for someone else. And I need to find out.

Brad let his hand gently fall away from the picture, taking a deep breath as he did so. He felt better. And he also knew what he was going to do. He was going to call Sam.

With a determined look on his face, Brad strode toward

the desk and reached for the phone—just as it started to ring. With a startled exclamation, he jerked his hand back, his heart jumping to his throat. Talk about strange timing, he thought, shaking his head and smiling ruefully. But it was even more strange when he recognized the voice on the other end.

"Sam?" he asked cautiously after the woman said his name questioningly.

"Yeah. Are you okay? You sound kind of…funny." Sam was a little thrown by the odd tone in his voice. She wouldn't exactly call it welcoming. Or pleased.

"You're never going to believe this," he said incredulously. "I was just reaching for the phone to call you!"

"You're kidding!"

Brad sat down in his desk chair and shook his head. "No. It's the truth. Talk about weird timing!"

That explained his strange tone, Sam thought with relief. At least it wasn't because he was sorry she'd called. "That's happened to me a few times," she said. "It is pretty weird. But I don't have any news on the house, if that's what you were calling about. I think I have a really good idea of what you want, and until I find the right one I don't want to waste your time."

"I appreciate that." No sense trying to explain the real reason for his call—especially since he wasn't sure of it himself. All he knew was that he wanted to hear her voice. But he couldn't very well say that. Better to let her think it was business. "So why were you calling, then?" he asked.

"Oh." Suddenly she felt uncertain, and she stared unseeingly at the contract on her desk, her fingers playing nervously with the phone cord. She took a deep breath, trying to steady the staccato rhythm of her heart. "Well, a client of mine has tickets for the symphony tomorrow night, and he's not going to be able to use them. He offered them to me, and I was wondering if…well, I know it's short notice and all…but if you're not busy, I thought…I thought maybe you might like to go." She finished in a rush, then drew a shaky breath, unconsciously holding it while she waited for his response.

Brad's eyes widened in surprise. Sam was asking him out! Okay, so it was only because she had free tickets and she knew he liked the symphony. Still, she could have asked someone else. But the symphony… He frowned. He hadn't been there since the last time he'd gone to a concert with Rachel. It wouldn't be easy to go back.

Brad hesitated uncertainly, knowing that if he accepted the invitation he would be bittersweetly reminded of the happy hours he'd spent there with Rachel. But what about his resolve to let go of the past and move on? he asked himself. This was his chance to implement that resolution. Only it was a lot harder to do than he expected.

As the silence lengthened, Sam felt her face flush. She'd obviously put him on the spot. When he'd suggested friendship, he clearly hadn't intended it to include something like this, she realized with disappointment. It had been a long shot anyway, she supposed. A minister wasn't likely to want to hang around with someone like her, not considering the "swinging" image she'd created all these years. He was too discreet and too kind to say that, of course, so she needed to get him off the hook.

"Look, I guess maybe this wasn't such a good idea," she said, striving for a light tone. "I know you're busy, and I guess I just took that friendship idea too literally. So just forget—''

"Whoa!" Brad interrupted, realizing she'd jumped to the wrong conclusion about his hesitation. "Did I say I wasn't interested?" His gaze fell on the calendar on his desk. "I'm just looking at my schedule for tomorrow. And if the offer is still open, I'd love to go."

"You would?" Sam said in surprise.

"Sure. I only hesitated because I haven't been there since the last concert I attended with Rachel. But it's time I went back."

"Well, that's great!" Sam suddenly felt more light-hearted. "The concert starts at seven, so I guess we could meet about—"

"Why don't you let me pick you up?" he asked.

"You don't need to do that," she assured him quickly, although she was touched by the offer.

"Maybe not. But you supplied the tickets. It seems only fair that I supply the ride."

"Well, if you're sure…"

"Absolutely. I've got a four-thirty appointment, so would six be okay?"

"Sure."

"Great. I'll look forward to it. And Sam…thanks for asking."

The husky tone in his voice sent a shaft of warmth through her, and she found herself smiling. "It's my pleasure," she replied. "I'm glad you can go."

"Me, too. See you tomorrow, then."

Brad slowly replaced the receiver. Talk about a turn of events! The last thing he had expected was a social invitation from Sam. Despite her revelation that she led a much more sedate social life than her image would suggest, Brad was sure she could have found someone more exciting to spend an evening with than him. He'd been honest with her about himself—he was a quiet, stay-in-the-background kind of guy, more interested in one-on-one relationships than crowd scenes or loud parties. Even if she wasn't quite the party girl he'd assumed prior to their lunch, she was still out of his league socially. And yet she'd picked him. Why?

Brad didn't have the answer. Maybe she just needed a friend, and he'd made himself available. But whatever the reason, he was pleased. Going out socially with a woman was a giant step forward for him. Okay, the symphony might be hard. But for some strange reason he had a feeling that with Sam by his side, it would be a whole lot easier.

It was funny, really, he thought as he pulled the stack of paperwork toward him. Initially he had been drawn to her because she seemed to need a friend—only to discover that he needed one just as badly. She had been good for him, prodding him to do things that he'd put off far too long already. Brad smiled to himself and shook his head. God really did work in mysterious ways.

Sam stared at her reflection in the full-length mirror and frowned. Maybe she was too dressed up. Maybe this outfit was too sexy. Maybe she should tone down her makeup. Maybe…

Sam cut the last "maybe" off in midthought. This was ridiculous, she admonished herself brusquely. It made absolutely no difference what she wore tonight. Brad's interest in her was purely as a friend. He'd said so himself.

He probably wouldn't even notice what she wore. Which was fine, she told herself. Even if he was interested in her romantically, things would never work out. Their backgrounds were too different. And if he ever found out about—Sam cut that thought off, too. All of this speculation was a waste of time, she told herself harshly. Romance and happy endings weren't in the cards for her. She'd have to settle for friendship. And that was better than nothing, she consoled herself.

Sam tugged one last time at the hem of her black skirt, but there was no disguising the short length. She always dressed in the latest fashion, but suddenly she wished she had something in her wardrobe that was a more demure, classic length. Oh, well, maybe the dark hose would help hide the fact that so much leg was exposed, she thought hopefully. At least her short-sleeved jewel-neckline satin blouse was modest, and the short strand of pearls added an elegant touch against the shimmery forest green fabric.

Sam ran a comb through her shoulder-length hair, thankful that it was a good hair day. The ends were waving under nicely on her shoulders, and her bangs had fluffed out just right. Okay, so her makeup was a little dramatic. But that was her, and if Brad didn't like it, well—

The ringing of the doorbell interrupted her second-guessing, and Sam's heart suddenly kicked into double time. For goodness sake, she admonished herself, get a grip! This is not a real date. Brad is just a friend. That's all. Just a friend.

The funny thing was that when she opened the door she could have sworn that the quick yet thorough appraisal he gave her was much more than just ''friendly'' in nature.

But she told herself she was reading far too much into a simple glance.

When his eyes returned to hers he smiled, and Sam's breath caught in her throat at the warmth in his gaze. "You look great," he said quietly, his voice shaded with a husky timbre that surprised them both. He'd been caught off guard by his own reaction to her discreet but alluring outfit, his gaze lingering just a moment too long on what the fashionably short skirt revealed—a pair of fabulous legs that just didn't quit. He'd have to be dead not to notice, he thought, trying to justify the surprising direction of his thoughts.

"Thanks." She tried to smile, but she suddenly felt shaky as her eyes took in his appearance. Tonight Brad did not look *anything* like a minister, she thought. His dove gray suit, starched white shirt and striking maroon and blue tie were more suited to a man of the world than a man of the cloth. If at lunch he'd made her think of an aftershave ad, tonight he looked like a successful executive or entrepreneur. The very faint brush of silver at his temples added a distinguished touch to his appearance and magnified his appeal. For just a moment she wondered what it would feel like to be held against his solid chest, to feel his gentle touch against her cheek, to— Disconcerted by the inappropriate direction of her thoughts, Sam abruptly took a step back and motioned him inside.

"Come on in. I'm ready. I just need to get my sweater," she said breathlessly.

Brad strolled inside and looked around with interest. The open room featured white walls and light gray modular furniture that could be easily moved into new configurations. Coffee and end tables were glass and chrome, and a fireplace was framed by a black screen. Throw pillows in magenta and cobalt blue added striking touches of color.

"Nice," Brad said as his gaze traveled around the room. "It makes me feel like I've stepped onto the pages of a decorating magazine."

Sam shrugged. "It's functional. And it suits my lifestyle. But I wouldn't exactly call it homey."

"It doesn't seem like 'homey' was what you were after," Brad said thoughtfully.

"You're right. It wasn't," she admitted slowly, surprised by his insight, realizing that she'd never consciously analyzed her decorating choices before. It was more as if she'd created a stage setting, a backdrop, for her as a single, socializing, professional woman, she thought, letting her own gaze circle the modernistic, picture-perfect room. In fact, it was almost as if no one actually lived here, she realized. And it certainly didn't reflect her real personality. Sam liked modern things, true. She wouldn't want Nick and Laura's old Victorian house, though she could appreciate its charm and realized it suited them. No, if she had a real home it would be contemporary, but she would intersperse the modern with the homey. A warm, hand-loomed throw on the sofa. A lovingly-stitched needlepoint pillow next to the fireplace. A brandy decanter on the mantel, with a pair of glasses for late-night toasts. A child's drawing framed and hung proudly on the wall....

Sam felt her eyes mist over at the last image. That was something she was never destined to have, she knew. She'd had her chance once, and she'd thrown it away. Better to live in this relatively sterile environment, where she could more easily pretend that those things were un-important to her, she thought resolutely.

Sam suddenly realized that Brad was watching her with those insightful brown eyes of his, and she turned away and reached for her sweater. "So, are we ready?" she asked with forced brightness.

He seemed about to say something, but apparently he thought better of it and instead silently followed her to the door.

By the time they were seated in his car, Sam had re-gained her composure, and they chatted about inconse-quential things during the drive into the city. As they en-tered the opulent lobby of Powell Hall, Sam looked around appreciatively, overwhelmed as always by the elaborate crystal and gilt decor, red carpet and sweeping grand stair-case. "I always forget how gorgeous this place is," she remarked.

When Brad didn't respond, she turned to look at him. He was frowning slightly, and his eyes seemed troubled. Sam assumed he was thinking about his last visit here, with Rachel, and she reached over to touch his arm.

"Brad?" It took a moment, but at last he looked down at her. "I'm sorry. I know this isn't easy for you," she said gently.

He sighed. "I'm the one who's sorry. I don't want to put a damper on our evening. It was just a jolt, coming through the door. I'm okay now."

"Are you sure?" she asked worriedly. "We don't have to stay."

"I'm fine, Sam. Really," he assured her. Then he smiled and reached for her hand. "But just stay close. That will help."

"Sure." A tingle ran through Sam as Brad's fingers closed over hers, engulfing them in a firm grip that gave her a comforting sense of protection and security. Okay, so he was only holding her hand to give him courage to see this evening through. But that didn't mean she couldn't enjoy it. She could even pretend for a little while that he was *really* holding her hand. What could it hurt?

When they reached their seats, Brad helped Sam off with her sweater, then reached for her hand again as the music started. A couple of times during the concert he absently rubbed his thumb across the back of her knuckles, and Sam felt her pulse rate quicken each time. She knew that he probably wasn't even consciously aware of the gesture, which made her reaction absurd. But she didn't seem to be able to control it.

When the last notes of the final piece died away, Sam turned to Brad and smiled. "Well, you made it," she said.

He returned the smile. "Yeah. Thanks to you."

"What do you mean?"

He lifted her hand, which he still held, and stroked his thumb across the back of it—consciously this time, she knew. "This helped a lot."

Sam flushed. "I didn't do anything," she protested, her heart rate once again quickening.

"Letting me hold your hand helped more than you know," he told her with quiet sincerity. "Sometimes a simple human touch goes a long way in giving people courage, in letting them know they're not alone."

Sam stared at him. She had faced her greatest crisis alone, so she knew what he meant. A simple caring touch, a choice offered in compassion, would have made a world of difference to her once. It could have changed her whole life, in fact. But there'd been no one there for her.

Her throat constricted and she squeezed Brad's hand. "You're not alone," she said softly, her voice uneven. Then she tried to smile, forcing a lighter note into her tone. "After all, what are friends for?"

Brad gazed at her speculatively. "You know, Sam, I think—" He stopped, and Sam looked at him curiously.

"You think what?" she prompted.

Brad cleared his throat. He'd been about to say that at the moment friendship was the furthest thing from his mind. It was true that at the beginning of the evening he'd sought her hand for courage. But she had nice hands— soft, with long, tapering fingers—and by the end he held on to it because it simply felt good. But that remark would surprise her. Good grief, the realization surprised him! And he sensed that now was not the time to reveal emotions he himself didn't understand. He glanced down toward their entwined hands with a frown, debating how to answer her question.

Sam followed the direction of his gaze, which seemed to be resting in the vicinity of her hemline, and removed her hand from his to tug self-consciously at her skirt. "You think my skirt's too short, don't you?" she said, embarrassed, misinterpreting the direction of his thoughts. "I suppose I'm not the type of woman a minister wants to be seen with. Listen, I understand. The friendship offer was probably made in haste, and—"

"Sam." Brad cut her off.

She stared at him, her eyes wide, taken aback by the touch of anger in his voice.

Brad frowned, aware that he sounded angry. And he

was. At himself. For some reason she'd felt disapproval in his gaze. Which had been the last thing on his mind as he'd gazed at their entwined hands.

"I'm sorry," she said contritely. "I didn't—"

"Sam," he repeated, more gently this time, reaching for her hand again. "I was *not* going to comment on your skirt."

"No?" She looked uncertain, and Brad wanted to pull her into his arms and just hold her. The impulse took him off guard. What was the matter with him all of a sudden? he wondered. He wasn't a man usually given to such inappropriate thoughts. So, using a self-restraint that required a surprising amount of effort, he kept his distance. But he also kept a firm grip on her hand.

"No," he repeated firmly. "I'll admit I noticed your skirt," he said frankly, deciding honesty was the best policy. "Or rather, what your skirt reveals—a pair of absolutely fabulous legs. I doubt whether any man still breathing could overlook them. And I hope you don't think that's some sort of insulting sexist remark. My intent is to flatter, not criticize or demean."

"Really?" she asked, wanting to believe his words but finding it difficult.

"Really," he assured her. "I may be a minister, but I'm also a man. And I'm proud to be seen with you—because of who you are, as well as how you look."

Sam stared at him. She couldn't doubt the sincerity in his eyes. "Then what were you going to say before?" she asked with a frown.

Brad's mind went into warp drive. "I think we should stop on the way home and get something to eat," he said with sudden inspiration. "My appointment ran late, and I haven't had dinner. Are you hungry?"

"As a matter of fact, yes," she said, surprised to find that she was suddenly ravenous.

"Good. I know just the spot."

Twenty minutes later they were seated in a small café not far from Sam's condo. Classical music played softly in the background, and the atmosphere was cozy and intimate.

"This is charming, Brad!" Sam said, glancing around approvingly. "I never even knew it was here."

"I wasn't sure you'd like it," he admitted. "It's pretty quiet."

"Well, I've had my fill of crowded, noisy, smoky bars, thank you," she said wryly. "This is perfect."

During the light meal, they discussed the concert, and when the waitress came to offer dessert, Brad looked at Sam inquiringly. "Are you in the mood to indulge?"

"Why not?" she said, wanting to prolong the evening. It had been a long time since she'd enjoyed herself so much in a man's company, and she hated it to end.

"Well, I can highly recommend tonight's special dessert," the waitress said. "Apple cobbler. It's a new recipe the chef's just trying out, and it's a winner."

"Sounds good to me," Sam said with a smile.

"How about you, sir?" the woman asked, turning to Brad.

He hesitated, and Sam looked at him curiously. He was frowning, but when he realized she was watching him, his face cleared and he seconded the order.

"Don't you like apple cobbler?" Sam asked curiously after the waitress departed.

"Yes...I do," he replied. "It's just that, well, Rachel made a wonderful apple cobbler. She was a great cook. It took me back for a minute, that's all."

"Oh." Sam looked down and stirred her coffee. Was there anything his wife couldn't do, she thought in despair? No wonder he still loved her. She sounded perfect.

Brad heard the woebegone tone in Sam's voice, even if she was unaware of it, and chided himself. If he was going to start dating again, he'd better *stop* singing the praises of Rachel in front of other women. No woman was likely to become interested in a man who was always talking about what a wonderful woman his late wife had been. A change of topic seemed to be in order, he thought, searching for some neutral, common ground.

"So...I understand Laura and Nick will be back this weekend," he remarked.

Sam looked up at him and forced herself to smile. What did she care how wonderful Rachel was? It wasn't like she and Brad's late wife were in competition for his affections or anything. Even if he *was* looking for a new romance, she was definitely not in the running. She'd better get that idea into her head once and for all.

"Yeah. I can't wait to hear all about it. Laura and I are going to have lunch next week," she replied.

"You and she seem to be very close."

"We are," Sam confirmed.

"What brought you two together in the first place?"

Sam shrugged. "I don't really know. We were both taking night classes at the junior college, and I used to run into her in the ladies' room. Not a very auspicious beginning," she said with a wry smile. "Anyway, she seemed kind of forlorn. There was this...haunted...look around her eyes. I found out later that her life was pretty awful at that point, so I guess she needed a friend, and I was available. I'm sure if she hadn't been so desperate she would have been a little more choosy,'' she said in a self-deprecating tone. ''But something clicked, anyway, and we've been through a lot together since then.''

Brad shook his head. ''Don't sell yourself short, Sam. Laura's an excellent judge of character. She obviously recognized a good person when she saw one.''

Sam stared at him, taken aback by the misplaced compliment. Then she lowered her eyes. ''Thanks. But save your praise for someone who deserves it,'' she said quietly.

Brad frowned. ''What's that supposed to mean?''

Sam shrugged and took a sip of her coffee. If he knew the truth about her, he wouldn't have to ask. But he didn't know, and she planned to keep it that way. ''I'm not such a great person,'' she said lightly.

Brad's frown remained in place. ''I don't think Laura would agree.''

''Maybe not.'' But then, Laura didn't know her friend's secret, either. Sam felt her throat constrict, and before she lost control she decided it was time to change the subject. ''Speaking of good people, tell me how you decided to become a minister. I've never known one before.''

Brad noted that Sam's eyes were suspiciously bright and realized that he'd touched a nerve with his remark. A very sensitive nerve, it seemed. She honestly didn't think she was a good person, he realized in surprise. But what on earth could account for her low self-image? Based on what he'd learned during their encounters, the real Sam was totally different from the image she'd conveyed. Different in a good way, according to Brad's Christian code of ethics. So why did she seem to feel somehow unworthy? He wanted answers, but one look at Sam's face told him that she wasn't going to provide them tonight. Reluctantly, he let it go and turned his attention to her question.

"I guess I've always known this is what I was meant to do," he said slowly, his expression thoughtful. "I grew up in a house where Christian values were not only taught, but lived. And unlike you, I knew a couple of ministers who were about as far from the 'fire and brimstone' variety as you could get. They were really great people, down-to-earth and humble, and they seemed to find great satisfaction in their work. After all, as one of them used to tell me, what could be more worthwhile than spreading the good news of Christianity? I had to agree. Besides, I've always been drawn to helping those in trouble, and being a minister allows me to spend my life doing that."

"But isn't it hard, getting involved in people's problems? I mean, I'm sure it's great when you're able to help, but what about when you're not?" She dealt with that issue every week at the counseling center. Maybe Brad could offer her some coping tips.

Brad sighed. "I haven't quite figured out how to handle that yet," he admitted. "I take things pretty personally, and it's hard for me to separate other people's problems from my own. Rachel used to worry about that, in fact. She said I needed to learn how to walk away sometimes, for my own mental health. But I've never quite gotten the hang of it."

Sam rested her elbow on the table and propped her chin in her hand. Dealing once a week with women in trouble was hard enough. He did that kind of work every day. "It all sounds pretty heavy. Don't you ever take time for fun?''

"Oh, sure. Mostly thanks to Rachel. Before she came into my life, I was a pretty serious guy."

"And you're not now?" Sam teased, her lips quirking up.

He smiled ruefully. "Touché. Okay, I'm still serious. I think it goes with the territory. But I have learned to give myself a break from work now and then. Not much in the past few years, but maybe I'm making a new start tonight. Going to the symphony was a big step for me."

Sam looked at him speculatively. She liked this man. He was nice, sensitive, attractive, a great conversationalist, had a good sense of humor. He was the kind of man, under different circumstances, that she would pursue. But given the present circumstances, getting involved with Brad Matthews was not an option.

Yet it didn't seem right that he should be alone—and lonely. Maybe she could help on that score. She knew some nice, single women she could introduce him to. After all, Brad had gone out of his way to be nice to her, offering her the hand of friendship when she'd desperately needed it. She should try to repay him in some way.

At the same time, she realized that the thought of him going out with another woman was extremely unappealing. But that was just being selfish, she berated herself. She should put his best interests first. And if that meant setting him up with some nice women, so be it.

"Brad, I think what you need to do is start dating again," she said bluntly, before she could change her mind.

Brad almost choked on the coffee he was swallowing,

and by the time he was able to speak, they'd attracted the attention of half the patrons in the café.

"Are you all right?" she asked with concern when he finally stopped coughing.

Brad dabbed at his lips with the napkin and stared at her. "May I ask where that remark came from?"

Sam shrugged. "I don't know. You just seem lonely. I know some nice single women you might enjoy meeting." She leaned closer and touched his hand. "I know you loved Rachel, Brad," she said softly. "But she's gone. You can't live on memories. Maybe I can help get you into circulation again."

Brad was speechless. Sam had voiced the thoughts that had been running through his head ever since the wedding. But they were just thoughts at this point. He had no immediate plans to move on them. Seeing Sam on a "friendship" basis was about all he was ready for at the moment.

"Look, Sam, I appreciate your concern," he acknowledged. "But I'm just not at that point yet. And, to be honest, I'm really rusty on the finer points of dating. Rachel was the only woman I ever seriously went out with, and that was a long time ago."

Sam frowned. "When you say 'seriously,' what do you mean exactly?"

He shrugged. "Honestly? I never got past a good-night kiss with any other woman."

"And you haven't gone out with anyone since Rachel died?"

"No."

Sam digested that information—and its implications. It was hard to believe that there was a man Brad's age alive in today's world who hadn't slept around to some extent before marriage and who would remain celibate for six long years after his wife's death. Certainly none of the men she knew. But here was one sitting right across from her, and she was impressed—and deeply moved. "I understand your reluctance," she said slowly. "It would be kind of scary to date again after such a long time. But you have to start sooner or later."

"I was sort of thinking along the lines of 'later,'" he admitted.

"Why?"

Brad shifted uncomfortably in his chair. Sam's reputation for directness was one thing Laura had *not* exaggerated. "Sam, I'm not even sure I remember how to talk to a woman—as a woman," he said frankly.

"Oh, that's silly," she replied, dismissing his comment with a wave. "You seem perfectly at ease with me."

"Yeah, I know," he admitted. "I guess maybe that's because we set the ground rules right up front—friendship. There are different pressures when you're actually dating."

Sam felt a sudden heaviness in her heart. He had just confirmed what she already knew—friendship was their destiny. But for some reason, when he put it into words, a little bit of the glow left her heart. With an effort she fought down the sudden melancholy that swept over her.

"That's true," she admitted, striving to keep her voice light. "But I think we can get around that. I know a woman who might be just your type. Sort of quiet, refined, likes music and books. She hasn't dated much, either, so she'll probably be just as nervous as you are. You'll be even on that score. Why don't you let me give her a call and see if she's interested?"

Brad shook his head. "I don't know," he said doubtfully.

"What do you have to lose with one date?" Sam argued.

Brad didn't have an answer to that. He'd told himself it was time to allow for the possibility of romance again. Sam was willing to help him. Why was he hesitating? He couldn't think of an excuse, so finally, with a sigh, he capitulated.

"You win. I can't think of any reason not to meet this woman," he said.

Sam felt her stomach sink to her toes, but she smiled. "Good. I'll give her a call tomorrow. By the way, her name's Stephanie Morris, and she's a librarian. Now why do you have that funny look on your face?" Sam asked suspiciously, when his lips turned up into a crooked smile.

"What funny look?" he asked innocently.

"You know what I mean," she asserted accusingly. "That look…like you're secretly laughing at something."

"I'm not laughing," he said with a smile, shaking his head. "I'm just amazed. First you get me out house hunting before I've really decided to do anything concrete about finding a new place, and now you're lining up dates for me—sooner, as you put it, rather than later. I'm just wondering what I'm going to get pulled into next."

Sam smiled. "You never know with Sam Reynolds," she warned. "Just ask Laura."

"I might. But you have to promise me one thing, Sam," he said, suddenly serious.

"What?"

"No singles bars."

Sam laughed, realizing that he was teasing her. "Don't

worry. I wouldn't even think about it. I just can't picture you in one of those places.''

"Well, I couldn't picture Laura there, either, and you managed to get her to a few."

Sam chuckled. "Yeah, but kicking and screaming. Besides, it didn't do any good. Although I must admit that the night we ran into Nick seemed to be a turning point in their relationship," she said thoughtfully.

"Sam," Brad warned, not liking the speculative look he saw in her eyes.

Her smile of response seemed somehow shadowed with sadness. "Don't worry, Brad. You're safe with me," she said quietly.

It was only later, after he dropped her off at her condo with a simple good-night and a warmly clasped hand, that he took time to analyze why her suggestion about arranging a date for him left him cold. He should feel something, he thought. Anticipation. Nervousness. Excitement. But he felt nothing. He just wasn't interested.

It was odd, really. It wasn't as if he was immune to women anymore. He'd noticed Sam's fabulous legs tonight. And he noticed the way her eyes could sparkle one minute and then suddenly cloud over with sadness the next. He noticed the way her striking red hair framed her heart-shaped face with vibrant color. He sensed her deep loneliness, which triggered an unexpected protective response in him—and something more, he admitted. Ever since he'd met her, there'd been occasions when he wanted to reach over and touch her for reasons that were not altruistic. His motivation had been purely physical, not spiritual.

So given his reaction to Sam, who was only a friend,

he was relatively certain that the right woman, someone like Rachel, could trigger a strong emotional response in him. He was also relatively certain that he was ready to allow someone new into his life.

Then why did he feel absolutely nothing about this date Sam was arranging? He should be looking forward to it. She sounded like a nice woman. They might have a lot in common. It could be the beginning of a whole new chapter in his life. He should be enthusiastic and optimistic. He *would* be enthusiastic and optimistic, he told himself resolutely. He would go to sleep imagining what Stephanie Morris looked like, he thought determinedly.

Funny thing was, try as he might to conjure up her image, every picture he created as he drifted off to sleep featured a woman with startling green eyes and striking red hair.

Chapter Four

Sam dashed into the café, muttering an unflattering comment about the weather as she paused to catch her breath. April was supposed to bring showers, not monsoons, she thought irritably. She'd been dodging raindrops all morning with two different clients, both of whom lingered far longer than expected at every house, and then she'd run into a major traffic jam. All of which meant she was twenty minutes late for her lunch with Laura.

Sam brushed her hair back from her face and sighed as she peered at her reflection in a small mirror just inside the door. She not only *felt* frazzled, she *looked* frazzled. For someone who was always meticulous about her appearance, it was a distressing realization. But then, she'd had a lot of distressing realizations lately, she thought wryly. This one was low on the scale of importance compared to the others.

Sam ineffectually ran her fingers through her hair and then gave up, acknowledging that it was a lost cause. With a sigh, she turned, scanning the room rapidly. It took her only a moment to spot Laura, seated at a quiet corner table, sipping a cup of tea, looking absolutely placid and dreamy-eyed, a faint smile on her face. That's what a honeymoon did for you, Sam supposed wistfully.

She was almost to the table before Laura saw her and smiled a warm welcome. "Sam! Oh, it's so good to see you!"

Sam slid into the seat across from Laura and grinned. "Well, better late than never. Listen, kiddo, I'm sorry. You wouldn't believe the morning I had. Two difficult clients, a traffic jam—"

"Sam, it's all right," Laura said. "I didn't mind waiting. But you look stressed out. Do you want some tea? Or would you prefer something stronger?" she asked with a smile.

"I'm on duty. Tea will have to do," Sam said resignedly. "I'll have whatever kind you're drinking—it seems to have a relaxing effect."

Laura grinned. "Well, I think my state of mind has more to do with three weeks in Hawaii," she admitted.

Sam studied her friend's face. The fine lines of tension that had always been around her eyes were gone, and the faint, parallel etchings on her brow had all but disappeared. "I have to say I don't think I've ever seen you look this…mellow."

Laura smiled. "I *feel* mellow. I don't know, Sam…ever since the wedding it's like a missing piece of my life has dropped into place. I feel…well…more alive, I guess. Nick is so wonderful…" Her voice caught, and she smiled ruefully. "I guess I still can't believe I really have him."

"Believe it, honey," Sam said. "And count your blessings."

"I do. Every single day," Laura said fervently.

"Okay, so enough of this mushy stuff," Sam declared. "Let's have some of the fun details. Tell me everything you did...other than the obvious," she said with an irreverent grin and a wink that brought a blush to Laura's cheeks.

Sam found herself smiling frequently at Laura's enthusiastic retelling of her dream honeymoon. Her face was animated and alive, and Sam's throat tightened at the soft, tender look that came into her eyes whenever she mentioned Nick's name. Clearly he was everything he seemed to be, and for that Sam was grateful. Laura deserved a caring, richly faceted relationship after her traumatic first marriage and the subsequent years of guilt and loneliness. It had taken Nick, with his patience, understanding and tenderness, to help her overcome her fear of commitment and find the courage to take a second chance on love. It was a classic story of triumph over tragedy, and Sam was truly happy for them both.

"And so it was really hard to come back," Laura concluded as they finished their dessert. "Hawaii is truly a tropical paradise, and I felt like I was in a dream. I don't think anyone ever had such a perfect honeymoon," she said with a sigh.

Sam grinned. "Well, based on everything you said, I think you're probably right. Do you know that you're actually glowing? And you look like you gained a few pounds, thank heavens."

"I did," Laura confirmed. "It was the first real vacation I've ever had. I mean, all we did was walk on the beach, eat fantastic meals, sleep and...well, you know," she said, a blush once more staining her cheeks becomingly.

Sam laughed. "Yeah, I know. And if Nick had anything to say about it, I have a feeling you did a lot of that 'you know' stuff."

Laura's blush deepened. "Well, after all, he waited patiently for a long time."

"I know. The man is a saint, if you ask me," Sam said with a grin.

"I won't argue with you there," Laura agreed. "But you know something, Sam?" she said earnestly. "I think we both feel like it was worth waiting for. The waiting made it even more special."

"Well, that's all that matters, then." Sam grinned. "I'll have to tell Brad that his theory about judging how much fun you had by how sleep deprived you looked was wrong."

"Brad?" Laura tried to recall which one of Sam's wide circle of male friends he was, but she came up blank.

"Yeah. Brad Matthews."

Laura frowned. Brad Matthews. She didn't recall Sam ever mentioning anyone by that name before. She tried to keep Sam's many admirers straight, but this one eluded her. "Do I know him?" she asked.

"Of course. Brad Matthews," Sam repeated. When Laura still looked confused, she laughed. "Your minister," Sam explained.

Laura stared at her uncomprehendingly. "Brad…my minister?" she repeated.

"Yeah. How about that?" Sam said, striving for a flippant tone. She supposed she shouldn't be surprised that Laura was shocked at the incongruous pairing. It was pretty bizarre, after all. Talk about two different kinds of people!

Laura still looked confused. "Now wait a minute. When did Brad say this? At the wedding?"

"No. On the phone after the wedding. He called me."

"Brad called you?" Laura knew she was beginning to sound like a parrot, but she was having a hard time linking her minister and her best friend in any way whatsoever.

"Uh-huh. They're going to tear the parsonage down, so he needs to find a house. He thought I could help," Sam explained.

"Oh!" That made a little more sense. Laura had told Brad that Sam sold real estate, and they *had* met at the wedding.

"He's a nice man," Sam ventured, keeping her tone light. "I'm surprised you and he never...clicked, you know what I mean?"

"Brad and me?" Laura said in surprise. "Oh, Sam, I grew up with Brad. He was more like a brother. And when he became a minister, I just started thinking of him in that role. I never even considered anything romantic. Anyway, he was married until six years ago, and at that point the last thing on my mind was romance. Besides, he was really in love with his wife."

"Rachel. Yeah, I know," Sam said, playing with her teacup. "It sounds like she was a wonderful person."

Laura studied her friend curiously. She seemed... *vulnerable* was the word that came to mind, although Laura had a hard time associating that characteristic with the self-confident, in-control Sam she'd always known. Yet it seemed to fit today. Why? And how did she know about Brad's wife? "Did Brad tell you about Rachel?" Sam asked curiously.

Sam shrugged. "It just sort of came up during our phone conversation, and then again at lunch."

Laura set her cup down carefully and folded her hands. "Now let me get this straight," she said slowly. "You and Brad had lunch?"

"Yeah. It was no big deal," Sam said lightly. "I took him out to look at a few houses, and we stopped for a bite to eat afterward."

"Okay. But how on earth did you get him to talk about Rachel? He never talks about her."

"He doesn't?"

"No. I've always gotten the impression that it was too painful for him. Her death was such a tragedy."

Sam frowned. "Yeah, he told me. It must have been awful for him." She took a deep breath. "I don't know why he talked about her to me," she admitted. "But he seems lonely. And sometimes people have to talk about things before they can let them go. Anyway, I think he's ready to consider romance again. Why else would he have agreed to the blind date I suggested after the symphony? Okay, so I pushed it a little, but—"

"Sam." Laura cut her off, starring at her friend uncomprehendingly. "Wait a minute. You went to the symphony with Brad? And he's going on a blind date?"

"Yeah." Sam shifted uncomfortably. "Listen, maybe he doesn't want anyone to know. You won't spread it around, will you?"

"No. Of course not. But...all of this happened in the three weeks I was gone?"

"Uh-huh."

Laura shook her head. "I don't believe it. How did this symphony thing come up?"

Sam shrugged. "I got some free tickets, and at lunch that day Brad mentioned that he and Rachel used to enjoy going. So I figured he might like it. After all, he was the one who suggested that maybe we could be friends, and offering the ticket seemed like a friendly thing to do. Besides, he's a really nice guy, Laura."

"Oh, I know. Absolutely. You couldn't find many guys nicer than Brad." Laura eyed her friend speculatively. Sam actually looked flushed—an unusual condition for her. Laura had never seen her ruffled or embarrassed by anything. "It's just that..." Her voice trailed off.

Sam grinned sheepishly. "You don't have to say it. Let me. Why in heaven's name—pardon the ecclesiastical pun—would someone like Brad be interested in having a friend like me? I asked him the same thing. He just said a person can't have too many friends, and then pointed out that you and I are really different, and we're friends. I couldn't fault his logic. Anyway, I like being with him. He's really solid, you know? And he's kind and empathetic and intelligent. Plus, he has a good sense of humor."

Laura took a sip of water. "He's not bad looking, either," she said innocently.

"Not bad looking?" Sam replied with a snort. "Honey, he's a hunk. Okay, if it's in bad taste to say that about a minister, I'm sorry. But let's give credit where it's due. He *is* a hunk."

"Yeah, I guess he is," Laura agreed, trying not to smile.

"Not that I'm interested in him in that way, you understand. Can you imagine that? Swinging single Sam and straight-arrow minister Brad. Not a good fit. Besides, I'm not really in the market for romance at the moment," she said with a careless lift of one shoulder.

"You're not?" Laura said in surprise. "I thought you were always looking for Mr. Right."

"Not anymore, kiddo. I've called a moratorium on the search. I'm just glad you found your Prince Charming."

"But why aren't you looking?" Laura persisted with a frown. For as long as Laura had known her, Sam had claimed to be on the hunt for a husband.

Sam waved the question aside. "It's a long story, hon. Too long to go into today." They were moving onto dangerous ground, which meant she needed to distract Laura. And the next topic was sure to do the trick, she thought wryly. "Besides, I have a favor to ask."

"Sure," Laura replied, still pondering Sam's last remark. What was the long story? she wondered.

"Now don't fall off your chair, kiddo, but I was wondering if I could go with you sometime to one of your Bible study classes," Sam said lightly.

Laura's eyes grew wide and she stared at her friend, speechless. It was about the reaction Sam expected. She'd felt sort of the same way when the idea occurred to her out of the blue, right after the lunch with Brad, which had given her a new "take" on religion. If a man like Brad had chosen to make it his life's work, and if someone of Laura's fragile sensitivity had found strength enough in her faith to carry her through the traumatic years of her marriage, then maybe it was worth checking out, Sam figured. She'd been off balance ever since the wedding, feeling lost and more alone than she had in years. She needed direction and support, and maybe she could find it in her long-neglected faith. It wouldn't hurt to try, and Laura was her entrée. *If* she ever got over her shock.

Sam smiled and reached over to teasingly snap her fingers in front of her friend's face. "Hello? Is anybody home?"

Laura blinked and made an attempt to regain her wits. Sam was always full of surprises, but today she'd outdone herself. "You want to go with me to Bible study class?" she repeated slowly, wanting to verify that she'd correctly heard Sam's request.

"Yep. I figured I'd give it a shot."

"Well, sure. Of course," Laura said, recovering quickly. She'd invited Sam a few times through the years, but without success. She had a feeling a certain minister was responsible for this change of heart. "We meet on Thursday from seven-thirty to nine."

"And this is a group of people from all over the area, right? Not just Brad's congregation."

"Right."

"And it's not at Brad's church?"

"No."

"Good. Listen, don't say anything about this to anyone, okay? It's jut a trial thing, really, and I'd rather keep it quiet."

"What about Brad? You're going to tell him, aren't you?"

"No. Not yet, anyway. You won't say anything, will you?"

"Not if you don't want me to," Laura promised.

"Good. Who knows? I might only last one session," Sam joked. Then, before Laura could probe any further, she glanced at her watch. "Oh, good grief! Have we been here two hours? I've got to meet a client in thirty minutes way out west. You may still be a lady of leisure for a few more days, but some of us aren't so lucky." Sam slung her purse over her shoulder and reached across the table to squeeze Laura's hand. "I'm really glad you had such a great time, Laura. You deserve it. Give Nick my best, okay? And let's talk soon."

"Oh, absolutely," Laura said. Real soon, if she had anything to say about it. There were an awful lot of holes in Sam's story that needed to be filled in. "I'll call you in a couple of days with details about the class."

"Thanks. You take care now." Sam said as she stood up.

"You, too," Laura replied.

Laura watched her friend walk toward the door, her self-confident saunter and swinging red hair the same as always. But there was something different about Sam. Something very different. Could it be that… Laura shook her head. Brad and Sam? No, it wasn't possible. Or was it? She'd have to run it by Nick and see what he thought. But Laura already knew what *she* thought. There was romance in the air.

"You've got to be kidding!" Nick looked up from the complex architectural rendering on his computer screen and stared at Laura.

"No! It's the truth!" Laura said excitedly, still out of breath from her dash up the stairs to Nick's second-floor home office in their sprawling Victorian.

"But Sam and Brad? That's ridiculous!"

"Why?"

"Oh, come on, Laura. Can you imagine two people any more different?"

"That's what Sam said," Laura replied impatiently.

"But I'm telling you, when she talks about him she gets this look in her eyes…" Laura's voice trailed off dreamily.

Nick smiled indulgently. "What look?"

"You know. That look, like he's special."

"Oh, *that* look," he said, his eyes twinkling.

"Nick, will you be serious!"

"How can I be? Sam and Brad?" He shook his head doubtfully. "Laura, sweetheart, you know I have great respect for your instincts. But I think you're jumping to the wrong conclusions in this case. This all started out as a business arrangement, remember? He called her to help him find a house. Period."

"Yeah, but then they had lunch, and they went to the symphony."

Nick shrugged. "Well, you know Sam. She can be pretty forceful. Brad probably just didn't want to hurt her feelings."

Laura frowned, somewhat deflated. "Well, he is going out on that blind date Sam's fixing him up with," she admitted. "But that doesn't mean he isn't interested in Sam, too," she declared stubbornly.

Nick stared at her. "Sam convinced Brad to go out on a blind date?" he asked incredulously.

"Yeah."

Nick chuckled and shook his head. "That woman is amazing." Then he sat forward and propped his elbows on the desk. "Look, Laura, I really like Sam. She's a great gal. But you might be stretching it just a little to think that she and Brad would get together."

"Well, opposites can attract," Laura pointed out. "And you know, the Lord often works in mysterious way."

"Yeah, but it would take Agatha Christie to figure this one out," he said with a grin.

"Oh, Nick," Laura said, coming around the desk and settling herself on his lap. "I just want Sam to be as blissfully happy as I am. Maybe I can sort of help things along and…"

"Laura." Nick's voice held a warning note. "We are not going to play matchmaker."

"Why not? Sam tried to fix me up plenty of times. I still remember those awful events for singles she used to drag me to," she said with a shudder. "I think turnabout is only fair play."

"I don't know," Nick said doubtfully.

Laura smiled and leaned down to nibble on his ear. "What don't you know?"

He drew in a sharp breath as a flash of heat ricocheted through him. "Are you by any chance trying to distract me?" he asked.

"Mmm-hmm. Is it working?" she murmured.

"You might say that," he replied huskily, his hands beginning to touch her in ways that sent a delicious shiver up her spine.

"Do you want me to stop?" she offered, pressing even closer against him.

"Stop?" He chuckled deep in his throat. "Sweetheart, you may not know it, but this is just the appetizer," he said, bending to claim her lips.

By the time the kiss ended, both of them felt breathless, and Nick slid his arm under Laura's knees and stood up. She nestled contentedly into his shoulder, her arms around his neck as he headed for the door, Sam and Brad forgotten—for the moment.

"Mmm," she murmured throatily. "I can't wait for dessert."

* * *

Sam's throat constricted as she gazed at the confused and frightened eighteen-year-old girl seated across from her, so alone and in need of love and understanding. Impulsively she reached for her hand, and the girl's icy fingers clutched hers convulsively.

"You've told me what everyone else thinks, Jamie," Sam said gently. "But what do *you* want to do?"

The girl chewed on her bottom lip, and tears suddenly flooded her eyes. "I—I don't know," she admitted helplessly. "My mom and dad and John and all my friends are sure it will ruin my life if I have the baby, but it feels so... so wrong to just...get rid of it."

Sam nodded understandingly, "I know what you mean. You'd like to believe there's not really a life at stake, because then your decision would be easy. But your heart is telling you there is."

"Yeah. That's exactly right," the girl affirmed, clearly grateful and relieved that someone at last seemed to understand how she felt.

"Let me ask you something, Jamie," Sam said slowly, choosing her words carefully. "Has anyone suggested that it might ruin your life if you *don't* have the baby? If you 'get rid of it' as you said."

The girl looked surprised. "No."

"You might want to give that some thought," Sam suggested, her voice still gentle. "Ask yourself how you'll feel in a few years when you see a little child that would be the same age as your baby. That's a hard thing to face, Jamie."

"But I'm not ready to be a mother! Especially a single

mother!'' the girl cried, her voice agitated and once more desperate. ''John doesn't want any part of it, and Mom and Dad are against it. I'd be totally on my own.''

''We can offer you a lot of support here,'' Sam said encouragingly. ''We can help with medical expenses, and I'm available to talk any time you need me. As for being a single mother, that's your choice, of course. And we'll help you in every way we can if you decide to take on that responsibility. But we have a list of dozens of couples, who, for whatever reason, can't have their own children. They'd welcome your baby with open arms and give him or her all the love they've stored up in their hearts. We've checked them out thoroughly, and they're all fine people, so you can be sure your baby would have a wonderful home.''

Jamie dabbed at her eyes. ''I just feel so confused,'' she said, her voice breaking.

''That's understandable,'' Sam empathized, her heart going out to the distressed young woman. ''It's a big decision, and it's hard to make a rational choice when you don't have much support from family and friends. But remember, Jamie—you do have a choice.''

There was silence for a moment, and then the girl sighed. ''I guess I'll just have to think about it some more,'' she concluded.

''That's a good idea. In the meantime, I'm here if you need me.'' Sam reached for a notepad and scrawled two numbers. ''The top number is the counseling center,'' she told Jamie as she tore off the sheet and handed it to her. ''The bottom one is my home phone. You can call me anytime, day or night, if you want to talk. Okay?''

The girl took the piece of paper and tucked it into the pocket of her jeans. "Okay. And thanks for listening tonight. It helped a lot."

"I'm glad. In fact, why don't we set up another appointment for next week? I can give you more details on our program and answer any questions you might think of between now and then."

"Okay."

After they chose a mutually agreeable time, Sam walked with her to the door. "Take care, Jamie," she said, letting her hand rest lightly on the girl's shoulder. "And call me in a couple of days, okay? Just to talk. Will you do that?"

"Yeah. Thanks."

Sam watched the rail-thin girl disappear down the hall, then closed the door. She walked slowly back through the counseling center to the director's office, a frown of concern etched on her face.

Carolyn looked up when Sam paused on the threshold. "How did it go?"

Sam shook her head and sighed. "I don't know. She's obviously trying to do the right thing, but it's equally obvious she's not getting any support at home. I'm just not sure I got through to her."

Carolyn set her glasses on her desk and gave her hardest-working volunteer a sympathetic look. "You did everything you could, Sam. That's all we can ask."

Sam looked at the motherly, gray-haired woman in frustration, then stuck her hands into the pockets of her slacks. "I just don't think it was enough this time. I don't have good feelings about this one."

Carolyn tapped her pen on the edge of the desk and studied the younger woman. "Sometimes I worry as much about you as the girls who come in here, Sam,'' she told her soberly. ''You take this so much to heart. I know it tears you up inside whenever you fail. And yet you keep coming back. I admire that kind of dedication.''

Sam waved the praise aside impatiently. ''Don't admire me, Carolyn. You know better.'' The director of the counseling center was the only person who knew even a piece of the tragic incident in Sam's past.

''Sam, whatever drives you to come here week after week and put yourself through an emotional wringer is your business. The motivation doesn't negate the good work you do. Thanks to you, a lot of children are here today—happy, healthy and enjoying the gift of life.''

Sam felt tears prick her eyelids, and she blinked to keep them at bay. ''But a lot of them aren't, Carolyn,'' she said dejectedly. ''And it's those children who haunt me.''

''Listen, Sam, I know it's an imposition, and I'm really sorry to put you on the spot like this, but it would save my life if you'd fill in.''

Sam frowned, trying to get Jamie out of her mind and focus on her friend's request. Normally she wouldn't hesitate to help Laura out, but it might be awkward. Since Brad had unenthusiastically reported to her on his date, they hadn't spoken. Doing a seminar at his church under those circumstances…well, it probably wasn't such a good idea. Even though he hadn't sounded terribly upset on the phone, he'd made it clear in their brief conversation that he didn't intend to go on any more blind dates.

''Sam?'' Laura prompted.

''Yeah, I'm still here. Listen, does Brad know about this?''

"What?"

"Me filling in."

"No. But these seminars are my responsibility and he doesn't usually get involved other than approving the topics."

"Explain to me again what this is exactly," Sam said, trying to buy some more time while she thought this through.

"Sure," Laura said patiently. "Brad believes that the church should offer assistance to people in all facets of living, not just spiritual. So about a year ago he got a committee together to plan some practical seminars for people in different phases of their lives. We decided to try it once a month for six months and see what kind of response we got. So far we've had seminars on how to choose child care, what to look for in nursing homes, planning for retirement and coping with loss. This month's topic is how to buy a home, and it's designed for young couples just starting out. About thirty people are signed up. You might even pick up some new clients," Laura pointed out.

"And it's this Saturday?"

"Uh-huh. One to three." Laura held her breath. It was sheer providence that their scheduled presenter, a member of the congregation, had to go out of town unexpectedly. And Laura intended to take advantage of it.

Sam frowned. She was available. And it really did sound like Laura was in a bind. Besides, Brad might not even be around. And Laura was right. Sam might pick up some new clients.

"Okay, kiddo. I'll be there," she said.

Laura let out her breath and smiled. "Great! And thanks a bunch, Sam."

"No problem. See you Saturday."

Laura hung up the phone, a satisfied smile on her face. Mission accomplished. Or at least phase one.

Sam didn't even notice when Brad slipped into a chair in the back of the room during her presentation. And she didn't see him during the lively question and answer session that followed, either. It wasn't until afterward, as she tried to collect her materials amid a barrage of one-on-one questions, that she realized he was the person handing her a cup of coffee. She paused midsentence as their eyes connected.

"I'll talk to you when you're finished," he said quietly, with a smile.

She nodded and forced her attention back to the eager young couples who were still plying her with questions.

When at last the final, lingering attendees departed, Laura stepped forward and gave her a hug. "You were a hit," she declared. "Great job! Why am I not surprised? See," she said, turning triumphantly to Brad as he joined them, "didn't I tell you she'd be great?"

Sam looked at Brad, and his warm smile played havoc with her metabolism.

"Yes. But I never doubted it. I know from personal experience that she's one sharp businesswoman." And she truly had been in top form today, he thought. Animated, wisecracking, high energy—she'd not only passed on important information, she'd kept her audience entertained in the process. "And the presentation was great. I wish my sermons were that dynamic," he said with a grin.

Sam felt a flush creep up her neck at his compliment and turned away on the pretense of putting some papers in her briefcase. "I just hope it was useful," she said.

"I know it was," Laura assured her. "Listen, Sam, I hate to run, but Nick and I have dinner plans tonight. Do you mind if I take off?"

"No, not at all. If I had someone like Nick waiting for me at home, you can bet *I* wouldn't be hanging around a church basement with a girlfriend," she said, turning to Laura with a grin.

Laura laughed. "I'll call you next week."

"Okay. Have fun tonight."

"Thanks. Brad, will you lock up?"

"Sure."

"Great. See you two later."

As Laura disappeared out the door, Brad turned back to Sam, and his smile seemed to grow even warmer. Or was it just her imagination, she wondered?

"You really were good, you know," he said.

She shrugged. "I'm glad I could fill in." She paused and took a deep breath, deciding she might as well clear the air about the date thing right up front. It had been on her mind ever since their one brief phone call following the less-than-successful event. "Look, Brad, I'm really sorry the date didn't work out. I understand if you're upset and felt I'd been too pushy, and I—"

"Who said anything about being upset?" he interrupted with a frown.

"Well, you didn't sound too happy on the phone afterward, and I haven't heard from you since, so I just assumed—"

"Sam." He took her hand, and a sweet shiver ran

through her at his touch. He had wonderful hands—gentle, but strong and sure. "Can we sit down for a minute, or do you have to rush off?"

"No. I have some time," she said, her voice suddenly hoarse. Must be from all that talking for the past couple of hours, she thought.

Still holding her hand, he led her to the first row of chairs and drew her down beside him. "First of all, I am not upset about the date," he said, angling himself toward her. "Stephanie is a very nice woman, and we had a lot in common. You made a good match. But...I don't know. If you've talked to her, she may have told you the same thing. There just wasn't any...spark."

He was right. At least, half-right. Stephanie liked Brad—a lot. But she sensed his lack of romantic interest.

"Maybe it's too soon, like you said," Sam suggested, employing the same theory she had used to console Stephanie.

Brad shook his head. "No. That's not it." He stood up and walked a few steps away, jamming his hands into the pockets of his slacks. "I should have felt something. I don't know why I didn't. She was very nice, and it was a pleasant, relaxing evening. Almost too relaxing, if that makes any sense. She was just too quiet. I guess I like people who are a little more...lively. I don't know," he repeated with a frustrated sigh, raking his fingers through his hair. "But for whatever reason, we just didn't click."

"Well, we can try again."

"No," he said quickly. At her surprised look, he amended his response. "I mean, not right away, anyway."

"Are you sure?"

"Yeah."

Sam shrugged. "Okay. If that's the way you want it." For some reason Sam wasn't inclined to push him this time. In fact, she was almost relieved that things hadn't worked out with Stephanie. Which was wrong, of course. But she couldn't help how she felt.

"I do appreciate your efforts, Sam."

"Hey, no problem. What are friends for? I'm just glad you're not mad. When I didn't hear from you, I got a little worried."

Brad sat down next to her again and closed his eyes, rubbing his forehead with the tips of his fingers. "I apologize for that. The week after that date was hectic, and for the last week I've had my father here visiting."

"Does he still live in Jersey?" Through the years Sam had heard a great deal about Laura's—and Brad's—hometown in southern Missouri.

"Yeah. My mom died about six months ago, and Dad's just never been able to regroup."

"I'm sorry," Sam said softly, reaching out to touch his hand.

"Thanks. It was hard on all of us. But I have my work, and Rebecca, my sister, has her restaurant in St. Genevieve, so life went on for us. But for Dad—well, Mom was always his main interest in life. They had a great marriage. Talk about two peas in a pod..." He sighed. "Anyway, he just kind of lost interest in everything when she died. Even his gardens, which were always his pride and joy. He hasn't even touched them this year. Rebecca and I have been really worried about him. She gets down there as often as she can. But since she opened the restaurant about a year and a half ago she hardly has a minute to call her own. I finally convinced Dad to come up here for a week, thinking maybe I could lift his spirits a little. But I can't say I've had much luck," he admitted with a sigh. Then his eyes grew thoughtful. "Say, I don't suppose there's any chance you're free tonight and would consider having dinner with a stodgy minister and his lonely old dad, would you?"

Sam stared at him, taken aback by the unexpected invitation. "Well, I don't know..." she said slowly, her voice trailing off.

Brad gave her a sheepish grin. "Look, never mind. It was a dumb idea. I'm sure you already have plans. And even if you don't, there are lots more exciting things you could do—like clean out your closets or vacuum the furniture."

Sam smiled. "As a matter of fact, Brad, I don't have plans tonight. And I'd love to have dinner with you and your dad. But he may not like having a third party there, especially if he's feeling down."

"Well, I think it would be good for him to meet someone like you," Brad said. "You're really great with people, and *I* always feel better around you. You have a knack for making me smile and feel lighthearted. Maybe you can do the same for Dad."

Sam had a feeling Brad didn't even realize that he'd just paid her a terrific compliment. Which was okay. *She* realized it, and that was the important thing. It was one of those lovely moments she intended to file away in her heart.

"I can certainly give it a try," she said with a warm smile.

"Great!" Brad glanced at his watch. "Let's see. It's already four...how about if we pick you up at six?"

"Are you sure you don't want me to just meet you somewhere?"

"I'd rather pick you up, if that's okay."

"But it's not a date or anything."

"Yeah, I know. Not too many guys would bring their fathers along on a date. I do remember that much," he said with a grin. Then he grew more serious. "But with the world what it is today, I'd just feel better seeing you to the door afterward."

"Well, sure, that would be great, if you don't mind."

"It's my pleasure," he said with a smile that warmed her right down to her toes.

"Is this going to be casual?" she asked.

"I think my dad would be more comfortable, if that's all right with you."

"Sure. I'll just run home and change." She stood up, and Brad followed suit, his gaze sweeping over her in a quick but appreciative appraisal.

"Too bad," he said. "I like that outfit."

Sam was surprised—and ruffled—by the compliment. She looked down and adjusted a button on her fitted short-sleeved tunic jacket, then smoothed down her short skirt. She'd debated whether to wear low, comfortable shoes or dressier two-inch heels, and she was suddenly glad she'd chosen the latter, which emphasized the shapely line of her legs.

"Are you wearing that?" she asked, nodding toward his khakis, blue shirt and lightweight off-white cotton sweater.

"Yeah. I was planning to."

"Then this is a little too dressy," she said.

"I could change," he offered.

She grinned, tilting her head to look up at him. "Do you like this outfit that much?"

He smiled. "Uh-huh."

"I'll wear it again sometime, then," she promised.

"It's a deal. But Sam..."

She looked at him curiously when he paused. "Yes?"

"I hope this doesn't sound too forward, but...maybe you could wear one of those short skirts? They look really great on you."

Sam stared at him in surprise, and a warm tingle raced along her spine. "Are you sure a minister should be asking a woman to wear a short skirt?" she chided teasingly, trying to keep her voice light...and steady.

"No," he promptly admitted. "But they suit you. And besides, sometimes when I'm with you I forget all about being a minister."

She smiled. "You know what?"

"What?"

"Sometimes I forget, too."

He looked thoughtful. "Maybe that's good."

"Why do you say that?"

"Well, I know your past experience with ministers hasn't been great. Maybe we get along so well because you do forget. So it might be a good thing."

"Maybe," she said slowly. Then she frowned. She was letting herself get too carried away here. It would be in both of their best interests for her to *remember* his profession so she was reminded of the impossibility of anything ever developing between them. She reached for her briefcase and turned to go, suddenly subdued. "Then again, maybe not," she said enigmatically. "See you in a little while, Brad."

Brad watched her leave, puzzled by her last remark. Had he been too forward, after all? He probably shouldn't have mentioned the skirt, he thought. In retrospect, it seemed out of line—and out of character. Maybe she'd gotten the impression that he wanted to change the status of their relationship from friendship to…something else. And maybe he did, he realized suddenly with surprise.

Brad frowned at that unexpected insight. Where on earth had that idea come from? Of course he was only interested in friendship. Sam wasn't his type. Okay, maybe he found her physically attractive. No, he corrected himself. There were no "maybes" about it. He *definitely* found her physically attractive. He'd had hormones kick in around Sam that had lain dormant for six long years. But physical attraction wasn't nearly enough to sustain a permanent relationship. And that was all they had, really. Or at least all *he* had. He had no idea whether Sam felt any attraction for him.

But what if she did? he suddenly wondered. An unbidden surge of adrenaline swept over him at the thought, but he quickly squelched it. Unfortunately it would never work between them. They were too different. Not that he didn't enjoy being with Sam. He enjoyed it a lot. She was lively, and that was something he hadn't had much of in his life. She was also attractive, intelligent, articulate, had a good sense of humor and was clearly a good person in many ways.

But even though her current social life was apparently much quieter than he'd imagined, he suspected that comparing the history of their romantic escapades would be like comparing Pollyanna to Madame Du Barry. His choices regarding intimacy had been grounded in a deep faith; hers…he didn't know her motivations, but her rules had clearly been much more liberal than his.

Even beyond differing philosophies on intimacy, though, it would be very difficult for him to become involved with someone who didn't share his basic Christian values, beliefs and life-style. Not to mention his strong faith. And Sam didn't seem to, apart from a few remnants that had survived from her Christian upbringing. While he had no doubt that she was highly principled and ethical—admirable qualities, to be sure—those attributes alone didn't make one a Christian.

No, Sam and he weren't right for each other. There were too many obstacles in the way of a romantic relationship. And yet…he felt drawn to her. He couldn't deny that. But what was he supposed to do about it?

Brad stood up in frustration and turned off the lights, then locked the door. Slowly he made his way upstairs, pausing at the church door. With a quick glance at his watch, he detoured inside and sat down in the last pew, bowing his head and closing his eyes.

Lord, I asked You to help me find the courage to put the past to rest and open myself to a new relationship, he prayed silently. *With Your help, I'm making progress. But now I have a new dilemma. Sam. I certainly never intended to feel anything more for her than friendship. And I don't want to now. But I forgot that the heart doesn't often listen to logic. I really like her, Lord. And I think it could grow to more than that. But we're so different… Could this possibly work? She says her reputation has been exaggerated, and I believe her. There is a sadness in her eyes, an honesty when she talks about it, that I cannot doubt. I believe that she's a very special lady who* hasn't seen enough kindness or caring in her life. And I'd like to show her both. But I'm not sure how to proceed— or even if I should—beyond a friendship basis. Please, Lord, help me to discern Your will.

But no matter what happens between the two of us, Lord, help Sam overcome her disillusionment about her faith and find her way home to You again. Because I believe that is the only way she'll find the lasting peace she seems to so desperately need.

Chapter Five

"I hope you won't be sorry," Brad said with a frown as he guided Sam toward his car, his hand at the small of her back. "Dad wasn't overly enthusiastic about having to carry on a conversation all during dinner with someone he's never met. He's gotten quieter and quieter these past few months. I'm afraid this could be uncomfortable."

Sam grinned. "Don't worry, Brad. I like a challenge," she assured him.

His features relaxed. "Thanks for being a good sport. And for agreeing to have dinner with us tonight."

"I think it will be fun," she said optimistically.

"I hope you still feel that way in a couple of hours," he replied dubiously.

They stopped beside the car, and a slight, thin man with fine gray hair climbed out of the back seat. Sam saw the resemblance immediately. Although Brad was a good four inches taller than his father, they had the same brown eyes and slightly angular nose. But while Brad's stance was typically relaxed, his father held himself somewhat stiffly, as if he felt awkward and would rather be somewhere else.

"Dad, this is Sam Reynolds," Brad said, his hand still at the small of her back. "Sam, this is my father, Henry."

Sam smiled and held out her hand. "It's very nice to meet you, Mr. Matthews. And thanks for letting me join you tonight for dinner. It's not often that a woman gets a chance to go out with *two* handsome men."

Her comment elicited only the smallest of smiles from Brad's father as he took her hand. "How do you do, Miss Reynolds. I'm very happy to meet you," he said politely.

"Thank you. And please call me Sam."

"Well, shall we go?" Brad asked, opening Sam's door. He gave her an I-told-you-so look as she slid into the seat, but she just winked and smiled confidently.

Brad's father remained quiet, answering her questions politely but in as few words as possible, during the drive to the restaurant. She tried to draw him out as they perused the menu, with little success. So once they had ordered she decided it was time to unveil her secret weapon.

"So, Mr. Matthews, Brad tells me you're a gardener," she said conversationally.

"Used to be," he replied, fiddling with his napkin.

"What do you grow?" she asked, ignoring the past tense.

"Roses. Perennials."

"What's your favorite rose variety?"

"Tea roses."

"Hmm. Me, too. Do you have any Double Delights?"

For the first time he looked directly at her, his eyebrows raised in surprise. "A couple."

"Best scent of any rose I've ever grown," Sam declared, helping herself to a roll from the basket.

He tilted his head and peered at her intently. "You grow roses?" he asked.

"Uh-huh. And perennials, too. I have a little garden at the back of my condo. But I have a feeling yours is a lot bigger."

Brad's father shrugged. "It's a fair size, I guess. Thirty-two tea roses, and a couple of nice-sized perennial beds."

"Thirty-two roses!" Sam repeated incredulously. "Gosh, I only have eight. And just a little strip of perennials. How long have you been at this?"

"All my life. I've always liked flowers. Lot of people don't bother with roses, though. Say they're too much trouble."

Sam gave an unladylike snort. "Hmm. Spray them once a week, feed them once a month, cover them up for the winter—how hard is that?"

"That's what I think," Henry nodded in vigorous agreement. "They're no trouble at all, considering they bloom all summer. What kind of spray do you use?"

As Sam and his father launched into a lively discussion about the merits of one kind of spray versus another, Brad just sat back and watched the exchange in awed amazement. He would never have tagged Sam, with her sophisticated clothes and perfectly polished nails, as a gardener. He was beginning to realize just what a multidimensional and surprising woman she was. With Sam, it was becoming clear that he'd better learn to expect the unexpected.

Such as this dinner. Brad would have laid odds that it would be a disaster, despite Sam's outgoing nature and optimism. But, amazingly, she had done what no else had been able to—she'd drawn his father into an animated conversation and brought the sparkle and interest back to his eyes. She even got him to laugh. And as far as Brad was concerned, that was a miracle.

By the time they arrived back at her condo after an extended dinner, Sam and his father were on a first-name basis.

"Now, Henry, you aren't going to neglect those poor roses anymore, are you?" Sam asked, as Brad's father climbed out of the car to say good-night.

"Nope. Think I'll tackle'em first thing when I get home tomorrow," he said purposefully. "And you won't forget to send me some of those perennial hollyhock seeds, will you?" he asked eagerly. "Sounds like a mighty pretty plant, and can't say as I've ever seen'em down in Jersey."

"I won't forget. I'll put them in the mail next week," Sam promised. She held out her hand, and this time Henry shook it vigorously.

"It's been a pleasure, Sam. And you're welcome anytime to come down and see my gardens. Course, give me a little time to get them in shape," he said. "Maybe Brad'll bring you down some weekend," he suggested.

"Well, he's a busy man," Sam replied quickly, avoiding Brad's eyes. "But I'll be sure to stop by if I get down that way." Before Brad could say anything, she hurried on. "Now you take care, okay, Henry? And try that spray I told you about. It really does work wonders in this Missouri humidity. I haven't had a touch of black spot since I started using it."

"I sure will. And...thanks for having dinner with us, Sam. I had a good time," he added almost shyly.

"Me, too," she assured him with a warm smile.

"I'll just walk Sam to the door, Dad," Brad said.

"No hurry. You two take your time," he replied.

As they made their way toward her condo, Brad was silent, and Sam wondered if he felt awkward about his dad's suggestion. Maybe she should bring it up, say she didn't expect—

"Sam!" Her elderly next-door neighbor opened her door halfway and peered out.

"Hello, Mrs. Johnson," Sam said.

"I'm sorry to bother you, Sam, especially since you have a gentleman friend with you, but I've been watching for you. Did you have a chance to pick up those things for me?"

"Of course. I'll bring them over in just a couple of minutes," she said.

"That would be fine, dear. You go ahead and say goodnight to your young man first."

Sam's face flushed again, and she turned to Brad helplessly. "Sorry about that," she apologized.

"What?"

"That 'your young man' business. And I'm afraid your father has the wrong impression about our relationship, too."

Instead of commenting on her remark, he nodded at her neighbor's door as they passed. "What was that all about?"

"Oh. That's Mrs. Johnson. She's eighty-five, would you believe it? Anyway, her kids want to put her in a nursing home, but she's hanging on to her independence for dear life. Literally, I think. And she's perfectly able to look after herself with just a little bit of help. Like she needs someone to do her grocery shopping every week and pick up a prescription now and then. It's no big deal to me, and if it helps her stay independent, I'm glad to do it,'' Sam said with a shrug as they stopped in front of her door.

''That's a very nice thing to do,'' Brad said, touched by her thoughtfulness.

She shrugged again. ''Who knows, maybe someone will do the same for me someday when I'm old and all alone,'' she said with a crooked smile, fishing for her key.

When she found it, Brad reached over and took it from her hand, and she looked up at him in surprise. He closed his fingers around it and leaned against the door frame with one shoulder, crossing his arms in front of his chest. ''What makes you think you'll be all alone?'' he asked quietly.

Sam lifted one shoulder and averted her face slightly. ''I don't know,'' she said evasively. When he didn't respond, she looked up at him. He was watching her with an odd expression that made her heart stop, then race on. ''Brad, your dad is waiting,'' she said, suddenly breathless as she tried to control the panic that swept over her.

''He said to take our time,'' Brad reminded her.

''Yes, but there's no reason to keep him waiting.''

''Maybe there is,'' he said quietly.

Sam looked at him uncertainly, her heart thumping painfully in her chest. ''What do you mean?'' she asked, a strange catch in her voice.

He paused, as if choosing his words carefully. ''Sam, I want to thank you for what you did for Dad tonight,'' he said slowly.

She dismissed his thanks with a shake of her head. ''It was no effort. He's a nice man.''

''Where did you learn so much about flowers?''

"I've always liked them."

"Do you really have a garden?"

She looked surprised. "Of course."

"You never told me."

She frowned. "I guess it just never came up."

"It seems like I learn something new about you every day," he said. "You're a pretty terrific lady, do you know that? And by the way, I like your skirt." He let his gaze flicker briefly down to the short hemline.

Sam blushed. His voice had a warm, intimate tone that set off alarm bells and made her nerve endings tingle. And she still hadn't figured out that look in his eyes. If she didn't know better, she'd think he wanted to kiss her. But of course that was ridiculous.

"Well, thanks," she said, her voice still uneven. "Um, Brad, you really ought to get back to your dad."

He frowned. "Yeah, I guess so." He paused and took a deep breath. "Sam, I—"

"Brad." This time the panic in her voice was evident. "It's getting late."

He remained unmoving for a moment, studying her face with his perceptive eyes. Finally, with a sigh, he straightened up. "Yeah, I know." Before she realized his intent, he quickly leaned down and gently kissed her forehead. Then he put her key in the lock and pushed open the door. "I'll call you soon, Sam," he said quietly.

She stared at him, her heart banging against her rib cage, her breathing shallow. "Okay," she whispered.

Brad lifted his hand, as if to touch her, then dropped it and turned away, striding quickly down the walk.

Sam closed the door and sagged against the frame, not

trusting her shaky legs to support her. Things were starting to get out of hand here.

When Brad had first suggested friendship, she'd been touched—and pleased. But she'd really never expected it to go beyond that. Oh, sure, he was an attractive man. He was fun to be with, intelligent, sensitive. He had all the qualities she most admired in a man. Husband material for sure. But she'd known from the beginning that there was no possibility of that. They were too different. And even if those differences could be worked out, he would never be able to accept what she'd done. Even *she* couldn't accept it. Which was why she'd long ago ruled out marriage. And now was not the time to start changing the rules.

But then again, she hadn't expected to actually fall in love.

Sam let her eyelids fall, and hot tears welled up behind them as she acknowledged intellectually what her heart already knew—she loved Brad. How could she have let this happen? she cried silently. She should have seen it coming. And she supposed she had. She'd just chosen to ignore it. Because she wanted to be with him, and she figured she could handle the inevitable emotional upheaval. But she wasn't so sure anymore.

And how did he feel? she wondered, as she began assembling the groceries for Mrs. Johnson. He seemed to like her. Sometimes she thought she even detected stronger feelings than that in his eyes. Like tonight. But maybe gratitude was the explanation for tonight. After all, even though he *had* kissed her, it had felt more brotherly than romantic.

And she should be glad that's all it had been, she reminded herself sharply. Because if he showed any deeper interest, she'd have to stop seeing him. Immediately. Otherwise she would be misleading him, building up false expectations, and that would be wrong. In the end he would be hurt, and the last thing in the world she wanted to do was hurt Brad.

Yet how could she walk away, if that became necessary? she wondered desperately. The thought of never seeing him again was almost too painful to consider. But how long could she hide her real feelings? Tonight she had wanted him to kiss her. Really kiss her. She had almost lost control, reached out to him. And that out-of-control sensation frightened her. Given the depth of her feelings, she ought to stop this thing before it was too late.

Except that she had a feeling it already was.

"Seems like a nice girl."

Brad looked over at his father as he backed the car out of the parking spot. He thought about telling him that "girl" wasn't the politically correct term, but he doubted it would do any good, so he refrained. "She is," he replied shortly.

"Known her long?"

"Since Laura's wedding. She was the maid of honor."

"Let's see, that's been…what? Two months ago?"

"Just about."

"Hmm."

Brad gave his father a warning look. "Don't get any ideas, Dad."

"Ideas about what?" his father asked innocently.

"Ideas about Sam and me," Brad said.

"Well, she's a nice girl," he persisted.

"Yes," Brad agreed. "She's a very nice *woman*. But there are a lot of nice women in the world."

"None that you've noticed in recent years, far as I can tell," his father countered promptly.

"You're right," Brad admitted. "I haven't been looking. And I'm still not. Sam and I are just friends."

"Humph" was his father's only response.

Brad looked over at him in exasperation. "Now what's that supposed to mean?"

"Son, I may be old, but my sight is just fine. I watched you tonight, and when you look at Sam I don't see 'friendship' in your eyes."

Brad frowned. He obviously hadn't given his father's powers of perception enough credit. He himself was only now coming to grips with his feelings for Sam, still struggling to understand their implications, and his father had summed it up in one accurate, pithy sentence.

"So?" his father persisted.

"So what?" Brad asked.

His father sighed heavily. "So what are you going to do about it?" he asked impatiently.

"Dad, it's too soon to be even thinking about that," he protested.

Henry snorted. "Baloney. I only knew your mother two weeks when I decided she was the one for me. Took her a little bit longer," he admitted. "But she came around. We were married six months later. So it's not too soon."

Brad shook his head. "I'm not ready for anything that serious."

"Why not?" Henry demanded. And then his voice gentled. "It's been six years, son. And you're still a young man. You could still have that family you always wanted," he said, reaching over to touch Brad's shoulder. "Rachel was a wonderful woman, but she's gone and she wouldn't want you to be alone. You know that."

Brad sighed. "Yeah, I know. But it's hard to let go."

Henry looked down and fiddled with his seat belt. "That's for sure."

Brad glanced over at him. Some of the life had left his father's eyes, and he berated himself for dampening the spark that Sam had so successfully fanned back into life.

"So you think I should pursue this, then?" he asked, more to refocus his father's thoughts than to prolong the conversation about Sam.

Henry looked up. "Course I do. Wouldn't have brought it up if I hadn't."

"I take it you like Sam."

"What's not to like? She's got spirit, that girl. Did you see the way her eyes shine when she talks about gardening? Does a person good to be around that kind of enthusiasm."

"I know. I always feel good around Sam."

"Well, there you go. Can't believe somebody hasn't grabbed her up by now," Henry said, shaking his head.

"She was married once, Dad. Years ago."

His father's head swiveled toward his son. "She was?"

"Yes. When she was eighteen she married a musician. He just walked out on her one day after only a few months. It sounds like he left her high and dry, to use a cliché. She never saw him again. He died a few years later of a drug overdose."

His father had a few choice words for Sam's former husband before he turned his attention back to Brad.

"Well, I bet the right man could get her to take the plunge again."

"Maybe," Brad admitted. "But Sam and I are different in a lot of ways, Dad. Too different to get seriously involved."

His father folded his arms across his chest. "Well, I don't see it. Seems to me like you two get along just fine. And it would do you good to be around somebody spunky like Sam. She'd sure keep life interesting."

Brad chuckled. "I can't argue with you on that."

"You think about it, son," Henry said. "Because those kind don't come along too often. It'd be a real shame to let Sam slip away without ever givin' it a try. I think you'd always regret it."

Later, as Brad prepared for bed, he recalled his father's words. He had a feeling that the older man was right about regrets. And also about his son's interest. Because what Brad had felt tonight for Sam as he said good-night had definitely *not* been friendship. He'd wanted to kiss her. She had looked so appealing, so sexy, so…wonderful, he thought.

And he kept discovering new facets to her personality. She had been absolutely fantastic with his father tonight, drawing him out with her easygoing manner and surprising knowledge of gardening. He had actually seen the spark in his father's eyes rekindle. For that alone he would be eternally grateful to her. And then he'd discovered the assistance she gave her elderly neighbor. Few people would put themselves out like that on an ongoing basis. It was the Golden Rule in action. Then there was her volunteer work on Tuesday nights. He'd never discovered just what that involved, only that she was dedicated to it, but he was beginning to realize that this was the way Sam operated. She did good things but never called attention to them. Whether Sam knew it or not, and whether she went to church or not, she was living the principles of the Christian faith.

Yes, Sam was quite a woman. And yes, he was attracted to her. But he'd promised her friendship, nothing more, and he had a feeling tonight that she'd sensed he had something else in mind. Something that she either hadn't considered before, so she'd been surprised, or considered and rejected. Why else would she have suddenly seemed so nervous and uncomfortable?

Brad hoped that the explanation for her reaction was surprise rather than rejection. Because he decided to follow his father's advice. If he didn't at least give this thing a chance, he'd grow old regretting it, wondering what might have been. And he didn't want to look back in twenty years and say, "What if?"

But how would Sam react to the notion of romance? They'd never actually gone out on a real date. She might even laugh at the suggestion. Then again, she might be willing to give it a try. What did he have to lose by testing the waters? He'd give her a call tomorrow and do just that.

It was Wednesday before Brad actually connected with Sam in person. Until then they communicated by voice mail, which was very handy for some things and very unsatisfactory for others—like asking a woman out on a first date. It wasn't something you left a message about.

Brad had thought the whole thing through and decided that a safe first "date" would be the annual church picnic. It would be a date, but not a "romantic" type date, which was probably a good way to start. *If* Sam was willing. And *if* he ever had a chance to ask her, he thought in exasperation. As her phone rang for the third time he sighed, certain that the answering machine was going to kick in any second. But just then a slightly breathless Sam answered.

"Sam? It's Brad."

"Brad! Finally! A live voice!" Sam sank down into a kitchen chair and pulled off her gloves.

"You sound out of breath."

"Yeah. I was working in my garden between appointments and I forgot to take the portable phone out with me. Oh, if you talk to your dad, tell him I mailed those hollyhock seeds."

"I will. He had a great time Saturday night, by the way."

"I'm glad. I enjoyed his company. He's a very nice man."

"Yeah, he is. So how's everything else going?"

Sam's eyebrows rose in surprise. Brad never called to just chat. He always had a purpose. And she had a feeling he did today, too, but for some reason he was taking the long way around to it. Which was all right with her. It felt good just to hear his voice.

"Oh, busy as always. I've got to go to Chicago next week for a few days, and trying to get everything squared away before I leave is always a hassle."

"You're going out of town?" he asked in surprise.

"Uh-huh. The company is having a regional seminar that I have to attend. It's a pain, but they do this every once in a while. It's only from Sunday night through Thursday."

"Then you'll just be getting back when I'm leaving."

"Where are you going?" Now it was her turn to be surprised.

"Jersey. When mom died Rebecca and I decided to go down together for a few days over the Memorial Day holiday, thinking we'd have some family time with Dad and try to lift his spirits. But thanks to a certain redhead, the trip probably isn't even necessary," he said, and the teasing warmth in his voice made her smile. "Dad's busy as a beaver with his garden, and he's going to meet his buddies again for cards. Frankly, I'd probably cancel except that Rebecca needs a vacation desperately, and if I don't go she probably won't, either."

"Well, I guess I won't see you for a while, then. But I hope you have a good time."

Did he detect a note of disappointment in her voice, he wondered? Or was it only wishful thinking? In any case, he'd have his answer soon enough, because she'd given him a perfect opening for the invitation.

"I guess not. We'll have to make up for lost time when we both get back. In fact, arranging a get-together was one of the reasons I called." He paused long enough to take a deep breath, feeling like a schoolboy about to set up his very first date. "We always have a church picnic the first weekend in June, and I was wondering if you'd like to go. One of the couples in our congregation has a farm about forty-five minutes from St. Louis, and we use it every year for the picnic. It's just a down-home kind of thing, but you might have fun."

Sam stared unseeingly at the refrigerator. Was Brad asking her out on a date? Or did he just think, as a friend, that she might enjoy meeting some of the people in his congregation? She didn't have a clue. Should she ask, she wondered? Part of her wanted to know and part of her didn't. If it wasn't a date, she could continue seeing Brad as a friend without worrying about misleading him. If it was a date, she would need to proceed with extreme caution. Maybe even consider ending their relationship. No, she decided, she didn't want to know. But she *did* want to go.

When Sam didn't respond immediately, Brad forced himself to laugh. "Is the thought of going to a church picnic that shocking? I promise this is not a revival meeting in disguise. There will be no sermon and no hymn singing. It's purely social."

Sam smiled. "I wasn't worried about that. Yes, I'd like to go. It sounds like fun."

"That's great!" he replied, feeling a strange, euphoric elation. "I'll call you when I get back to arrange the details. In the meantime, have a safe trip."

"You, too. And thanks for asking, Brad."

"My pleasure," he said warmly. "See you in a couple of weeks."

"So…are you going to tell me about Sam?" Rebecca asked as they sat on the back porch of their childhood home eating ice cream cones.

Brad had been waiting for this question. He'd seen his sister's speculative look when they arrived earlier in the day and his father immediately asked about Sam. Brad took a leisurely bite of his ice cream before turning to Rebecca.

"What about Sam?" he asked innocently.

Rebecca rolled her large, hazel eyes. "What about

Sam?'' she mimicked. "Give me a break, big brother. You know exactly what I mean. What's the scoop?''

"You're eating it,'' he teased, pointing to her double-dip ice cream cone.

She rolled her eyes again. "Spare me the bad puns. I hope you do better than that in your sermons,'' she said with a grin. "But don't try to change the subject. Who's Sam?''

"She's my real estate agent,'' Brad replied.

"Oh.'' Rebecca's face fell momentarily, but then she glanced at him suspiciously. "Then why does Dad know her?''

Brad chuckled. "You know her, too.''

Rebecca frowned. "I do?''

"Uh-huh. You met her at Laura's wedding. She was the maid of honor.''

"Oh, yeah! The redhead,'' she said thoughtfully. "I remember. She seemed really nice. Kind of perky and upbeat.''

"Yep,'' he confirmed, crunching into the cone.

"Brad Matthews, are you going to tell me anything? Or do I have to give Dad the third degree?'' she said in exasperation.

Brad chuckled again. He and Rebecca had a good rapport, an easy give and take, and he always enjoyed teasing her—within limits. But he also knew when to stop. She had a sensitive nature that made her vulnerable to hurt, and he was always mindful of that. "Okay, what do you want to know?'' he capitulated.

Her longish russet-colored hair, usually secured in a French twist, swung freely tonight as she turned toward him eagerly. When it was loose like this she looked so youthful that it was hard for him to believe she was already thirty-two. "Everything," she said simply.

"Everything is a big order," he replied with a smile.

"Okay." She frowned in concentration, the evening shadows highlighting the delicate bone structure of her face. "Why does Dad seem to know her so well?"

"She had dinner with us when he was in town. In fact, she's responsible for that miracle." He nodded toward Henry, who was energetically weeding the perennial bed. "She and Dad had a lively discussion about gardening, and the next thing I knew they were sending seeds back and forth in the mail." He shook his head and smiled tenderly, his eyes growing soft. "She is one amazing woman."

Rebecca studied his face, her own eyes widening in surprise. "Why Brad Matthews—I don't believe this!" she said softly. "You're in love!"

He turned to stare at her, his smile evaporating. "I wouldn't go that far," he protested.

Rebecca grinned smugly. "I would. It's written all over your face. Maybe you haven't admitted it yet, but your heart knows the truth. I can see it in your eyes. And I'm happy for you," she added softly.

Brad continued to stare at her. He liked Sam. A lot. And he was definitely attracted to her. That's why he wanted to pursue a romantic relationship, see where it led. But he didn't think he was actually in love. At least not yet.

"Don't jump to any conclusions, Rebecca," he warned. "I only met her two months ago."

She shrugged. "It doesn't take long if it's the right person."

"Now how would you know?" he teased.

Rebecca's hand paused imperceptibly as she raised the ice cream cone to her mouth, then moved on. It was a nuance, but Brad saw it and realized he'd spoken too rashly. She'd always been sensitive about the lack of romance in her life.

"Becka…I'm sorry," he said contritely, reverting to her childhood nickname.

She shrugged, but there was a stiffness in her shoulders that hadn't been there before. "It's okay. You're right. I'm certainly no authority on the subject."

Brad frowned. He didn't understand why his sister remained unmarried. Even as a child she loved romantic stories, dreamed of having her own home someday, talked of the children she would lovingly raise. But at some point she simply stopped mentioning those things. She rarely dated, as far as he knew, instead devoting all her time to her business. It had never made sense to him.

"Becka." He reached over and touched her arm, but she averted her gaze, and he saw her swallow convulsively. "Becka," he repeated more gently. He was treading on off-limits territory, and he knew it. But he worried about her, and there was rarely an opening like this to discuss the subject. "You have so much love to give," he said carefully. "You should have a husband and kids to share it with. Is there some reason you don't? Would you like to talk about it?"

She glanced down, and there was a long moment of silence. When at last she looked up at him she was smiling, but he saw the glimmer of unshed tears in her eyes. "Thanks for the offer, big brother. I can see why you're such a good minister. But I'm fine. Please don't worry about me. I have a good life."

Brad let it drop. She wasn't going to tell him anything, and that was her choice. But she was such a loving, giving, caring person that it seemed wrong for her to live a solitary life. Despite the challenges and demands of her business, which kept her extremely busy, she had to be lonely. And loneliness, as he well knew, was a heavy cross to bear.

"Well, I'm here if you ever need a sympathetic ear," he said.

She nodded. "I know. And thanks. But we were talking about *your* love life, remember?" She touched his arm gently. "I hope this works out for you, Brad. Rachel was a wonderful woman, but maybe it's time to let go. I'd hate to think of you spending the rest of your life alone. You could still have that family you always wanted, you know? You'd make a great father."

"That may be jumping the gun just a little," he cautioned her. "But I have to admit a family would be really nice," he added with a wistful smile. "It's one of those dreams I gave up when Rachel died. But maybe there's hope after all."

Rebecca squeezed his arm. "I'll keep you in my prayers." She smiled, and for a moment in the growing darkness their eyes connected, further solidifying the brother-sister bond that seemed to grow stronger with the passing years. Then Rebecca dropped her hand and crumpled her napkin, turning to look toward her father. "Well, do you think we should drag Dad in before the mosquitoes finish him off?" she said with a laugh, lightening the mood.

Brad grinned. "Yeah. I don't know how he can see in the dark, anyway."

It wasn't until much later, as he lay in the familiar bed

of his childhood, that Brad had a chance to think back on his conversation with Rebecca. Her instincts were probably correct, he suspected. His relationship with Sam seemed to be heading in a serious direction. He wouldn't call it love yet, but the possibility was certainly there. And that left him with a deep feeling of hope and happiness.

At the same time he was troubled by his sister's loneliness. She would deny it, of course, but he knew it was true. And he also knew instinctively that a solitary existence was not the life the Lord had intended for her. She had *chosen* it, he suspected—for reasons she didn't want to share.

As he drifted to sleep, he took a moment to send a request to the Lord. Help Rebecca to find a man deserving of her love, he prayed. And help her overcome whatever it is that holds her back from sharing that love.

When the morning of the picnic finally dawned, Sam felt as if a lifetime had passed since she'd seen Brad. This was their longest separation since Laura's wedding, and she had missed him more than she expected. His mere presence brought a spark to her life, and without him the days seemed dull and lifeless.

Even talking to Laura a couple of times a week at Bible class—which Sam was actually enjoying—or on the phone didn't help much. Besides, when Laura found out that Brad had asked her to the picnic, she began firing questions that Sam either couldn't answer or wouldn't consider. So their conversations were brief and unsatisfactory. Sam would have liked to talk with Laura about her feelings—she desperately needed to talk to somebody!—but she couldn't very well say she had a dilemma without saying why. And she wasn't about to share that secret with anyone.

Sam eyed herself critically in the full-length mirror in her bedroom. Her khaki shorts, which Laura had assured her were perfectly appropriate, were of a modest length, and the short-sleeved madras cotton blouse cinched in with a hemp belt flattered her figure without being flashy. Her hair was sedately French braided and she'd used only a little makeup. She looked very respectable for a church picnic, she thought with a satisfied nod. Now it was just a matter of waiting for Brad to arrive. Except the waiting wasn't easy.

By the time the doorbell rang twenty minutes later, Sam was a bundle of nerves. She still hadn't resolved the "date" issue—was it or wasn't it?—but it sure *felt* like a date. Except that she was never this nervous before an ordinary date. And it only got worse when she opened the door and Brad smiled at her.

"Hi, Sam."

She swallowed. She'd seen Brad in many types of attire, but today was the most casual so far. He had on those well-broken-in and oh-so-nice-fitting jeans he'd worn for their house hunting expedition, and a light blue golf shirt hugged his broad chest. The sleeves called attention to his impressive biceps, convincing her that he must visit a gym on a regular basis. A vee of brown hair was visible at his neck, and her eyes got stuck there just a moment too long as she completed what she hoped had been a discreet perusal.

But not discreet enough, she realized, when her eyes returned to his and he was grinning.

"So...do I pass?"

She blushed, but pretended to misunderstand his meaning. "I'm just glad you dressed down. I was afraid maybe my outfit was too casual."

He gave her a thorough, lazy appraisal that didn't even pretend to be discreet, and her breath caught in her throat. "I'd say you look perfect," he declared huskily, his deep brown eyes smiling into hers. Then he propped one shoulder against the door frame, crossed his arms and gazed directly into her eyes. "I missed you, Sam," he said quietly.

Sam stared at him. He was acting...different...today. Undisguisedly interested. And not just in friendship, either, if she was reading his body language correctly. But she couldn't be sure with Brad. She had plenty of experience picking up signals from men, but Brad wasn't the type of man she typically dated. So maybe she was wrong.

"Um, thanks," she said, finding her voice at last. "Let me just grab my purse and we can get started." She turned away and reached for her shoulder bag on the hall table, willing her heart to behave and her lungs to keep working. Since she wasn't sure exactly what to make of his behavior, the best plan for today was to act the same as always, she decided. Ignore anything that indicated otherwise. Then later, when she was home and alone and more rational, she could analyze the situation logically and consider what to do next. But the first order of business was to get through this day without giving away her own feelings to this perceptive, virile man.

Fortunately for Sam's blood pressure, their conversation during the drive to the farm focused on "catching up." She described some of the houses she'd looked at—and rejected—for him, and he told her about his visit to Jersey.

By the time they arrived she felt much more relaxed and in control.

Her first view of the crowd behind the barn, however, made her step falter slightly. Sam didn't mind crowds. She could schmooze and make small talk with the best of them. But this was a different kind of crowd. These were religious people, and this was a church picnic. What on earth would she find to say to them? And why did it seem that everyone was staring at her assessingly in the sudden hush that descended over the group at their appearance?

Brad's eyes narrowed imperceptibly at the group's reaction to their arrival. It had never occurred to him that Sam—as his date—would attract so much attention. But it should have. Most of these people were long-time members of the congregation. They had known and liked Rachel, watched in sympathy as he deeply mourned her loss and then spent the subsequent years alone and bereft. If he chose to bring a woman to a church event, they would correctly assume it was because she was someone special. As a result, she was bound to be scrutinized. Even Sam, with her outgoing personality and self-assurance, was bound to feel some unease in a setting that was both awkward and unnatural for her.

He took her arm reassuringly, and she looked up at him with an uncertain smile. "Time to run the gauntlet, I guess," she tried to joke, but he heard the underlying tension in her voice.

"It won't be that bad," he promised, praying his words were truthful. These were all good people. But they were human, too, and Sam might not fit their image of a suitable date for their minister. *Please, Lord, let them find it in their hearts today to practice Christian charity and make Sam feel welcome,* he silently implored.

Brad stayed close, acutely aware of her nervousness, his hand comfortingly—and possessively—exerting gentle pressure in the small of her back.

They made their way around the small groups clustered near the barn, and Sam tried to relax. She couldn't fault anyone's manners—they were all pleasant. But she sensed a reserve, a withholding of approval, as if they weren't yet sure whether to accept this intruder who had caught their minister's eye—and maybe his heart. Sam supposed she couldn't blame them. Compared to Brad's first wife, she was sure she fell short. Her spirits took a nosedive, and she suddenly wished that this picnic, which she had looked forward to so eagerly, was ending instead of just beginning.

As they made their way toward two older women, Brad leaned down. "So how are you doing?" he asked in a low voice.

Not so good, she thought. But she couldn't very well say that. "Okay," she replied. "They all seem nice."

The two women looked at her pleasantly when they approached, and Sam summoned up a smile.

"Rose, Margaret, I'd like you to meet Sam Reynolds. Sam, this is Margaret Warren and Rose Davies. Rose is our wonderful organist. Her playing always inspires me to sing," he said, giving Sam a conspiratorial wink over their heads. Sam stifled a smile at Rose's pained expression, remembering Brad's comment at Laura's wedding about his lack of singing ability.

"It's very nice to meet you both," Sam said.

"Well, we're certainly glad you could make it, my

dear," said Rose. "Do you by any chance sing? We're always looking for good voices for the choir." She emphasized the word good, and Sam tried not to grin, relaxing for the first time.

"I'm afraid I'm not much in the voice department," Sam admitted. "I'm more the I-like-to-sing-in-the-shower-but-you'd-need-earplugs-if-I-sang-in-public type."

"Well, I'm sure you have many other talents," Rose declared, reaching over to pat her arm reassuringly. "And I always think it's good when we can recognize our own limitations. For example, if you really can't sing, then it's better to just not sing. Don't you think so, Reverend?"

Brad looked at her solemnly. "Oh, absolutely."

Sam choked back a laugh at the look of defeat on Rose's face, coughing to camouflage her smile. "Let's get you some lemonade, Sam," Brad said solicitously, his eyes twinkling as he took her arm. "Excuse us, ladies."

As soon as they were out of earshot, Sam laughed and shook her head. "You're awful, do you know that?"

"Why?" Brad asked innocently as he poured her a cup of lemonade.

"As if you don't know," she accused.

Now it was Brad's turn to chuckle. "Poor Rose. I guess I do give her a hard time. I ought to just shut up and make her life easier, but I really do like to sing. I have toned it down, though. So I don't think she minds quite as much."

"Sam! Brad!"

They turned in unison to see Laura heading their way, waving two pieces of paper with identical numbers on them, a burlap sack draped over her arm. "Will you two help me out? I'm supposed to be organizing the games, but nobody seems to want to be the first to sign up. So I put you down for the three-legged race. Do you mind? I think once I have a couple of names down, it will break the ice.''

Sam eyed her doubtfully. "The three-legged race?"

"Don't worry. It's a piece of cake," Laura assured her. "We're going to start in five minutes."

"Laura, I'm not the athletic type," Sam protested.

"But you don't have to be. It's a short race. Brad, talk her into it, will you, while I try to round up a few more people?" Laura implored over her shoulder as she dashed off to recruit two more victims.

Sam looked up at Brad, who seemed to be taking Laura's strong-arming in stride. "I don't know about this. What do you think?" she asked with trepidation.

He smiled and shrugged. "I'm game if you are."

Sam bit her lip. She'd heard of three-legged races, though she'd never seen one, and she assumed that there was some physical proximity involved. She had a sudden suspicion that Laura had set them up, but her friend had long since made herself scarce. Purposely, no doubt, Sam thought grimly.

"So what do you think?" Brad asked, pulling her back to the matter at hand.

She frowned. If Brad could make her heart go into triple time with just a look, what would it do to her metabolism to actually be physically touching him? But it was just a race, an impersonal thing, in front of his congregation. Nothing could possibly happen. In fact, it was a safe context in which to get close to him. Maybe she ought to enjoy it. The opportunity might never come again.

"All right," she capitulated. "But I wasn't kidding

when I said I'm not the athletic type. If you want to win, I'd suggest you find another partner.''

''I'll take my chances with you,'' Brad told her with a smile. ''Turn around so I can pin your number on.''

Sam did as instructed, but her fingers seemed to have a mind of their own when it was her turn to do the pinning. She'd never quite realized how broad his shoulders were, she thought, as she fumbled with the uncooperative piece of paper. And was it her imagination, or were the two of them once more drawing speculative glances from his congregation?

''Is it on?'' he asked over his shoulder.

It was slightly crooked, but Sam didn't trust herself to touch him anymore when the urge to run her hands over his back was so strong, despite the watchful eyes she felt riveted on her back. ''Yes.''

''Okay, step in,'' he said, leaning down to hold the burlap bag open. ''Try your left leg.''

''What?'' she asked blankly.

He looked up with a grin. ''We each have to put one leg in the sack,'' he explained patiently.

She swallowed convulsively at the unbidden image that flashed across her mind. But judging by his matter-of-fact expression, Brad was oblivious to the double entendre. With a determined effort she tried to stifle her overactive imagination as she silently followed his instructions.

He straightened up and put his leg in beside hers, and the next thing she knew he slipped his right arm around her waist and pulled her close, until they were touching along the entire length of their bodies, from ankle to shoulder. Sam drew in her breath sharply, vowing to seek revenge on her so-called friend Laura for making her endure this sweet agony.

"Can you hold on to this excess burlap?" Brad asked, apparently unaware of her distress and seemingly unmoved by their proximity. So much for her concern about his interest level, she thought wryly.

Sam reached down to take hold of the fabric, noting for the first time that his left hand was ringless. When had that happened, she wondered?

"Maybe we should practice a little," Brad said easily. "I know there's a trick to this. You have to be in sync, establish a rhythm, I think. You want to try it?" he asked.

She was still staring at his bare left hand, trying to comprehend the significance, and it took a moment for his words to penetrate her overloaded sensory circuits. "Sure. Why not?" she replied helplessly, not at all certain that her legs would cooperate.

He grinned and gave her a squeeze that sent a hot wave shooting through her entire body. "Okay. Let's give it a whirl."

As it turned out, just staying upright demanded her full and undivided attention, and hormones quickly gave way to hilarity as they stumbled around awkwardly, giggling like teenagers at their uneven gait. She even momentarily forgot about their audience.

"Hey, you two, no fair!" Laura called as she passed. "If you practice ahead of time you'll have an advantage."

"I don't think you have to worry," Brad assured her as they dissolved into laughter after another misstep.

His words proved prophetic. They made a good start when the gun went off a couple of minutes later, but in the heat of the race Sam apparently pulled too hard on the edge of the canvas bag she was holding. The next thing she knew she lost her footing, and she clutched at Brad to regain her balance. Unfortunately, he was in no better shape, and suddenly they both pitched forward. As they fell Brad twisted toward Sam and yanked her against his chest, bringing her down on top of him to cushion her impact.

For a moment after they hit the ground, neither of them moved. Sam was sprawled over Brad's firm body, her head pressed to his shoulder, his arms around her protectively. It took her only a moment to decide that she was just shaken, not hurt. But the trembling of relief she felt quickly turned to another kind of trembling as her mind—and body—absorbed their intimate position. Her heart seemed to stop, then race on, and her breathing became erratic as a surge of longing swept over her. She didn't want to move. Not now. Not ever. It felt so good in his arms!

But they couldn't stay like this. Reason told her that, even while her heart directed her otherwise. What would people think? They had to get up before his congregation suffered a collective heart attack.

Except that Brad hadn't moved, she suddenly realized with a frown. Maybe he'd struck his head or something, she thought in panic. But at least he was still breathing. And she could hear the hard, uneven thudding of his heart against her ear.

Quickly she backed off, bracing her hands on either side of his head so she could look down at him.

It was immediately obvious that Brad wasn't unconscious. Not even close. In fact, the ardent light in his brown eyes made her realize that physical injury was the *last* thing on his mind.

''Are you hurt?'' she whispered, her eyes locked on his.

His arms molded her even more firmly against him and his hands stroked her back ever so slightly. ''No. Are you?''

Mutely she shook her head, her breath catching in her throat as his hands moved to frame her face, his thumbs gently caressing her cheeks. Sam stared at him in shock at the blatant intimacy of his touch.

Only a few seconds passed during the entire mishap. And Sam knew they'd only fallen a short distance and spoken barely half a dozen words. But she also knew that in that brief interlude they'd traveled to a whole new world. Because one thing was now very clear. The original ground rules for their relationship might have been based on friendship. But the rules had just changed.

Chapter Six

"**H**ey, you two, are you okay?"

Sam was so mesmerized by the compelling intensity of Brad's eyes that it took a moment for Laura's concerned voice to register. But when it did, she also became aware once again of her suggestive sprawl on top of the hard planes of Brad's body. Her cheeks flamed in embarrassment, and she rolled sideways, frantically trying to untangle her leg from the burlap sack. When it was finally free, she scrambled to her feet, studiously avoiding Brad's eyes as he stood up beside her and brushed himself off.

"I'm fine," she said breathlessly. "Just a little shaken up."

"Brad?" Laura turned to him, and Sam ventured a glance in his direction. He flexed his shoulder gingerly, and she saw a flicker of pain cross his face, but his words didn't reflect that momentary flash of discomfort.

"A few minor bruises, I think. Nothing serious," he replied with an easy smile. He didn't seem at all embarrassed by their position of moments before, Sam noted in surprise.

Relief washed across Laura's features. "Thank goodness! Listen, you guys have been good sports, but why don't you find a cool spot and just be spectators for a while? I think you've had enough games for today."

Brad's clear, direct eyes locked on Sam's and refused to let go. "Yeah. I'd say our games are over," he replied quietly.

Sam swallowed convulsively. The man obviously wasn't talking about three-legged races.

Laura looked from one to the other, a smug expression on her face, and decided that three was a crowd. "Well, I'll talk to you two later," she said, tossing the words over her shoulder as she turned to make a hasty exit.

When she faced forward again she ran squarely into Nick, who steadied her with two firm hands on her shoulders.

"Why do I have a feeling you're up to some matchmaking tricks?" he admonished her with mock sternness. Then his mouth quirked up into a smile and he leaned down, his lips close to her ear. "Your ploy was a little obvious," he said in an undertone.

She grinned impishly and shrugged. "It worked, didn't it?"

He laughed and draped an arm around her shoulders. "It sure looks that way," he agreed, glancing back at Sam and Brad, who were still staring at each other, transfixed. Then he shook his head. "I would never have believed it. Maybe I should go over and rescue Brad before it's too late," he said, making a halfhearted attempt to turn back.

Laura grabbed his arm. "Don't you dare!" she said,

tugging him in the opposite direction. "Besides, it's too late, anyway," she added with a smug smile.

Sam was thinking the same thing as she stared at Brad, the flame in his eyes speaking more eloquently than words of his desires. She tried to disguise her own feelings, but she knew she was failing miserably. The attraction was almost palpable, and neither could deny it.

"Sam?" Brad's voice was gentle, his gaze sharp and probing.

She licked her lips, which had suddenly gone dry, and his eyes released hers as they dropped to her mouth. Which did nothing at all to slow her metabolism. She wasn't ready to deal with this yet, she thought in desperation. At least not this level of intensity. She had to calm down, think rationally. And she sure wasn't going to be able to do that with Brad standing just inches away.

"I...I think I'll find the ladies' room," she stammered breathlessly. "Will you excuse me for a couple of minutes?"

Before he could respond, she fled toward the house, grabbing her purse en route.

Brad watched her flight, realizing that was exactly what it was. For all her sophistication and experience with men, she was thrown by his overtures. Thrown, but not unreceptive, he reminded himself, recalling how his own desire had been mirrored in her eyes. But for some reason she was running scared.

He frowned as she disappeared into the house. Had he come on too strong, he wondered, revealing his feelings too soon and too intensely? But he was an honest man, and game playing wasn't his sport. He figured it was better to lay his cards on the table, be up-front. But Sam might be used to men who did play games. If so, his direct, open approach could have thrown her.

She was probably surprised, too. After all, he himself had only recently come to grips with the fact that despite their differences, a relationship was worth exploring. Maybe she hadn't come to that realization yet. The attraction was there, certainly; the air between them had practically sizzled in the moments following their fall. But rationally she might still be hung up on their differences.

His congregation certainly seemed to be, he mused, glancing around at the group. He'd sensed their reserve, and he was sure Sam had as well. She wasn't a stereotypical minister's date, that was clear. And maybe, given their obvious differences, he was wrong to think they could build a relationship. Maybe his life-style as a minister wouldn't suit Sam in the long run. Then again, maybe it would. And despite the vibes he was picking up from his congregation, his heart told him that he should pursue this attraction, see where it led. Sam didn't seem as certain as he was about that, but he felt confident that once they talked things through, he could convince her to give it a try.

Yes, a nice long talk was exactly what they needed, he thought, speculatively eyeing the door where Sam had disappeared. Folding his arms across his chest, he leaned against a convenient tree, determined to wait her out. He wasn't sure he agreed with Rebecca about being in love. But now that she'd voiced that observation, he was giving it a lot of thought. Maybe he wasn't in love yet. But he knew with certainty that there was a good possibility he could be.

* * *

Once Sam reached the privacy of the bathroom, she closed the door and sagged against it. Things were moving *way* too fast. She'd suspected that Brad might consider this a real date. What she hadn't suspected was the depth of his attraction. Okay, so maybe she'd had a *few* clues, she admitted. Like the night he took her home after dinner with his father, when she'd thought he wanted to kiss her. She'd attributed the look in his eyes then to gratitude. Talk about a wrong call! Considering all the men she'd dated she should be an expert at picking up signals. So why had she been so far off the mark with Brad?

The answer was obvious, of course—she cared too much, and she didn't *want* to pick up his signals. Because she'd known all along that if his feelings ever deepened beyond friendship, she'd have to end their relationship. To do otherwise would be misleading and grossly unfair to him.

Well, she couldn't ignore the signals anymore, she admitted resignedly. Brad had made it clear that he wanted more than friendship. And unfortunately that was all she could offer, even if her heart was willing to give more. Much more.

Sam drew a deep, shaky breath and leaned over to inspect her face in the mirror. She *looked* pretty much the same. A little pale, maybe, although her makeup disguised most of that. But she sure didn't *feel* the same. Earlier she had been filled with a tingling sense of anticipation and happiness as she looked forward to a day in Brad's company. Now she was overwhelmed by sadness and a feeling of hopelessness as she realized that it was the last such day they would have together.

Her eyes filled with tears, but she brushed them away

angrily. She had no one but herself to blame for this mess. If she'd had the courage to deal with her own deepening feelings sooner, she wouldn't be in this position now. She'd already waited too long, and it would only get worse if she let more time pass.

Sam smoothed back her hair and straightened her shoulders. She'd survived without Brad before, she told herself resolutely. She could again. The difference, of course, was that before she could only *imagine* what she was missing. Now she *knew*. Because she'd had a tantalizing taste of what it was like to be cared for by a decent, sensitive, sincere—and passionate—man.

The passionate part was what really threw her. Up until a few minutes ago, Sam had thought of Brad as a very disciplined, in-control person. But the glimpse of fire she'd just seen in his eyes told her there was a whole other, exciting facet to this man. And it was a facet she yearned to explore. In fact, the very thought of doing so sent shafts of desire ricocheting through her. But that was not in the cards. Brad was a fine man who deserved a woman equally fine and, unfortunately, she didn't qualify.

As if to reinforce her self-assessment, the voices of two passing women suddenly penetrated the door.

"...so surprised when they walked in."

"She's nothing like Rachel, is she?"

The other woman gave a humorless laugh. "That's putting it mildly! Whatever do you think he saw..."

The voices faded away.

Sam gritted her teeth and took a deep breath, ruthlessly blinking back her tears. She had to pull herself together, make it through this day. And later, when they got back to her condo, she'd find a way to tell Brad that she couldn't see him anymore. She didn't have a clue yet just how she was going to do that, or what she was going to say, but maybe something would come to her. In the meantime, the easiest way to survive the day was to make sure that she and Brad were never alone.

Much to Brad's consternation, Sam executed her plan quite successfully. He finally admitted defeat, watching her from a distance as she laughed and chatted with members of his congregation, seemingly lighthearted and happy. But he knew her well enough to realize that the real Sam was hiding behind a facade. Her eyes were a little too bright, her smile a little too forced. And she was avoiding him like the plague.

Clearly, he wasn't going to have an opportunity to talk with her at the picnic, he realized, watching her disappear into the barn several hundred feet away with Laura and a few other women to retrieve the food. But he consoled himself with the knowledge that he'd have her all to himself on the drive home. And they *were* going to talk then.

Brad's musings were interrupted by several members of his congregation, who wanted to discuss plans for an upcoming meeting, and he didn't turn back to the barn until a startled voice drew everyone's attention.

"Watch out everybody! A bee's nest just fell by the door!"

A murmur of alarm ran through the crowd, which moved as one away from the barn, and Brad's eyes swept the throng, searching for Sam. Near the food table he spotted Laura and the other women who'd been with her, but there was no sign of Sam. And she was easy to find in a crowd, with her striking red hair. Was she still inside? And if so, had she heard the warning? he wondered in alarm.

A sudden surge of adrenaline propelled him toward the door, just as she stepped out balancing a tray holding two cakes.

"Sam! Get back inside!" he yelled desperately, increasing his speed to a flat-out run.

She gave him a puzzled look and stopped. "What?" she called.

"Get back—" It was too late. She was directly on top of the swarm, and her puzzled tone suddenly changed to a startled cry of pain as the first few bees simultaneously pierced her tender flesh. She dropped the tray and glanced down, trying to wave the bees away. The sweet frosting on the ground diverted the attention of most of the swarm. But a few bees preferred Sam to the cake. She panicked and began to run, attempting to elude them.

Brad reached her in seconds, just as she began to stumble. He steadied her with one hand, waving away the remaining bees with the other. He felt a sharp sting or two on his hand, but was almost oblivious to the discomfort, aware only of Sam's gasps of fear and pain as she writhed in his grasp.

By the time the last bee was banished, Sam's complexion was as white as the coconut frosting on the cakes she had carried, and she was shaking badly. There was a sting just above her lip, another over her left eye, and both were already swelling ominously.

Linda Perkins, the owner of the farm, came up behind Brad, her face a mask of concern. "Let's get her inside," she said, worriedly. "Sandy's here and she can help."

Brad turned toward the physician, sending a "thank you" heavenward that her hectic schedule had allowed her to attend today's picnic.

"I sent John for my bag in the car," she said crisply as she stepped forward, her eyes on Sam's face. "Sam, are you allergic to bee stings?" she asked.

Sam shook her head jerkily.

Sandy gave the other woman a quick but thorough look. "Brad, do you think you could carry her inside? She's got a lot of stings on her ankle, and she seems too shaky to walk."

Brad's jaw tightened, his own face almost as colorless as Sam's. "Yeah." He put one arm around her shoulders, the other under her knees, and lifted her in one smooth motion, cradling her in his arms. His gut wrenched as she clung to him and whimpered softly, her arms around his neck, her face buried in his chest. He could feel the tremors that ran through her body, and he lengthened his stride, desperate to relieve her misery as soon as possible.

Linda led them to the guest room, and Brad gently deposited Sam on the bed. Her pain-filled eyes stared up at him helplessly, and his gut clenched as he tenderly brushed some stray strands of hair off her face.

"Brad, she may need to undress so I can assess the damage," Sandy said. "You'd better wait outside."

He didn't want to leave her. Not when she looked so hurt and vulnerable. But she was in good hands. He couldn't add anything except moral support, and Laura, who had slipped in behind him, could provide that. He nodded curtly. "I'll be right outside if you need me."

Brad reluctantly left the room, gently closing the door behind him, then began to pace. He didn't even notice when Nick joined him until the other man laid a hand on his shoulder, causing him to flinch.

Nick frowned. "Are you okay?"

Brad glanced at Nick and shook his head dismissively. "I guess I bruised my shoulder when I fell. It's nothing. I'm more worried about Sam."

Just then the door opened, and as Laura slipped out both men turned to her questioningly.

Seeing the tense line of Brad's jaw, she reached out to touch his arm reassuringly. "She'll be okay," Laura said quickly. "She's got about a dozen stings, enough to be very uncomfortable but not enough to be dangerous."

Brad raked his fingers through his hair and expelled a long breath. "Thank God!"

"It looks like Sam wasn't the only victim," Laura noted with a frown, her eyes on his hand.

He glanced down. He had two welts on the back of one hand, but he only vaguely remembered the sharp stings. They were throbbing now, he realized. But compared to what Sam must be experiencing—he waved Laura's concern aside. "I'm fine. Listen, would you two go out and try to keep the party going? I know Sam would feel awful if this incident disrupted the picnic any more than it has already. I'd do it myself, but I'd rather stick close here."

"Sure," Nick said. "Come on, Laura."

"Maybe I should stay in case Sam…"

"Come on, Laura," Nick repeated more insistently. "Brad will be here if she needs anything," he added meaningfully.

"Oh. Right. Well, I'm sure you'll want to take Sam home after this, Brad, so just tell her I'll call tomorrow, will you?"

"Okay."

Brad watched them leave and then resumed his position outside the door. Another ten interminable minutes passed before Sandy appeared, and by then Brad was on the verge of going in, invited or not. He was in no mood for small talk when she appeared at the door.

"Well?" he said tensely, without preamble.

Sandy smiled. "Relax, Brad. She's okay. Uncomfortable, but okay."

Brad felt the tendons in his back and neck loosen slightly, and the rigid line of his shoulders relaxed as he closed his eyes. "Can I take her home now?"

"Yes. She's not going to feel too hot, though. I've already told her what she needs to do, but I'm not sure she took it all in, so let me repeat it for you—aspirin every four hours as needed, put this on the stings," she handed him a bottle of lotion donated by Linda, "and keep an ice pack on the swelling on her ankle. She has multiple stings in very close proximity there, which is going to make walking difficult for a couple of days. After that, the swelling and redness will dissipate. In a week she'll hardly even know this happened."

"Can I go in now?" he asked.

"Sure. She's decent. And since I know I'm leaving her in good hands, I think I'll head outside and have some food before it's all gone," she said with a wink.

Brad waited until Sandy disappeared down the hall, then took a deep, steadying breath before he turned the knob and walked inside.

Sam was sitting on the edge of the bed, holding an ice pack, her pale face and the lines of strain around her eyes providing silent but eloquent evidence of her pain. She gave him a wan smile, and he crossed the room in three strides, dropping to one knee in front of her.

"I guess I look a mess, huh?" she said, a tremor in her voice.

He swallowed convulsively. "You look just fine to me," he replied sincerely, his own voice husky. Objectively speaking, however, her words were more accurate than his. The welts near her upper lip and above her eye were an angry red, but as he surveyed the rest of the damage, he realized her right hand and left ankle had taken the brunt of the attack. Two of her fingers were swollen, and her ankle was puffy and covered with crimson welts.

When his gaze traveled back to her face, he saw the glint of unshed tears in her eyes, and his throat constricted painfully. He wanted to pull her close, to hug away all of her hurt, but he knew that in this case physical proximity would probably exacerbate the pain. So he refrained, contenting himself by running a gentle finger down one cheek.

"Oh, honey, I'm so sorry," he said, his eyes anguished.

"It's not your fault," she replied, her voice still unsteady. "Listen, Brad, I know this is a big event for your church, and everyone expects you to attend. I can just rest here until you're ready to leave." At least the attack gave her an excuse to skip out on the rest of the event, she thought, trying to look on the bright side.

He stared at her. Did she really think he'd let her lie here and suffer while he was out socializing? "Sam, I'm taking you home right now," he said, in a tone that brooked no argument.

"But I don't want to ruin your day," she protested.

Brad shook his head in amazement. Despite her pain she was worried about ruining *his* day.

"You have *not* ruined my day," he said firmly. Before she could reply, he stood up and held out his hand. "Can

you make it to the car, or do you want me to carry you?"
he asked.

Sam tried to smile again, but the effort seemed to be too
great, and she only managed a slight grimace. "The next
thing we'll be dealing with is a back injury if you have to
keep lugging me around. I think you did that once today
already."

Sam had very little recollection of the recent disaster.
She remembered coming out of the barn, and Brad's frantic waving. Then everything was shrouded in a cloud of
sharp, stinging pain that had washed over her in wave after
wave. She did have a vague memory, though, of being
swept into Brad's arms, followed by a floating sensation
as he carried her into the house.

"I don't mind doing it again," he told her with a smile.

"Thanks. But I think I can manage." She took his hand
and he eased her up, noting the way she bit her lip to keep
from crying out.

"Sam, I—"

"I'm okay, Brad," she said. "Just…give me a minute."

He watched her silently as she took several deep breaths,
and the fact that she wouldn't meet his eyes convinced
him that she was struggling to mask her pain before she
looked at him. When at last their gazes met, it wasn't her
eyes that gave her away, but the tight, narrow line of her
mouth and her deeply knit brow.

"Okay. I'm ready."

Brad thought about protesting. She didn't have to put
up a strong front for him. But at this point he didn't think
she could handle an argument. He suspected it was requiring all of her energy and willpower just to remain upright. So he put his arm around her waist for support, and

they slowly made their way out the front door, avoiding the crowd in the back. Sam leaned heavily on him the whole way, favoring her injured ankle.

By the time they reached the car and she carefully eased herself into the front seat, she was breathing heavily and the lines in her forehead were etched even deeper.

"Listen, Sam, maybe I should get Sandy again," Brad said worriedly.

"No. I'm all right."

Her answer didn't surprise him, but neither did it convince him. However, Sandy *had* assured him that her condition wasn't serious, just uncomfortable. He figured the best thing he could do was get her home as quickly as possible.

Sam didn't speak at all during the drive back into the city. Brad couldn't tell if she was asleep or just trying to conserve her strength. But in either case, he didn't bother her. He had some thinking to do, anyway. Because even though he'd intended this to be a "date," a turning point in their relationship, a lot more had happened than even he'd expected.

First, there was his intense, purely physical response when she'd fallen on top of him and he'd felt her soft, supple curves molded against his body. That physical response, more than the fall, was what had taken his breath away.

Then there was his emotional reaction to her distress. When he saw her engulfed in that swarm of bees... His stomach turned over and his jaw clenched at the memory. Her startled cries of pain would haunt him for a long time. The fear he experienced, his sheer terror at the threat to her physical safety, went far beyond simple empathy.

Even now, he felt as if his heart was being squeezed in a vise when he looked at her. She seemed so fragile and defenseless, and the fierce surge of protectiveness that had engulfed him when he'd carried her into the house earlier returned with renewed intensity. He desperately wanted to ease her hurt and simply take care of her.

It was that sense of desperation that made him realize how deeply his feelings ran. It surprised him, and it had clearly surprised Sam. Yet her feelings matched his, he knew. He'd seen the fire smoldering in her eyes when they'd stared at each other after they'd fallen, their faces only inches apart. But she was running scared.

Brad shook his head ruefully. The day had certainly not turned out the way he'd expected. If this was a first date, they were not off to an auspicious beginning. Between the tumble and the bee incident, *disaster* might be a better term than *date*. But he'd learned a lot about himself and Sam.

He glanced over at her again, wanting to talk this thing through, knowing she wasn't up to a heavy discussion today. But as soon as she was feeling more like herself, he intended to find out why she was so frightened of the idea of a romantic involvement. And then he intended to put those fears to rest. Because after today, he knew beyond a shadow of a doubt that their days of being "just friends" were over.

"Sam?" he touched her shoulder gently, and her eyelids flickered open. "We're home."

Sam wasn't really asleep. She'd been drifting in a sort of self-induced trance as she tried to shut out the pain that seemed to radiate through her hand and ankle. She'd succeeded marginally, managing to reduce the pain to a dull throb, but the thought of moving was extremely unappealing. Unfortunately, however, she couldn't very well stay in the car.

"Okay," she mumbled.

"Stay put till I come around," Brad said.

Sam didn't argue. She'd stay here all night if he would let her. But a moment later her door swung open and he leaned down, his face a mask of concern.

"Do you feel any better?" he asked.

"Well, the stinging isn't quite so bad," she said. Thankfully, that had subsided somewhat.

"I think I can read between the lines on that answer," he said grimly. "And the offer of a lift—literally—is still open."

She managed a shaky smile. "Thanks. But what would the neighbors say?"

"Oh, I have a feeling Mrs. Johnson would approve. After all, she thinks I'm your young man." He tilted his head and gave her a crooked grin. "Come to think of it, maybe she needs her vision checked. *Young* is hardly an accurate description."

"It's all relative," Sam replied with a faint smile. "Remember, she's eighty-five."

"You have a point," he admitted. Brad knew Sam was attempting to psyche herself up for the walk to her condo, and he gave her the time she needed.

"Brad?"

"Mmm-hmm?"

"I'm sorry about today. This really messed up your plans."

She didn't know the half of it, he thought. But he'd

make up for lost time later. "Don't worry, Sam. There will be other picnics."

She took a deep breath. "Okay, we might as well go in."

"How can I help?"

"If you could hold this," she said, handing him the ice pack, "and just let me lean on you when I get out, I think I'll be fine."

Sam bit her lip as she struggled out of the car, then leaned against the door for support. Brad moved beside her and slipped his arm around her waist, and they made their way slowly up the steps and down the walkway.

By the time they reached her front door, there was a thin film of perspiration on her upper lip. As she fumbled for her key, the look of exhaustion and strain on her features convinced Brad that she needed to lie down as soon as possible.

When Sam at last withdrew the key, Brad took it from her trembling fingers, fitted it into the lock and pushed the door open. Then he guided her inside and toward the couch, where he eased her gently onto the cushions. As she sank down, she expelled a shaky breath and closed her eyes, letting her head drop back wearily.

"I'll refill the ice pack," Brad said quietly.

He completed the task as quickly as possible and then sat down beside her, careful to jostle the cushions as little as possible. He reached for her uninjured hand and she opened her eyes, giving him a tired smile.

"I bet you're sorry you asked me to that picnic," she said ruefully.

"No. Just sorry about everything that happened." Well,

not quite everything, he corrected himself silently. But certainly the bee incident.

She glanced at her watch and frowned. "I guess it's too late for you to go back, isn't it?"

Brad looked at her steadily. He'd already thought this through, and he was ready to argue the point if necessary. Maybe his congregation wouldn't approve. Maybe what he was about to suggest flew in the face of the propriety he always so carefully observed. But at the moment he cared more about Sam than propriety. Besides, abandoning her, alone and in pain, just seemed wrong. "Sam, I have no intention of leaving here until tomorrow," he informed her, his voice firm.

She stared at him. "What do you mean?"

Brad knew that Sam wasn't seriously ill or injured. But neither was she in any shape to function on her own. She could hardly walk. And he didn't intend for her to try, at least for tonight. "I'm staying until morning," he replied.

"But...why?" she asked in bewildered surprise.

"Because I want to. Because you're in no condition to be left alone." Because I care about you more than you're willing to acknowledge, he added silently.

"But...you can't," she said in panic, instinctively sensing danger. It would *not* be a good idea to have Brad in her condo all night. "I'll be fine," she assured him.

He'd expected a protest. He'd also decided that the subject was not open for discussion. "Look, Sam," he said, rubbing his thumb gently over the back of her hand. "Let's not make a big deal out of this, okay? I can't just walk out and leave you in pain to fend for yourself."

Sam's throat contracted convulsively at the tenderness in his voice. No man had ever cared for her this much before. She tried not to cry but she was powerless to stop her reaction.

Brad had expected resistance. Instead, he watched her face crumple, saw the tears fill her eyes and silently spill onto her cheeks, heard the muffled sob. Throwing aside his resolution to keep his distance until she was fully recovered, he pulled her into his arms and pressed her fiercely against his chest, stroking her back with one hand as his other gently caressed her nape.

"It's okay, Sam," he murmured, his lips in her hair. "Let it out. You deserve a good cry after the day you've had."

Sam clung to his shirt, her fists balling the fabric, as she struggled for control. She didn't want to cry. Crying never solved anything or made a hurt go away. But the combined emotional and physical trauma were no match for her shaky control. She couldn't stop the tears, so she simply tried to stifle the sobs as much as possible.

Brad just held her, rocking her gently in his arms and murmuring soothing words, his cheek against her hair, until her sobs subsided and she rested quietly against him.

Sam would have liked to stay right where she was indefinitely, drawing comfort from the strength and compassion of Brad's arms, but at last she drew a shaky breath and ventured a glance at him. "Sorry about that," she apologized with a tremulous, watery smile. "I don't usually cry."

"You had good reason," he replied, stroking her cheek gently with the back of his knuckles.

Sam's breath caught in her throat at his touch and at the tender caring in his unguarded eyes. She couldn't let him stay tonight, she told herself, much as she'd like to. It would only complicate things even more.

"Brad, about tonight…"

"Sam. Let it rest, okay? For me."

When he put it like that, how could she refuse him? she thought helplessly. Besides, she simply didn't have the strength to argue. She'd just have to deal with the consequences tomorrow, she thought, capitulating with a sigh. "I think there's some microwave stuff in the freezer. And there's some extra bedding in the closet in the office. If you need to—"

"Sam," he said, his voice gentle but firm. "Stop worrying. You don't have to play hostess. I'll be fine. I'm used to coping on my own. And I'm a master at microwave. In fact, why don't I fix us both something to eat?"

She shook her head wearily. "Thanks. But I think I'll pass. To be honest, all I want to do is lie down and try to sleep."

Brad didn't argue. Rest would probably be better for her tonight than food, anyway. "Okay." He stood up and then reached for her, carefully drawing her to her feet. "Come on, let's get you to the bedroom," he said as he put his arm around her waist.

At any other time that comment would have set a thousand butterflies loose in her stomach and inspired all sorts of romantic fantasies. But the stings were beginning to throb with renewed intensity, and her sole priority was the oblivion of sleep, which would bring welcome relief from her misery.

Brad gave her bedroom a cursory glance as they entered. Like the living room, it featured ultramodern decor. So modern, in fact, that it was almost stark, he realized, the predominant color a cool blue. Not at all the sort of boudoir he'd imagined for Sam, he thought in surprise. This sterile, monotone room definitely did not seem designed to induce romance.

Sam's quiet sigh effectively refocused his attention on the woman beside him, and he reined in his wayward thoughts as he guided her to the bed. She sank down carefully, and he squatted in front of her, his concerned eyes searching her wan face.

"I'll get some water and aspirin, and I'll bring in the lotion that Linda sent," he said gently.

"Thanks."

When he returned, he found Sam struggling with her hair, hampered by two swollen fingers that rendered her right hand almost useless.

Brad deposited the collected items on the nightstand and sat down beside her. "Can I help?"

Sam sighed in frustration. "If I don't unbraid my hair before I go to sleep it will be too tangled to even get a comb through tomorrow," she said, her voice quavering. "But my fingers aren't working right."

"Then let me do it for you," he said, grasping her shoulders and gently angling her away from him. Brad eyed the tucked-under French braid with a frown. He had very little experience with women's hairstyles. Rachel had favored a short, simple cut, and he didn't have a clue where to begin with this complicated style.

"Okay, I give up," he said at last. "Where are the pins?"

"Down at the bottom," Sam replied, her voice muffled as she bent her head.

There was something endearing about Sam's trustingly

submissive posture, and an unexpected surge of desire jolted through Brad as he looked at the vulnerable and enticing expanse of skin that was exposed at her nape. Although a sharply indrawn breath was the only auditory evidence of his acute physical reaction, Sam picked up on it.

"Brad?" Her voice was uncertain, and Brad forced himself to focus on the task at hand. Now was *not* the time to wonder how that patch of creamy skin would feel against his lips, he told himself sharply.

"Just trying to figure out where to start," he said, hoping his voice sounded more in control than he felt.

"I think I got one pin partly out," she volunteered, her voice still hesitant.

He scanned her hair and finally saw the pin in question. "You're right," he said, reaching over to gently extract it. Then he took a deep breath, trying to slow the pounding of his heart, and with unsteady fingers began to probe the soft hair at the base of her head for the elusive pins. Gradually he located them, carefully withdrawing them one by one until the bottom of the braid hung free.

"I think that's it," he said at last, hoping his voice didn't betray his elevated hormone level. The intimate nature of his task had set his heart pounding, and try as he might, he couldn't stop his imagination from creating a picture of what this scene might mean in another context.

Sam reached around with her good hand and made an unsuccessful attempt to loosen the braid, but Brad stilled her uncooperative fingers with his own.

"I started the job. I might as well finish it," he said, his voice oddly hoarse.

Sam hesitated momentarily. The feel of his hands in her

hair was sending electric currents through her body, over-
riding the pain of the stings, and a tightly wound coil of
tension began to pulsate deep within her. The intimate nature of the act wasn't lost on her, either, despite her injuries. It was sweet agony to sit passively and let this man
run his fingers through her hair when what she really
wanted to do was turn in his arms and taste his kisses. The
struggle of trying to stifle that impulse was actually making
her quiver.

Brad's hand was still covering hers at the back of her
head, and he could feel her trembling. Or at least he
thought it was her. He was so shaky himself at this point
that he couldn't be sure.

"Sam?" he asked questioningly.

The best thing right now would be for him to leave the
room, she thought frantically. But what about her hair? It
would be impossible to handle tomorrow if she left it
alone, and he'd gone this far. How much worse could it
get? Drawing an unsteady breath, she removed her hand
from under his and let it fall to her lap in silent acquies-
cence.

Brad didn't say anything, either. He no longer trusted
his voice.

A muscle in his jaw twitched as he began to methodi-
cally unbraid her hair, trying desperately to keep his imagination and hormones in check. It had been a long time
since he'd touched a woman like this, and he was stunned
by the impact it was having on him physically.

When at last her hair was loose, he reached for the brush
he'd seen earlier on her nightstand. "I'll get some of the
tangles out for you," he said quietly, and before she could
protest he began to gently run the brush through her hair.

Sam had never had a man brush her hair before, and the pure sensuousness of the gesture sent a shock wave down her spine, producing a surge of desire that radiated all the way to her toes.

It was also a first for Brad, and the effect on him was exactly the same. Sam had incredibly soft hair, and as it slipped through his hands it awakened nerve endings in his fingertips that he didn't even know existed. What would she do if he tossed the brush aside and ran his fingers through her hair instead? he wondered recklessly. If he pressed his lips to the silky strands, and turned her head to taste—

Brad's flight of fancy was abruptly halted when the brush dislodged a small object from Sam's hair. She glanced down as it fell on the bed beside her and, with a sudden shriek of terror, she shot to her feet and backed away, staring at it in horror.

Brad was so startled by Sam's reaction that it took him a moment to identify the cause—a bee. A very dead bee, actually. With one quick motion he scooped it up, crushed it inside a tissue and deposited it in the trash. In the next instant he was beside her, gathering her into his arms and pressing her face to his chest.

"Sam, it's okay. It's dead. It won't hurt you. Nothing's going to hurt you," he whispered, his breath warm on her forehead.

The rigid lines of her body suddenly went limp, and a sob caught in her throat as she sagged against him. "I think I'm go-going to have a bee pho-phobia for life," she gasped.

She was shaking again, and Brad gently but firmly guided her back to the bed, steadying her with one hand as he pulled back the covers before easing her down. She lay docilely as he applied lotion to her stings, swallowed the aspirin he handed her, and felt him press the ice bag gently against her ankle.

Sam watched him as he pulled up the sheet and sat down next to her, her wide eyes still slightly glazed. Brad took her good hand in his and studied her face as he laced his fingers through hers.

"I'll be close by, Sam," he said softly. "Will you call me if you need anything?"

She nodded mutely.

He hesitated, then slowly leaned down and gently, lingeringly, pressed his lips to her forehead. Her eyes seemed even wider when he straightened up, and he tenderly brushed some stray strands of hair back from her forehead.

"Remember that I'll be here for you," he said, his eyes compellingly locked on hers. Then he rose, and with one last glance back at her supine form, gently shut the door behind him.

For a long time Sam drifted in a place somewhere between sleep and pain-dulled reality, Brad's pledgelike words echoing through her mind. But even as she clung to them, suspecting a deeper, longer-term meaning, she knew they applied only for tonight. Because soon Brad, like his words, would be just a distant, treasured memory that was filed carefully and lovingly away in her heart.

Chapter Seven

The beeping of the microwave timer diverted Brad's gaze from his view of Sam's small but well-tended garden. He strode quickly across the room to turn it off before the high-pitched tone disturbed her. As he withdrew the container of fettuccini, his stomach reacted loudly to the savory aroma, and he glanced at his watch—8:00 p.m. No wonder he was so hungry. His last meal had been more than twelve hours ago, and that had consisted of a bagel and black coffee before his early service.

Brad downed the first several forkfuls quickly to appease his grumbling stomach, but then slowed his pace as a bone-deep weariness suddenly overcame him. It didn't seem possible that he and Sam had arrived at the picnic only five hours ago. It felt like a lifetime had passed since then. Sam had the right idea about sleep, he decided. They could both use a good night's rest.

He remembered her mentioning something about extra bedding in the office closet, so when he finished his meal he went exploring. He'd given the office only a quick glance earlier as he passed, but his first impression of a neat, businesslike setup was confirmed as he stepped inside and flipped on the light to reveal a no-nonsense, work-oriented room.

Brad found the extra pillows, blankets and sheets stacked in the large closet, as Sam had said, and he reached up to retrieve what he needed, only to halt in surprise when his shoulder twinged painfully. He frowned and lowered his arm quickly, flexing it gingerly before reaching up again, this time more carefully, to remove a pillow and blanket. A sore shoulder seemed to be *his* souvenir of their outing, he thought ruefully.

As Brad closed the closet door something on a lower shelf tumbled onto the floor. He opened the door again and bent to retrieve several videotapes, glancing at the titles as he replaced them. He quickly came to the obvious conclusion—for all her apparent sophistication, Sam was a romantic at heart. And she liked happy endings. The shelf was filled with classic romantic movies, including what appeared to be a complete collection of Cary Grant and Rock Hudson/Doris Day flicks. Brad smiled and shook his head as he closed the closet door. No question about it, Sam was full of surprises. And pleasant ones, at that.

Brad deposited the bedding on the couch in the living room and stretched wearily. A shower would sure feel great, he thought longingly. And under the circumstances, he doubted whether she would mind if he took one.

He rummaged around in the hall linen closet, emerging triumphantly a moment later with a towel. Then he stepped into the guest bath and quietly closed the door, glancing in the mirror as he passed the sink. The image reflected back at him, however, made him stop dead in his tracks.

His hair was tousled, a five-o'clock—no, make that nine-o'clock—shadow was darkening his face and his shirt was streaked with dirt. Disreputable would be a kind way to describe his appearance. But at least the shower should help, he consoled himself.

Brad crossed his arms to pull off his shirt, pausing abruptly as his shoulder once again protested. Moving more slowly, he stripped off the shirt in one smooth but careful motion, then turned his back to the mirror and glanced over his shoulder to check out the damage.

Brad's eyes widened in surprise at the large, ugly black-and-blue mark that marred his skin. He'd known at the time that he'd taken the brunt of their fall—purposely—and it had hurt, but he hadn't had a clue about the severity of the bruising.

He supposed he should put some ice on it, he thought halfheartedly. But he was just too tired.

Brad took a longer shower than usual, angling his injured shoulder away from the warm, soothing spray, and by the time he finished and combed his wet hair, he felt much more human. Not to mention cleaner. Unfortunately, he couldn't say the same for his clothes, he thought, surveying them critically. He shook out his jeans, which helped a little, and pulled them back on, not bothering with the belt. But he quickly came to the conclusion that washing was the only thing that would improve his shirt. He'd noticed Sam's small washer and dryer earlier in the utility room next to the kitchen, and with one more distasteful glance at his shirt, headed in that direction.

While he waited for the wash cycle to finish, he made a makeshift bed on the living room couch and checked his voice mail at the parsonage. He also spent a few minutes in contemplative prayer, as had become his custom at the end of every day. He'd gotten into the habit after Rachel died, when that quiet time alone with the Lord had provided a special source of strength. But even in normal times he found the practice to be refreshing and renewing.

By the time Brad heard the washer shut off, he was beginning to fade. As he headed for the utility room and tossed his shirt into the dryer, he yawned hugely. Maybe he'd lie down and rest until it was done, he thought wearily, padding back to the couch to stretch out. Then he would follow Sam's lead and get some sleep.

But half an hour later, when the dryer signaled the end of its cycle, there was no one awake to hear it.

Sam emerged from sleep slowly, feeling groggy and out of sorts. She squinted at the window, where bright light was trying to penetrate the blinds, then turned to peer at the digital clock on her nightstand, which said 8:30 a.m.

Her brain felt muddled, and she frowned as she stared at the ceiling. What on earth was wrong with her? Could she be coming down with the flu or something? In June? That hardly seemed likely. She threw back the sheet, preparing to rise, only to discover to her amazement that she was fully dressed. What was going on here? But as Sam sat up and swung her legs to the floor, the sight of the angry red welts and swelling on her ankle brought her memory back in a flash. She shuddered as she recalled yesterday's nightmare.

She stood up carefully, grateful that the stinging sensation had finally disappeared. The swelling and redness might not look pretty, and the area around the stings was tender, but the worst of her discomfort seemed over, thank goodness.

Sam limped to the bathroom and leaned against the sink to peer cautiously into the mirror. The two stings on her face were more subdued today, though still quite apparent, and although she was naturally fair, her complexion was paler than usual. Yesterday was one day she never wanted to repeat! she thought ruefully. She just hoped the incident hadn't completely disrupted the picnic. She'd have to ask Brad about that. The poor man…

Brad! Her eyes widened and she straightened up abruptly. He'd said he was going to spend the night. Had he? She held her breath and listened, but her condo was silent.

Sam moved to the door of her room and paused to listen again. Still no sound. Gently she eased it open and peered down the hall. Nothing. Walking slowly and stiffly, her feet silent on the thick carpet, she passed the empty kitchen, hesitating on the threshold of the living room. He must be on the couch, she thought. But it faced away from her, toward the fireplace, so she couldn't tell for sure. Slowly, trying to still her suddenly rapid pulse, she moved closer and peeked over.

Brad was there, all right—lying on his stomach, one arm bent under his head, the other trailing to the floor. But it wasn't his position that caught her attention—it was his attire. Or lack thereof, she corrected herself.

He didn't have a shirt on. That registered immediately. Except for one shoulder partially hidden by a throw pillow, his broad back was totally bare. And totally masculine, she thought, her heart rate increasing dramatically. Her eyes traced its strong contours, down to the edge of the sheet which was draped over the lower half of his body, the edge of his jeans just visible.

He shifted slightly, dislodging the throw pillow, and Sam took a steadying breath. She forced her eyes back toward his shoulders, and that's when the next impression slammed home, taking her breath away for another reason.

Sam had seen bruises. But she'd never seen one like Brad's. It was almost totally black, with traces of purple at the edges, and it had to be four inches square. She knew he'd purposely taken the brunt of their fall, and she remembered seeing him wince as he flexed that shoulder yesterday when Laura asked if they were all right. She'd meant to ask him about it later, but events had taken several unexpected turns, and it had completely slipped her mind. But she couldn't forget about it now, not when that bruise was staring up at her in living color.

Sam frowned. It looked really bad. Bad enough to need medical attention, perhaps. Maybe she should suggest that he get his shoulder X-rayed. But she couldn't very well do that while he was sleeping. Should she go back to her bedroom and wait till he woke up? she debated silently. Or rattle around the kitchen a little to alert him to her presence? Or maybe…

The decision was taken out of her hands when he suddenly sighed, turned over and opened his incredibly gorgeous sleep-hazed eyes to stare directly up at her.

For the briefest moment he seemed disoriented, but Sam didn't mind. She needed the time to recover from the powerful impact of his naked chest, with its T of curly dark brown hair, and to notice the day's growth of stubble on his chin that for some reason made her pulse flutter even more than it already was. She was used to seeing him impeccably groomed, and his magnetism was strong then, but in this "natural" state it was almost overwhelming.

Unfortunately Sam was still trying to absorb the assault on her senses when Brad's eyes cleared.

Her voice came out in a kind of squeak, and she cleared her throat and tried again. "Good morning."

He pulled the sheet off, swinging his jeans-clad legs to the floor and faced her, planting his hands on his hips.

"How are you feeling?" he asked, his astute eyes not missing a thing as they raked over her.

"Better than yesterday."

She did look better, he thought. She had more color, and the welts on her face weren't quite as red or swollen. "How's your ankle?"

She glanced down. It was a good excuse to tear her eyes away from his chest. "Well, I don't think I'll be entering any races in the near future. It's still pretty swollen, and the stings are tender. But compared to yesterday I really do feel a lot better."

Relief flooded his face, and she saw the lines of tension visibly ease around his mouth and eyes. "Thank God! And I mean that literally. You had a really rough day."

"So did you." She nodded toward his shoulder. "You've got an awful bruise," she said, her eyes reflecting her concern.

For the first time Brad seemed to realize that his shirt was missing, and he glanced down with a frown. The last thing he remembered was putting it in the dryer. He gave Sam an apologetic smile. "Sorry about this," he said sheepishly, gesturing toward his torso as he moved toward the kitchen. "I washed my shirt last night and I must have fallen asleep before it finished drying."

"It's okay," she called after him. She heard him open the dryer, and a moment later he reappeared, tucking in his shirt as he padded barefoot back to her. "But what about your shoulder?" she persisted. "It looks bad. Maybe you should have it checked out."

He shrugged aside the suggestion. "It's just a bruise. Believe me, you got the worst of the deal yesterday. I think in the future we'd better include an 'attend at your own risk' disclaimer on the picnic announcement. The two of us look like the walking wounded."

Sam smiled. He looked great to her, but she couldn't very well say that without starting something that she wasn't up to dealing with just yet.

"How about some breakfast?" he said. "You didn't eat anything last night."

"Yeah, I am kind of hungry," she admitted. "I've got some eggs and cheese in the kitchen. We could have omelettes. And there's juice and English muffins."

"A veritable feast!" he declared with a grin.

"Let me just take a quick shower and change, and I'll fix something," she said.

"No hurry," Brad replied. "My morning is free."

Sam's eyes widened, and she covered her mouth with her hand. "But mine isn't! I'm supposed to meet a client at ten-thirty!"

Brad frowned. "I think you ought to take it easy today, Sam. Do you really feel up to traipsing around, showing property?"

As a matter of fact, she didn't. Her ankle was beginning to throb already and her right hand was still too swollen to be of much use. She sighed and glanced at her watch. "I guess I could try to cancel."

"Good idea. Go ahead and make your call and freshen up. I'll wait."

Sam was able to reschedule her appointment, and by the time she showered, washed and blow-dried her hair and applied a little makeup she was feeling almost human. As she slipped into a short-sleeved knit top and denim jumper she realized that despite her hunger, she would gladly settle for a muffin and juice for breakfast. Her energy level just wasn't up to par, and preparing even a simple meal seemed like far too much effort. But she owed Brad, after all his kindness. It wouldn't kill her to make a couple of omelettes.

However, it appeared that Brad had taken matters into his own hands. By the time she stepped into the hall tantalizing aromas were wafting from the kitchen, and she paused in the doorway to find him slipping a huge omelette onto a platter.

He glanced her way and smiled. "I figured we could split this," he said. "Go ahead and sit down. Coffee's ready, and I just took the muffins out of the toaster."

"But...but Brad, I would have made breakfast," she said, surprised and deeply touched by the thoughtful gesture.

"I know. But I didn't have anything else to do," he replied easily. "Come on. Let's eat before it gets cold."

He held out her chair, and Sam sat down carefully, giving him a crooked smile over her shoulder. "This is a first," she said.

"What?"

"Being waited on in my own kitchen."

He looked at her as he took his seat, his gaze direct and unwavering, and when he spoke his voice was quiet.

"We've had a lot of firsts in the last twenty-four hours, haven't we, Sam?"

Her fork was halfway to her mouth, and her hand froze for a brief second before continuing on its journey. It was a good thing they were eating eggs, which slid down easily, she thought, or she was sure the food would stick in her throat. As it was, she swallowed with difficulty and then stared at him, completely at a loss for words. She wasn't up to a heavy discussion this morning.

When she didn't speak, Brad took a slow sip of coffee, his eyes never leaving her face. "We have to talk, you know."

She tore her eyes away from his and looked down at her plate. Denying the obvious would be foolish. They did need to talk. Only the talk wasn't going to end the way Brad expected. And Sam just wasn't up to the emotional scene that was sure to occur when she told him she couldn't see him anymore.

She took a deep breath and toyed with her food. "I know. But—"

"But you're not up to it today." He completed the sentence for her, as if reading her mind, and she looked over at him gratefully.

"Right."

"I didn't think you would be. But I just wanted to make sure we both agreed that the topic of our relationship needs discussing. And the sooner the better."

"Yes."

"Good," he said with a satisfied nod. "Now go ahead and eat my culinary masterpiece before it gets cold," he added with a grin.

Sam smiled, relieved that he hadn't pressed the issue today, grateful for the reprieve.

Brad kept the conversation light during the rest of the meal and then insisted on cleaning up when they were finished, despite her protests.

"It's not a big deal, Sam. I've got another few minutes. Actually, I'd stay longer, but I have an appointment at one and I need to return some calls before that. And I have a church board meeting tonight. Can we get together tomorrow for lunch or dinner?"

Sam shook her head. "I'll be swamped, considering I'm taking today off. And I have my volunteer work in the evening."

Brad frowned. "Wednesday morning I'm driving down to see Dad, and I had planned to spend the night. How about dinner Thursday?"

Sam shook her head again. "I'm taking a class on Thursday nights."

Brad looked at her in surprise as he rinsed the last dish. "When did that start?"

"About a month ago."

"Something work related?"

Sam shifted uncomfortably. She didn't want to tell Brad about the Bible class. He might think she was going to please him, and that wasn't the case at all. It was just that she'd become increasingly aware of the emptiness and despair in her life, along with a troubling spiritual vacuum. And though she'd originally gone to the class more out of desperation than with any great confidence that it would help, surprisingly enough she now looked forward to the Thursday-night study group. But her reawakening faith was still too new and fragile to discuss. "No. Just... personal interest."

Brad turned away and squeezed the dishcloth, then carefully hung it over the sink. He recognized Sam's tone of voice. It meant Keep Out. So he did.

Sam looked at Brad's ramrod-straight back. He was probably hurt by her refusal to discuss a seemingly innocuous subject, she realized. But she wasn't trying to shut him out, and she needed to make him understand that. Suddenly an idea occurred to her. Why not invite him to dinner on Friday night? After all, she owed him big-time after everything he'd done for her in the past twenty-four hours. And maybe it would make up a little for her reticence just now.

"Brad, since we both have such busy schedules this week, why don't you come over Friday night for dinner?"

He turned in surprise. "Here?"

She grinned. "Yeah."

"You mean for a home-cooked meal?"

Actually, she planned to order dinners from a local gourmet shop. Cooking wasn't her forte. It always seemed too much bother just for herself. But she couldn't disappoint him, not when he had that look of hopeful anticipation on his face.

"Uh-huh."

"That would be great! But are you sure you want to go to all that trouble?"

"Why not?" she said recklessly. After all, how hard could it be? There were plenty of cookbooks out there. She even had a couple in a closet somewhere. She could read as well as the next person, and cooking was just a matter of following a recipe, after all. It wasn't rocket science.

"Do you think you'll feel up to it?" he asked, a frown of concern suddenly marring his brow.

"Well, the doctor said the swelling would go down pretty fast. And I feel a lot better already."

Brad poured himself another cup of coffee and sat back down at the table. "Dinner here will be nice," he said with a smile, the intimate warmth in his eyes soaking into her pores like sunshine.

Sam was saved from having to reply by the sudden ringing of the phone. She started to rise, but Brad restrained her with a hand on one shoulder and stood up to take it off the hook, passing it to her as he sat back down.

Sam gave him a smile of thanks as she greeted the caller. "Hello?"

"Sam? It's Laura."

"Hi."

"You sound better."

"Yeah, well, yesterday wasn't exactly my day."

"Are you okay?"

"Uh-huh. The stings are pretty red and swollen, but at least they don't hurt as much."

"Thank heavens! We were all so worried. And Brad was a wreck."

Sam looked over at the man in question, who smiled disarmingly, making her heart flip-flop. "Really?"

"Yeah. I thought he was going to have a heart attack or something while he was waiting for Sandy to come out and report on your condition."

"Hmm," was Sam's only response.

"So did he stay long when he took you home?" Laura

asked, her studiously casual tone not fooling Sam. Laura was fishing for information, and Sam decided to have a little fun.

"Uh-huh."

There was silence, and when it became clear that Sam wasn't going to offer any more information, Laura tried another tack. "I'll probably give him a call later this morning and see how he is. Nick thinks he hurt his shoulder in the fall. We were all so worried about you that no one really paid attention to him."

"Do you want to talk to him now?" Sam asked innocently.

There was a long moment of stunned silence. But at last Laura found her voice. "You mean he's there?" she asked cautiously.

"Uh-huh. We just had breakfast."

By now Sam was grinning, and Brad raised his eyebrows questioningly. Sam just shook her head. She was enjoying this. Laura was too discreet to come right out and directly ask a personal question, but Sam knew she was dying of curiosity. So she waited her out.

"Well...that's nice," Laura said finally. "He must have come over really early."

"No. Actually, he never left. And Nick was right. His shoulder is badly bruised."

By now Brad was on to her game, and he leaned back with a smile and shook his head, sipping his coffee.

Sam knew Laura's brain was in overdrive, so before things got too out of hand, she stepped in. "He slept on the couch, Laura," she said deliberately.

"I'm sure he did," Laura replied quickly. "I mean, I've known Brad a long time, and he's a real gentleman. Besides, sleepovers aren't his style.'' She paused. ''Listen, Sam, I wasn't trying to pry or anything, so…''

''Yes, you were,'' Sam interrupted with a chuckle. ''And it's okay. I gave you the third degree plenty of times when you were dating Nick, remember? After all, what are friends for?''

Laura's soft laugh came over the line. ''Yeah. I do remember. Well, take care of yourself. And tell Brad to do the same. Will I see you Thursday night?''

''I'll be there. And thanks for calling, Laura.''

''Like you said, what are friends for? 'Bye.''

Sam replaced the receiver, and Brad chuckled as he set his cup down on the table. ''I think I got the gist of that conversation.''

Sam flushed. ''Sorry about that. I couldn't resist putting her on a little.'' Then she frowned in sudden concern. ''Oh, Brad, I probably shouldn't have done that! I mean, you're a minister and all, and I wouldn't want to start any rumors or anything.''

Brad rose and smiled down at her. ''Don't worry. Laura's known me too long to jump to the wrong conclusions.''

Sam's face cleared as she stood up as well. ''Yeah, you're probably right. She did say you were a gentleman, and a gentleman wouldn't…well…you know.''

''Wouldn't he?'' Brad asked softly, moving closer.

Sam backed up in alarm, her heart accelerating to double time. ''Brad…let's put things on hold till Friday, okay?''

It wasn't okay as far as he was concerned. He wanted to talk things out right now. In fact, he wanted to do more than talk. But they'd agreed to wait until Friday, and Laura was right—he was a gentleman. And a gentleman kept his word.

"Okay," he capitulated. "I've got to get going, anyway."

Sam walked him to the door, and he paused on the tiny porch, turning back to gently touch her hair, remembering the way it had felt in his hands the night before. Exercising great restraint, he took a deep breath and then bent down and gently kissed her forehead, carefully avoiding the puffy welt above her eye.

"Will you take it easy for the next few days, Sam?"

She nodded, trying to swallow past the lump in her throat. "Uh-huh."

He gazed down at her, clearly reluctant to leave, and finally let out his breath slowly in a long, heavy sigh. "Well, I know one thing for sure," he said at last.

"What?"

"It's going to be a long week."

Sam wearily fitted her key in the lock and pushed the door open. Not only was it turning into a long week, it had also been a long night. There were times when she found her work at the counseling center very rewarding. And then there were other times, like tonight, when it left her emotionally drained and depressed.

She dropped her purse on the hall table and stepped out of her shoes, arching her back and tilting her head back and forth to relieve the tension in her muscles. Was there something else she could have done, or said, or offered that would have made a difference? she wondered futilely. It was the same question she always asked on nights like this, and she came up with the same answer: maybe. But she didn't have a clue what.

As Sam mechanically prepared for bed she wondered how Jamie was doing, both physically and emotionally. Her decision had been made under pressure, Sam knew. The last thing her boyfriend wanted to deal with as a college freshman was a baby. And her parents were apparently of the opinion that a scandal would be worse than the alternative.

They were wrong, of course. Dead wrong. But they'd obviously convinced Jamie. Maybe, in the end, they'd threatened not to pick up her college tuition if she had the baby. Maybe they'd told her they would throw her out of the house. Only Jamie knew which pressure had finally pushed her to make a decision Sam knew she would live to regret. Because Sam also knew that the girl had had serious moral concerns. But Sam had seen the desperate, frantic look in her eyes both times they'd met and she knew that despite her best efforts, there was a good chance Jamie would go through with the procedure. Sam had done everything she could think of to prevent that from happening, even giving the girl her home phone number and encouraging her to call at any hour. But Jamie hadn't taken her up on the offer. She might call now, though, after the fact. Some of them did. And at that point all Sam could do was listen and share their anguish.

Sam lay awake a long time, staring at the dark ceiling. Jamie was probably doing the same thing right now. And if she was half as sensitive as Sam thought she was, similar nights lay ahead of her. Nights filled with regret and remorse and sadness. Maybe someday she would go on to marry, have other children, lead a fulfilling life. Most women did. But Sam suspected that even those who seemed able to put the decision behind them and move on still had moments of deep sadness and guilt.

As Sam finally drifted to sleep, she did something she hadn't done in a very long time. She turned to the Lord for help. Not for herself, but for Jamie. She asked him to watch over the girl in the difficult months—and years—ahead. She would need all the help and support she could get. Ending the life of an innocent child—by choice or through irresponsibility—often took only minutes. But it exacted a price that lasted a lifetime.

Sam thrashed on the bed, frowning in her sleep. She heard a child's anguished cry of fear and pain, followed by the plaintive utterance of a single word...*Mama*...that slowly turned into a scream of terror that went on and on and—

With a strangled sob, Sam awoke abruptly, her heart pounding, her breathing erratic. It was a familiar, if dreaded, scenario, and Sam knew what to do. She sat up quickly and turned on the light, forcing herself to take slow, deep breaths as she focused on the Monet painting strategically hung across from her bed. It was a coping mechanism she'd learned a long time ago.

She continued to breathe deeply, letting the beauty of the painting seep into her soul until the ugly images in her mind began to fade, and gradually her heart rate returned to normal and her respiration slowed. She was still shaky, though, her hands trembling as she reached for the sheet and pulled it up as she leaned back against the headboard.

Sam's eyes filled with tears. With every fiber of her being she wished she could forget that day, pretend it had never happened. Sometimes she managed to force the memory into a dusty corner of her mind, but always the nightmare would return, the images so vivid, the sounds so real, that for those brief moments before awakening she relived the horror in all its original intensity. Choking back a sob, she lowered her head to her knees and huddled on the bed, reliving once again that terrible time in her life....

"How could you let this happen? We've only been married two months! I don't want a kid, Sam. Get rid of it or I'm out of here."

Randy's voice was angry and his face expressed shock, but Sam was more shocked at the harshness of his words. She didn't really want a child, either, at this point in her life. She was too young and too inexperienced and too frightened of the responsibility. Nor did she want to lose Randy. Since she'd alienated her parents by marrying him, he was all she had. There was no one else to turn to, and she had no job, no money, no place even to live without him.

Yet she couldn't bring herself to end the life growing within her, despite Randy's threats. The very thought of it was abhorrent to her. But as the days wore on and his threats intensified, she grew more uncertain and desperate. There just didn't seem to be any other option. Sleepless night blended into sleepless night as she struggled alone with her decision, and she grew pale from exhaustion and strain.

The night of horror began with Randy's angry parting words as he left for his band job.

"I told you to get rid of that thing, Sam. Make your choice now—it's me or it."

Sam watched him leave, the tears silently coursing down her cheeks. Wearily she lay down on the bed, staring at the ceiling in the latest of the impersonal, nondescript motel rooms that had become her home. Sleep. That was what she craved. Her body needed the rest and she needed the oblivion. But sleep had been a stranger lately.

Suddenly she remembered the pills Randy took. The blue ones and yellow ones; uppers and downers, he called them. He never seemed to have any trouble sleeping when he took the downers, she thought. It couldn't hurt to take one or two, could it? She needed the sleep so badly! She couldn't even think straight anymore, she was so tired.

Sam got up and filled a glass with water in the bathroom, then rummaged in his suitcase, finally withdrawing a small container. She hesitated for a brief second, then resolutely shook out two of the innocuous-looking pills and tossed them into her mouth, downing them quickly with a gulp of water.

Sam replaced the container and lay down, waiting for her eyelids to grow heavy. But instead, as the minutes ticked by, she started to feel strange. Lightheaded. Sensitized. Her nerve endings began to tingle, and she grew more alert rather than sleepy. As the feelings intensified, she frowned in confusion. This wasn't supposed to happen. Unless—

With growing, frightening certainty, she swung her feet to the floor and rummaged through Randy's suitcase again, once more retrieving the bottle of pills. She stared at it, then searched for the other bottle, pulling it out as well. With a sickening jolt, she realized that she'd taken the wrong pills.

Sam began to pace, frightened by the frenetic energy

coursing through her veins and the erratic pounding of her heart. She had to find a way to tone down the effects of the pills, she thought in panic. Fresh air. That would help. Lots of fresh air. Maybe she should take a drive and just let the air rush against her face. Yes. That was a good idea. It couldn't hurt, anyway. Mike, the drummer, had picked Randy up in his van, so at least the car was here.

Frantically she searched for the keys, sighing with relief when her fingers closed over them in the pocket of Randy's jeans. She grabbed her purse and dashed for the car, rolling the window all the way down despite the light rain that was falling. Then she set out aimlessly on the unfamiliar roads of the small town.

Sam drove for almost two hours until gradually she began to feel better. As she waited at a red light on the outskirts of town, she decided it was time to return to the motel. She felt normal again—physically, at least. Maybe tonight she'd be able to sleep, she thought hopefully.

When the light turned green, she stepped on the accelerator, gaining speed as she crossed the intersection. And that's when it happened.

The subsequent sequence of events was a disjointed blur in her mind and was destined to remain so even years later.

A child's bike, suddenly darting in front of her through the deepening dusk.

The squeal of brakes.

A frantic attempt to turn the unresponsive steering wheel.

A dull thud against the bumper.

The sensation of slow-motion gliding as the car slid off the wet pavement and into a ditch.

The sharp impact of her head against the windshield as the car slammed into a telephone pole.

And then blackness.

Sometimes Sam wished that the story had ended there. That she'd never reawakened. But the horror had continued. Her next conscious memory was distorted faces, peering at her as she lay in the hospital, grotesquely moving in and out of focus. But the words were what would remain most indelibly burned into her memory.

The child's mother, leaning over the gurney as they wheeled her into the emergency room, as she shouted over and over: "You killed my baby! You killed my baby!"

The nurses, talking in low voices over the background noise of a child crying in pain somewhere else in the emergency room. "She has internal injuries. We can't save the baby."

The doctor, standing by her bed. "I'm sorry. We did everything we could, but there's a good chance you may never be able to conceive again."

And finally Randy, with his warped attempt at humor. "Well, you could have found an easier way to take care of the problem. But at least it's over."

Sam drew a shaky breath and reached for a tissue on her nightstand, focusing once more on the Monet painting. No, she thought in despair, it was never over. Not the next day. Not the next month. Not even seventeen years later. She lived with the oppressive guilt every day of her life.

It wasn't that anyone had blamed her. Witnesses said the collision was unavoidable. But Sam knew differently. If she hadn't taken those pills, she wouldn't have felt the need for fresh air and gone for a drive with less-than-sharp reflexes. And she wouldn't have taken the pills if she hadn't felt so alone and in such deep despair. If only there had been someone to turn to, to talk with, she thought futilely. She had been so young and so desperate—and so very wrong. The bottom line was that because of her irresponsibility two innocent lives had ended that night. Those were the cold, hard facts. And they were irrefutable.

Sam knew she couldn't restore to those children the gift of life she had snatched away. All she could do was try to help other young girls who found themselves in her situation, let them know they weren't alone, that someone cared, that there were other options available that didn't include destroying a life. It was heartbreaking work, and she didn't always succeed. Like tonight. But sometimes she did, and in those successes she found consolation. She felt that in some small way it helped her to make reparation for her own wrong. Quite simply, the counseling center work appeased her conscience enough to allow her to go on living.

The dull, pounding ache in her head that was the typical aftermath of her nightmare intensified, and Sam rose and went to the kitchen in search of aspirin. As she filled a glass with water, her glance fell on the answering machine, and she noted that she had one message. She'd been so tired and upset when she arrived home that she hadn't even checked, an unusual lapse for her. Failing to return messages promptly was a no-no in the real estate game.

But it wasn't a business-related message after all, she realized, as soon as she punched the play button.

"Hi, Sam." The warmth of Brad's voice washed over her like a soothing balm. "I know you're not home, but I'm leaving for Dad's early in the morning and I was afraid

I'd wake you if I called then. I just wanted you to know that I'm counting the days till Friday.'' He paused, as if debating his next words, then continued. "And I wanted to tell you that I miss you. See you soon.''

The line went dead, and Sam leaned against the counter, overcome by an almost painful yearning. She missed him, too. On a night like this, it would have been so nice to turn to his strong, steady arms for comfort. But she doubted whether he would offer those arms if he knew the reason she needed them.

As she headed back to bed, Sam suddenly thought about her last Bible class, where the topic had been forgiveness. She'd been especially attentive that night. It had even given her a brief moment of hope. Until she realized that the concept, noble though it was, seemed too lofty for the human condition. In a perfect world, people might be able to practice that principle. But the world was far from perfect, and people were judgmental. It was a fact of life. Maybe the Lord could forgive her. Maybe. People were another story. Certainly not that child's mother. Even Brad, who was not only a minister but the finest, most decent man she had ever had the privilege of knowing, would have a very hard time dealing with what she'd done. If *she* couldn't accept it, find a way to forgive *herself,* how on earth could she expect anyone else to? No, it would be too much to hope for. Besides, even if the Lord could forgive her, as they taught in Bible class, she still didn't feel that she deserved a happy ending, let alone someone like Brad.

Wearily Sam climbed back into bed, the light still burning. After one of her nightmare episodes she could never bear to be alone in the dark. Brad had said he was counting the days till Friday, she recalled sadly. So was she. But while he looked forward to it with eager anticipation, she felt only dread. Because that was the last time she would see him. Calling off their relationship was the right thing to do, for both of them, she told herself resolutely. But it wasn't going to be easy.

Chapter Eight

Sam had hoped to have some time Friday before Brad
arrived to mentally prepare for their discussion and to very
carefully formulate her wording about why their relationship had to end. Breaking things off was going to be difficult, no matter what she said, but the right words might
help.

However, things didn't work out quite the way she
planned. In fact, it was a day of disasters, beginning with
a flat tire, followed by a difficult client who insisted on
seeing a house at precisely one o'clock and then arrived
half an hour late, ending with a quicker-than-expected contract response requiring an unscheduled stop at the office
to redo some paperwork.

By the time Sam arrived home, frazzled and exhausted,
it was nearly four o'clock. The good news, she told herself
consolingly, was that she still had time to prepare dinner.
The bad news was that she didn't have time for anything
else. As she hastily pulled on a pair of jeans and headed
for the kitchen, she decided that she'd just have to wing

her discussion with Brad and hope that the right words came when she needed them. Because right now dinner was going to require her undivided attention.

A few minutes later, after poring over the complicated instructions in the cookbook she'd dug out of the closet earlier in the week, Sam quickly came to the conclusion that she should have made time to familiarize herself with the recipes—beyond shopping for the ingredients—before Friday at four o'clock. Maybe, just maybe, she'd been a little too ambitious with the menu, she acknowledged reluctantly. Chicken *Cordon Bleu,* twice-baked potatoes and green beans *almondine,* not to mention homemade biscuits, would be something Laura could whip up in an hour. After reading the instructions, Sam wasn't sure she could do it in half a day, let alone the allotted two hours. She eyed the preparation times on the recipes skeptically, quickly concluding that they were for people who knew what they were doing, not novices. And she was *definitely* a novice.

A wave of panic washed over her, and she accelerated her pace, reaching into the refrigerator for the cheese. Thank goodness dessert was finished, she thought with relief, her glance falling on the English trifle she'd made the night before. However, because it had been deceptively easy to put together, it had given her a false sense of confidence about today's foray into the culinary arts. But that confidence was rapidly deteriorating.

Sam stared at the chicken recipe, her brow knit in concentration. It said to flatten the breasts, but how in the world did you do that? She tried pressing on them with the heel of her hand, but that had little effect. Would a hammer work? she wondered in sudden inspiration, rummaging around in her tool drawer. Yes, she thought triumphantly a moment later after giving one a whack.

The next step—layering the breasts with ham and cheese and then rolling them up—wasn't so easy. Maybe the breasts were still too thick, she thought with a frown, finally managing to get one of the uncooperative bundles into a semicylindrical shape. Why didn't these books have step-by-step pictures? she wondered in frustration. She brushed her hair back from her face with one hand and clutched the rolled-up packet of chicken, cheese and ham in the other as she checked the recipe. It said to dust the breasts in flour, dip in a beaten egg, roll in bread crumbs, then secure with a toothpick. Sam's frown deepened. If she tried to do any of those things they would fall apart. Maybe she could just sprinkle them with crumbs after they were in the pan, she thought hopefully. Sure. That ought to work, she decided, impaling the meat with a generous number of toothpicks. Besides, she'd already devoted way too much time to this recipe.

Sam moved on to the potatoes. She'd put them in the oven earlier, but when she removed them and tried to slice off a long end so she could scoop out the interior, the skin was too hard. She frowned and checked the recipe. Bake for one hour and fifteen minutes at four hundred degrees. That's what she'd done, wasn't it? She glanced at the temperature gauge on the oven. Apparently not. It read five hundred, not four hundred, she realized with dismay.

She looked at her watch and her panic intensified. It was already five-thirty, and Brad was coming at six. And she hadn't even started on the vegetable or salad yet. She put the chicken in the oven, then ruthlessly she crossed the homemade biscuits off the menu, concluding that English muffins would have to do instead.

Sam tackled the potatoes with renewed vigor. She finally managed to cut through the crusty skin, but in the process much of the shell shattered. Resolutely she forged on, scooping out the shriveled insides and adding the other ingredients before placing the mixture in what was left of the skins.

Finally she turned her attention to the green beans. The sauce sounded easy enough—just onion and slivered almonds sautéed in butter. She chopped the onion as rapidly as possible, dumped everything into a small frying pan, and set the heat on low. Maybe she could change clothes while the sauce cooked, she thought, distractedly running her fingers through her hair. Then she could throw the salad together at the last minute.

Sam headed for the bedroom, shedding her T-shirt as she went. What a day! And the most difficult part was still to come. At least now she had a minute to think about how she was going to break the news to Brad. She reached for the deep purple silk blouse she'd chosen, pulling it on rapidly, debating her approach. It might be best if she—

The harsh buzzing of a smoke detector made her jump, and she dashed toward the kitchen, her heart pounding. She paused for a brief second on the threshold, her eyes riveted to the smoke seeping out of the oven, then moved toward it and yanked open the door, only to be engulfed in a billowing gray cloud. Coughing, she tried to wave the smoke away as she peered inside, but it was difficult to see with her eyes watering so badly. As nearly as she could determine, it appeared that the cheese had leaked out of the chicken breasts and was now burning. In rapid order, she grabbed the pan and removed it, turned on the exhaust fan, opened a window and began waving a towel at the smoke detector to clear the air.

When the piercing alarm finally fell silent, Sam leaned back against the counter, her heart pounding. She surveyed the sad-looking chicken, desperately trying to figure out a way to salvage the unappetizing mess. Maybe if she scooped the cheese back in and—

Suddenly she sniffed and glanced suspiciously toward the stove. The almonds and onions in her butter sauce were turning black, and she flew across the room to remove the pan from the heat before the smoke alarm went off again. As she stood there holding it, her glance fell on the potatoes waiting to go into the oven. They looked pathetic, too. The skins had pretty much disintegrated, and the filling was already spilling out.

Sam thought she had felt panic before. Now she realized that had been mere concern. *This* was panic. She opened her refrigerator and looked inside in desperation, hoping that by some miracle a solution to her dilemma would appear. But no such luck. She had dessert, and she had salad, she thought, her eyes visually ticking off the ingredients—lettuce, tomatoes, mushrooms, parmesan cheese, red onion, Italian dress—Sam frowned. Where was the dressing? It had been on her list. She remembered that clearly. But as she frantically rummaged through the refrigerator, it became equally clear that it hadn't made the transition from list to reality. She must have forgotten it!

Sam stood numbly before the refrigerator, forced to admit the obvious—her dinner was a disaster. And Brad was expecting a home-cooked meal! The kind that Rachel used to make. Instead he was getting a culinary catastrophe.

How was she ever going to face him? And what was she going to do about dinner? She didn't even have any microwave stuff left in the freezer! Maybe she could still call the gourmet shop and—

The ringing of the doorbell startled Sam, and she froze, her stomach sinking to her toes. With sickening certainty, she slowly checked her watch. Six o'clock. As usual, Brad was punctual. She looked longingly at the back door, and for the briefest moment she actually considered sneaking out and just disappearing. But of course she couldn't do that. Could she?

The bell rang again, and distractedly she pushed her hair back. She had to face him. There was no way out. Her heart pounding in her chest, she forced her legs to carry her toward the door. She hovered there, her hand on the knob, until a third ring forced her to respond. Taking a deep breath, she pulled it open.

Peripherally, she realized that Brad looked great. He was dressed in tan slacks and a blue-striped open-necked shirt, and his navy blue blazer sat well on his broad shoulders. He was also carrying a bottle of wine, which Sam figured they were both going to need before this so-called dinner was over.

Brad's smile of welcome slowly faded to a frown, then changed to a look of concern as he took in Sam's appearance. Her normally well-groomed hair hadn't even been combed, and there was a trail of bread crumbs across her face. Her silk blouse was attractive—but she was wearing it, untucked, over scruffy jeans. She was also barefoot. As Brad completed his quick but thorough scrutiny, alarm bells began ringing in his mind.

"Sam? Are you all right?"

She managed a shaky laugh. "Oh, sure. Why wouldn't I be? I mean, it's just a little dinner for two, right? Anyone should be able to handle that. Laura could. And I'm sure Rachel would have managed with no problem."

His frown deepened. "What are you talking about?"

"Your dinner. Or what was supposed to be your dinner. It's a disaster."

"Sam, let's go inside," he said carefully. She seemed on the verge of tears, but surely a recipe gone awry wouldn't make her almost hysterical. Not Sam, who took everything in stride.

She moved aside so he could enter, then shut the door behind him as he deposited the bottle on the table in the tiny foyer and then turned to her. He placed his hands on her shoulders, his eyes probing and concerned.

"Let's start over, okay?" he said, struggling to keep his voice calm. "Now what happened?"

Suddenly she felt tears welling up in her eyes. "Dinner. It's ruined," she said, sniffling.

"I don't mind if everything's not perfect," he assured her.

He didn't seem to understand. "Brad, it's inedible," she said.

"Oh, come on, it can't be that bad."

She nodded. "Yes it can. It is. Trust me on this. It's not a pretty picture in the kitchen."

"But what happened?" he asked, frowning in puzzlement.

"I don't spend much time in the kitchen. I didn't realize cooking was so time consuming or involved, so I guess I overextended myself with the menu. And I don't even have any microwave stuff in the freezer!"

Brad put his arm around her shoulder and drew her toward the couch. "Relax, Sam," he said easily. "It's not the end of the world. We'll make do. What turned out the best?" he asked encouragingly.

"Dessert. And it's not just the *best*. It's the *only* thing that turned out."

He kept his arm around her as they sat down, and though he was trying to remain calm, he was concerned and bewildered. He didn't understand why she was so upset. It wasn't like her to be thrown by something like this.

"Okay, then how about Chinese? I passed a place a few blocks from here."

"But I promised you a home-cooked meal."

"Can I tell you something, Sam? A home-cooked meal would have been nice. But food is *not* the reason I came tonight."

That was good news on the dinner front, solving one dilemma. But it only reminded her of the other, far more important one.

When she didn't reply, Brad removed his arm from around her shoulders and stood up. "I'll be back in twenty minutes," he said. "Will you be all right?"

She nodded. "Yes."

He hesitated uncertainly, not sure he should leave her alone in her present state. She looked up at him, saw the concern in his eyes, and managed a shaky smile. "Go on. I'll be fine," she said reassuringly.

He nodded. "Twenty minutes."

Sam heard the door click shut behind him and drew a long, shaky breath. He didn't seem all that upset about the dinner shambles, after all. But that was only because his attention was focused on another issue. And she'd better start thinking fast about how she was going to handle *that*.

Sam glanced down, and her eyes widened in surprise. She still had on her jeans! With a startled exclamation, she rose and made her way to the bedroom, quickly substituting a black skirt and leather flats for the jeans and bare feet. She was almost afraid to look in the mirror, and she did so tentatively, groaning as her worst fears were confirmed. Her face had been largely wiped free of makeup from the steam in the kitchen, there was a trail of bread crumbs across one cheek and her hair looked like it hadn't been combed since yesterday. She was going to have to work fast to make herself presentable before Brad returned.

By the time the doorbell rang, she'd not only dressed, combed her hair and repaired her makeup, she'd also finished setting the table—a job she'd abandoned earlier in the afternoon as the kitchen crises began escalating. She'd also discarded most of the evidence of her culinary disaster, wrinkling her nose in distaste at the unappetizing mess she'd created. Martha Stewart had nothing to worry about from her, she thought ruefully.

When Sam answered the door this time, she was calmer and much more in control. Brad noticed the difference immediately as he stepped inside, carrying two large white bags which were emitting tempting aromas.

"Feeling better?" he asked, turning to her with a smile still tinged by concern.

"Much," she assured him. "I can't even imagine what you must have thought when you arrived the first time," she said, feeling a faint flush of embarrassment creep across her cheeks.

"Worried," he replied quietly, his eyes searching hers

as if to assure himself that she was all right. When he seemed satisfied, he nodded toward the bags. "Should we put these in the kitchen?"

"Uh-huh. Here, I can take one," she offered, reaching for a sack.

He followed her, pausing on the threshold to look around cautiously before entering.

Sam glanced back and laughed. "It's safe. I destroyed most of the evidence while you were gone."

Brad grinned. "Then let's eat. But first…how are you feeling? Are the stings any better?" he asked, his voice suddenly serious. "I meant to ask the minute I got here, but we sort of got sidetracked."

"Yeah, you might say that," she said with a wry grin. "Actually, I feel fine. Most of the stings have faded and the tenderness is slowing disappearing. How's your shoulder?"

"In working order," he said, flexing it to demonstrate. "It's still not very pretty to look at, but the color palette has changed from black and blue to blue and yellow. It doesn't hurt as much, either."

"Well, I have to say that when you ask someone out, you do show them a memorable time," Sam said with a laugh.

"So do you," he countered, nodding to the kitchen.

"Touché," she acknowledged. "But at least my disaster didn't involve injuries."

He grinned sheepishly. "True. Next time I ask you out, things will be better, I promise."

Sam's face clouded, and she turned away to hide her reaction, reaching into the bags to remove the food. "Why don't you go on into the dining room? I'll put this in bowls and be right there.''

Sam hadn't turned away quickly enough, however. Brad saw the look on her face, and he didn't like what it implied. Clearly she was still skittish about the notion of a romance between them. But he wasn't leaving here tonight until he persuaded her to give it a try. And the first order of business was to find out *why* she was reluctant. It wasn't lack of interest, he was sure of that based on the smoldering look he'd seen in her eyes at the picnic. No, it was something else. Something quite serious, apparently. Nevertheless, he was convinced they could overcome it. Now he just had to convince her. But there would be time for that later, after dinner, when they'd both had a chance to relax a little.

''I'll open the wine,'' he said.

''That would be great.''

By the time she brought the food into the ''formal'' dining area next to the living room, Brad was waiting to pull out her chair. ''I got beef and broccoli and chicken cashew. I hope that's okay,'' he said as she sat down.

''Mmm. Great!'' she replied, spooning generous servings of both onto her plate to make up for the lunch she'd skipped. ''Let me tell you, this is much better than what we'd be eating if I tried to salvage the dinner I cooked,'' she said ruefully.

''That bad, huh?'' he teased.

''Let's just say that cooking isn't my forte. I wish I'd learned how. You were lucky to have a wife who was good at it.''

Brad chewed thoughtfully. This was the second time tonight that she'd mentioned Rachel. Maybe she thought he was comparing her to his late wife, and she felt intimidated and less suitable for him because she wasn't as "domestic." If so, he needed to diplomatically dispel that concern.

"Rachel was a good cook," he acknowledged slowly. "But I've found that everyone has their own unique talent. None are better or worse than the other. Just different. For example, you have a wonderful talent for drawing people out and making them feel happy. I can speak from personal experience on that one."

Sam flushed and glanced down. "Not very practical, though," she said.

He shrugged. "Depends on how you define *practical*. Joy and happiness are great foundations for coping with the trials and tribulations of everyday life. It seems pretty practical to me."

Sam felt a warm rush of pleasure at his words. Or maybe it was from the wine, she thought, speculatively eyeing her half-empty glass. She'd had a glass and a half already. Given that her usual drink was mineral water she'd never developed much tolerance for alcohol. But tonight she figured she needed a drink. Or two. Maybe it would mellow her out a little after the kitchen disaster, help her find the words to tell Brad she couldn't see him anymore.

The very thought of that discussion usually made her panic, but surprisingly, this time, it didn't. She just felt very relaxed and content. Must be the alcohol, she concluded. "The wine's good," she said with a smile, taking another sip.

"Yes, it is. I like to have it on special occasions."

"Is tonight a special occasion?" she asked.

"Maybe," he said noncommittally, his deep brown eyes

watching her over the rim of his glass as he lifted it to his lips.

What a stupid question, she berated herself! Very deliberately and carefully she set her own glass down. No more wine for her. She cleared her throat—and tried to clear her too-foggy mind—before she spoke. "Well, how about if we have dessert and coffee in the living room?" she said brightly.

"Sounds good. Can I help."

"No!" she replied quickly. "I mean, thanks, but I can manage," she added, before escaping to the kitchen.

As Sam scooped out the trifle and waited for the coffee to perk, she took a deep breath. This was the moment she'd dreaded. How was she ever going to tell this wonderful man to get lost? And essentially that was what she had to do. He wasn't going to like it, even though she knew that in the long run it would be better for him. But making him understand that without revealing her secret would be tough. Yet telling him the truth wasn't an option. Because as hard it would be to lose him, it would be even worse to see the horror and recrimination in his eyes as *he* rejected *her* if she shared the terrible secret from her past with him.

Sam carefully poured the coffee and placed it on a tray, adding the bowls of trifle, cream, sugar and napkins as she tried to think of some way to delay her entry. But she'd have to deal with this sooner or later, and she might as well get it over with, she realized with a resigned sigh. Waiting wasn't going to make it any easier.

Brad was standing by the mantel when she returned, and he moved toward her and took the tray, setting it carefully on the coffee table.

"Dessert looks good," he said.

Sam tried to smile. "Well, the proof is in the tasting. I'm not making any promises." Even to her own ears her voice sounded strangely tight, and she hoped Brad wasn't picking up on her nervousness.

Her hope was in vain. He'd known this wasn't going to be an easy sell, and he'd been keenly attuned to her signals all evening, debating the best approach to use to convince her to give a romantic relationship a chance. He'd ultimately settled on the one thing he knew they had in common—physical attraction. That wasn't enough on which to build a long-term relationship—but it wasn't a bad starting place for his persuasive efforts.

"Well…shall we sit?" he said, when she remained on her feet next to the table. "Unless you want to eat dessert standing up?" he teased.

"Oh! No, of course not." She sat down on the couch, careful to allow room for a discreet distance between them. But Brad apparently had other ideas. He sat down very close to her, his arm brushing hers as he reached for his dessert. Sam's instinct was to scoot into the far corner of the couch, away from danger, out of the magnetic range of the attractive man sitting next to her. But she couldn't figure out a way to do that without being obvious, so she remained where she was, her back stiff, trying vainly to control the staccato beat of her heart.

"Sam?"

Brad was offering her one of the servings of trifle, and she reached for it automatically. He picked up his as well, then leaned back and took a bite, chewing thoughtfully. Then he took another bite. And another. Finally he turned to her with a grin. "Well, the rest of your dinner may not have turned out, Sam, but this makes up for it. It's great! Go ahead, try some,'' he said, helping himself to a generous mouthful.

Sam did as he suggested, mostly because she couldn't think of anything else to do. She certainly wasn't hungry, although she had to admit that the creamy concoction was tasty. She continued to eat so she wouldn't have to talk, trying to buy herself a little thinking time while she figured out a way to break the news to the man sitting next to her.

She was only half-finished by the time he'd demolished his serving, topping it off with a sip of coffee before wiping his lips on one of the napkins. "You can make that for me anytime," he said, turning to her with a smile.

As he angled himself toward her, he jostled her arm, and Sam, who was just about to take another bite of trifle, missed her mouth. Fortunately the concoction stayed on the spoon, although a streak of whipped cream ended up on her cheek.

"Sorry about that," he said with a sheepish grin. "Here, let me."

He reached over and carefully dabbed at the sweet trail, and Sam literally stopped breathing. He was only inches away, and the magnetism she'd felt earlier was multiplied exponentially.

Suddenly Brad's hand stilled on her cheek, and the natural brown color of his eyes darkened perceptibly as they sought and held hers compellingly. Without releasing her gaze, he laid the napkin on the back of the couch and took her dessert out of her trembling hands, setting it on the coffee table in front of him.

Sam knew she should say something. Anything. She had to break the spell he was weaving with his passionately eloquent eyes before it was too late. But her voice deserted her, and she seemed incapable of fighting the powerful emotions that were sweeping over her like a relentless tide, igniting her body in their wake.

Brad reached over and stroked her hair, pushing it back from her face and letting it glide through his fingers. Silently he repeated the motion again. And again. And still again, until Sam thought her heart was going to explode in her chest.

"You have beautiful hair, Sam," he said softly at last, continuing to play with it.

"Thanks." Her voice sounded like a croak, and she cleared her throat. "It's the real thing, too. I'd never pick this color on purpose," she said nervously.

"Why not?"

"Why would anyone want red hair? It clashes with everything."

"Red? I wouldn't call your hair red," he mused, finally releasing her gaze to study the strands he held in his hand. "It's more…burnished. Like the color of autumn."

Sam struggled to take a deep breath. This wasn't working out at all as she'd planned. She thought they were going to have a nice, rational discussion about their relationship. She hadn't expected Brad to…well…do this. It was throwing her off balance, making it hard to breathe, let alone think.

"Um, Brad, I…"

He pressed a finger to her lips, effectively silencing what he supposed was going to be a protest. She gazed at him wide-eyed and swallowed convulsively, a pulse beating frantically in the hollow of her throat.

His gaze dropped to that very spot, and then he transferred his fingertip to the faded welt near her upper lip, letting it rest there gently. "Is this still tender?" he asked, his own voice strangely hoarse.

She shook her head as the touch of his finger sent a tremor rippling through her body. "No," she whispered.

"Good. Because I don't want to hurt you, Sam, but I'm not sure I can wait any longer to do this."

Very slowly, very deliberately, he leaned down and pressed his lips to hers, gently, tentatively testing her response, gauging her reaction. He was fairly certain that she would welcome his kiss—if she listened to her heart—but there was a chance he'd misread her attraction. This was the real test. He moved his lips over hers coaxingly, seeking a response, waiting for an unspoken invitation to continue.

As Brad's lips worked their magic, Sam suddenly felt as if she'd consumed the entire bottle of wine instead of just two glasses. She was dizzy and light-headed and drowning. And she was also fighting a losing battle with her resolve. She knew this was *not* the right way to go about ending their relationship. She needed to think rationally, and she was only going to be able to do that if she backed off, put some physical distance between them.

Logically, Sam knew that was what she should do. But it felt so good, and so right, being close to Brad. What could it hurt, just this once, to let herself enjoy a moment of tenderness with a man who seemed to care about her very much—as a person, not just for her physical assets, not just because he was looking for a good time or hoping for a one-night stand? Maybe it would be okay, she told herself, as long as things didn't get out of hand. And they wouldn't, not with Brad. That wasn't his style. So just this once, maybe she could let herself respond.

Except there was still a problem, she realized. It wasn't that she was uncertain *how* to respond. She'd been kissed by enough men in her time to have developed *some* technique. But this was a unique situation. Brad was... well...different. He was religious. How much response did he expect? She didn't want to come on too strong. Maybe he played this game by different rules. And if so, she didn't have a clue what they were.

Brad felt her hesitate, and reluctantly he backed off slightly, enough to look down into her eyes. They were troubled, but he could also see the ardent spark glowing in their depths, could feel the trembling desire in her body as he held her in his arms. Yet she was holding back. "Sam? What is it?" he asked gently, his lips traveling across her forehead, leaving a trail of fire in their wake.

She swallowed. "I...I don't know how to kiss a minister," she whispered.

Brad's soft, throaty chuckle of relief did strange things to her metabolism. "I'll tell you what, Sam," he suggested, his voice husky with emotion, the leashed passion in his eyes making her breath catch in her throat. "Just try kissing a man." And with that he pulled her into his arms and lowered his lips to hers once again.

This time Sam threw caution to the wind. She could feel the hard, uneven thudding of his heart against her breast as he held her tightly, and a powerful surge of longing ricocheted through her body. If this was going to be her only chance to taste Brad's kisses, she might as well take full advantage of it. So she did exactly what he asked. She kissed a man. Thoroughly, completely, without reserve.

Brad had hoped for a response. What he got was an earthquake. Not that he minded. Far from it. It was just that the intensity of Sam's passion surprised him. The kiss that had started off gentle and tentative quickly became much more consuming as they both allowed the passion that had simmered below the surface for weeks to explode.

Sam moaned softly as Brad molded her slim, pliant body to his with strong, sure arms, deepening the kiss until their smoldering passion became a consuming flame. His mouth moved over hers with a fierce intensity, and Sam couldn't be sure whether the drumming pulse she heard was her own or his. But it didn't matter. The only thing that mattered for this moment in time was the oneness she felt with this man, whose surprisingly deep passion was turning her world upside down. She put thoughts of tomorrow aside as they explored the wonderful magic of the attraction that had pulled them together almost since the beginning, long before either was consciously aware of it.

When they at last drew apart, both were shaken and breathless, and Sam's face was flushed.

"Wow!" Her voice was hushed and awed, her eyes dazed, her lips still throbbing from the touch of his. "I didn't know ministers could kiss like that!"

Brad managed a crooked grin as he struggled to calm his own raging pulse. "Neither did I," he admitted. The response she had drawn out of him surprised him as much as it had obviously surprised her.

As Sam struggled to get her own pulse under control, she looked at him suspiciously. "Brad, are you sure you haven't, well, done more of this than you said?"

"No. In fact, to be honest, I was a little bit intimidated," he admitted.

She looked up at him in surprise. "Why?"

He shrugged and pulled her close again, liking the way her head nestled naturally into his shoulder. "Because I *haven't* done much of this. I wasn't kidding when I said my experience was limited. Rachel was the only woman I was ever intimate with, and other than that it was just a simple good-night kiss for the few other women I dated. Let me tell you, in my book this was *not* a simple good-night kiss," he said with a throaty chuckle. "Anyway, I guess I was afraid that I would fall short of…well, I know you've dated a lot more than I have, and…" His voice trailed off.

Sam pulled away slightly and looked up at him. "Brad, just for the record, I'd like to clear up some misconceptions you seem to have about my dating background," she said with a frown.

"Sam, it's not necessary. All that matters to me is what we have together. I've known you long enough to get a very good sense of the kind of person you are *now,* and whatever happened in your past dating history isn't relevant."

"But I'd still like you to know. Because my 'past dating history,' as you put it, wasn't nearly as wild as I have a feeling you think it was."

"You don't have to do this, Sam," he said, his eyes sincere and direct.

"I know. But I want to, okay?" She drew a deep breath. "Randy was the first man I was intimate with, and only after we were married. When he ran out on me, I didn't want anything to do with men for quite a while. For one thing, you can imagine what his leaving did to my newly acquired and very fragile self-image. But after a year or so, I started to feel very lonely. And I needed to find out if I was attractive enough to get dates, I guess. That's when I joined a singles group and started to socialize more.''

Sam's eyes skittered away from his and she glanced down, playing with a button on her skirt. ''There were a couple of times in those next few years when the loneliness got so bad that I thought intimacy would help, even if it was only for a night or two,'' she said slowly, her voice soft. ''So I...I tried it. But I was wrong. It only made things worse. And after two episodes like that, I swore off one-night stands—and any other kind of stands. Besides, I guess some of my Christian upbringing stuck, because I just felt it was morally wrong.''

She looked up then, her eyes connecting directly with his. ''I've dated a lot, Brad. But that's all I do—date. Most guys aren't interested in dating indefinitely without a pay-off, so my dating roster changes frequently. But even casual dating has gotten old in the last year or so. To be honest, I rarely date at all anymore. So now you know.''

Sam was right to assume that Brad had envisioned her social life to be much more...active. It was certainly the impression he'd picked up from Laura. But he couldn't doubt the sincerity in Sam's eyes. He would stake his life that she was telling him the truth.

''Will you forgive me if I say I'm glad that my impression was inaccurate?'' he said. ''It wouldn't have made any difference, because I think that the Sam I know is terrific. But I have to admit that it was hard to reconcile the image I had of your past with the woman you are now. I'm glad that I don't need to.''

''So the fact that I've had two...encounters...doesn't bother you?'' she asked carefully, her voice soft.

"Sam," he drew her close again, cradling her head against his chest. "People have reasons for what they do. They make mistakes. They have regrets. We all do. You survived a very difficult, lonely period in your life in the only way you knew how at the time. And you learned from it. That's the best we can hope for in this imperfect, human world. What matters most to me is that the Sam Reynolds I know is a wonderful person. And I'm glad she's part of my life."

He'd given her the perfect opening to bring up their relationship, she realized. But she simply didn't have the strength to do it, not when his lips were in her hair, and his hands were working magic again, and her heart was his willing partner.

Finally he drew back and smiled at her. "I'll tell you what, Sam. It's still early. I could pick up a video, if you like. Or better yet, we could just watch one of those old romantic classics from that collection you keep hidden in the office closet."

Sam looked up at him in surprise, color stealing onto her cheeks at his teasing tone. "You saw them when you stayed that night, didn't you?"

"Uh-huh," he replied, his eyes twinkling.

"So my secret's out, I guess."

"Yep. Sam Reynolds—a closet romantic. Literally. And a softie under that sophisticated career woman image." He put a finger under her chin and gently tipped her head up so she had to meet his eyes, which were warm and tender. "And I like you just the way you are," he added with an intimate smile before draping his arm around her shoulders. "Now, personally, I vote for Cary Grant. He's always been one of my favorites. What do you say?"

She nodded, her throat tight. "Okay."

And so they watched her old romantic movie, cuddling on the couch, missing some of the screen action as they played out their own romantic scenes. Then they had more dessert and coffee, prolonging the evening as much as possible, neither wanting this special moment in their relationship to end. But at last Brad reluctantly removed his arm from around her shoulders and looked at his watch.

"I have to go, Sam," he said with a sigh. "It's nearly two o'clock."

Her eyes widened. "You're kidding!"

"No. I wish I were."

He took her hand as they walked toward the door, lacing his fingers through hers. "How about dinner tomorrow?" he said.

"Not here, I hope," she said with a wry grin.

He chuckled. "No. I thought we'd go out."

"Good choice."

"So…is it a date?" he asked, stepping outside and turning back to face her.

When he looked at her like that, it was impossible to refuse. Besides, despite what had happened tonight, she hadn't changed her mind about breaking things off. Brad had said some nice things earlier about mistakes and regrets and doing the best one could in the circumstances. But a one-night stand, wrong as that was, was *not* equivalent to an irresponsible action that senselessly took two young lives. She doubted whether he would be as understanding about that "mistake." Ending their relationship was still the right thing to do.

"Yes," she said, forcing herself to smile.

"Great. I'll pick you up at six.?"

"That would be fine."

He reached for her then, and she went willingly, closing her eyes as she hugged him fiercely, the hard planes of his body solid and strong against her slender curves. And as his lips claimed hers in a warm, lingering kiss, she knew that saying good-bye to this wonderful man was going to be the hardest thing she had ever done in her life.

Chapter Nine

Sam glanced at her watch for the dozenth time and frowned. She was sure Brad had said six o'clock. It was now six-twenty. Restlessly she moved to the front window and pushed the curtain aside to stare at the gray shroud of rain that had been falling relentlessly all afternoon. She peered into the gloom, her eyes scanning the grounds and parking lot, but there was no sign of him. With a sigh she let the fabric fall back into place. This wasn't like him, she thought worriedly. Brad was *never* late.

Sam ran her fingers through her hair distractedly and wandered toward the kitchen, pausing on the threshold. Had she come in here for some reason? she wondered. If so, it escaped her. She shook her head and sank down at the dinette table, drumming her fingers on the glass top. Brad could have gotten caught in traffic, she reasoned. It did happen, even to punctual people. He'd probably be along any minute, she reassured herself, trying to remain calm.

By six-thirty, when she dialed his number and got only

the answering machine, Sam wasn't calm anymore. By six forty-five, she started to panic.

She knew he hadn't forgotten their date. No way, not after last night. And if something else had come up requiring him to cancel or delay, he would have called her. That was just the kind of man he was. Which left only one possibility—an accident.

Sam began to pace. She tried to figure out the best course of action, but in her agitated state, her imagination was working overtime, and it wasn't easy to think rationally. She could start calling the hospitals, she supposed. Or the police. They might have an accident report. But what if Brad had injured himself at home? Maybe he'd fallen down the basement steps and was lying there unconscious!

With sudden decision, Sam rose and quickly scribbled a note to Brad, telling him she was going to the parsonage and to call her cellular number if he showed up. Then she grabbed her purse, taped the note to the front door and headed for her car. She knew this might be a wild-goose chase, but action was preferable to just sitting around. If she found no sign of him at the parsonage, she'd start calling the police and hospitals, she decided.

Sam drove quickly, pulling into Brad's driveway in record time. She'd never been inside the modest, one-story parsonage, but it stood right next to the church, and she'd seen it the day she gave the home-buying talk.

She slammed on the brakes and almost before the car came to a complete stop, threw open the door and raced up the steps, unmindful of her umbrella. Her heart thumped painfully in her chest as she pressed the bell. She waited impatiently, trying to ignore the string of frightening scenarios conjured up by her vivid imagination.

When the doorbell produced no response, Sam knocked and waited again, but still there was no response. She pressed the bell once more, with the same result. If Brad was in the house, he obviously couldn't get to the door.

She glanced around, debating her next move. The garage! That was it! Check the garage and see if his car was still here. Dodging raindrops, she dashed toward the detached structure and made her way to the side, cupping her hands around her face to peer in the smudged window. As her eyes adjusted to the gloom, her stomach dropped to her toes. The car was here. So where was Brad?

Sam looked back toward the house uncertainly, panic etching her features. Maybe she should break a window. Or would it be better to call the police first? But if Brad was hurt, it might not be wise to wait until the police arrived to get to him. Sam twisted her hands together and closed her eyes, leaning against the side of the garage. She hadn't yet developed the habit of talking to the Lord on a regular basis, but Bible class must be rubbing off on her, she thought, because in this moment of crisis she suddenly felt the need for higher guidance. Please, Lord, let him be okay, she prayed silently. He's such a fine and good man, and he's already had more than his share of pain and sorrow. Show me what to do to help him.

When she opened her eyes, her gaze drifted to the adjacent church, and suddenly, with a degree of certainty that startled her, she intuitively knew that Brad was inside.

Sam straightened up and slowly made her way toward the building, pausing at the door as a powerful feeling of dread engulfed her. She sensed darkness and desolation, could feel it as palpably as she felt the rough iron of the door handle beneath her fingers, and it frightened her. The sensation was weird and unsettling.

Sam didn't want to go in. But she couldn't just walk away. Because just as she sensed despair, and the vacuum of hopelessness, she also sensed that Brad needed her. And so, drawing a deep, shaky breath, she opened the door and stepped inside.

The vestibule was empty and silent as she closed the door softly behind her. Cautiously she moved forward to the double doors that led into the church proper. She gently eased one door open to slip inside, then let it shut silently against her back.

Sam stood unmoving, her shoulders pressed against the wooden door. When her eyes grew accustomed to the dimness, she scanned the church quickly. It seemed to be empty, she realized with a frown. But Brad was here. She was certain of it. She could *feel* his presence. She let her eyes sweep over the church once more, this time more slowly and carefully.

She almost missed him again. In fact, she would have if he hadn't reached up to run a hand wearily over his face just as her gaze swept past.

He sat in a pew near the front, off to one side, half-hidden in the shadows. With his head bowed and his shoulders slumped, his posture spoke silently but eloquently of defeat and sadness. A cold knot of fear slowly formed in Sam's stomach, then tightened painfully. Something bad had happened. Very bad. He'd obviously sought solace here, with the Lord. Maybe three was a crowd in a situation like this, she thought, suddenly uncertain. Maybe he needed to be alone and would consider her presence an intrusion. Should she quietly leave, wait outside until he emerged? she wondered.

A sudden ragged breath, sounding to Sam like a choked sob, echoed softly in the church and made her decision easy. Brad was hurting, and she wanted to help. It was as simple as that.

Instinctively she moved forward, pausing a few steps behind him to softly call his name. When he didn't respond, she tried again, this time a little louder.

"Brad?"

Her voice penetrated his consciousness the second time, and he lifted his head and slowly turned to look at her.

Sam's eyes widened in shock at his appearance. *Wretched* wasn't a word she dusted off very often, but it was the only one in her vocabulary that came anywhere close to describing Brad's face. His eyes stared back at her with a haunted look and his skin was stretched tautly, almost painfully, across his cheekbones. The deep grooves etched in his brow were matched by equally deep furrows on either side of his mouth. Sam found it hard to believe that this was the same man who had held her in his arms and laughed with her last night. He stared at her dazedly, as if he didn't even recognize her. The hand he passed across his eyes, as if to clear his vision, shook badly.

Trying to quell her panic, which was approaching epic proportions, Sam moved closer and sank down on the pew beside him. She reached out to touch his face. "Brad? What is it? What's wrong?" she asked urgently.

Slowly his eyes cleared, focused, and he stared at her in confusion. "Sam? Why are you here?"

"We had a date," she reminded him, speaking slowly.

"When you didn't show up, I got worried and came looking for you."

"A date?" he repeated blankly.

"Uh-huh. For dinner. Remember?" she prompted, struggling to keep her voice calm.

He frowned, as if trying very hard to do just that, and then he closed his eyes and sighed, raking his fingers through his hair. "Dinner," he repeated. "Sam, I completely forgot. I'm sorry. Just let me change and—"

"Brad," she interrupted gently but firmly. "Forget dinner, okay? Just tell me what happened. Is it your dad?"

"My dad?" he repeated blankly.

"Is he all right?"

He turned and stared toward the chancel, nodding his head jerkily. "Yeah."

When he didn't offer any more information, Sam reached for his hand. "Then what is it? What's wrong? Can you tell me?" she asked, a tremor of fear running through her voice.

His fingers crushed hers painfully, but she didn't flinch. It was almost as if he needed a lifeline to grasp, and her hand was serving that function.

"I don't want to burden you with my problems," he said, and her heart ached at the raw pain in his voice.

"Brad, I care about you." She spoke slowly, deliberately, her voice intense. "I care a *lot*. I want to help if I can. Please…tell me," she pleaded.

"It's too late to help," he said dully.

"But it's never too late to talk. Come on, Brad. Please. Talk to me. Tell me."

He exhaled a long, shuddering sigh, and after a moment of silence he turned to her. "Remember I told you once that I tend to get too personally involved in the lives of my congregation? Well, tonight is the downside of that.''

''What do you mean?''

He drew a shaky breath. ''There's a middle-aged couple with a 'problem' teenage son. I've been counseling them for the past few weeks,'' he said, his voice so low she had to lean close to hear him. ''Based on everything they said I eventually came to the conclusion that he was probably depressed—maybe clinically depressed—and that they needed to get him professional help. The only trouble is, I came to that conclusion too late.'' He wiped his hand across his eyes, and when he continued, his voice was uneven, laced with devastation. ''He committed suicide this morning.''

''Oh, Brad!'' With her free hand, Sam reached over and touched his cheek. His whole body was shaking, and she could feel the grief emanating from every pore.

''What kind of minister am I that I couldn't prevent a tragedy like this?'' he asked in anguish, his voice harsh with desolation, his grip on her fingers tightening.

Sam placed her free hand flat against his cheek and exerted gentle pressure, forcing him to turn his head so she could look directly into his devastated eyes. ''Brad Matthews, don't you ever doubt the fact that you are a fine man and an equally fine minister,'' she said fiercely. ''Your only problem is that you care too much. Surely this boy's parents aren't blaming you?''

''I don't know,'' he said, shaking his head. ''But *I* blame me. There *was* a way to prevent this. I just didn't know what it was. And when they called today, looking for comfort, I failed them then, too. I couldn't find a way to explain what happened, why a young life was wasted.

All I could do was go to them, tell them that I'm sorry and that we can't always understand the ways of the Lord.''

"Maybe that's what they needed to hear," Sam said gently.

He shook his head. "A minister should be able to do better than that, find more words to ease their pain."

"But you're also a man, remember? You told me that yourself. You're human, Brad. You did the best you could to help. That's all the Lord can ask. That's all this boy's parents can ask."

"Maybe. But it doesn't bring him back," he said sadly. He was still clutching her hand, but his grip had loosened imperceptibly, and the tremors that had racked his body were subsiding.

"No," Sam agreed. "But even when we don't understand why something happens we have to accept God's will."

He looked at her wearily, and the ghost of a smile touched his lips. "You're the one who sounds like a preacher."

"Hardly," she said, her mouth twisting wryly. Then she reached up and smoothed the hair back from his forehead. "How long have you been sitting here?"

He shrugged. "I don't know."

"Well, I think you need to focus on something else for a while. Have you eaten anything today?"

He frowned. "I had a bagel this morning."

"That's what I thought. Now I'm not going to offer to cook or anything, so don't panic, but why don't we raid your refrigerator? I can whip up something simple, and I'll feel better if you have a meal. I think you will, too."

"You don't have to do that, Sam."

"Maybe I want to."

"Are you sure?"

"Of course I'm sure. Come on. We'll make do."

An hour later, as they finished their simple meal of spaghetti and salad, Brad reached for her hand across the table. "I do feel a little better, Sam. Thank you. For everything."

"I didn't do much."

"You were here when I needed you," he said, rubbing his thumb across the back of her hand. Suddenly she winced, and he glanced down with a frown. Faint purple marks had appeared on her flesh, and he looked up at her in concern. "I did this, didn't I?" he said slowly. "In the church, when you took my hand."

She shrugged off his question. "Don't worry about it, Brad. You needed to hold on to a hand. Mine was convenient. I didn't mind."

He sighed. "I'm sorry, Sam. The last thing I'd ever want to do is hurt you."

"Brad, it's nothing. Really," she assured him. "Now how about some dessert? I saw ice cream in the freezer."

He shook his head. "Not for me, thanks. But go ahead if you want some."

"No. I'm full."

He took a sip of water and his lips quirked up ruefully. "You know, I'm beginning to wonder if we're ever going to have a normal date."

Sam smiled. Now was *not* the time to bring up their relationship. He'd had about all the stress he could handle for today. "I know what you mean," she said noncommittally.

"Well, given tonight's episode, I wouldn't blame you if you ate and ran. But I'd really like it if you could stay awhile. Maybe there's a good movie on TV or something."

"Just try to get rid of me," she said with a grin. She wasn't about to leave yet. Brad had suffered a terrific shock, and caring human contact was the best thing for him right now.

He gave her a grateful smile. "Thanks." He rose and reached for her hand, lacing his fingers carefully through hers. "Let's see what the tube has to offer."

They lucked out with a classic comedy, but the emotional trauma took its toll on Brad, and halfway through he fell asleep beside her, exhausted, his head dropping to the cushioned back of the couch.

For a long while Sam didn't move, content to sit close beside him, listening to his deep, even breathing and letting her mind rest. It had been an eventful two days, she mused, with nothing going according to schedule. She'd come here tonight to say goodbye to the man next to her. Instead she felt more linked to him than ever. It was almost as if, in the face of tragedy, they'd forged an even deeper bond, taking their relationship to a new, more intimate level. In many ways it was beginning to seem as if they really did need each other.

When the movie ended, Sam carefully reached for the remote and clicked off the set. She looked over at Brad, the harsh lines of anguish in his face now softened in sleep. With a sudden rush of tenderness she reached over and ever-so-gently brushed his hair back from his forehead. He sighed softly, and his head dropped to her shoulder. She really ought to go, she knew. It was getting late. But she hated to wake him just yet. He was so exhausted. She'd wait just a little while longer, she decided, tilting her head so she could feel his hair against her cheek.

As she sat there in the dim room she, too, began to grow drowsy. And as her eyes drifted shut, her last conscious thought was that this evening had certainly turned out differently than she expected. Falling asleep with Brad's head on her shoulder had definitely not been on the agenda.

A sudden pressure against his chest made Brad sigh, and he shifted slightly, coming partially awake. Subconsciously he was aware of a feeling of warmth, contentment and...for some reason the word *completeness* came to mind. He was just beginning to drift back to deep sleep when a soft, feminine sigh pulled him sharply back to reality.

Brad opened his eyes. The room was dim, illuminated only by a low-wattage lamp on a table near the door, giving the contents a fuzzy, slightly out-of-focus appearance. But one thing was very clear. Sam was wrapped in his arms, her head nestled against his chest, her glorious hair spilling over his arm.

As that realization penetrated his consciousness, Brad suddenly, abruptly, came fully awake. It had been more than six years since he'd awakened in a woman's arms, and he'd almost forgotten the intense, sweet joy of that experience.

Sam smelled good, he thought, inhaling the spicy fragrance that emanated from her skin, noting at the same time that she looked different in sleep. Younger. More vulnerable. And definitely appealing. Very appealing. His arm rested at her waist, and gently he traced her slender curves with his fingers, suddenly finding it difficult to breathe as a powerful, consuming surge of desire raced through his body.

Deliberately he stilled his hand. He had to get himself under control, he thought, his jaw tightening. Think rationally. He took a deep breath. Then another. That was better. First of all, he reasoned, it was late. Second, Sam needed to leave. Third, despite points one and two, he couldn't wake her up just yet. Not until he'd calmed down a little. Except that being snuggled up next to her soft curves wasn't helping in the least. Focus on something else, he told himself deliberately. Think about your sermon for tomorrow. Or maybe it was today already. Pretend Sam isn't even here.

Clearly, *that* was an unrealistic goal. But eventually he would feel under control enough to face her. It just might be a long wait.

Sam was having a wonderful dream. She was wrapped in Brad's strong arms, her head nestled against his shoulder, the musky scent of his aftershave drifting in the air. She didn't want to wake up. But someone was calling her name. Persistently. So slowly, reluctantly, she opened her eyes—to find Brad's only inches from her own.

"Hi, sleepyhead," he said huskily, his lips curving up into a smile.

Sam frowned. Was she still asleep? Or was this real?

The gentle pressure of Brad's hand at her waist was real enough, all right, and suddenly the events of the evening came back to her in a rush. "What time is it?" she asked, her voice thick with sleep.

"I don't know. You're leaning on my arm, and it's asleep," he replied, his voice tinged with amusement.

For the first time, Sam became conscious of her position. Sometime after she'd fallen asleep she'd apparently turned toward Brad and cuddled shamelessly against him. Her face flaming in embarrassment, she quickly extricated herself.

Pushing her hair back from her face, she leaned over to search for her shoes, which she'd kicked off earlier in the evening.

"I'm sorry," she said, her voice muffled.

"Why?"

"I should have left when you fell asleep instead of..." She paused, fishing for the right phrase.

"Cuddling?" he supplied matter-of-factly. He didn't seem at all embarrassed, Sam realized in surprise.

"Yeah," she replied, tucking her hair behind her ear in a very uncharacteristic but endearing little-girl-like gesture.

"I'm glad you stayed, Sam," he said with quiet sincerity. "And there's nothing wrong with cuddling when two people care for each other." Then he glanced at his watch and gave her a wry grin. "Unfortunately, as a minister, I have to be concerned about propriety. Even if things *were* perfectly innocent, I doubt whether my congregation would appreciate discovering that a woman spent the night here."

She flushed. "I'm sure they wouldn't. I didn't mean to fall asleep, Brad. I was only going to stay a few minutes," she said apologetically.

"It's okay," he assured her. "Having you here helped a lot. To be honest, I wish you could stay the rest of the night."

Sam tore her gaze from his with difficulty and rose, smoothing down her skirt. So did she wish that, she thought as he stood beside her. But she left the words unsaid.

"Let me drive you home," he offered.

"But my car's here," she reminded him.

"Oh, yeah." He frowned. "I could drive you home in your car and then take a taxi back," he suggested.

She glanced at her watch. It was one in the morning, and he had an early service. "I appreciate the offer, Brad. But I can get home safely by myself. I have a phone in the car. Besides, you need to be awake in the pulpit tomorrow."

"You have a point," he admitted. "Still, maybe I'm old-fashioned, but I don't like the idea of—"

"Brad…I'll be fine," she interrupted gently. "I'll call you when I get home," she promised.

He capitulated with a sigh. "You win. But be careful."

"I will." She reached for her purse, then hesitated, frowning. "Brad…are you sure you'll be all right here by yourself?" she asked, gazing up at him worriedly.

He smiled sadly. "Yes, the darkest hours have passed. I'll be okay now."

They walked to her car in silence, and when she turned at the door to look up at him his eyes tenderly traced the contours of her face. The rain had stopped, but a fine, soft mist hung in the air, giving the world an ethereal quality. As he reached over to run a gentle hand down her cheek, Sam felt almost as if she had stepped into a scene from one of her favorite old romantic movies. And she *definitely* felt that way when Brad reached over and cupped her neck with his hand, then drew her close and lowered his lips to hers.

Sam didn't protest. She was past protesting. Her body was his ally. So was her heart. It was only her mind that fought this attraction. And her mind was not functioning too well at the moment.

Brad's lips moved over hers, gently, yet sensuously, drawing an ardent, breathless response from her. He pulled her closer, until her body melted against his. Sam's breath caught in her throat as his touch worked its magic.

By the time they drew apart, both of them were breathless.

Brad stared down at her, his eyes smoldering. He wanted Sam. To pretend otherwise would be foolish. For the first time in his life he truly understood the powerful temptations of the flesh. Brad had never experienced anything like the attraction he felt for Sam. Rachel and he had shared a quiet, deep passion. *Wild* was not a word that described the physical expression of their love. But it very definitely—and accurately—described his reaction when Sam was in his arms. The simmering, consuming need he felt for her was very hard to resist. Yet giving in to his desires went against everything he believed. It just wasn't his style.

Brad drew a long, deep breath and reached over to cup her face in his hands, gently stroking his thumbs over her cheekbones. Sam could feel him trembling. And this time it wasn't from shock and grief. He wanted her, just as much as she wanted him. But giving in to desires wasn't his way. She knew that, and she was grateful for his restraint, because in her present state she wasn't sure she would have had the strength to resist him if he'd pushed for further intimacy.

"I'll call you tomorrow," he said softly, his voice unsteady.

She nodded, not trusting her voice, and after one last, lingering kiss, she slipped behind the wheel.

As she pulled away from the parsonage, she glanced in the rearview mirror. Brad was illuminated in the mist by a streetlight, and the glow it cast around him added to the unreal, dreamlike quality of the scene. But it was real enough, Sam knew. Her lips were still tingling from the pressure of his mouth on hers, and her body was quivering with desire.

As she drove home through the mist, Sam thought about the similarity between their parting of moments before and so many of the old, romantic movies she collected. Of course, the movies had happy endings. Real life didn't, necessarily.

But for the first time, Sam felt a glimmer of hope. There were problems to deal with in their relationship, of course, obstacles to overcome. For a happy ending to become a reality, both she and Brad would have to make peace with her past, as well as her potential inability to have children. Both her age and her medical history were working against her on the latter, and she knew that he loved children and deeply desired a family. Accepting all of these things would require him to be very forgiving and to love her very, very deeply.

Sam knew it was a long shot even for a man like Brad. And she might be jumping to the wrong conclusions, she reminded herself. She knew Brad liked her. What she didn't know was just how serious he was about their relationship long-term. She suspected that he was the kind of man who would think this relationship out very deliberately and allow plenty of time for things to develop before jumping to any conclusions. *Impulsive* was not a word she associated with Brad. Love might not even have entered his mind yet. She couldn't be sure of his feelings, only hers. And the simple fact was that she had fallen in love with him.

Sam didn't know exactly when it had happened. All she knew was that it had. And she also knew that the love she felt for him was deep and irrevocable. But she was in no hurry to deal with those feelings. Time was good. It would give her breathing space to seek a way to resolve the guilt that had been part of her life for seventeen years. And it would give their relationship a chance to grow and deepen, provide her the opportunity to choose the perfect moment and the right words to tell him about her past. Not to mention the time to build up her courage.

Sam knew she was taking a chance. In the end, even if Brad came to love her, he might not be able to accept what she told him. It was risky. But for the first time in many years, she was beginning to believe that maybe she *could* have her own happy ending. And for the possibility of a happy ending, she was willing to take the risk.

Chapter Ten

~~

"Surprise!"

Sam looked at Henry's stunned face, then at Brad, and smiled. They'd pulled it off, after all. Instead of the sedate seventieth birthday dinner with Brad, Rebecca and Sam that he expected, Henry was the guest of honor at a gala party in the Jersey American Legion Hall. The three-piece combo broke into "Happy Birthday," and fifty voices gave a rousing rendition of the song.

As the crowd moved forward to surround Henry, the three conspirators stepped back.

"I'd say he was surprised," Brad commented with a grin.

Rebecca laughed. "That's putting it mildly. This was a great idea, Sam. Left to our own devices, I'm afraid Brad and I would have come up with something much less imaginative. And definitely more boring."

"I doubt that," Sam demurred. "But surprises are a lot of fun. So I figured your dad might get a kick out of it."

Brad glanced at his father, flushed and laughing in the

midst of the high-spirited crowd, and smiled. "I'd say your instincts were right on target."

The band struck up a fox-trot, and Sam turned to Rebecca. "Maybe you and your dad should have the first dance," she suggested.

Rebecca shook her head doubtfully. "I don't know if we'll be able to coax him onto the dance floor. He never was much of a dancer, even when Mom was alive. She always had to drag him out there. But maybe..." She directed a speculative look at Sam. "Why don't you try? He might dance if you asked him."

Sam hesitated. "Do you really think so?"

"Rebecca's right," Brad concurred. "You're the most likely person to get him out there."

Sam shrugged and smiled. "Okay. I'll give it a shot."

Three hours later, Rebecca gazed at Brad across the table and shook her head incredulously. "Do you believe this? Dad—line dancing! And did you see him in that conga line a little while ago?"

Brad chuckled. "Yep. Leave it to Sam. I told you, she's one amazing woman."

Rebecca smiled. "Speaking of which...anything new to report? It's been almost three months since we talked on Memorial Day."

The band shifted gears, and the melodic strains of "The Very Thought of You" drifted over the room. Brad looked toward the dance floor and rose. "I think it's about time I reclaimed my date," he said, glancing back at Rebecca, a mischievous glint in his eyes.

"You're not going to get off that easily, you know," she informed him pertly. "We'll talk tomorrow."

Brad grinned. "We'll see."

"Count on it," she called after him.

As Brad approached Sam and his father, his grin softened into a tender smile. She looked fabulous tonight, in an elegant black dress that enhanced her slender curves, the skirt slit to reveal an enticing glimpse of leg. He'd been wanting to dance with her all night, longing to feel her melt into his arms as she had at Laura's wedding, while they moved in time to a romantic melody. But Henry monopolized her after the first dance, and Brad was reluctant to interrupt. After all, it *was* his father's party. But enough was enough. He deserved at least one dance with his date.

Brad tapped on his father's shoulder and smiled. "Sorry to interrupt, Dad, but I think this dance is mine."

Henry stepped back. "'Bout time you danced with the prettiest lady here," he declared, giving Sam a wink.

The smoky look Brad sent her way made Sam's nerve endings sizzle. "I agree," he said, the husky timbre of his voice playing havoc with her pulse.

She moved into his arms, and he pulled her close as they swayed in time to the melodic refrain. With a contented sigh, she closed her eyes, enjoying the gentle but firm pressure of Brad's hand in the small of her back, his cheek against her hair, his fingers entwined with hers. It felt so right to be in his arms. So good. And so natural.

Sam thought back over the past two months, since the day she'd found Brad in the church, despondent over the young boy's suicide. That time of tragedy had been a turning point in their relationship, she realized in retrospect. Until then, Sam had fought her attraction to him, refusing to believe it could ever work between them. But that night, as she consoled Brad, a tender hope had been born. It was a fragile thing, requiring careful nurturing, but little by little it grew stronger as their relationship deepened and developed.

Slowly Sam had begun to believe that maybe—maybe—there was a future for them together. According to everything she was learning in Bible class, the Lord offered forgiveness to those who repented. And if the Lord could forgive her, maybe, just maybe, Brad could, as well. She even began to harbor a precarious hope that if he loved her enough he might be able to accept the possibility that theirs could be a childless union.

Sam knew she was juggling a lot of "maybes." There were issues she needed to resolve with Brad. And she would. Soon. But not tonight. Not when he was holding her so tenderly, his hand stroking her back, his lips in her hair. There would be time to face reality later. For tonight, for this moment, she just wanted to lose herself in the magic of his arms. And so, with another contented sigh, she molded herself even more closely against the hard planes of his body and refused to think about tomorrow.

Brad felt Sam move closer and glanced down at the top of her head. Her cheek was pressed to his shoulder, her glorious red hair resting softly against the front of his jacket. It was becoming more and more difficult to imagine his world without her, he realized. She was lively and energetic and fun, bringing joy and renewed life to his existence. She was also tender and compassionate and loving, and those qualities touched his heart, filling him with a deep yearning that grew stronger each day. He no longer wanted to part from her at the end of an evening together and return to his empty house—and empty bed. He wanted to fall asleep with her every night, his last conscious sensation her soft body snuggled against his, and wake up each morning to find her burnished hair spilling over his arm, her gorgeous green eyes merely inches away as they smiled sleepily into his. He wanted her to share everything with him, from his morning coffee to his last waking thoughts. In other words, he wanted her to share his life. Anything short of that was becoming less and less acceptable.

Weeks before, Rebecca had said he was in love. Brad had denied it then, but now he was forced to admit the truth. Rebecca was right. He loved Sam. And maybe it was about time he told her.

The music came to an end, and reluctantly he loosened his hold. Sam released a small sigh and stepped back slightly to look up at him, her unguarded eyes seeming to mirror his deepest feelings.

Yes, he decided. It was time he gave voice to what was in his heart.

"Okay, big brother, you've got fifteen minutes," Rebecca said with a glance at her watch. She poured herself a glass of orange juice then joined him at the kitchen table, where Brad was enthusiastically working his way through a gargantuan waffle.

"For what?" he mumbled between bites.

"To finish the conversation we started last night."

He looked at her innocently, twirling a bite of waffle in the syrup. "Which conversation was that?"

Rebecca took a sip of juice and pointed out the window, where Henry and Sam were in deep discussion next to the rose garden, apparently oblivious to the oppressive late-August humidity. "About you and a certain redhead. Who I like very much, by the way."

Brad smiled. "I like her, too."

Rebecca chuckled. "Yeah, I know. So why are you dragging your feet? Is it serious or not?"

Brad's hand stilled and he turned to look out the window, his eyes lovingly tracing Sam's profile. "It's very definitely serious," he affirmed quietly.

Rebecca reached over and touched his arm. "I'm happy for you, Brad," she said softly, all traces of her teasing tone vanishing.

"Thanks. I just hope she feels the same way."

Rebecca turned to look thoughtfully out the window. She had no doubt that Sam loved Brad. It was obvious. Yet she sensed some sort of tension, almost worry, in the other woman that she couldn't quite get a handle on. But maybe it was just her overactive imagination, she told herself. There was probably no reason for concern.

"Why so quiet all of a sudden?" Brad asked cautiously, wondering if Rebecca harbored doubts about Sam's suitability as a minister's wife. Sam wasn't stereotypical, that was for sure. Her flamboyant nature and less-than-active religious life had given him pause as well. They were issues he still grappled with on occasion. Yet he knew beyond the shadow of a doubt that he loved Sam. The rest he had put in the Lord's hands.

Rebecca suppressed her wayward thoughts and turned back to Brad. "Just thinking about what a nice couple you two make," she said, much to his relief. "And as for hoping she feels the same way—you won't know till you ask her," she pointed out. "But I wouldn't worry too much. The lady is definitely in love," she added with a smile. Then she swallowed the last of her juice and stood up. "Sorry to run like this. But Rose and Frances held the fort for me last night at the restaurant, and I don't want to impose too much.''

Brad grinned, picturing the two maiden sisters who were combination hostesses, cooks and mother hens for Rebecca. "You were lucky to find them."

Rebecca smiled. "Don't I know it! They're a treasure! That's why I don't want to leave them in the lurch to handle the Saturday crowd alone. I'll just say goodbye to Dad and Sam on my way out," she said, pausing at the door. "And keep me informed," she added, smiling.

Brad watched as Rebecca joined Henry and Sam, giving each of them a lingering hug. She said something that made Sam laugh, and then, with a wave, she was gone. Henry and Sam went back to their gardening discussion, and Brad tackled his waffle again, spearing a bite and chewing thoughtfully. Rebecca was right. He wouldn't know how the lady felt till he asked her. And he would. Just as soon as the right opportunity presented itself.

"Well, I'd say the party was a success," Sam said as they approached St. Louis. "Your dad seemed to have a great time. And I like your sister. She's very nice."

"Yeah. I'm kind of partial to her," Brad replied with a smile. "She liked you, too, by the way."

Sam returned his smile. "I'm glad."

There was a moment of silence, and Brad suddenly sensed an undercurrent of excitement. He glanced at Sam curiously, in time to see her tuck her hair behind her ear— a gesture he'd come to recognize as a sign of nervousness or excitement. Something was very definitely up.

Sam drew a deep breath and turned to him. "I guess

this is the weekend for surprises,'' she said with studied casualness. ''I have one for you, too.''

He looked at her and quirked an eyebrow questioningly. ''You do?''

''Mmm-hmm. Just follow my directions when we get in a little closer.''

He did as she asked, pulling to a stop a short time later in front of a contemporary ranch-style house.

She turned to him eagerly, no longer trying to restrain her excitement, her eyes sparkling with enthusiasm. ''Well, this is it!'' she declared.

He looked at her quizzically. ''This is what?''

''Your house! I found your house!''

''My house?''

''The one you need, remember?'' she teased. ''I've been keeping my eyes open, but I just couldn't find the right one. This came on the market Thursday, and I took a quick look, even though it hasn't been officially listed yet. But I've got the key.'' She reached into her purse and withdrew it, dangling it in front of him enticingly. ''Do you want to take a look?''

He grinned. ''Absolutely.''

For the next hour they poked through every corner of the house and the yard, and Brad had to admit that Sam's instincts were right on target. Even he hadn't known exactly what he wanted. Until now.

''So...what do you think?'' she asked anxiously, when they'd completed their tour and stood once again under the vaulted ceiling in the living room.

He shook his head. ''I don't know how you did it. But it's perfect.''

A smile of relief brightened her face. ''Thank goodness!

I thought this was the sort of house you had in mind, but I wasn't absolutely sure. And it's close to your church, too.''

"What do *you* think of it?" he asked.

"I think it's great!" she said enthusiastically. "It's modern—but not too much so. And it's bright and airy and spacious. I know it's a little more than you want to spend, but I really think it's worth it, Brad. This is a solid neighborhood, and the prices have steadily risen here. So it'll be a good investment.''

"I'll take your word on that. And it does seem ideal.'' He took a deep breath. "Okay. Let's make an offer.''

"Great! I'll get the paperwork ready.''

He glanced at his watch, a thoughtful look on his face. "I've got to take care of a few things this afternoon. How about if I stop by your place around seven? Would that work?''

"Sure. I'll be ready for you. I'll even chill a bottle of wine so we can celebrate.''

"That would be perfect,'' he said with a smile. And if things went well, he thought, they'd be celebrating a whole lot more than buying a house.

Brad nervously fingered the small velvet box in the pocket of his jacket as he waited for Sam to answer the door. He hadn't planned to move quite this quickly, but the opportunity he'd been waiting for had unexpectedly presented itself, and it was too good to pass up. What better time to ask Sam to marry him than when he was buying a house they would hopefully share? He'd spent the afternoon at the jewelry store, emerging lighthearted and excited with his purchase, but now that he was actually faced with posing the question, his confidence faltered. Maybe he'd misread Sam's feelings. Despite Rebecca's assessment, maybe Sam just liked him. Maybe that's as far as it went with her. What if she said no? he thought in sudden panic.

The door opened, and Sam's tender smile and warm, welcoming eyes allayed some of his doubts.

"Hi," she said, her gaze sweeping over his cream linen blazer, open-necked blue shirt and crisply pleated tan slacks. "You look nice," she added approvingly, her eyes returning to his.

"Thanks. So do you," he replied, returning the compliment with a warm smile. Then he reached for her, and she went willingly into his arms, her ardent, breathless response rapidly dispelling the rest of his doubts. His wavering confidence steadied.

When Brad released her after a lingering kiss, Sam smiled and stepped back, emitting a small sigh of pleasure. "Mmm. Nice. But you'd better keep your distance until we fill out the paperwork on the house. If you distract me too much I might add a zero to your offer or something," she warned with a laugh as he entered. She closed the door behind him, leading the way toward the kitchen. "I've got all the paperwork ready. It's on the table," she said, heading in that direction.

"Sam."

An odd note in his voice stopped her, and she turned to give him a questioning look. "What's wrong? Are you having second thoughts?"

He shook his head. "Far from it." He raked his fingers through his hair and gestured toward the couch. "Could we sit down for a minute?"

"Sure." She moved toward the living room, watching him with a worried frown as he sat down beside her and reached for her hand, cradling it between his. "What is it, Brad? Is the price too high? I know it's a little more than you wanted to—"

"The price is okay, Sam," he interrupted her.

She fell silent. Something was wrong, though she didn't have a clue what. She'd just have to wait for him to tell her in his own way.

Brad smiled at her tentatively, his thumb gently stroking the back of her hand. "You'll have to forgive me if I seem a little nervous. But I've only done this one other time."

Something in his tone triggered a faint alarm bell in the back of her mind, and a knot began to form in her stomach.

"I know we've only been dating for five months, Sam. But as my father and sister told me, that's long enough when you meet the right person. And I have."

He gazed at her, and she stared at him, mesmerized by the soft glow of love reflected in his eyes. "Before you came into my life, there was a cold, empty place in my heart that desperately needed light and warmth. I found those things in you. And somewhere along the way, I also found something else. I found love."

He reached into his coat pocket and withdrew the small velvet box, flipping it open to reveal a sparkling solitaire.

"The simple fact is, I love you, Sam. I want to spend the rest of my life waking up next to you, laughing with you, sharing with you. I want us to grow old together surrounded by our children, with wonderful memories of a life filled with love and joy and discovery." He paused and took a steadying breath. "Will you marry me?"

Sam continued to stare at Brad, her eyes now wide with

shock. This wasn't supposed to be happening. Not yet. Brad wasn't the impulsive type. He was the kind of man who should believe in a long courtship. She thought she had plenty of time to bring up the secrets from her past. But obviously she had thought wrong.

With all her heart Sam wanted to throw herself into his arms and say yes, to forget her past and think only of the wonderful future Brad offered. But that wouldn't be fair to him. He deserved to know exactly what he was getting. There were issues that had to be faced. And they had to be faced now, whether she was ready to address them or not. Carefully Sam withdrew her hand from between his and rose, nervously lacing her fingers together as she began to pace, trying to formulate the words that needed to be said.

Brad sat perfectly still, tuned in to every nuance of her response. While he had limited experience with proposals, this was *not* the reaction he had hoped for. He had expected surprise, yes. But not shock. And Sam was clearly shocked. She looked agitated and distracted, and the fact that she was putting physical distance between them was not a good sign. He felt his stomach clench, and his throat grew tight with tension. Had he misread her interest after all? He waited with trepidation for her to speak, but as the seconds slowly ticked by she remained silent, pacing nervously, her eyes almost desperate. Something was very, very wrong.

Finally Brad couldn't stand the silence any longer. "Sam?" he prompted, striving to keep his voice even, trying not to reveal his tension.

She ignored him, so he tried again. "Sam?" His voice was gentle, but a bit more insistent, and this time she paused, slowly turning to face him. Brad frowned at the fear and despair reflected in her eyes. "What is it?" he asked, suddenly afraid himself.

Sam drew a shaky breath, realizing she'd run out of time. She was backed into a corner and there was no escape. "It's just so...unexpected, Brad," she said, the explanation for her reaction sounding lame even to her ears.

"I realize that," he conceded, struggling not to betray his panic. "But I'm also getting the impression that it's unwelcome," he said cautiously.

"Oh, no! No! It's not that," she cried.

Brad couldn't doubt the sincerity in her voice or her eyes, and he breathed a little easier. His instincts had been right—she cared about him deeply. But something—apparently of a very serious nature—was holding her back. "Then what's wrong?"

"Oh, Brad!" She didn't even know where to start. Maybe it was best to begin with the lesser concerns. "Think about it. We're so different. How could this ever work?"

"We're not as different as you seem to think we are." She was stalling, avoiding the real problem, and he knew it. But eventually she'd have to tell him, and all he could do was wait until she was ready.

"But...well...there are issues."

"Like what?"

"Like...I don't want to quit working," she said, groping for excuses.

"I don't expect you to," he assured her. "Lots of ministers' wives work. Besides, we could use the extra money. Especially if we buy that house you found," he said teasingly, trying to lighten the mood of doom that now hovered menacingly over the room.

"I'm not the domestic type, either. And I can't cook."

"Trust me, I know," he replied, his mouth twisting into a wry grin. "But I'm used to microwave food."

She frantically racked her brain for other excuses. "I probably make more money than you do," she pointed out.

He shrugged. "Does that bother you?"

She stared at him, taken aback. "Well, no. But— Oh, Brad, I'm not religious enough to be a minister's wife!"

"We'll work on it," he said easily. "I think that more of your Christian upbringing survived than you realize. It's just a matter of giving it a chance to develop."

Sam was out of excuses. This was the moment of truth. She reached for a throw pillow, crushed it between her fingers and hugged it in front of her like a shield before turning to face him.

Brad frowned, his perceptive eyes missing none of her distress. She looked pale, almost ill, and once more his gut clenched as he braced himself for whatever was to come.

Sam drew a deep, steadying breath, and when she spoke, her tone was no longer frenetic or agitated, but resigned. "Brad, there are things you don't know about me," she said slowly, her voice subdued.

"I know everything I need to know," he assured her, but for the first time she detected a slight hesitation in his voice.

Sam swallowed convulsively and shook her head jerkily. "No. You don't." She walked over to the window and stared out silently for a moment, still gripping the pillow protectively. "But it's time you did," she affirmed quietly, taking another deep breath before she forced herself to turn and face him. "You know that volunteer work I do on Tuesday nights?"

He nodded. "Yes."

"It's at a counseling center. We work with young un-married pregnant girls, giving them the support they need to carry their baby to full term instead of destroying it."

"That's good work, Sam. It's admirable," he said care-fully, unsure where this was leading.

"No," she replied, her voice choked. She turned away, unable in the end to look at him. "I don't do it for altruistic reasons. I do it because…because of guilt."

There was a moment of silence as Brad absorbed her words, and though her face was averted, Sam could feel a slight withdrawal, a distancing, even though neither had moved.

When he spoke again, his tone was measured, his voice cautious. "Do you want to explain that?"

No, she cried silently. What she wanted to do was forget it! To erase it from her memory forever and be free to live her life without the shadow of guilt that darkened her days. But that was a futile wish. And it was time he knew the truth.

And so she told him. Of her pregnancy. Of Randy's threats. Of her indecision and desperation. Of the pills and the drive and the accident. She told him how her irrespon-sibility had caused two deaths and left her potentially un-able to conceive. She spared him none of the details, plac-ing the blame squarely where it belonged—on herself. Because this man, who had just offered her his heart, had a right to know the burden she carried—and would always carry—in hers.

Not until she finished, tears running down her face and

her voice choking on the last few, choppy sentences, did she turn with dread to face him.

Their eyes met, hers filled with anguish, his with shock. They stared at each other silently across the room, now shrouded in gloom by the fading twilight. Brad's lips were compressed into a thin, grim line, and there were deep furrows etched in his brow. His eyes were no longer warm, but distant, horrified and dazed. It was exactly the reaction Sam had feared, and she reached up to wipe the back of her hand across her eyes, trying to stifle a sob.

"I'm sorry, Brad," she whispered brokenly. "I should have told you all this a long time ago, before…" Her voice trailed off. She had started to say, "before we fell in love," but the words lodged in her throat. "I'm so sorry," she repeated helplessly.

Brad didn't say anything. He just bowed his head and passed one hand wearily over his face.

Sam watched him, her heart breaking. She knew his reaction was what she deserved but she wished with all her being that it had been different. In the last few weeks she'd allowed herself to hope that maybe she could find her own happy ending, as Laura had. But now she was forced to acknowledge that her hope had never been more than a fragile illusion. One that was crumbling now before her eyes as she stood by helplessly, unable to do anything but watch.

Sam felt ready to crumble herself, and she suddenly knew that the one thing she couldn't handle was Brad telling her it was over. The words he would say would be forever burned in her memory, replaying over and over again in the lonely years ahead. She couldn't deal with that. It was better if she ended it herself.

Sam moved shakily toward the coffee table and picked up the velvet box in her trembling fingers, allowing herself one last look at the ring, the sparkling symbol of the dream that might have been. Then she closed the lid. The finality of the snap echoed hollowly in the heavy stillness that suddenly lay between them. She put the ring carefully into his hand and walked unsteadily to the door.

"I think it will be easier for...for both of us if we just...say goodbye, Brad." Her words were choppy, her breath coming in short gasps. "I hope someday you can find it in your heart to...to forgive me for not telling you all this sooner. I guess I hoped that...well, it doesn't matter now. Please...just leave."

Brad stared down at the ring box, almost as if he didn't understand how it had come to be in his hand, then walked toward her. "Sam, I..."

"*Please,* Brad," she repeated in a choked voice. "Just go. Please."

He stood only inches away from her, but the chasm between them felt so deep and wide it might as well have been an ocean. Sam opened the door and stepped back. He paused on the threshold to look at her, his eyes still glazed with shock, the porch light mercilessly highlighting the haggard planes of his face. He almost seemed like a stranger, she thought. The warmth and love and passion she'd grown so used to finding in his eyes had vanished. In their place she saw only...emptiness.

"Goodbye, Brad." Without waiting for him to respond, she gently eased the door shut and slipped the lock into place.

Sam sagged against the frame and closed her eyes as the tears ran unchecked down her face. It was over. She was alone. Again. Just as she'd been for the past seventeen years.

Except—maybe the Lord was still with her, she thought suddenly. And in her despair she turned to Him with a desperate plea. Forgive me for what I did to that wonderful man, she prayed fervently. I let him fall in love with me, knowing what would likely happen when he found out about my past. That was wrong. And, Lord, please…please forgive me, also, for what I did that night seventeen years ago. I've never asked for Your forgiveness before, because I never felt I deserved it. And I probably still don't. But I've carried the burden of guilt and sorrow for so many years. I don't think I can carry it any longer. Even if Brad can't find it in his heart to forgive me, I hope that You can. Because I need to feel Your love and forgiveness, and to know that I'm not alone. Please help me.

Laura frowned and replayed the answering machine one more time.

"Laura, it's Sam. I just wanted to let you know that I'm going out of town for a few days, in case you try to reach me. And would you do me a favor? Tell Brad that Leslie Nelson at my office will handle the contract for him. Thanks, kiddo. I'll call you when I get back."

Laura's frown deepened. Despite the straightforward content of her message, Sam didn't sound at all like herself. Her voice was…funny. Rough, ragged, like she'd been crying. And the message had been left at eleven-thirty. If she and Nick hadn't stopped for a late bite after the theater she would have been there to talk to Sam directly. Now all she could do was wonder—and worry.

"What do you make of it?" Laura asked Nick, who entered in time to hear the last play-through.

Nick shook his head, frowning. "I don't have a clue. But that sure doesn't sound like Sam."

"Do you think I should call Brad?"

Nick glanced at his watch. "It's twelve-thirty. I'm sure he's in bed by now."

She sighed resignedly. "You're probably right. I guess I'll just have to wait and talk to him after church tomorrow. I just hope he knows what's going on."

One look at Brad's face the next morning was enough to convince Laura that he knew exactly what was going on. There were dark circles under his eyes, as if he hadn't slept all night, and he had an uncharacteristic pallor. Obviously, Sam's problem was also Brad's.

Laura waited in the church after the service while Nick went down to the coffee room. The moment Brad emerged she rose. He saw her immediately and strode toward her quickly.

"Laura! I was hoping you'd wait. Do you know where Sam is?" he asked without preamble.

She shook her head helplessly. "I thought maybe you did. I had a message on the answering machine when we got home last night that she was going out of town for a few days. And she said to tell you to work with Leslie Nelson in her office on the contract, if that makes any sense."

He nodded impatiently. "Yeah, it does. The contract part, anyway. I'm getting ready to put a bid on a house. Listen, Laura, do you have any idea where she went?"

"No. None." She reached up and touched his arm, her

voice etched with concern. "Brad, what happened? She sounded awful. And pardon me for saying so, but you don't look so great yourself. I have a feeling there's a connection there."

He raked his fingers through his hair and sighed. "You're right. There is. Sam and I...well, she told me some things last night...I guess I was just in shock or something.... I've been calling her, but I keep getting her machine. I don't know what to do...." He sighed again, his frustration almost tangible. "Frankly, Laura, I acted like an idiot," he admitted bluntly. "She needed me, and I wasn't there for her."

Laura couldn't follow Brad's disjointed rambling, but obviously something serious had happened between him and Sam the day before, which Brad now regretted. And if Brad was in this almost incoherent condition, Laura suspected that Sam's mental state was as bad, if not worse. Laura desperately wanted to help, but she had no idea where to even begin looking for her friend.

"I'm sorry, Brad," Laura said helplessly. "I don't know what happened between you two, but Sam sounded devastated." She frowned worriedly. "I hate to think of her being alone, feeling like that."

"So do I," he said, his voice raw with pain. He reached around and wearily massaged his neck, his eyes desolate. "Look, Laura, if you hear from her, would you ask her to call me? Or find out where she is, at least?"

"I'll do what I can, although I have a feeling she won't call until she gets back. But if she's going to miss Bible class I'm sure she'll let me know," she added hopefully.

Brad stared at her uncomprehendingly. "Bible class?"

Laura bit her lip and frowned at her indiscretion. "I

wasn't supposed to mention anything about that," she said slowly.

"Sam goes with you to Bible class?" Brad repeated incredulously.

Laura nodded reluctantly. "She has been for months. But she didn't want me to say anything."

Brad closed his eyes, and a muscle twitched in his jaw. All these months, while he'd been wrestling with the notion of getting involved with someone who didn't actively practice her faith, she'd been going to Bible class. Probably learning all about mercy and forgiveness and withholding judgment—the very principles he'd neglected to demonstrate last night, he thought bleakly.

He was a minister, a man who had dedicated his life to spreading the Lord's principles, who preached every Sunday about the importance of living the words in the good book—not just reading them. Oh, he talked a good show. But when push came to shove, when he'd been dramatically called on to put those principles into action, he'd fallen short.

Brad shook his head helplessly. "I can't believe how I failed her," he said, his voice shadowed with despair and self-recrimination. "She needed support and understanding, and I just shut down. I don't know how I can ever make it up to her."

Laura reached over and once more touched his arm. "Brad, do you remember the sermon you gave last Christmas Eve?" she asked gently. "About mending relationships and saying 'I'm sorry'? It gave me new hope when I needed it the most. And those two words really do make a difference. Maybe you just need to follow your own advice." She paused to pick up her purse, then turned to him again. "Call me if I can do anything to help, okay?"

"I will. Thanks, Laura."

Brad watched her leave and then sank down on the pew, his head bowed. It had taken him hours last night to sufficiently emerge from his shock to think coherently. He had spent the long, sleepless hours that followed pacing, trying to sort out his feelings. On the one hand, he was appalled by Sam's story. The deaths of two young children, one yet unborn, was tragic. And the tragedy *was* her fault. That was the undeniable fact. There weren't many things that tested Brad's tolerance, but irresponsible behavior that hurt others was one of them.

And yet—who was he to judge her? That was the Lord's prerogative, not his. All he knew was that Sam would no more purposefully hurt anyone than he would. Seventeen years ago she'd been a frightened teenager, driven by deep despair and desperation, coping as best she knew how. Yes, she'd made mistakes. But the tragic event that had taken two lives had been an accident. Yet, she'd shouldered the blame without excuses, and she'd paid for those mistakes every day of her life since. Did the Lord expect her to do so for the rest of her life? Hadn't she done her penance? Didn't the Lord offer forgiveness and a second chance for those who repented? That's what Brad preached. It was what he believed. But he hadn't expected his belief to be tested quite so dramatically—and so unexpectedly.

He had still been trying to come to grips with the first revelation when she dropped her second bombshell—that should they marry, theirs might be a childless union. Brad had been stunned. He loved children. And while his dreams of a family had died with Rachel, they had been born again in the past few weeks as he fell in love with Sam. Giving that dream up the first time had been tough. He had never expected to be asked to do so a second time. It was a tremendous blow, and he knew his resolve to marry Sam had faltered momentarily.

An image of her desolate, tear-streaked face last night as she said goodbye at the door flashed suddenly across his mind. She loved him, and had hoped he loved her enough to accept the tragic secrets from her past, so that together they could create a future that gave full expression to their love. His shocked reaction had clearly convinced her that those hopes were in vain.

But as he'd discovered during his long night of soul searching, they weren't. Because, despite the impression he'd given her last night, he did love her enough to accept her past. And even enough to accept a childless union, if that was to be their fate.

Brad sighed and wearily rubbed his forehead. The ways of the Lord were often difficult to understand. For some reason He was erecting obstacles in the path of this relationship, testing their commitment to the limit. Brad didn't know why. All he knew was that he loved Sam—with or without children, and regardless of the tragic event in her past. Because in her he'd found a love he'd never hoped to find again. She was so much a part of his life now, that he couldn't even imagine a future without her.

The challenge was to convince Sam of these things. Considering the haunted, empty look in her eyes when she said goodbye, it wasn't going to be easy. It had been a look of—*resignation* was the best word he could think of to describe it. As if she felt rejection was what she deserved, that she was somehow unworthy of love or happiness.

With sudden insight, Brad realized that that was *exactly* what she felt. He thought back to some of their earliest conversations. Once, he recalled, she'd admitted that she was lonely. But when he'd asked her why she'd never remarried, her reply had been trite. "Too picky," she'd said. Even then he hadn't quite bought that explanation. Her flippant tone had somehow seemed underlaid with sadness. And then there was the time he'd remarked that she was a good person. Her face had grown sad at his comment, and she'd told him to save his praise for someone who deserved it.

In the intervening months those conversations had receded in his memory. But now, as he reconstructed them, the pieces suddenly fell into place. With uncanny certainty, he realized that they formed the basis for a self-imposed punishment. She had sentenced herself to a solitary existence as a penance for her mistake. And his shocked, judgmental reaction last night had only confirmed the validity of that sentence.

Brad closed his eyes and made a heartfelt plea to the Lord. Please help Sam to feel Your forgiveness, to know that she's punished herself enough and that it's all right to allow love into her life, he prayed. And help me find a way to let her know that I don't hold her past against her, and that her love alone, even without a family, will be more than enough for me. Because I need her, Lord. I need her today. And tomorrow. And for always.

Chapter Eleven

"Laura? It's Brad."

"Did you hear from Sam?" Laura asked tersely.

"No. But I checked, and she's been calling into the office, so I know she's okay. Physically, at least. And she has to come back soon. Listen, I need your help with something. I need you to get Sam to Bible class Thursday night."

Laura frowned. "That could be a tall order, Brad," she said slowly. "I'm not sure she'll even be back in town. And if she is, I can't guarantee she'll go. She sounded really down in that message she left."

"I'm sure she'll be back," Brad said, with more confidence than he felt. "You know Sam. She won't neglect her work for long. But you're right about the class," he admitted with a sigh. "She didn't exactly see Christian principles in action the other night. I've left all kinds of messages on her machines at work and home, trying to apologize. She just isn't responding. But I have an idea that might work, if you can get her to the class."

"I'll do my best," Laura promised.

"Thanks. And sit in the front, okay? That way she won't be able to leave without causing a stir."

Laura nodded. "Okay. And Brad...good luck."

He sighed. "Thanks. I have a feeling I'm going to need it. Plus a little help from Someone upstairs."

"Hi, kiddo. Did you think I dropped off the face of the earth?"

"Sam! Thank heaven!" Laura said in fervent relief. It was Thursday afternoon, and no one had expected Sam to disappear for this length of time. Especially Brad, who grew more frantic each day. "We've been worried sick! Where are you?"

"I'm back. Home, sweet home. Just walked in the door, in fact. Listen, I'm really sorry about that weird message last Saturday night. I probably sounded like a fruitcake. But I was upset about something, and I just needed to get away—quickly. I didn't even stop to think about how it would sound to you. I hope you'll forgive me."

"Of course," Laura assured her. Obviously Sam wasn't going to mention Brad, so Laura didn't either. "Where were you?"

"Chicago." She'd taken the train up, not trusting herself to drive, and spent days just walking, thinking, grieving. In the end, she made some semblance of peace with her situation, though now her heart felt cold and empty. "I just got in, but I wanted to talk to you about Bible class tonight. I know it's my turn to drive, but I'm thinking about skipping. Would you mind?"

Laura took a deep breath. She'd worked this all out ahead of time, asking the Lord for forgiveness even as she fabricated her story. But it was for a good cause, she consoled herself. "Well, no. I can figure something else out, I guess," she said, with just the right amount of hesitation. "It's just that I agreed to lead one of the discussion groups tonight, and my car's in the shop. Nick has a dinner meeting, or I could use his. But I can check around for a ride. I was going to, anyway, if you hadn't called."

There was silence for a moment, and Laura knew Sam was waging an internal debate—her friend's needs versus her own. Laura crossed her fingers and held her breath, hoping Sam's sense of responsibility was strong enough to overcome her reluctance to attend class. It was.

"Well, I don't want to leave you in the lurch," Sam said slowly at last. "Okay, I'll be by. The usual time?"

"Yes. Thanks, Sam. Listen, I don't want to pry, but…is everything all right?" Laura already knew the answer to that question. Even though Sam sounded more normal, Laura detected an undertone of strain in her voice, as if her light tone was forced. But Laura wanted Sam to know that she was willing to lend a sympathetic ear, though she suspected that Sam wasn't ready to talk yet. And her friend's next words confirmed that suspicion.

"I'll live, kiddo," she replied, but her voice sounded empty and sad. "Maybe one of these days I'll tell you all about it."

"Well, I'm here if you need someone to talk to."

"Thanks. I appreciate that, Laura. I'll see you tonight."

Sam hung up quickly and reached for a tissue. Two more seconds and she'd have lost it. It had taken all her self-discipline to make it through the practical part of their conversation without breaking down. She couldn't handle a personal discussion.

She filled the kettle and set it on the stove, gazing out the window unseeingly as she waited for the water to boil, her thoughts returning to last Saturday. It was a scene she'd replayed over and over in her mind these past few days, and with each review her sympathy for Brad had grown. Of course he'd been shocked by her startling revelations, coming totally out of the blue like that. He was only human, after all, even if he was a minister. And she had thrown a lot at him all at once.

But she knew he hadn't meant to hurt her. It simply wasn't in his nature. That's probably why he'd left so many messages during the week, checking to make sure she was all right. Not that she'd listened to any of them. As soon as she heard his voice, she hit the Erase button. It was easier that way. Because even if he was sorry for hurting her, his initial reaction had been the honest one— shock, recrimination and withdrawal. He blamed her, just as she blamed herself, for the deaths of those children. And the final blow had been her revelation that she might never be able to give him the family he wanted so badly. He was probably hurt, and maybe even angry, that she'd withheld that information from him. And he had a right to be.

The kettle whistled, and Sam poured the steaming water into a mug, absently dunking an herbal tea bag. The motion reminded her of the day she'd received Laura's postcard from Hawaii, five months before. That was also the fateful day Brad had called about needing a house. It seemed like years ago, she thought wearily. So much had happened in the intervening months. And yet so little had changed. She'd been alone then. She was alone now. Her brief fling with romance, and the soaring hope that now lay shattered, simply affirmed what she'd always believed. There would be no happy ending for her.

"Laura! Laura!" Sam hissed urgently, reaching ahead to physically restrain her friend, who was blithely heading toward the front of the meeting room.

Laura turned in surprise. "What's wrong?"

"Let's sit in the back," Sam said in a low voice.

"But Marion's up front. She's led a study group before, and she promised to save us seats so she could fill me in on the protocol before the lecture starts."

Sam sighed tiredly. It was too much of an effort to argue. "Okay. Fine."

Sam said hello to Marion, then sank into her seat. She hadn't prepared for tonight's class, since she hadn't intended to be here. Maybe she'd duck out after the lecture, go have a cup of coffee or something, and come back for Laura later.

The moderator stepped up to the podium, and the room grew silent. "Good evening, everyone. Welcome. It's my pleasure tonight to introduce our guest lecturer. Reverend Williams can't be with us, but we are fortunate to have as a replacement Reverend Brad Matthews. He's a wonderful speaker, as you'll soon discover, and I'm sure his talk will provide us with plenty of ideas for our discussion groups. Reverend Matthews' topic tonight is forgiveness."

Sam felt the color drain from her face as Brad entered the room from a side door and moved to the podium. For a moment she actually felt dizzy, and she forced herself to take several deep breaths.

"Sam? Are you all right?" Laura leaned over and eyed her friend worriedly.

"Did…did you know about this?" Sam asked, still fighting a wave of blackness. She turned to her friend, and one look at Laura's guilty, flushed face gave her the answer. Sam's gaze swung to Brad, who was now opening a folder from behind the podium. This was a conspiracy, she realized. Laura had lured her here falsely, made her sit in the front of the room so she couldn't leave without causing a stir and calling attention to herself. And Brad had put Laura up to it. Sam stared at her friend, the shock in her eyes giving way to uncertainty and then hurt. How much did she know?

Laura could easily track Sam's changing emotions in her unguarded eyes, could imagine her train of thought, and she reached over to touch her friend's arm. "Brad just asked me to get you here," she said quietly. "I don't know what happened between you two, but I do know that he's been a basket case all week. And you didn't sound much better on that message you left. I'm sorry if I did the wrong thing, but I hoped maybe this might help."

Sam was saved from having to respond by Brad's opening comments. She glanced longingly at the distant door, but there was no escape. She was stuck, plain and simple. She felt Laura squirm uncomfortably beside her, and a twinge of guilt tugged at her conscience. Laura had only done what Brad asked, and her heart had been in the right place. Sam couldn't hold that against her. Laura had no way of knowing that there was no simple fix for the problems she and Brad faced. Sam touched her arm, and when Laura looked over, Sam forced her lips up into the semblance of a smile. "Don't worry, kiddo," she whispered. "I know you meant well."

Laura squeezed her arm. "Thanks," she said gratefully, relief flooding her eyes.

Sam glanced back at Brad. Tonight he was in clerical garb, the first time she'd seen him dressed in his "work" clothes since the wedding. He made a nice appearance, she thought, studying him surreptitiously. He had a certain presence that radiated strength and solidness, inspiring confidence and trust. But his face seemed different than it had a few days before, she reflected. Older, somehow, and weary. There were lines at the corners of his eyes, and the shadows underneath spoke of sleepless nights and worry. Even the glint of silver that brushed his hair on each side seemed more prominent than before. Last Saturday's scene had obviously taken a heavy toll on him, she thought guiltily. And she could have prevented it if she'd had the courage to reveal the truth earlier in their relationship, before love complicated their lives. She could only hope that he quickly realized the truth—that he was better off without her. Maybe he already had.

But then why arrange this elaborate ruse to get her here tonight? she wondered with a puzzled frown. It wasn't as if he was giving her any special attention. In fact, except for a brief glance in her direction when he entered, as if to assure himself that she was there, he hadn't made eye contact with her once. Which was fine, of course. She preferred it this way. It would be much more difficult to keep her emotions in check if he looked at her with those probing, insightful eyes of his.

But still the question remained: Why did he want her here tonight? Sam didn't have a clue.

Brad launched into his well-prepared talk, and Sam was struck by the mellow, soothing quality of his voice, which she'd first noticed at Laura's wedding. Now, as then, she found it restful and comforting. Of course, his topic was another story. As she'd discovered, the notion of forgiveness was good in theory. But practical applications were another matter. Some things, obviously, just couldn't be forgiven.

As Brad neared the end of his talk, Sam began to plan her escape. She figured he must be hoping to waylay her after the lecture, and she didn't intend to give him the chance. As soon as he finished, she would head for the exit door to her right. She started to lean over to tell Laura that she'd be back later to pick her up, but Brad suddenly closed his notes and looked directly at her. His intense eyes locked onto hers with a riveting gaze, and the words died in her throat.

"Tonight we've talked about the Biblical context of forgiveness and the theory behind it," he said. "And as we've seen, this topic receives a great deal of attention from Scripture writers. But before I close, I'd like to focus for a few moments on the practical applications of forgiveness."

Sam swallowed with difficulty, and she suddenly found it hard to breathe. She stared at him, frozen in position, as she listened to words that seemed directed at her alone.

"Forgiveness is a concept that all of us embrace as Christians. I preach about it frequently, in fact. It is an admirable quality that we all strive to practice. But because we're human, we often fail.

"We know what the Scripture says. Matthew tells us not to judge, so that we may not be judged. And he tells us that we must forgive not seven times, but seventy times seven. In his letter to the Ephesians, Paul reminds us that we should be kind to one another, and merciful, forgiving each other as the Lord generously forgives us. And when he wrote to the Colossians, he repeated that message. In Ezechiel we read about the new life that comes to those who repent and do what is right and just. And he offers us hope, promising that none of our wrongs will be remembered if we practice virtue.

"My friends, those are powerful words. They capture one of the most beautiful elements of our faith—the recognition that people are human and do make mistakes, but that the Lord offers forgiveness and a 'second chance' to those who repent.

"As we strive to practice our faith, let us also remember that judgment belongs to the Lord. That while we can judge whether a *behavior* is right or wrong, only the Lord can judge a person. Because only He knows what is in our hearts. If we have judged someone, and hurt them by doing so, let us resolve to mend that hurt. Let us find the courage to say 'I'm sorry' and ask for their forgiveness. If the Lord is willing to give us a second chance, can we do any less for each other?

"And while we're forgiving each other, let us not forget to forgive ourselves. Sometimes that's the hardest kind of forgiveness of all to practice. Maybe we carry a burden of guilt over something from our past, which continues to color our lives today. Let us go to the Lord with that guilt, and let us place it in His hands, along with our request for forgiveness. I promise you, He won't turn away.

"I know that forgiveness isn't easy to practice, especially when someone you love fails you, or hurts you, or doesn't truly hear your plea for understanding. But don't turn away. Don't cut that person off. Give him another chance. Forgive him for not being there when you needed him most. For failing to demonstrate his love. Give him the chance to say 'I'm sorry.' Remember that broken relationships *can* be mended. All it takes is forgiveness born of love. And love is the key. Because, as the Bible tells us, love never fails.''

Sam sat numbly as the audience responded to Brad's words with enthusiastic applause. He continued to hold her eyes, as if trying to read her reaction. She knew his beautiful words of healing, spoken from the heart, had been meant for her. Was it possible that he had accepted her past, after all, that he still loved her? she wondered incredulously. Somehow it seemed too much to hope for. She gazed at him uncertainly, questioningly…and at the warmth and reassurance in his eyes a tiny flame of hope stirred among the cold embers of her heart.

The moderator stepped forward to thank Brad, and he reluctantly turned away to shake the woman's hand. Sam blinked rapidly and groped for a tissue in her purse, trying to calm her frantically beating pulse.

Laura leaned over and whispered in her ear. ''Sam, don't worry about giving me a ride home. Nick's picking me up later. We arranged it ahead of time.''

Sam nodded mutely, too overwhelmed with emotion to speak.

Laura gave her arm an encouraging squeeze and joined the crowd moving toward the door. Sam remained seated, her eyes on Brad, who was still talking to the moderator. Eons passed before the woman finally shook his hand and exited.

For a long moment Brad gazed at her in silence from the small stage. Then he slowly moved toward her, lowering himself to an adjacent folding chair when he reached her. Sam's eyes lovingly tracing the strong line of his jaw and his firm but tender lips, connecting at last with his eyes to bask in their tender warmth. He angled himself toward her, draping an arm across the back of her chair, and Sam had a sudden urge to reach over and smooth away the deep lines of fatigue in his face. She stifled the impulse with difficulty, clasping her hands tightly together in her lap instead, waiting apprehensively for him to speak.

"Thank you for coming tonight, Sam," Brad said quietly.

"Laura didn't give me much choice," she replied softly, glancing down. The rapid rise and fall of her chest clearly indicated her unsteady emotions, but she was powerless to control her physical reaction to this unexpected turn of events.

"Don't hold it against her. It was my idea."

"I figured as much."

"When you wouldn't return my calls, I couldn't think of any other way to tell you how I felt."

She ventured a glance at him. "It sounded like *you* were apologizing to *me*," she said hesitantly.

"I was."

"But...but I'm the one who should apologize. I should have told you a long time ago about my past."

"Why didn't you, Sam?" he asked gently. There was no recrimination in his voice, only curiosity.

She looked down again. "I guess because I...I was afraid you'd reject me. I never felt worthy of your love, and I figured once you found out about my past you'd feel the same way." She looked up at him, her eyes pleading for understanding. "I meant to tell you, Brad. Honestly I did. But the more involved we became, the less I wanted to lose you. And so I just kept waiting...and waiting...until finally it...it was too late," she said, her voice breaking.

He reached over and stroked her cheek, and Sam quivered beneath his tender touch. "It's not too late, Sam," he said gently. "At least, I hope not."

She looked up at him, the flame of hope in her heart beginning to blaze more brightly. "What do you mean?" she asked cautiously.

"I mean I love you," he replied with simple, straightforward honesty. "I did last Saturday, before all this happened. And I do now."

"But how can you? After what I did?" she asked uncomprehendingly. "And it...it didn't seem like you did last Saturday. You were so...distant...that night."

He sighed. "My only excuse is that I was in shock. I was having a hard time coping with everything you told me. It was like information overload or something. And I was judgmental, which was wrong," he admitted. "Only you and the Lord know what was in your heart seventeen years ago. You were a desperate teenager, pregnant with a child your husband didn't want and with no one to turn to for help. I didn't know you then, Sam. I can only grieve for your pain and the burden of guilt you've carried all these years. But I know you now. And I know that you're one of the most sensitive, considerate, caring people I've ever had the privilege to meet. And I think you were that kind of person back then, too. I think that's why you were so devastated by what happened."

He reached for her hand, cradling it between his. "That's why you never married again, isn't it?" he said gently. "Because you felt that by denying yourself the happiness and joy of love, you could in some way make amends for what you did."

"Yes," she confirmed, her quavering voice barely audible as she lowered her head in shame.

"Well, let me tell you what I think, Sam," he said, his own voice steady and sure. "You spent seventeen years alone and lonely, atoning for what you did. I suspect the Lord would ask no more than that. And neither would I."

Tentatively Sam raised her head and stared at him. His gaze was direct and unwavering, and she couldn't doubt the sincerity of his words. But there was still another issue.

"What about...what about the family you always wanted, Brad? I can't promise you that."

"I know. I thought about that a lot," he admitted. "I love children, Sam. I've never made a secret of that. I think a loving family is the greatest gift the Lord can bestow. You and I happen to know, going in, that the odds are against us. But even if they weren't, there's no guarantee that we'd be blessed with children. Rachel and I weren't. There was no reason that the doctors could detect. It just never happened. We finally accepted it as the Lord's will."

He paused and looked down, running the tips of his fingers over the back of her hand for a moment before continuing. "The fact is, Sam, my love for you isn't contingent on whether you can have children. I'd like children, yes. But if that means giving you up, there's no contest. Maybe we'll have children. Maybe we'll adopt. I don't know. I do know that I love you, and with or without children I believe we can have a full and rich life together.'' Brad paused, reached into his pocket and withdrew the familiar small velvet case. Sam's heart stopped, then raced on.

"I got the house, Sam," he said.

She nodded, her eyes locked on the case in his hands. "I know."

"You do?"

"Leslie told me."

"Ah. I should have guessed. Well, it's a great house, Sam. But I really don't want to live there alone." He paused, and Sam tore her eyes away from the case to gaze up at him. The smile he gave her was warm and tender and filled with the hope of spring, even though the month was August. "I tried this once before without much success, but I'm nothing if not persistent," he said with a crooked grin. He flipped open the case, and Sam stared down at the solitaire sparkling against the velvet lining. "The offer is still open, Sam, if you'll have me. Will you marry me?" he asked huskily.

She gazed up at him and nodded mutely, overcome by a flood of emotions. Joy. Gratitude. Relief. Awe. And love. Mostly love.

Brad smiled and removed the ring from the case, cradling her hand in his as he slipped the solitaire on her finger.

Sam gazed down at it for a moment, but the dazzle of the sparkling stone paled in comparison to the radiant glow on her face when she looked back up at him. "I love you, Brad Matthews," she said, her voice choked with emotion as her eyes caressed the contours of his face.

"The feeling is definitely mutual," he replied, his own voice none too steady. And as his lips closed over hers, in a tender kiss that spoke more eloquently than words of commitment, caring and the promise of a future shared, Sam's last, lingering doubts vanished. Here, in his arms, was where she belonged. For always.

"I guess we're on, Sam," Henry said nervously, adjusting the unfamiliar bow tie.

Though her own nerves were quivering, she smiled reassuringly and linked her arm in his. "I guess we are."

"You sure do look pretty," he said shyly.

Sam glanced down at the cream-colored lace sheath. The scalloped hem ended modestly just above her knees, and the long sleeves were demure. But the neckline—cut straight across, the scalloped edge revealing an enticing glimpse of creamy skin on her shoulders—gave the dress "Sam pizzazz," to use Laura's term.

"Thanks, Henry. So do you. That tux suits you."

"Do you think so? I never wore one before."

"It's perfect."

The music suddenly changed, and Sam drew a deep breath, her fingers tightening on the small bouquet of cream-colored roses and holly sprigs in her hand. "Well, this is it."

The doors opened, and they moved forward slowly into the candlelit church. Christmas was still two days away, but Brad's congregation had pitched in to complete the decorating in time for the wedding. Poinsettias adorned the altar, and fir trees draped in twinkling white lights stood on each side, adding a magical touch to the scene. Sam's gaze skimmed over the sea of smiling faces, coming to rest on Rebecca and Laura who stood in front to the left. Their elegant, gored, forest-green velvet dresses, with cowl necklines and low-cut backs, complemented the festive setting, as did their bouquets of red roses and holly.

Sam's gaze connected with Laura's, and for a long moment of linked eyes—and hearts—a wealth of understanding passed between them. Both had come so far in such a short time. Nine months before, when Sam had made her way down this aisle as Laura's maid of honor, she would never have believed that it would soon be her turn to walk down the same aisle as a bride. And yet it had happened. Thanks to Brad.

Sam turned then to gaze at the man who would soon be her husband. Her husband, she repeated in silent wonder, still finding it hard to believe. Lovingly she let her eyes drink in his tall form. Not surprisingly, he looked wonderful in his tux. Handsome. Distinguished. *Stalwart.* It was an old word, but it fit him.

It was his eyes, though, that held her spellbound. Tender, caring, softened by love, and—simmering in their depths—just a hint of the passion he'd held carefully in check all these months. A passion that he would soon be able to allow free rein, Sam thought with a sudden, delicious tingle of anticipation.

As Henry relinquished his hold, Brad smiled down at her and tucked her arm in his, protectively covering her hand with his own. And as they moved forward to take the vows that would unite them as man and wife for all time, Sam's heart overflowed with joy. The holiday might still be two days away, she thought, but she had just received the most wonderful Christmas present of all—her very own happy ending.

Epilogue

Fourteen months later

Brad gazed tenderly at Sam's face, serene in sleep, and reached over to gently press his lips to her forehead. She stirred slightly at his touch, and he smiled in anticipation as she burrowed a little more deeply into the pillow, then emitted a small sigh. He never tired of watching her awaken. First there was the flutter of her burnished lashes against her creamy cheeks. Then came the slightly unfocused confusion in her vivid green eyes. Finally there was the smile that warmed her face as her eyes cleared and connected with his, a smile filled with deep, abiding love that never failed to make his breath catch in his throat. Not a day went by that he didn't thank the Lord for sending this special, cherished woman into his life.

"Hi there, sleepyhead," he said softly, lightly brushing a stray wisp of hair off her forehead as their gazes met.

"Hi," she mumbled sleepily, rubbing her eyes with the

backs of her hands in a little-girl-like gesture, endearing because it was so at odds with her usual sophisticated demeanor.

A sudden rush of tenderness swept over him, and his throat constricted as he delicately stroked her cheek. The gray tinge of fatigue that had earlier shaded her face was gone, he noted thankfully, leaving in its place an almost luminous glow. "How do you feel?" he asked.

She considered the question thoughtfully. "Good," she said at last, a contented smile softening her face. "And happy. And very grateful."

"My thoughts exactly," Brad replied huskily. "And I might also add, very blessed." Then he withdrew a single, perfect, long-stemmed rose from behind his back and handed it to her. "Happy Valentine's Day, darling," he said tenderly.

Sam smiled mistily, overwhelmed as always by the bountiful love in his expressive eyes, and inhaled the sweet, rich fragrance. "It's beautiful, Brad," she whispered. "Thank you."

"There are twenty-three more over on the table," he told her, nodding toward an overflowing vase.

Sam's eyes grew wide. "Oh, Brad! That's such an extravagance!"

"Well, only a dozen are for you," he admitted.

"Oh?" she said, quirking an eyebrow.

"Yes," he confirmed solemnly. He took her hand between his. "I must confess, Sam…there's another woman in my life now. The other dozen are for her."

"And what might this other woman's name be?" Sam asked, her lips curving up into a sweet smile.

"Emily." He said the name wonderingly, as if savoring the sound of it on his tongue.

A tender light suffused Sam's face. "And where is Emily?" she asked softly.

Brad reached behind him and carefully lifted a tiny pink bundle, which he placed in Sam's outstretched arms. "She's right here. Waiting patiently for her mommy to wake up."

With one finger, Sam carefully touched the tiny but perfect nose, stroked the fuzz of reddish hair, stared down in awe at the wide blue eyes that gazed up at her so trustingly. She had never been this happy in her whole life, or overcome by so many emotions. Her throat tightened, and a tear spilled out of one eye to trail down her cheek.

Brad reached over and delicately traced its path with one fingertip, then wiped it away with a featherlight touch. "No more tears, Sam," he said, his voice firm but gentle. "Our time for weeping is past. This is our time to laugh— and to love." Then, one hand resting on their new daughter, the other on Sam, he reached over to tenderly claim the lips of the woman who had brought him joy beyond measure.

Sam closed her eyes, and in the moment before the magic of his kiss drove all thoughts from her mind, she was overcome by a profound sense of joy and fulfillment and gratitude. And by something else as well—the peace of true forgiveness. It was as if a burden had suddenly been lifted from her heart, and for the first time she felt truly free from her past.

And as Brad's lips closed over hers, her heart soared. For here, in this circle of love that the Lord had blessed her with, she had at last found her redemption.

* * * * *

Dear Reader,

I've always enjoyed reading romances, so as a writer I suppose it was inevitable that I would eventually pen my own romantic tales. I especially enjoy writing inspirational stories, because they allow me to focus on the three things that last—faith, hope and love.

A Groom of Her Own was a special pleasure to write because it embodies all three of these elements. Sam's faith gives her the courage to hope, and the love she and Brad share is strong enough to free her from her past. As this story illustrates, nothing is impossible with God, and love really does conquer all. If that isn't inspirational, I don't know what is!

The tremendous power of love is a recurring theme in romances, and it appears again in the third and final book of my VOWS series, *A Family To Call Her Own*, which features Brad's sister, Rebecca. It is a story of vulnerability and of innocence lost, and how love transforms the lives of three very special people.

I hope the VOWS series touches your heart. And as you journey through life, may your path always be paved with faith, hope and love.

Irene Hannon

THE WAY HOME

THE WAY HOME

Not as man sees does God see, because man sees the appearance, but the Lord looks into the heart.
—*1 Samuel* 16:7

To Tom—my friend, my hero, my love…always

Chapter One

"There's your man!"

Amy Winter turned in the direction her cameraman was pointing and quickly scanned the group of people milling about in front of the courthouse.

"Where?"

"Straight ahead. Tall, dark hair, gray suit, intimidating. Carrying a black briefcase."

It took Amy only a moment to spot Cal Richards. "Intimidating" was right. As he strode purposefully through the group of people clustered on the sidewalk and headed toward the door, his bearing communicated a very clear message: "Back off." But clear or not, it was a message Amy intended to ignore. She took a deep breath and tightened her grip on the microphone.

"Okay, Steve. Let's go."

Without waiting for a reply, she headed toward her quarry and planted herself directly in his path.

Cal Richards didn't notice her until he was only a couple of feet away. Even then, he simply frowned, gave her a distracted glance and, without pausing, made a move to step around her. Except that she moved, too.

This time he looked right at her, and their gazes collided for one brief, volatile moment that made Amy's breath catch in her throat. The man had eyes that simultaneously assessed, calculated, probed—and sent an odd tingle up her spine. But before she had time to dwell on her unsettling reaction, his gaze moved on, swiftly but thoroughly sweeping over her stylish shoulder-length light brown hair, vivid green eyes and fashionably short skirt before honing in on the microphone in her hand and the cameraman behind her. His frown deepened, and the expression in his eyes went from merely annoyed to cold.

"Excuse me. I have work to do." The words were polite. The tone was not.

Amy's stomach clenched and she forced herself to take a deep breath. "So do I. And I was hoping you'd help me do it." Though she struggled to maintain an even tone, she couldn't control the slight tremor that ran through her voice. And that bothered her. She resented the fact that this stranger, with one swift look, could disrupt the cool, professional demeanor she'd worked so hard to perfect.

"I don't give interviews."

"I just have a couple of questions. It will only take a minute of your time."

"I don't have a minute. And I don't give interviews," he repeated curtly. "Now, if you'll excuse—"

"Look, Mr. Richards, this trial is going to get publicity whether you cooperate or not," she interrupted, willing her voice to remain steady. "But as the assistant prosecuting attorney, you could add a valuable perspective to the coverage."

Cal expelled an exasperated breath. "Look, Ms...." He raised an eyebrow quizzically.

"Winter. Amy Winter." She added the call letters of her station.

"Ms. Winter. As I said before, I don't give interviews. Period. Not before, not during, not after a trial. So you'll save us both a lot of trouble if you just accept that right now. Trust me."

Before she could protest, he neatly sidestepped her, covered the distance to the courthouse door in a few long strides and disappeared inside.

Amy stared after him in frustration, then turned to Steve, who gave her an I-told-you-so shrug.

"Okay, okay, you warned me," she admitted with an irritated sigh.

"Cal Richards has a reputation for never bending the rules—his own or the law's. Everyone in the news game knows that. Did you see anyone else even *try* to talk to him?"

Steve was right. The other reporters in front of the courthouse, most longtime veterans of the Atlanta news scene, hadn't even approached the assistant prosecuting attorney. They'd obviously learned a lesson she had yet to master after only six months in town. Then again, she wasn't sure she *wanted* to learn that lesson. If she was ever going to win the anchor spot she'd set her sights on, and ultimately a network feature slot, she had to find a way to make her coverage stand out. This story had potential. And getting Cal Richards's cooperation would be a coup that could boost her up at least a couple of rungs on the proverbial career ladder.

She turned once more to gaze thoughtfully at the door

he had entered. Maybe Steve was right. Maybe the assistant prosecuting attorney wouldn't bend. Then again, maybe he would. And until she tried everything she could think of to induce a change of heart, she wasn't about to let Cal Richards off the hook.

Cal closed the door behind him, tossed his briefcase on the couch and wearily loosened his tie. The first day of jury selection had been frustrating and largely unproductive. Which was about what he'd expected, given the high-profile nature of this trial. Whenever a public figure had a run-in with the law, it was big news. Especially when that public figure was someone like Jamie Johnson, a well-liked sports hero, and the charge was so explosive—manslaughter. If any average citizen had been involved in a drunk-driving accident that left a pedestrian dead, they'd throw the book at him. But Jamie Johnson had public sentiment on his side. And since the victim was a homeless drifter, his death was being treated as no great loss.

Cal didn't see it that way. Manslaughter was manslaughter, as far as he was concerned. It didn't matter who the victim was. But Johnson was going to walk unless they came up with a rock-solid witness. Though the sports hero didn't dispute the drunk-driving charge, he claimed that the victim had stepped off the curb and into his path. And at the moment, it was his word against no one's. With his clean-cut good looks and apparent sincerity and remorse, he had the public eating out of his hand.

But he was guilty as sin, and Cal knew it deep in his gut. Johnson had had other minor run-ins with the law, was known to be a drinker, had demonstrated his irresponsibility in any number of ways the police were well aware of. Unfortunately, none of that was admissible as evidence.

Cal jammed his hands into his pockets and walked over to the window of his apartment. There were many things he liked about his job. The harsh reality of this kind of trial, where the odds of seeing justice done were minuscule, wasn't one of them. He would do his best, of course. He always did. But he'd been in this business long enough to learn that no matter how high your ideals were when you started, disillusion was your legacy. There were just too many instances where the "little guy," for lack of money or power, was shortchanged by the law. Cal worked hard to keep that from happening, and sometimes he won. That was what kept him going—knowing that in at least a few instances justice had been served because of his efforts. It was a deeply satisfying experience, but it happened too rarely.

Cal looked down at the glittering lights of the city and drew a long, slow breath, willing the tension in his shoulders to ease. It was a pretty view, one that his infrequent visitors always admired. But it wasn't home. Never would be. And, as usual, it did nothing to help him relax.

So instead he closed his eyes and pictured the evening mist on the blue-hued mountains outside his grandmother's cabin in Tennessee. He could almost feel the fresh breeze on his face, smell the faint, woodsy aroma of smoke curling from distant chimneys, hear the whisper of the wind in the pine trees and the call of the birds. As he let the remembered beauty seep into his soul, his mind gradually grew still and he was filled with a sense of peace.

When at last Cal opened his eyes, he felt better. Calmer. He'd lived in cities for almost half of his thirty-four years, but only Gram's cabin fit the definition of "home." It was still his refuge, the place he went when he couldn't handle the impersonal, fast-paced city anymore, when the frustration became too intense, when he needed to regain perspective. And he'd been going there a lot lately. Even after all these years, he felt like a stranger in the sterile environment of steel and concrete. Only in the mountains was he able to ease the growing restlessness in his soul.

But how could he ever explain that to his father? he asked himself dispiritedly for the thousandth time. Cal raked his fingers through his hair and sighed. Jack Richards would never understand. All his life, all the years he'd labored as a tenant farmer, he'd wanted a better life for his only offspring. And "better" to him meant an office job, a lucrative career, life in the big city. He'd instilled that same dream in his son, though it wasn't a dream Cal had taken to naturally. Unlike his father, he'd always loved the land. But somewhere along the way his father had convinced him that his destiny lay elsewhere, far from the blue-hazed Smoky Mountains. And the day Cal graduated from law school with an enviable, big-city job offer in his pocket, his destiny had seemed settled, his "success" assured.

In the intervening years, however, he'd begun to realize that deep inside he had never really shared his father's dream. The mountains called to him more and more strongly as the years passed. And it was a call he was finding harder and harder to ignore, especially on days like this. Yet how could he walk away from the life he'd built for himself, throw away all the long hours he'd invested in his career in Atlanta? Frustrating as it often was, there were also moments of deep satisfaction when he was able to help someone who really *needed* his help, who might be lost in the system without his intervention. That was why he had gone into law, why he still enjoyed it. And as he took on more and more responsibility, he would be in a position to do even more to further the cause of justice. It somehow seemed wrong to even *consider* leaving a job where he could be such an instrument for good. And further compounding the situation was his father. How could he disappoint the man who had worked so hard to give him a better life?

With an impatient shake of his head, Cal turned away from the window. He'd been wrestling with this dilemma for months, praying for guidance, but resolution was still nowhere in sight. And until his prayers were answered, he'd simply have to maintain the status quo. At least until his patience ran out. Which might not be too far down the road, he thought ruefully as he headed toward the kitchen.

The red light was blinking on his answering machine as he passed, indicating three messages, and he paused. Fortunately, his unlisted number kept crank calls and solicitations at bay. Only his close business associates, family and a few select friends were privy to his private line.

Despite the protest of his stomach, Cal deferred dinner for yet another few minutes. He straddled a stool at the counter, pulled a notepad toward him and punched Play.

The first two messages were easily dispensed with. The third was more disturbing.

"Mr. Richards, this is Amy Winter. We met this morning at the courthouse. I don't like to bother people at home, but I'm not having much luck connecting with you at your office, and I really would like to continue our discussion. As I told you, I'm covering the Johnson trial and your input would add a valuable perspective to the coverage. I realize, of course, that you can't discuss the trial in any detail, but perhaps you can suggest an angle I might investigate, or offer some other insights that would be helpful. Let me give you my work number and my home number…''

As she proceeded to do so, Cal's frown deepened. He didn't like reporters in general, and he especially didn't like pushy reporters. Which was exactly the category Amy Winter fit into. How in the world had she managed to get his unlisted number? And did she really think he'd return this call when he'd ignored both of the messages she'd left at his office earlier in the day?

Resolutely he punched the erase button. Obviously she was new on this beat or she'd know that his ''no comment'' meant exactly that. But she'd learn. In the meantime, if she continued to call his home number, he could always file a harassment complaint. He hoped it wouldn't come to that, but he didn't have time to play games. Sooner or later she'd get that message.

Apparently it was going to be ''later,'' Cal thought resignedly when he spotted the persistent reporter on the courthouse steps the next morning. At least she'd left the cameraman back at the station this time, he noted.

''Good morning, Mr. Richards.''

She sounded a bit breathless as she fell into step beside him, and he glanced over at her. The chilly, early-spring air had brought a becoming flush to her cheeks, and her jade-colored jacket complemented the startling green of her eyes. She was a very attractive woman, he realized. Then again, that seemed to be a prerequisite for broadcast news. As far as he was concerned, TV stations would be better off if they paid more attention to solid reporting skills and real news and less to cosmetics and sensationalism. He picked up his pace.

"If this keeps up, I'll have to wear my running shoes next time," she complained breathlessly, trotting beside him.

He stopped so abruptly that she was a step ahead of him before she realized he'd paused. When she turned back he was scowling at her.

She ignored his intimidating look. "Could you maybe signal the next time you're going to put on the brakes?" she suggested pleasantly.

"I'm hoping there won't be a next time."

"Gee, you sure know how to make a girl feel wanted."

"I thought I made myself clear yesterday, Ms. Winter. I don't talk to the press. And I did not appreciate the call to my home. I consider that invasion of privacy, not that you reporters know the meaning of that term. But if it happens again, I'll file a complaint. Is that understood?"

She flushed, and something—some odd flash of emotion—darted across her eyes. It was there and gone so quickly, he wondered if he'd imagined it. But he didn't think so. Suddenly the word *cringe* came to mind, and he frowned. How odd—and unlikely. Reporters were a thick-skinned lot. You couldn't hurt their feelings if you tried. Obviously he had misread her reaction.

"Look, Mr. Richards, I'm sorry about the call to your apartment. It seemed like a good idea at the time, but it won't happen again. However, I won't promise to stop calling your office or talking to you here at the courthouse. That's my job." She tilted her chin defiantly on the last words, giving him a good look at her classic oval face, clear, intelligent eyes and determined, nicely shaped lips. His gaze lingered on those lips just a moment too long before he jerked it away, disconcerted by the sudden, unaccountable acceleration of his pulse.

"And my job is to see justice done," he countered a little too sharply as he moved forward once again.

"Why should our two jobs be incompatible? And why do you hate the press so much?" she persisted, struggling to keep pace with his long strides.

They reached the door of the courthouse and he turned to her, his jaw set, his eyes flinty. "They shouldn't be incompatible, Ms. Winter. Justice should be a mutual goal of the press and the law. But the only things TV stations care about are ratings and advertising revenues. If that means sensationalizing a trial at the expense of justice to gain viewers, so be it."

"That's a pretty cynical attitude."

His mouth twisted into a humorless smile. "Let's just call it realistic. How long have you been in this business, Ms. Winter? Two years? Three?"

"Seven."

His eyebrows rose in surprise. She didn't look more than a year or two out of school, but she must be close to thirty, he realized.

"Then you should know that it's hard enough to see justice done when everything works right. It's impossible when the press takes sides."

"I take it you're speaking from personal experience?"

He hesitated, then gave a curt nod. "Five years ago I handled a trial very similar to this one. High-profile figure, well liked. He was charged with rape. He was also the proverbial golden-haired boy. Popular, wealthy, powerful, a churchgoing man with a list of philanthropic endeavors to rival Albert Schweitzer. He had the press eating out of his hand. In fact, the news media did everything it could to discredit and harass the victim. She finally caved in under the pressure. We didn't stand a chance.'' The bitterness in his voice was unmistakable.

"And…''

At her prompt, Cal turned to her, his rapier-sharp eyes cold as steel. "Two years ago he was charged with rape again. But this time he picked the wrong victim and the wrong place. She was a fighter, and she was determined to make him pay. Not to mention the fact that there were witnesses.''

"So in the end, justice was served.''

He shrugged. "No thanks to the press. And it depends on what you mean by 'justice.' Yes, he was convicted. But he's still appealing. Worst case, he'll serve a couple of years and be back on the streets. I hardly consider that justice, given the crime.''

Amy gave him a quizzical look. "So why did you go into law, if it's so hopeless?''

He gazed at her thoughtfully. "Frankly I've been asking myself that question a lot lately,'' he replied soberly, surprising her—and himself—with his candor. "I guess I thought I could make a difference. And once in a great while I can. Every now and then, because of my efforts, justice is served and the little guy wins. That's what keeps me going. That's what makes it worthwhile.''

His tone once more grew brusque. "Look, Ms. Winter, I can't stop you from covering this trial. But I can—and do—decline to participate. I'll give you one piece of advice, though. Don't fall into the trap those reporters did in the case I just told you about. Don't be taken in by appearances. Do your homework. Dig. Don't assume that the image Jamie Johnson projects publicly is the real man. You'll do everyone a great service if you treat him as you would any other defendant. And while you're at it, take a look at the issue itself. Too many times people blame liquor for drunk driving instead of focusing on the real problem—irresponsibility. That's a harder issue to tackle. But some thoughtful coverage might go a long way toward placing the blame where it belongs—on the person, not the object. Think about that, Ms. Winter. Try to go for substance over sensationalism.''

She looked at him silently for a moment. ''No matter what I do, I have a feeling nothing will change your mind about the news game,'' she said at last.

Cal's mouth settled into a grim line. ''When somebody dies, it's not a game.''

Amy met his intense gaze steadily. ''I agree. And I appreciate your candor and suggestions. They were very helpful. In fact, I'd welcome any other input or ideas you might have as the trial progresses.''

''Don't hold your breath. As I said, I try to stay as far away from the press as possible.''

''I'll keep trying, you know.''

He shrugged and turned away. ''Suit yourself.''

Amy watched as he disappeared inside, a thoughtful expression on her face. For somebody who didn't talk to the press, he'd certainly given her an earful just now. Which meant he might do so again. And maybe next time he would offer a piece of information that would give her just the edge she was looking for in her coverage.

In the meantime, she intended to take to heart what he had said. While she didn't agree completely with his assessment of the press, he had made some valid points. And he'd given her a couple of ideas for related stories that could round out her coverage when there wasn't much to report on in the trial itself. All in all, it had been a productive morning, she decided. She had some good ideas, and she had a ray of hope—which was probably the last thing Cal Richards had intended to give her, she thought, a wry smile quirking the corners of her mouth.

As she turned to go, she glanced back at the door through which the reticent assistant prosecuting attorney had disappeared. He was an interesting man, she mused. Not to mention good-looking. Too bad they were on opposite sides—in his opinion, at least. Not that it mattered, of course. He wasn't her type anyway. Not even close.

Besides, even if he was, she didn't have time for romance. She had a career to build.

"If looks could kill…"

Cal stopped abruptly outside the jury selection room, the scowl on his face softening as he glanced at his colleague.

"It's not that bad, you know. We'll get this jury. If not in this century, then surely in the next."

This time Cal smiled. Bill Jackson, who could go for the jugular in the courtroom better than anyone Cal had ever encountered, also had an amazing ability to ease the tension in any situation. It was a pretty unbeatable combination in an attorney, and Cal was glad he was assisting on this trial.

"Believe it or not, I wasn't even thinking about the jury."

"No? Then what put that look on your face?"

"A run-in with the press."

"No kidding! I thought you had them all trained to keep their distance."

"So did I. I think this one's new."

"What's his name?"

"It's a her. Amy Winter."

Bill gave a low whistle, and Cal raised his eyebrows. "You know her?"

"Unfortunately, no. But I've seen her on TV. Man, she's a looker! And you're right. She's only been around a few months. Must be good, though, to get an assignment like this so quickly."

"She's pushy, anyway."

Bill shrugged. "Same thing in the news game."

"Yeah, well, I don't appreciate being called at home."

Bill looked at him in surprise. "How'd she get your unlisted number?"

"Beats me. I didn't ask. I just told her to back off."

"And how did the lady respond to that?"

Cal's scowled returned. "Let's just say I don't think I've seen the last of Amy Winter."

Bill chuckled as he reached over to open the door. "This could be interesting. Two people equally unwilling to bend. You'll have to keep me informed. In the meantime, we'd better get on with the jury selection or there won't even be a trial to write about."

As Cal followed Bill into the room, he gave one last fleeting thought to Amy Winter. Bill had called her a "looker," and his colleague was right. But that wasn't why she lingered in his memory. He'd met plenty of attractive women, and he'd rarely given them a thought once out of their presence. No, it wasn't her *looks* that intrigued him. It was the *look* that had appeared in her eyes, then quickly vanished, when he'd spoken harshly to her. For the briefest of moments she had seemed somehow… *vulnerable* was the word that came to mind. Yet that seemed so out of character for someone in her profession. Reporters got the cold shoulder all the time. Surely they built up an immunity to it. Why would she be any different?

And she probably wasn't, he told himself brusquely. Most likely he'd imagined the whole thing. Besides, why should he care? Amy Winter was a stranger to him. And a reporter to boot. She was aggressive, ambitious, competitive, single-minded, brash— qualities he didn't particularly admire in either gender. He ought to just forget her and hope she honored his request to back off.

Except he didn't think she would.

And for some strange reason, he didn't think she was going to be so easy to forget.

Chapter Two

Amy took a sip of her drink and glanced around glumly. A charity bachelor auction was the last place she wanted to be on a Saturday night. If her TV station hadn't bought a table and their lead anchorwoman wasn't the MC—making this a politically expedient event to attend—the proverbial wild horses couldn't have dragged her here. Spending an entire evening watching women bid on dates was not exactly her idea of a compelling way to use her precious—and rare—free time.

"Why the long face?"

Amy turned to find one of the younger copywriters from her station at her elbow. She shrugged, groping for the woman's name. Darlene, that was it. "I can think of other places I'd rather be."

"Yeah? Spending an evening mingling with a bunch of hot-looking guys doesn't seem so bad to me. Have you checked out the program?" She waved it in front of Amy's face. "It's got all their pictures and bios."

"No. I'm not planning to bid."

"I wasn't, either, until I got here. But I met several of the auctionees during the cocktail hour and now I've got my eye on Bachelor #12—over there, by the bar." She gazed at him longingly. "Man, a date with that dude would be *worth* a couple hundred bucks! Did you meet anyone interesting?"

Amy shook her head. Actually, she'd only just arrived, putting off her appearance as long as possible. It had been a grueling and frustrating couple of weeks and she was exhausted. Though she'd tried repeatedly to contact Cal Richards—even waylaid him a couple of times enroute to the courthouse—and spent hours in the courtroom after the trial began, he'd hardly spoken to her. Apparently he'd said everything he intended to say at the one encounter when he'd made it clear what he thought of the news media.

Amy sighed. She hadn't given up on finding an angle on this story. But the assistant prosecuting attorney wasn't making it easy, that was for sure. Still, she was due for a break. In fact, she *deserved* one. After all, she'd paid her dues. She'd put in the long hours, sacrificed her personal life, worked the midnight shift in the newsroom, all in the name of career advancement. And she'd accomplished a lot. But not enough. She had her sights set on an anchor slot. And she'd get there, just like Candace Bryce, she vowed, as the celebrity MC stepped to the microphone.

"Ladies, please take your seats so the wait staff can serve dinner—and we can get to the *real* purpose of this evening. You'll have about an hour to enjoy your food and plan your strategy. Bon appétit!"

"Our table's over there," Darlene indicated with a nod, leaving Amy to follow.

Amy knew most of the women from the station either by name or face, although she didn't consider any of them "friends." The broadcast news business was too competitive to foster real friendships. She smiled pleasantly and sat down in the one empty chair, her back to the stage. Obviously her table mates had vied for the seats with the best view, she thought wryly. As far as she was concerned, they could have them. She'd much rather focus on the chocolate mousse promised for dessert than the dessert the other women had in mind.

By the time the mousse was served, Amy was beginning to plan her escape strategy. She'd put in her appearance, been noticed by Candace and stopped on the way to the ladies' room to chat with the station manager. Her duty was done. In another few minutes she could sneak out, head back to her apartment, take her shoes off, put on some mellow jazz, dim the lights and do absolutely nothing for what little remained of the evening. It sounded like heaven!

As Candace stepped once more to the microphone, a buzz of excitement swept over the room and there was a rustling of paper as the women reached for their programs. While the ladies focused on the stage, Amy focused on her dessert.

The first auctionee was introduced to cheers and whistles, and Amy rolled her eyes. How could grown women behave in such a sophomoric way? she wondered in disgust. And *they* complained that *men* acted juvenile! She eyed the exit longingly, but it was too soon to leave. The bidding had barely begun. Resignedly she reached for one of the programs and fished a pen out of her purse. She might as well put the time to good use. In the car this evening, on the way to the dinner, she'd had some ideas about the trial coverage and she wanted to jot them down before they slipped her mind.

As Amy made her notes, she tuned down the surrounding cacophony of sound until it was no more than a background buzz. She'd learned that technique early in her career, when she realized she would often have to compose broadcast copy in the midst of chaos for live feeds. It was a skill that had served her well in the years that followed.

In the one real conversation they'd had, Cal Richards had suggested some angles for her coverage that she hadn't yet explored. She'd also picked up a few ideas since sitting in on the first couple of sessions of the trial. They had all been filed away in her mind for emergency use, just in case she wasn't able to break through his wall of reserve. Up until now, she'd been confident she'd find a way to do that. But her confidence was beginning to slip, she admitted. She'd tried everything she could think of, and the man simply refused to budge. It was time to put some of her emergency plans into action.

Amy ran out of room and turned the page to continue her scribbling. Her name fell on Bachelor #5 just as Candace introduced him.

"Now, ladies, here we have a real coup. One of Atlanta's most eligible and elusive bachelors, who only agreed to participate because of his interest in Saint Vincent's Boy's Club, which will benefit from this event. He's gorgeous, articulate, charming and *very* available. If I wasn't already married, I'd bid on this one myself. Ladies, please welcome one of Atlanta's finest assistant prosecuting attorneys, Cal Richards."

Amy practically choked on the sip of coffee she'd just

taken as the room erupted into wild applause and more catcalls. She stared at his name and photo in the program, then jerked around to confirm that her nemesis was, indeed, present. Sure enough, there he was, looking incredibly handsome in his tux—and extremely uncomfortable in the glare of the spotlight, judging by the flush on his face and his strained smile. Cal Richards, who shied away from publicity, was allowing himself to be ogled by a roomful of raucous women and auctioned off for charity! It was incredible! It was unbelievable! It was…the chance she'd been waiting for, she realized with a jolt! If she bought a date with him, he'd *have* to talk to her, she reasoned, her mind clicking into high gear. Sure, there was a chance he wouldn't tell her anything of value. But she was pretty good at ferreting out information. It couldn't hurt to try, considering she'd run out of other options.

Amy turned to Darlene. "How much are these guys going for?"

Darlene gave her a distracted glance. "What?"

"How much are these guys going for?" Amy repeated impatiently.

"So…someone caught your eye." Darlene glanced back at the stage and gave Amy a sly smile. "I can't say I blame you. He's a hunk. Even if he wasn't a prosecuting attorney, my defenses would crumble with him in five seconds flat."

The bidding had already started, and Amy needed information—fast. In the interest of time she restrained the impulse to throttle Darlene. "It's for a good cause," she replied with a noncommittal shrug.

Darlene wasn't buying. "Yeah, right."

Amy gave up the pretense of disinterest. "So how much?" she repeated urgently.

"The last guy went for three-fifty."

Amy cringed and glanced back toward the stage. Was it worth the gamble? Cal Richards didn't strike her as the kind of man who would bend. But even if she got one lead, one piece of information that gave her an edge, it would be worth the money. It was almost like an investment in her career, she rationalized.

Amy glanced around. Women were holding up numbers and calling out their bids. She turned back to her table, spotted the large number in the center and reached for it as the bid rose to three hundred.

She waited until the bidding slowed at four-twenty-five.

"Okay, ladies, is that it? Any more bidders? No? All right, then…" Candace raised her gavel. "Going… going…"

Amy took a deep breath, turned her head slightly away just in case Cal Richards could see past the glare of the spotlight, and held up her number. "Four-fifty."

There was a momentary hush, and her heart thumped painfully against her rib cage.

"Four-seventy-five," someone countered.

Amy gulped. "Five hundred."

A murmur swept the room.

"Now, ladies, that's what I call a bid!" Candace said approvingly. "Do I hear five and a quarter?"

Amy stopped breathing. Five hundred was about her limit, especially when the odds of hitting the jackpot were about on a par with winning the lottery.

"No? All right, Bachelor #5 is going, going, gone, to table thirty-two and one very lucky lady."

As enthusiastic applause swept the room and her table

mates congratulated her, Amy hoped Candace was right. Because she could use a little luck about now.

"Cal, there's a woman on the phone who says she won you in an auction. Is she a nut, or is there something you haven't told me?"

Cal closed his eyes and felt the beginning of a headache prick at his temples. He hadn't mentioned the auction to anyone in his office, especially not Cynthia. She was a great friend and legal assistant, but ever since she'd walked down the aisle a year ago, she'd made it her personal goal in life to watch him do the same. And she was nothing if not tenacious. "She's not a nut, Cynthia, and yes, there's something I haven't told you."

As the silence lengthened, he could feel her growing impatience over the line.

"So are you going to come clean of your own free will or do I have to drag it out of you?" she finally demanded.

A bemused smile tipped up the corners of his mouth. "Have you ever thought about going into police work, Cyn? You'd be great at the third degree."

"Hah-hah. Spill it, Richards."

He sighed. There was no way around it. He and Cynthia had been co-workers and friends a long time, and she wouldn't rest until she had the whole story. "I agreed to be one of the bachelors auctioned off at a charity dinner last Friday. A good chunk of the money goes to Saint Vincent's, so I couldn't say no."

"No kidding! Mr. Particular, who finds fault with everyone I suggest as a potential date, is actually going to go out with some strange woman?"

"I certainly hope she's not strange."

"Very funny. So do you want to talk to her or not?"

Cal sighed again. No, he didn't. But he'd have to face this sooner or later, and he might as well get it over with. "Yeah, I guess so."

"Do try to restrain your eagerness," Cynthia said dryly. "Remember, this woman paid good money for you. You could at least show a little enthusiasm. How much, by the way?"

"Five hundred."

She gave a low whistle. "All I can say is, you better make this date something to remember. I'll put her through."

"Wait! Did she give you her name?"

"No. Don't you have it?" Cynthia asked in surprise.

"I cut out early that night. She hadn't gone back to pay yet. They said she'd be in touch with me."

"Well, it's payoff time now. Have fun, lover boy."

Cal grimaced and took a deep breath. This was the most awkward thing he'd ever done, even if it was for a good cause. He just hoped the woman could at least carry on a decent conversation, or it would be one very long evening.

He heard the call go through and, remembering Cynthia's comment about how much money the bidder had paid, forced a pleasant note into his voice. "Cal Richards speaking."

"Mr. Richards, I believe we have a date."

He frowned. The voice was oddly—and unsettlingly—familiar, and a wave of uneasiness swept over him.

"Yes, I think we do," he replied warily. "I'm sorry, I didn't get your name the night of the dinner, although I have a feeling we've met."

"Yes, we have. This is Amy Winter."

Amy Winter? The *reporter?* Impossible! Fate wouldn't be that unkind, not after he'd endured being auctioned off in front of hundreds of women, let himself be humiliated for charity. It couldn't be her!

"Mr. Richards, are you still there?"

It was her, all right, he realized with a sinking feeling. Now that she'd identified herself, he recognized that distinctive, slightly husky voice. His headache suddenly took a turn for the worst, and he closed his eyes. "Yes, I'm here. Look, Ms. Winter, is this a joke?"

"Hardly. I paid good money for this date. And I have the receipt to prove it."

"But why in the world…?" His voice trailed off as her strategy suddenly became clear. He wouldn't talk to her in a business setting, so she figured he'd have to in a social situation. A muscle in his jaw clenched, and his headache ratcheted up another notch. "It won't work, you know," he said coldly.

"What?"

"Don't play innocent with me, Ms. Winter. You're still trying to get me to talk about the trial. Well, forget it. You wasted five hundred dollars."

"It went to a good cause. Besides, how do you know I didn't bid on you because I really wanted a date?"

"Ms. Winter, anyone who looks like you doesn't need to buy dates at an auction. Let's stop playing games. You bought a date, I'll give you a date. And that's all I'll give you. How about dinner Friday night?"

"How about sooner?"

"Sorry, that's the best I can do."

"Okay. Just name the time and place."

"I'll pick you up. That was part of the deal."

"Don't put yourself out."

Cal frowned. She sounded miffed. And she had a right to, he conceded guiltily. As Cynthia had said, she'd paid good money for their date, whatever her motivation. He took a deep breath and forced a more pleasant tone into his voice. "I'll be happy to pick you up. Just give me your address."

She hesitated, and for a moment he thought she was going to refuse. But in the end she relented and they settled on a time.

"I'll see you Friday, Mr. Richards. It should be interesting."

That wasn't exactly the word he would have chosen, he thought grimly as he hung up the phone, reached for his coffee and shook out two aspirin from the bottle he kept in his desk drawer. On second thought, he made it three. Amy Winter was definitely a three-aspirin headache.

As Amy replaced the receiver, she realized her hand was shaking. The strain of keeping up a breezy front with the recalcitrant assistant prosecuting attorney had clearly taken a toll. She'd always been outspoken and assertive, but "pushy" wasn't her style. Which was unfortunate, given the career she'd chosen. Though she'd learned to be brash, she hadn't yet learned to like it. The in-your-face approach just wasn't her. But it *was* part of the job, and she figured in time it would get easier. The only problem was, she'd been telling herself that for years now.

Amy took a sip of her herbal tea and gave herself a few minutes to calm down. Cal Richards didn't like her, and though she knew she shouldn't let that bother her, it did. She liked to be liked. But she'd chosen the wrong business for that, she reminded herself wryly. Investigative reporters didn't usually win popularity contests. Acrimony went with the territory.

For a fleeting moment Amy wondered if she might have been happier using her reporting skills in some other way. But she ruthlessly stifled that unsettling thought almost as quickly as it arose. It was way too late for second-guessing. She'd invested too much of her life and energy building this particular future to question it now. She'd very deliberately set her sights on a career as an anchor-woman, and she knew exactly why.

First, she liked the glamour. She enjoyed being in the spotlight, relished her pseudocelebrity status.

Second, she liked the big-city lifestyle. Unlike her sister, Kate, who had actually enjoyed small-town farm life, Amy had always dreamed of the bright lights and the excitement of the city. If the lights were more garish than dazzling up close, well, that was more a reflection of the nature of her work—which often took her to seedy areas—than of the actual city, she assured herself.

Third, she liked the money. Or at least the freedom it gave her. The freedom to travel to the Caribbean on exotic vacations, the freedom to live in an upscale town house, the freedom to walk into any store in Atlanta and buy whatever designer outfit she chose without having to give up something else to do so. Money had always been tight on the farm. Her parents had done their best, but she had vowed to put the days of homemade prom dresses and hand-me-downs far behind her.

Fourth, she liked feature reporting, especially human-interest stories that uplifted and inspired and made people feel optimistic about the goodness of the human race. True, those rarely came her way. Someday, though, when she made her mark, she would be able to pick and choose her assignments, decide when and if she wanted to come out from behind the anchor desk. But that was still a long way down the road. In the meantime, she did what she was told and worked hard to get the best possible story. Including bidding on a date with a man who clearly disliked her.

Amy sighed and took another sip of tea, trying to find something positive in the situation. She thought back over their conversation and suddenly recalled Cal's comment about her not needing to buy a date. So he thought she was attractive, she mused. It wasn't much, she acknowledged, but it was a start.

"Hi, Gram. How's everything at home?"

"Cal? My, it's good to hear your voice! We're both fine. Jack, it's Cal," she called, her voice muffled as she apparently turned her head.

Cal smiled and leaned back, resting his head against the cushion of the overstuffed chair as he crossed an ankle over his knee. Just hearing the voices from home made him feel better.

"Your dad'll be right here, son. How's life in Atlanta?"

"Okay."

"Hmph. I've heard more enthusiasm from old Sam Pritchard."

Cal smiled again. Sam Pritchard was legendary in the mountains for his blasé reaction to life. As usual, his grandmother had tuned right in to Cal's mood. Probably because she was one of the few people who knew of his growing dissatisfaction with city life.

"Sorry, Gram." He modified his tone. "I can't complain. The job is demanding and stressful, but it's worth-while work, and I've been blessed in a lot of ways.''

''Are you taking any time for fun?''

Cal pondered that question. Fun? The only time he really had any fun was when he went home, and that wasn't often enough. When he was in the city, he was too busy for much socializing. His job ate up an inordinate amount of his time, and most of the little that remained he spent at Saint Vincent's.

''I get out once in a while,'' he hedged.

''You need to take some time for yourself, son,'' the older woman persisted, the worry evident in her voice. ''A body needs more in life than work and responsibilities. You meet any nice women lately?''

For some reason, his social life—or lack thereof—had become a hot topic over the past year. His grandmother seemed to think that if he got married and had a family, many of his doubts and issues would be resolved. Frankly, he thought a romantic entanglement would just complicate matters. He needed to get his life in order, make some decisions about his future, before he got involved in a relationship. That was only fair to the woman. And it was that sense of fairness, not lack of interest, that kept him from serious dating. In fact, in the past couple of years he'd begun to long for the very things his grandmother was suggesting, had become increasingly aware of an emotional vacuum in his life. He'd lain awake more nights than he cared to admit yearning for warmth, for a caring touch, for someone who would listen to the secrets of his heart and share hers with him. He *wanted* to fall in love. It was just that now was not the time.

''Cal?'' his grandmother prompted. ''It wasn't a hard

question. 'Course, if it's none of my business, that's okay.''

"Actually, I have a date Friday night," he offered, to appease her.

"Well! Now that's fine."

He could hear the surprise in her voice, could tell she was pleased, and he felt a twinge of guilt. He should explain the situation. After all, it wasn't a real date.

"It's no big deal, Gram. Just dinner."

"Everything has to start somewhere. Where did you meet her?" she asked eagerly.

He felt himself getting in deeper. "At the courthouse. But Gram, she…"

"Is she a lawyer, too?"

"No. She works in TV. Actually, that's how…"

"My! That sounds interesting. What's her—oh, your dad's ready to talk to you. We'll catch up some more later. You call us again over the weekend, okay?"

Cal sighed as the phone was passed on. He'd certainly handled that well, he berated himself. Now his grandmother would get her hopes up, jump to all sorts of wrong conclusions. But he'd be better prepared when he called the next time. He'd use the old "we just didn't click" routine, and that would be the end of that.

"Cal? How are you, son?"

Cal settled deeper into the chair. "Hi, Dad. Fine. How's everything there?"

"Same as always. Quiet. Things don't change much in the mountains, you know. But tell me about you. I know there's a lot more going on in Atlanta than there is here."

Cal relayed some recent events that he knew his father would enjoy hearing about—the black-tie dinner, though he made no mention of the auction part of the evening, a meeting he'd had with the mayor earlier in the week, the publicity the Jamie Johnson trial was receiving. As usual, his father ate it up.

"My, son! You sure do lead an exciting life. But you deserve all your success. You worked hard for it. And I'm proud of you. I was just telling Mike Thomas about the governor's commission you were appointed to. He was real impressed."

Cal felt the old familiar knot begin to form in his gut. His father was a kind, gentle, decent man who'd never had a break in his entire life. He'd spent his youth and middle age barely scraping by, handicapped by limited education and limited opportunity as he struggled to support a son and an ailing wife. He'd worked with his hands all his life, accepting that as his lot but dreaming of better things for Cal. Now he was living Cal's success vicariously. If his son returned to the mountains, in whatever capacity, the older man would be sorely disappointed, Cal knew. But there had to be a line somewhere between responsibility to his father and to himself. He just wasn't sure where it was.

Up until now he'd done everything that was expected of him—by others and by himself. He gave his job one hundred percent, and did his best to make a contribution to society. He'd provided well for Gram and his dad. They'd refused his offer to move to Atlanta, both reluctant to leave the only home they'd ever known, but he made sure they lived comfortably, that neither had to work anymore. By choice, Gram still put in a great deal of time at the craft co-op she'd founded. His father, however, who had always disliked working the land, had walked away from his job without a second look, content to spend his time helping out at the church or reading, a pastime he'd had little opportunity to indulge in most of his life. *They* were both happy. Unfortunately, the vague discontent that had been nagging him for years had intensified dramatically in the last few months, leaving *him* restless and searching.

"You coming home to visit soon, son?" His father interrupted his thoughts.

"I hope so, Dad." The sudden weariness in his voice reflected the burden of decision he was struggling with, and he tried for a more upbeat tone. "It's hard to get away, though. Things are pretty busy."

"I understand. You have an important job. I'm sure they need you there. But your room is always waiting, anytime you can get away. You'll come up sometime later in the spring, won't you?"

"Of course. Have I ever missed spring in the mountains?"

The older man chuckled. "Can't say you have. One thing about you, son. You're reliable. We can always count on you."

The knot in Cal's gut tightened. "I'm not perfect, Dad."

"Maybe not. But I sure wouldn't trade you in. You take care, now."

"All right, Dad. Tell Gram I said goodbye."

Cal replaced the receiver and wearily let his head drop back against the chair. He needed to make some decisions, and he needed to make them soon. There were rumors that he was being considered for a promotion to the coveted position of prosecuting attorney. He should be happy. It was what he was supposed to have been working toward all these years. Instead, it just made him feel more pressured, more trapped. If he was going to make a change, this was the time, before he got so deeply entrenched in his urban career and lifestyle that he couldn't get out.

Cal closed his eyes. He wanted to go back to the mountains, back to the place where he felt more in touch with nature, with himself and with his God. Cal hadn't let his spiritual life slip since coming to the city. It was too important to him to neglect. But it was harder here to retain a sense of balance, to stay focused on the really important things in life. There were too many distractions, too many demands, too much emphasis on materialism, power, prestige and "getting ahead."

Cal's priorities had always been different. Position and money meant nothing to him personally. Their only value, as far as he could see, was that they gave him the means to help others who were less fortunate. In his job, he did his best to see justice served, which helped humanity in general. That, in turn, provided a good income, which allowed him to make life better for Gram and his father. And he was able to contribute both time and dollars to the causes he believed in, such as Saint Vincent's. So plenty of good had come from his career choice. Was he being selfish to consider changing the status quo?

Cal rose, walked restlessly over to the window and stared pensively out at the city lights. In his heart, he wanted to go home, back to the mountains where he could spend his days free of the confines of concrete and steel and glass. There was a part of him deep inside that had always yearned to share the beauty of nature with others hungry for nourishment for their souls. Though he had no specific plans for it, he'd completed a degree in forestry last year by going to night school. It was just something he'd wanted to do, and he'd shared the accomplishment with very few. Even Gram didn't know.

Cal sighed. He knew that few people would understand his feelings about the mountains. Certainly no one in the city, and very few at home. Gram did. But not his father. And the last thing he wanted to do was disappoint the man who had sacrificed so much for him. As his father saw it, Cal was his one success in life. If Cal scaled down his lifestyle, gave up his high-profile job and moved back home, his father would feel that all his efforts had been for nothing, that he was a failure after all. And Cal didn't know if he could do that to the man who had given him life and love so abundantly. Nor was he sure he should walk away from his present job, knowing he was good at it and that he did, sometimes, make a difference.

Cal jammed his fists into his pockets and looked up at the sky, trying to discern the stars that shone so brightly in the mountains but here were dimmed by the glare of city lights.

Lord, I need Your guidance, he prayed. *I want to do the right thing, but I need direction. I need to know Your will. You know I want to go home, that my heart is most at peace in the mountains. But maybe my dad's needs and my work here are more important. Please help me make the decision that best serves You. And, Lord—please do it soon. Because I feel like a man in limbo. I'm torn between two worlds, and I don't think I can give my best to either until this issue is resolved.*

Chapter Three

Amy took one last look in the mirror, nervously brushed a stray strand of hair back into place and glanced at her watch. Cal Richards was late.

For a moment she wondered if he'd stood her up, then quickly dismissed her doubt. There might be many things she didn't like about the assistant prosecuting attorney, but somehow she sensed he was a man of honor who played by the rules and kept his promises. If he was late, there was a reason.

Amy had no idea where they were going for dinner, so she'd chosen a middle-of-the-road outfit—nice enough for a dressy place, but not too dressy for a casual restaurant. She looked at herself critically. Since the only pleasant thing Cal Richards had ever said to her related to her appearance, she'd taken pains to look especially nice tonight. Her fashionably short, slim black skirt and two-inch heels enhanced the line of her legs, and the jade-green, jewel-neckline jacquard silk blouse softly hugged her curves and shimmered in the light. A wide, black leather belt emphasized her small waist, and a clunky hammered gold necklace and matching earrings added an elegant touch. She'd softened her usual sleek, businesslike hairstyle by blow-drying her fine hair into gentle waves that fluffed around her shoulders, and she'd added a touch of eye shadow that brought out the green of her eyes.

Amy studied her image for another moment, then gave a satisfied nod. This was definitely the right look, she decided. She could be any young woman going out on a Friday-night date. The fact that there was an ulterior motive—well, if she was lucky, Cal Richards would quickly forget all about that.

The doorbell rang and Amy's pulse kicked into high gear. She forced herself to take a couple of deep, steadying breaths, squared her shoulders, plastered an artificial smile on her face and then walked purposefully toward the door, determined to give this evening her best shot. As she reached for the knob, the image of a boxing match, complete with a gong followed by the voice of an announcer saying "Round one," suddenly flashed through her mind. An appropriate analogy, she reflected, her lips quirking wryly. Then, with her adrenaline pumping for the battle of wits ahead, she opened the door.

The sight that greeted her instantly wiped the smile off her face. It appeared Cal Richards had already fought round one—and lost. His tie was askew, his hair was mussed and he was holding a bloody handkerchief to his nose and sporting a rapidly blackening eye.

She stared at him speechlessly for several seconds before she found her voice. "Good heavens, what happened?" she finally sputtered, her face a mask of shock.

"Where's your phone?"

"What?"

"Your phone. I need to report a mugging."

Her eyes widened. "You're kidding!"

He glared at her, his voice muffled behind the handkerchief. "Do I look like I'm kidding?"

"No. I mean...I can't believe this! Look, come in. Sit down. Are you all right?" She took his arm and guided him toward the couch, pushing the door shut with her foot. Once he was seated she scurried for the portable phone and handed it to him. "I'll get some ice. And a towel."

"Don't bother."

She ignored him and headed toward the kitchen. By the time she returned, the phone was lying on the coffee table and he was trying vainly to staunch the flow of blood with his very inadequate handkerchief. She thrust the towel into his hand.

"Here. Use this. And tilt your head back. Then put this on your eye." She placed the ice bag in his other hand.

"Has anyone ever told you you're bossy?" he grumbled, wincing as he gingerly settled the ice bag against his bruised skin.

She grinned. "I think my sister might have said that a few times through the years."

"Well, she was right. Listen, the police will be here in a few minutes. I'm sorry to put you in the middle of this."

"Do you want to tell me what happened?"

"Two thugs jumped me in the parking lot. I didn't even see them coming," he said in disgust. "I'm usually more alert than that." And he would have been tonight, too, if he hadn't been so preoccupied with this obligatory date, he thought ruefully.

Amy frowned and sank into the nearest chair. "I've never heard of anything like that happening here before."

"There's always a first time. No place is really safe, Ms. Winter. You ought to know that. You cover the crime beat."

She sighed. "Look, can we move past the 'Mr.' and 'Ms.' business? It's starting to seem kind of silly."

Even with only one good eye, his piercing gaze was intimidating, and she shifted uncomfortably. But instead of responding, he suddenly closed his eyes and leaned wearily back against the couch.

Amy frowned. He looked pale. Maybe he was hurt worse than he was letting on, she thought worriedly as a wave of panic swept over her.

"Look, Mr. Richards, are you sure you don't need an ambulance or something?" She rose and hovered over him nervously.

He opened his good eye and she thought she saw a glimmer of amusement in its depths. "Just make it Cal. And no, I'll be okay. But thanks."

The doorbell rang, and with one last worried glance at him, she hurried to answer it.

For the next few minutes she stayed in the background while the officer and Cal spoke. They obviously knew each other, and their mutual respect was evident. Cal described the two young men as best he could, told the officer they'd only been interested in the hundred dollars in his money clip and roughing him up a bit, and once more declined medical assistance.

"I've been taken care of," he said, directing a brief smile toward Amy.

"Okay, then." The officer stood and closed his notebook. "I'm awfully sorry about this, Cal."

"It's not your fault, Mitch. You guys do the best you can. You can't be everywhere at once."

There was a warmth in Cal's voice that Amy had never heard before, and she looked at him curiously. Up until now, she'd only seen two sides of him—the incisive prosecuting attorney at work in the courtroom, and the reticent, abrupt, potential news source who held her profession, and as a result, her, in low esteem. This human side, this warmth, was new. And quite refreshing. Not to mention appealing, she realized with a jolt.

"We haven't had much trouble in this area before." The officer frowned and sent a troubled look toward Amy. "Have you heard or seen anything suspicious recently, ma'am?"

"No. Never. But I've only lived here six months."

Mitch stared at her for a moment. "Aren't you on TV? One of the news shows?"

"Yes."

"This would have to happen on my beat," he said in dismay. "Listen, you're not going to…"

"No!" Cal and Amy answered in unison, and with equal vehemence. He sent her an amused look and she flushed.

"There's more important news to report than a mugging," Amy said with a shrug.

"Yeah." Mitch frowned and turned his attention back to Cal. "This was probably just a freak incident. Still, we'll beef up patrols in this area for a while. And if we get any leads on those two, we'll let you know."

"Thanks."

Amy let the officer out, then returned to the living room. Cal was standing now, the ice pack still clamped against his eye, but his nose had stopped bleeding. "Could I use your bathroom? I'd like to clean up a little."

"Sure. Right down the hall."

She watched him disappear, then sank onto the sleek, modular couch. She'd speculated all week about how this evening would play out, but never in a million years would she have dreamed up this scenario!

Cal was gone a long time, and when he returned the only lingering physical evidence of the mugging was the black eye. Aside from that, he looked great, she realized, getting past his face for the first time all evening. His dark gray suit sat well on his broad shoulders, and she figured he must put in time at a gym to maintain such a trim, athletic appearance. Despite the trauma of the past hour, his white shirt still looked crisp, and his elegant red-and-navy-striped tie was now ramrod straight. He'd restored order to his thick, dark brown hair, as well, and for once his brown eyes seemed friendly rather than adversarial.

"Feeling better?" she asked.

"Much. I rinsed out the towel. It should be okay after it's washed, but I'll be happy to replace it if you prefer."

Amy waved his suggestion aside. "Don't even think about it. I'm just sorry about all this." She sighed and leaned back. "Well, so much for our date."

He weighed the ice pack in his hand and raised his brows quizzically. "Are you calling it off?"

She looked at him in surprise. "Aren't you? I mean, you were just mugged! You can't possibly feel like going out."

He shrugged. "I'll admit those two thugs hurt my pride.

And my pocketbook. But not my appetite. And I still have my credit cards. I'm willing to give it a shot, as long as you don't mind being seen with a guy who has a shiner. Besides, this way I can get all the unpleasantness out of the way in one night—a mugging and this date.'' His teasing tone and crooked grin softened his words.

Amy stared at him. He was actually smiling at her! Genuinely smiling! And suddenly her pulse did the oddest thing. It started to race. Not the way it did when she was nervous about confronting a hostile source for a story. No, this was altogether different. This was almost a pleasant sensation. And why on earth had a thrilling little tingle just run up her spine? Good heavens, if she didn't know better, she'd think she was attracted to the man! Which was ridiculous. After all, this wasn't even a real date. It was a strategy. And she would do well to remember that, she admonished herself.

Amy swallowed and tried for a flippant tone. ''Putting my date on par with a mugging isn't the most flattering comparison I've ever heard.''

He smiled again. ''You must admit there is a similarity. The muggers wanted money, you want information. But I guarantee they were more successful than you'll be.''

''Maybe I should resort to strong-arming, like they did,'' she replied pertly, getting into the teasing spirit.

He eyed her speculatively, the quick sweep of his gaze lingering just a bit too long on her shapely, crossed legs. ''Unless you're a black belt, I don't think that will work. Or maybe you're referring to something besides physical force,'' he countered with a lazy smile.

Amy stared at him. The man was actually flirting with her! The buttoned-up, stuffed-shirt, play-by-the-rules assistant prosecuting attorney was letting his hair down! The transformation in his demeanor was amazing! Apparently he had a sense of humor after all.

Or did he? she wondered, her eyes suddenly growing troubled. Maybe he *wasn't* teasing. Maybe he was hinting that he might be willing to answer her questions if she cooperated in other ways. He *had* made it clear that he thought she was attractive. He hadn't struck her as the type to even think along those lines, but, after all, she hardly knew him. And it wouldn't be the first time someone had suggested such a thing. She just hadn't expected it from him, she admitted, oddly disappointed. He seemed somehow to radiate integrity and honor and…well, goodness, corny as that might sound.

Amy hoped her first impression was right, that his last remark had just been innocent flirting, but in case she was wrong, she needed to clarify the parameters of this date right now. She rose, tilted her chin up and gazed at him levelly.

"Look, Mr. Richards, don't get the wrong idea. I—"

"I thought we were past the 'Mr.' stage."

"Maybe. Maybe not. I don't know what you're thinking right now, and I might be jumping to conclusions, but let me make something very clear. I want to find a way to make my coverage on the Jamie Johnson story stand out. I want that very much. Enough to go to some pretty extreme lengths, including spending five hundred dollars for a date with a man who dislikes me on the slim chance that I might get some piece of information I can use. But I don't intend to make a…personal…investment in this story. That's not my style. It never has been, and it never will be."

Now it was Cal's turn to stare. Good heavens, did she really think he was insinuating that for the right "personal investment," as she put it, he might be willing to offer her a few crumbs of information? What kind of man did she think he was? he thought indignantly. He opened his mouth to set her straight, then suddenly recalled some advice Gram had once offered, which had always held him in good stead: Think before you speak. And put yourself in the other person's shoes before jumping to conclusions.

He stifled his sharp retort and instead took a moment to study the woman across from him, looking for the first time past her superficial beauty. There was spirit in her deep green eyes, and intelligence and sensitivity, he realized. Her posture was defiant, but the subtle quiver in her hand as she reached up to brush a stray strand of hair back from her face was more revealing. To the world she might appear brash and assertive and so ambitious that she was willing to push the bounds of ethics for the sake of a scoop, but suddenly he knew better. Amy Winter had principle. And character. Yes, she wanted success. But not at any price.

He admired her for that, admired her for setting clear boundaries and taking a stand. After all, she really didn't know him, he reminded himself, and the crime beat was filled with seedy characters. With her looks, she'd probably been propositioned more times than she could remember as a trade-off for information. Once more he felt a surge of anger. Not *at* her this time, but *for* her. She'd obviously been subjected to offensive behavior and suggestions often enough to make her suspect his motives.

Instinctively he reached out to touch her arm, but at her startled jerk, he withdrew his hand immediately. He could feel her tension quivering almost palpably in the room. She was like a young colt, he realized. Skittish and suddenly unsure and ready to bolt at the slightest provocation. It was not the behavior he'd expected from the sophisticated, glib, always-in-control newswoman he'd encountered up until now.

"Look, let's sit down for a minute, okay?" he suggested gently.

She eyed him warily, trying to read the expression in his eyes. The man was like a chameleon, changing from moment to moment. She could deal with the difficult, evasive assistant prosecuting attorney. She was used to that type. She could also deal with men who thought they could barter for favors. Unfortunately, she'd had experience with that type, too. But the way Cal Richards was looking at her now—with compassion and concern and a disconcerting insight—threw her off balance. And for a woman who liked to be in control, that was *not* a pleasant sensation. After all, *she* might know that confrontation made her uncomfortable, but she'd always done a good job hiding that from the world. Until now. For some reason, she had a feeling Cal had picked up on it. And that was downright scary. A "danger" signal flashed in her mind, and somehow she sensed that it would be a lot safer if he left right now, if they forgot about this date and—

"Please."

The single word, quietly spoken, and the warmth in his eyes, melted her resistance. Even though she had a feeling she was making a mistake, she did as he asked and gingerly sat on the couch, folding her hands tightly in her lap. He sat beside her, keeping a modest distance between them.

"I think we need to clear the air here," he said, his gaze locked on hers. "I was only teasing a few minutes ago. For the record, I do not indulge in, nor condone, physical affection except in the context of a committed relationship. It seems that might be one of the few things you and I agree on. Besides keeping my mugging out of the news, that is."

He smiled then, his eyes reassuring and warm, and Amy looked down, twisting her hands in her lap, feeling like an idiot for overreacting. There was no way she could doubt his sincerity, and a flush of embarrassment rose to her cheeks. Drawing a deep breath, she forced herself to meet his gaze.

"I'm sorry I jumped to conclusions," she said quietly.

"I have a feeling you had reason to."

She conceded the point with a nod. "I don't always meet the most ethical people in my work."

"I can imagine."

She looked down again. "Listen, why don't you just go home and get some rest? You've been through enough tonight. Just forget about the date, okay?"

Cal frowned and studied her profile: smooth forehead, finely shaped nose, firm chin, the slender sweep of her neck. At the moment she looked more like a fragile and vulnerable woman than a brash reporter. An unexpected surge of protectiveness swept over him, and his frown deepened. Now what was *that* all about? He didn't even *like* Amy Winter! And she'd just let him off the hook, released him from the obligation to go on the date he'd been dreading. This was his chance to make a quick exit. Except, strangely enough, he suddenly didn't want to leave.

When the silence lengthened, Amy glanced up cautiously and tried to smile. "Are you still here? I thought you'd be out the door in three seconds after that reprieve."

So had he. Why was he still sitting here? For a man who spent his days finding answers to difficult questions, this one left him stumped. Maybe it was simply his sense of fairness, he rationalized. After all, she'd paid good money for this evening, and he owed her dinner. That was certainly the easy answer—even if he had the uncomfortable feeling it wasn't the *right* one. But now was not the time to analyze his motivation for wanting to stay. He could think about that later. In fact, he *would* think about it later—whether he wanted to or not, he realized ruefully. And he had a feeling that the answer was going to be a whole lot more complicated than simple fairness. Still, it was a good enough response to Amy's question.

"I owe you dinner. And I pay my debts."

She hesitated. Then, with a little shrug, she capitulated. "We could at least make it another night, if you'd prefer."

"Like I said, as long as you don't mind having an escort who attracts attention, I'm game."

With or without the black eye, Cal Richards would attract attention, Amy thought. Tall, distinguished, handsome—he'd turn women's heads in any room he entered. If he thought the black eye was the only reason he'd be noticed, he was either slow or totally without vanity. And she knew it wasn't the former. The fact that it must be the latter was refreshing. In her world, appearance—for both men and women—was at least as important as skill and often received far more attention. To discover someone who seemed totally unaware of his appeal was a rare—and pleasant—occurrence.

"I'm used to attention," she hedged.

"I'm sure you are. Even Mitch recognized you. I imagine that gets old."

She shrugged. "Not yet. It's still kind of fun, most of the time."

Cal shook his head. "Well, to each his own. Personally I prefer anonymity."

"Then maybe we *should* cancel tonight. Because between the two of us, I guarantee we're going to attract attention."

He frowned. "Well, I have an idea, although it's not much of a date for five hundred dollars," he said slowly.

"What?"

"Let's have dinner here."

She stared at him. "Are you serious?"

"Absolutely."

Amy hesitated, then shrugged. "Okay." She took a quick mental inventory of her freezer. "I think I have a couple of frozen microwave dinners. And I might have a—"

"Whoa!" He held up his hands. "I wasn't asking you to supply the food."

She frowned. "Then what did you have in mind? Pizza?"

He grinned. "Hardly. Will you trust me on this?"

She shrugged. "Why not? Nothing else tonight has turned out the way I expected."

"Look at the bright side. The evening has to get better, because it can't get any worse."

Amy had to admit that he was being an awfully good sport about the whole thing, and she smiled in return. "Too true."

"I'll just need to use your phone again."

"Okay. I'll set the table."

"We'll salvage this evening yet," he promised with an engaging grin as he reached for the phone.

As Amy got out plates and silverware, she glanced once or twice toward Cal. He was mostly turned away from her, but she caught a glimpse of his strong profile now and then. He wasn't exactly handsome in the classic sense, but there was something about his face, some compelling quality—call it "character" for lack of a better term—that touched her. It was odd, really. In an evening full of surprises, this was the most surprising of all—the discovery that she was actually starting to *like* Cal Richards. It didn't make any sense, of course. She was still convinced they were polar opposites in many ways, not to mention at odds professionally. Nevertheless she had a strange feeling that somewhere deep inside, at some core level, they were more alike than either had suspected. It was an intriguing, unsettling and surprising thought.

But the surprises for the evening weren't over yet, it seemed. When she returned to the living room, Cal had put on one of her favorite jazz CDs.

"I like your taste in music," he commented.

"Thanks."

"Dinner will be here shortly."

"Can I ask what we're having?"

He grinned. "I think I'll surprise you."

She tilted her head, a small smile lifting her lips. "I like surprises."

"Really? I'll have to remember that."

She started to say "Why?" then caught herself. It was just a meaningless remark. After tonight, the only time their paths would cross would be in the courtroom, she reminded herself, surprised at the sudden slump in her spirits. She forced herself to focus on the present, reminding herself she had a job to do tonight. That was what this evening was all about after all. With an effort she smiled. "Would you like something to drink?"

"That would be great."

"Would you like a soft drink, or something stronger?"

"Do you have any wine?"

Amy bit her lip. She was pretty sure she had some wine left from a gathering she'd had at Christmastime. "I think so."

"It's not something I indulge in often, but I could use a glass tonight."

Amy returned to the kitchen and rummaged around in the refrigerator, triumphantly withdrawing a bottle of merlot. She had just enough for two glasses, which she carried back to the living room, handing one to Cal.

He waited until she was seated, then lifted his glass. "May the rest of the evening be better," he said.

She raised her glass. "I'll second that."

Amy wasn't sure if it was the toast or the wine or just the fact that they both seemed to let their guard down, but from that moment on, the evening took a decided turn for the better.

By the time they'd finished their wine, dinner arrived, and it was like no "carryout" Amy had ever seen. It came via courier—two gourmet dinners from one of the city's finest restaurants, on china plates inside domed food warmers, complete with salad and a chocolate dessert to die for.

Amy could only stare in awe as Cal arranged the food on the table, shaking her head in wonder the whole time.

"Well, if you can't go to the restaurant, bring the restaurant to you," she murmured finally. "I'm impressed. You must have good connections to get this kind of treatment. I didn't think 'carryout' was even in their vocabulary."

Cal shrugged. "The owner and I go way back. Trust me. I'll owe him for this," he said over his shoulder with a grin. Then he stepped back and surveyed the table. "Now, all we need is a little candlelight, and we can pretend we're actually at the restaurant."

"That I can supply."

As they leisurely made their way through the dinner, Amy realized that she was truly enjoying herself. Cal was a good conversationalist, moving with ease from topic to topic, displaying an impressive knowledge and insight on everything from world events to Broadway musicals. The more they talked, the more she realized how much they had in common. Their tastes in art and music were similar, and they were surprisingly in sync politically. It wasn't until they started talking about more personal things, especially their careers, that their differences emerged.

"So tell me why you went into broadcast news," he said as they sipped their coffee and dug into the rich dessert.

Amy cupped her chin in her hand. "For the glamour. And the excitement. Not to mention it pays well," she said with a grin.

"Is money that important?"

"It is when you don't have it."

"So I take it you don't come from a wealthy background."

She made a face. "Hardly. I grew up on a farm in Ohio. We weren't poor, but there was never any money to spare.

It never bothered my sister, Kate. She was perfectly content with that life and had no desire to leave the farm. I, on the other hand, was drawn to the lights of the big city. I figured there was more to life than cows and plows, and I was determined to find it.''

"Have you?"

She looked surprised. "Sure. I mean, this—" her arm swept the room, with its panoramic view of the city lights "—is what I've always wanted."

"And you've never looked back? Never questioned your decision?"

Amy shifted uncomfortably under his suddenly intense gaze. Funny he should ask that, when she'd done that very thing not long ago. But as she'd told herself then, it was too late for second thoughts. And anyway, she *did* like her life and her job.

"Not really. Sure, there are some parts of my job that I don't particularly care for. But someday, if I play my cards right, I'll snag an anchor slot and have the freedom to pick and choose the kind of stories I cover."

"Such as?"

"Human-interest pieces. Stories about ordinary people who do extraordinary things. Feature reporting, more in-depth than what I do now, where you have the time to do stories that leave people uplifted and inspired. I get to do a bit of that now, but not nearly enough. It's really satisfying to shine the light on good, decent people instead of the dregs of humanity who usually dominate the news. There *are* good people out there, and I like to find ways to give them their moment in the spotlight. I think it would also help young people to see that nice guys don't always finish last.''

Amy had gotten more and more passionate as she spoke, and Cal's attentive—and approving—gaze, as well as the sudden warmth in his eyes, brought a flush to her cheeks. She didn't usually get so carried away, nor did she typically reveal so much about her personal feelings. She had no idea why she'd done so tonight. She *did* know it was time to shift the focus. "So now you know all the reasons why I left the farm and never looked back," she finished lightly. "And how about you? What's your background? How did you get into law?"

He gave her a quick smile. "I guess turnabout is fair play. I grew up in Tennessee, in the shadow of the Smoky Mountains. Unlike you, I had to think long and hard about leaving."

"Why did you?"

He shrugged. "A lot of reasons. For one thing, law seemed like a career where I could do some good, help people, advance the cause of justice. I was pretty idealistic in the early days."

His reasons for his career choice made many of Amy's sound shallow and self-serving, she realized, and she took a sip of coffee while she mulled over his answer—especially the past tense in the last sentence. "And you aren't idealistic anymore?"

His eyes grew troubled. "When the system works the way it's supposed to, when I can really help someone and justice is served, it's incredibly satisfying," he said slowly. "Unfortunately, that doesn't happen nearly often enough."

"Is it happening in the Jamie Johnson case?"

"I guess we'll see when the verdict comes in."

"But you think he's guilty."

"I'm prosecuting him."

"You're avoiding the question, Counselor."

"That's right."

She sighed. He'd easily deflected her few subtle probes about the trial during the evening. So far, she had nothing usable, no lead that would give her the edge she so badly wanted. Then again, she hadn't pressed all that hard. For some reason, her heart just hadn't been in it. Besides, it had quickly become apparent to her that while she was a good reporter who knew how to ask the right questions, he was an even better attorney who knew how to avoid answering them.

"I'm still going to try and find an angle to make my coverage stand out," she warned.

"I wish you luck." He took a final sip of his coffee, then glanced at his watch. "Well, for an evening that almost ended before it began, we've managed to make a night of it."

She checked the time and her eyes grew wide. It was after eleven. "I had no idea!"

He smiled, then rose and began clearing the table. "I promised Joe I'd have all this stuff back safe and sound tomorrow."

She stood also. "Let me help."

When everything was carefully packed, Cal lifted the box and Amy followed him to the door. He turned to her, but the simple good-night he'd planned to say stuck in his throat. Suddenly he didn't want to leave the softly lit room, where the candles cast flickering shadows on the wall in the dining alcove and sensuous jazz played quietly in the background. He drew in a slow, unsteady breath, inhaling the faint, pleasing fragrance that emanated from Amy's hair. Suddenly Cal felt warm. Too warm. He cleared his throat and shifted the box.

"Well…"

"The evening didn't turn out exactly as we planned, did it?" Amy said softly, her green eyes luminous in the golden light.

"Not quite."

"Take care of that eye."

"I will. Listen…thanks for being a good sport about the dinner."

"You were the one who was a good sport. And I had a great dinner."

"You can't go wrong with Joe's food."

Amy *had* enjoyed the food. But the dinner had been great for a lot of other reasons, she realized as she stared up at Cal. The assistant prosecuting attorney had turned out to be an incredible date, even if she hadn't gotten the hoped-for lead. In fact, this evening had been well worth the five-hundred-dollar price tag. It had been a very long time since she'd enjoyed a date this much. And the truth was, she was sorry it was over. Mostly because she knew there wouldn't be a next time.

"Well…" Cal repeated. "I guess I'd better go. It's late."

"Right."

Still he hesitated. Cal wasn't sure why. For some reason the unexpected events of the evening had thrown him off balance. And he wasn't thinking only of the mugging, he realized, as he looked into Amy's appealing green eyes. Their gazes locked for several eternal seconds, and he wished he knew what she was thinking. Was she suddenly as confused as he was? Had her pulse lurched into overdrive, too? His gaze dropped to her lips. Was she fighting the same surprising and powerful urge he was?

Cal had no idea. All he knew was that he was glad he was holding the box of dishes. Because as he said a very rapid good-night and escaped into the hall, he knew that if his arms weren't otherwise occupied, he would be very tempted to put them to another use. And he didn't think that would be wise at all.

Chapter Four

"Amy? Have I caught you at a bad time?"

Amy smiled and grabbed her tea as she headed for the couch. "Not at all. It's great to hear your voice, Kate." She sat on the couch and tucked her feet under her. "How's St. Louis?"

"It's too soon to tell, after only a week. But it doesn't matter where we live, as long as I'm with Jack."

"Still crazy in love with that handsome hunk you married, I see," Amy teased.

"Absolutely. You should try it sometime."

"Well, when I meet the right handsome hunk, I just might do that." For some reason, an image of Cal flitted through her mind, and she frowned. How odd. If ever two people had different philosophies of life, it was them. Though they did agree on some things, their basic priorities and motivations were at opposite ends of the spectrum. Not a good omen for a long-term relationship—even if they were interested in pursuing one. Which, of course, they weren't.

"I'm sure you meet all kinds of handsome men in your business," Kate scoffed.

"With egos to match, too," Amy countered dryly.

"Oh, come on. You must meet *some* guys who aren't self-centered."

Again Amy thought of Cal. "Actually, I did meet one recently."

"Well, that's more like it! Tell me all."

"I bought a date with him."

There was a beat of silence on the other end of the line before Kate spoke. "Do you want to explain that?"

Amy grinned. "I bought a date with him at a charity auction."

"You've resorted to buying dates? Things must be worse than I thought!"

This time Amy laughed. "I had an ulterior motive. He's the prosecuting attorney in a high-profile case I'm covering, and I was hoping he'd let something slip that would give me an angle."

"Oh." The disappointment in Kate's voice was obvious. "So it was just a business thing."

"Yeah. But I actually had a good time."

"Did you get your angle?"

"Unfortunately, no. But he was surprisingly pleasant, considering that we'd clashed in every previous encounter. And he was a really good sport." Amy recounted the story of the mugging.

"He sounds nice," Kate commented. "Are you sure you don't want to pursue this?"

"Trust me, Kate. I am the last person Cal Richards wants to see again. He admitted himself that he was dreading our date, so the odds of—" The ringing of the doorbell interrupted her. "Can you hold a minute? There's someone at the door."

"Sure."

Amy set her mug down and strode toward the door, pausing to peer through the peephole. All she could see was a large, green blob, so she cautiously cracked the door, leaving the chain lock in place.

A face appeared around the blob, which Amy now realized was a flower arrangement wrapped in green paper. "Amy Winter?"

"Yes."

"These are for you."

Amy gave the young man a puzzled frown. "Are you sure?"

He recited the address, and her frown deepened. "Well, you've got the right place," she conceded. She closed the door and slid the chain across, then opened it. The young man grinned and placed the vase in Amy's hands. "Enjoy."

As he disappeared down the steps, she stared at the cloud of green tissue. Who in the world would be sending her flowers?

Suddenly she remembered that Kate was waiting. Shoving the door shut with her foot, she moved quickly back to the couch, placing the vase carefully on the coffee table.

"Kate? Sorry."

"Do you need to hang up?"

"No. It was just a delivery. Flowers believe it or not."

"Flowers? Okay, sister dear, you've been holding out on me. Who are they from?"

"I haven't a clue," Amy confessed.

"There must be a card."

Amy poked at the tissue, discovered a small white envelope and rapidly scanned the note inside.

"Please accept my apologies again for the change in plans last night. And thanks for being such a good sport. Cal."

Amy stared at it, stunned. "I don't believe it!"

"What?"

"They're from Cal Richards!"

"No kidding! And this is the man who was never going to contact you again, huh?"

Amy ignored Kate's jibe and tore the paper away from the vase, letting out a soft exclamation of pleasure. "Oh, Amy, you should see this arrangement! It's gorgeous! A dozen peach-colored roses with baby's breath and fern. It's stunning!"

"Sounds like there could be potential here after all," Kate mused.

Amy looked at the card again. "It's just an apology, Kate. For the change in plans. That's what the card says. After all, I did pay five hundred dollars for that date."

"Five hundred dollars!" Now it was Kate's turn to sound incredulous. "Wow! Still, he could have sent carnations and daisies. Or just a note. Or nothing at all."

Amy fingered the card thoughtfully. "He told me last night that he always pays his debts. I guess he felt he owed me more than an eat-in dinner."

"He sounds like a *very* nice man, Amy."

"He is. He's just not for me," Amy declared, refusing to read more into the gesture than she was sure Cal intended. "Now tell me more about you. Are you adjusting okay since the move?"

"That was a pretty abrupt—what do you call it again in

your business? A segue? But I can take a hint. Pretty well, actually, though the move is only the first in a series of adjustments.''

"What do you mean?''

"I have some other news.''

Amy heard the undertone of excitement in Kate's voice and held her breath. "You have my full attention.''

"We're going to have a baby!''

Amy's heart soared. Kate and Jack had been trying unsuccessfully for five years to start the family they both wanted, but it had been a frustrating and disheartening process. Amy knew that over the last year Kate had begun to lose hope, had struggled to come to grips with the fact that perhaps it simply wasn't meant to be. And now this!

"Oh, Kate, I'm thrilled! When are you due?''

"October 26. I've known for a couple of weeks, but we wanted to make sure everything was okay before we told anyone.''

"I bet Mom is excited.''

"Ecstatic. A grandmother at last!''

They chatted excitedly for a few more minutes, but when Amy at last replaced the receiver, her euphoric mood suddenly evaporated. She was happy for Kate, of course. That went without saying. She knew how much her sister wanted a family. But she also had an odd and unexpected feeling of melancholy, which puzzled her. It wasn't as if she would want to change places with Kate. She liked her life, had worked hard to make her ambitious goals a reality and was now beginning to reap the rewards of all her hard work. But the price had been high. Too high, according to her mother, who made it a point to occasionally remind her younger daughter that her success had come at the expense of other things. Like a personal life. And a husband. And a family.

As if she didn't know, Amy thought with a sigh. She took a sip of her now-tepid tea and leaned back against the couch. It wasn't that she didn't want those things. It was just that now was not the time for them. Which didn't mean that she was immune to loneliness, she admitted. There were times when she yearned for a caring touch, or a simple, loving look, or the comfort of knowing that someone was waiting for her at the end of the day. But throughout the years she'd learned a lot about self-discipline and delayed gratification. Someday she'd go after those things, applying the same single-minded determination with which she was now pursuing her career goals. But she couldn't do both at once, and right now her career took priority.

Her gaze drifted to the roses, and she reached out to gently touch a velvety petal. She had to admit that she'd enjoyed her rare social evening last night. She'd been pleasantly surprised by Cal Richards, had begun to see him in a new and appealing light. He seemed like a decent, caring, considerate man. Under other circumstances, maybe something could have developed between them, despite their differences. But Amy didn't have the time. And she was pretty sure Cal didn't have the inclination.

"So how did the big date go on Fri—good grief! What happened to you?"

Cal glanced up at Cynthia, who was staring at him wide-eyed. "I have a black eye," he replied dryly.

"I can see that. Was there a brawl at the restaurant or something?"

"We didn't go to a restaurant. We stayed at her place and ordered in."

Cynthia's mouth dropped open. "For five hundred bucks you give her takeout? Well, that explains it. I'd have socked you, too, after paying that kind of money for a date."

Cal smiled. "That's not quite what happened."

Cynthia dropped into the chair across from his desk. "I didn't think so. Tell me everything."

"I got mugged in the parking lot of her apartment."

Once more Cynthia's eyes grew wide. "Mugged! You're kidding!"

"Those were *her* exact words when she opened the door. And, as I said then, do I *look* like I'm kidding?"

Cynthia eyed him speculatively. "I guess not. What happened?"

"Two thugs jumped me. They got my money, I got a bloody nose and a black eye. Considering the circumstances, she very graciously consented to eat in."

"So what did you get? Pizza?"

"You're two for two, now. Her words, again. And no, we didn't get pizza. I have a friend in the restaurant business who sent something over."

"What restaurant?"

When he told her, she gave a low whistle. "Now *that's* a carryout! I bet the lady was impressed."

"She seemed to enjoy it."

"So…are you going to see her again?"

He looked at her in surprise. "Why would I?"

"Didn't you like her?"

Cal frowned. As a matter of fact he had—despite himself. She had many qualities that he found appealing—and intriguing. She was a woman of paradoxes—gung-ho about her career, as well as smart, savvy, ambitious and willing to push hard to get the job done, but also a woman who seemed to find aggressiveness and the in-your-face demands of her profession distasteful and who clearly had solid moral and ethical values.

However, it was equally clear that the two of them had very different priorities. Even under ideal conditions—and the fact that she was a newswoman pursuing him as a source was definitely *not* ideal—he doubted whether anything serious could ever develop between them.

"Well, if you have to think that long about it, I guess I have my answer," Cynthia said dryly. "But not to worry. We'll find you somebody yet, Cal."

Cal shook his head. "Give it up, Cyn. I don't have the time."

"You should *make* the time."

"Now you sound like my grandmother."

"I'm sure she's a very wise woman."

"She is. And you're both right. And I'll get around to it one of these days."

"Hmph. By the time you get around to it, there won't be anything left to get," she said pertly as she turned to go.

Cal watched her exit. At thirty-four, he didn't exactly consider himself over-the-hill. But he *was* well past the age when most of his friends and acquaintances had married. In fact, many of them had a couple of kids by now. Though he'd admitted it to no one, the notion of "settling down," as his grandmother would say, held more and more appeal for him these days. It would be nice to have a wife and children to come home to at the end of the day.

Trouble was, his *day* often didn't end until well into the *night*, which wasn't conducive to family life. At least, not the kind of family life he wanted.

Which brought him back once again to the tough choice he was facing. Stay in the city to fight for justice and continue building his promising career, or make a radical lifestyle change and return to the mountains where his soul was most at peace. Considering his unsettled state, it wouldn't be fair to pursue a romance. Besides, only a very special woman would understand why he was discontent with his life in the city, why he was drawn so strongly to the mountains, when in the eyes of the world he seemed to have it all—success, prestige, the potential for power. And he seriously doubted whether Amy Winter was that woman.

Cal frowned. Why in the world had Amy popped into his mind again, and in such an odd context? It didn't matter in the least if she understood his motivations. Their contact in the future would be limited, and purely of a professional nature.

A week ago that scenario would have made him happy. But for some inexplicable reason, it now left him feeling vaguely depressed.

"That should do it, Steve," Amy said as she closed her notebook.

The cameraman extinguished the light and took the Minicam off his shoulder as Amy turned back to Michael Sloan, the director of the youth center.

"All we need now is some B-roll footage as background," she said. "Can we do a walk-through, see some of the activities in progress?"

"Sure." He rose and led them down the hall to a small but well-equipped computer lab. Boys ranging in age from seven or eight to mid-teens were using every available piece of equipment under the supervision of an older man, who smiled at them when they entered.

"That's John Williams, one of the volunteers," the director told Amy. "As I mentioned earlier, our volunteers are the backbone of this place. They not only provide much-needed manpower, but act as great role models for the boys, many of whom are from broken homes without a father figure."

He introduced Amy to the volunteer, and with the man's consent, she spoke with him for a few minutes on camera.

They stopped in a few other rooms, where a variety of activities, from woodworking and drawing to rehearsal for a theater production, were in progress.

"The other big part of our program is sports," Michael told her as he ushered them down the hall toward the gym. "We have athletic activities scheduled every night. Tonight it's basketball, and we are incredibly fortunate to have a prominent local attorney as one of our coaches. He's working with the young-teen team right now. He's a bit camera-shy, but I'll see what I can do to convince him to give you an interview."

Amy frowned. An attorney. Camera shy. Saint Vincent's Boy's Club. Her step faltered. Wasn't Saint Vincent's the charity Candace Bryce had referenced when she introduced Cal at the charity bachelor auction? Hadn't she said something about him participating only because Saint Vincent's would benefit? Amy hadn't made the connection until now. But surely there were other attorneys who volunteered here, she reassured herself. It would be too much of a coincidence if he happened to be here the very night she'd come to do her story. Yet somehow, deep inside, she sensed that, coincidence or not, it was him.

Amy's heart began to pound. She didn't want to intrude on Cal's off-duty "turf." It was too...well, personal. Since their "date" two weeks before, their only contact had been in the courtroom, and then only an occasional, fleeting connecting of gazes. He hadn't acknowledged the thank-you note she'd sent him for the flowers, nor had she expected him to. Their limited contact had been impersonal and therefore safe. Which was fine with her. Something strange had happened that night as he was leaving her apartment. The unexpected sizzle of electricity that had sparked between them had left her rattled. For whatever reason, Cal Richards was a distraction, and distractions were not something she needed at this point in her career.

Michael stopped at the gym door and pushed it open for her to enter. "A lot of the boys in here would be on the streets if it wasn't for people like Cal Richards," he said, confirming Amy's premonition.

Her heart stopped, then raced on. She hesitated, and both the director and Steve looked at her questioningly.

"Something wrong, Amy?" Steve asked.

She forced herself to take a deep breath. She knew her reaction was totally illogical. After all, she'd covered any number of stories that had put her in physical danger or resulted in threats of bodily harm, and she'd always remained calm and cool. This situation was a piece of cake compared to that. She could handle this, she told herself reassuringly.

But as she stepped to the door, the sight of Cal in his tank T-shirt and sweatpants, with biceps to rival a Mr.

World candidate she'd once interviewed, made her long for the relative safety of a bank robbery or an impending tornado. However, since both Steve and Michael were staring at her curiously, she was left with no choice but to enter the gym.

"Just taking a moment to observe," she replied belatedly to Steve's question. His skeptical look as she brushed past told her he didn't buy her response, but it was the best she could do.

"I'll see what I can do about that interview," Michael said. "Excuse me for just a minute."

"So what gives?" Steve asked the moment the director was out of earshot.

Amy gazed after Michael as he headed toward the group of boys clustered around Cal. "It's just that the assistant prosecuting attorney and I have…clashed…a few times."

Steve followed her gaze. "You and every other member of the press in Atlanta. Join the club. Haven't you given up on him yet?"

"I don't give up," Amy said determinedly. "I still go to the courthouse almost every day. But so far, no luck."

Just then Cal looked her way, and their gazes met for one brief moment before he turned back to Michael and said a few words. Then he directed his attention to the boys, and Michael rejoined them.

"No luck on the interview, I'm afraid," he apologized. "Cal's one of our biggest supporters—in a lot of ways— but he keeps it low-profile. His motives are purely altruistic, and he has no interest in personal recognition or accolades. However, when I explained to him that this feature would be good for Saint Vincent's and might encourage others to support our work, he did agree to some—what did you call it—B-roll filming?''

"That will be fine, Michael," Amy assured him. "I think we have plenty of other shots, so we'll just film for a few minutes here and then wrap it up."

"Great." He glanced at his watch and frowned. "I hate to run, but my daughter is in a school play tonight, and I'll just be able to make it if I leave now. Would you mind if I took off while you finish up?"

"Not at all," Amy assured him. "Thank you for your help."

"Thank *you*," he replied, shaking her hand. "You can't imagine how much this kind of publicity will mean to Saint Vincent's."

"I hope so. You do good work here, and you deserve all the support you can get."

"Thanks." He shook hands with Steve, as well. "Feel free to spend as much time as you like here. Cal just asked that you try to keep him in the background as much as possible when you film."

"No problem," Steve assured him, hoisting his Mini-cam into position.

"I'll wait over there," Amy said, nodding toward the corner where a youngster sat alone on a folding chair, watching them curiously. "Good night, Michael."

"Good night."

As Steve scoped out the gym for angles, Amy wandered over to the little boy of about seven, who was sitting on his hands, his legs wrapped around the legs of the chair. She sat beside him and smiled.

"Hi. My name's Amy. What's yours?"

"Mark." He spoke softly and hung his head.

"Well, it's nice to meet you, Mark." She nodded toward the court. "Do you play basketball?"

He shook his head. "I'm too little."

"But not for long. Pretty soon you'll be just as big as those guys out there."

He looked up at her shyly. "I hope I can play as good as my brother. He's on the team. Mr. Richards says I have po-po-potential."

He struggled with the complicated word, and Amy smiled. "Then I'm sure you do."

"Mr. Richards lets me watch. He says I can learn a lot by watching. And sometimes, when the practice is over, he shows me how to hold the ball and how to throw."

"Sounds like he's very nice."

Mark nodded vigorously. "I like to talk to him. He listens real good." Mark glanced toward Steve. "What's he doing?"

"He's shooting some video for a story we're going to do on the news about Saint Vincent's."

"Wow! You mean we're going to be on TV?"

"Yes."

"How come?"

"Because Saint Vincent's is a good place, and we want to let other people know about it."

"I like it here," Mark affirmed. "Sometimes it's not real nice at home, when my mom is sick, so Troy—that's my brother—and I come here and do stuff."

"That should be a wrap, Amy. You want anything else?"

She looked up at Steve. "I think we're done. Thanks, Steve."

"No problem. Want me to walk you to your car?"

"Sure." Saint Vincent's wasn't in the safest neighborhood, and Amy didn't take unnecessary chances.

"Let me just check in and see where I need to go next."

"Do you want to use my phone?" She reached for her purse, but he shook his head.

"Mine's in the bag. I'll stow this stuff, then call. Just give me a couple of minutes."

Amy turned back to Mark. "So you like coming to Saint Vincent's?"

He nodded emphatically. "It's neat. After school they give us cookies and milk. And the grown-ups here don't yell or throw things or anything. They talk nice to us and listen to what we say, like we're important. It makes me feel good to come here."

Amy leaned closer and laid her hand on his. "You know something, Mark? You *are* important. Every person is different, and every single one is important in his own way. There's nobody else in the whole world just like you, and nobody could ever take your place. You remember that, okay?"

Mark smiled shyly. "You're nice, Amy. I wish my mom talked like you."

"Ready to do a little practicing, Mark?"

Mark and Amy simultaneously looked up at Cal. She was glad for Mark's eager response, which momentarily distracted Cal, because for a second her voice deserted her. It was one thing to look at Cal in his workout clothes from across the gym, and quite another to have him standing only two feet away. His tank T-shirt clung to his broad chest, and with one hand on his hip and the other arm hugging the basketball to his side, his well-defined biceps made her breath catch in her throat. The man was in absolutely perfect physical condition, she realized, from his pecs to his abs. There wasn't an ounce of excess flesh on his well-toned body. Muscled chest, tapering waist, flat stomach, slim hips. To use one of Darlene's favorite expressions, Cal Richards was one hot-looking dude. If during their date she'd been impressed by the man's mind and ethics, today she was equally impressed by his physical attributes. He radiated a virility that literally took her breath away and made her respiration go haywire.

As Cal finished his brief conversation with Mark, handed him the ball and watched him scamper off, Amy reached for her purse and made a pretense of looking for her keys, trying to buy herself a few moments to restore her poise. No man had ever wreaked such havoc on her emotional and physical equilibrium by his mere proximity. That Cal Richards should be the one man who *could* seemed like a nasty trick of fate. Why couldn't some *compatible* man have had this effect on her—and about two or three years down the road?

Cal turned back to Amy, planted his hands on his hips and took a moment to study her bowed head as she searched through her purse. Her light brown hair swung forward, hiding her face, and he was glad for the momentary reprieve. He hadn't planned to speak to her. But as he'd watched her interact with Mark, he'd been struck by the quick rapport she'd established with the shy little boy, who—for good reason—had a real problem with trust and rarely said more than a few words to strangers. The fact that she had quickly broken through his reserve and established a comfort level with him said a lot. It was yet another appealing side of this intriguing woman, and he'd found himself walking over to her without making a conscious decision to do so.

Amy withdrew her keys and slung her purse over her shoulder before she looked up.

"Hello, Cal."

Her voice seemed more throaty than usual, and he suddenly found it difficult to swallow. "Hello, Amy. This is a surprise. Isn't this a bit off your normal beat?"

She shrugged. "I go where the stories are."

He glanced at his watch. "How many hours a day do you work? You were in court at nine this morning."

She looked at him steadily. "How ever many it takes."

He frowned. "But why would they assign you to two stories twelve hours apart?"

"They didn't assign this one. I proposed it and got permission to put a piece together. I'm hoping it's good enough to win airtime. But the rest of my work still needs to get done. So I do these kinds of stories after hours."

His frown deepened. "Have you had dinner?"

The impulsive question surprised him as much as it obviously did her.

"No."

He hesitated, unsure what had prompted that query. But he was in too far now to back out, and he didn't have time to analyze his motives. "Would you like to grab a bite with me? I came here directly from the office, and I'm starving."

She stared at him. Was he actually *initiating* a date? With a woman he'd gone to great lengths to avoid? "Could you repeat that? I think my ears are playing tricks on me," she said cautiously.

Cal gave her a crooked grin. "Would you believe me if I told you I'm as surprised by the invitation as you are?"

She couldn't doubt the sincerity in his eyes. "Yes."

"So how about it?"

She tilted her head and looked at him quizzically. "Can I ask why?"

He paused to consider. "That's a fair—but tough—question," he replied candidly. "Frankly I have no idea. Maybe because I feel I still owe you a dinner. Maybe because I enjoyed our evening together. Maybe because it would make my grandmother happy."

She eyed him warily, but now there was a slight twinkle in her eye. "I'm not even going to ask about that last reason."

"Good. So?"

She studied him for another few seconds, then gave a slight shrug. "Why not?"

He smiled, and the warmth in his eyes brought a flush to her cheeks. "Great. Give me ten minutes to shower and change."

Cal headed back toward the boys still on the court as Amy stared after him.

"What was that all about?"

With an effort she tore her gaze from Cal's retreating figure and looked up to find that Steve had returned. "He asked me out to dinner."

Steve's eyebrows rose. "No kidding! What brought that on?"

"I have no idea."

"Well, maybe it will give you a chance to pump him for that angle you're after."

"Maybe."

But oddly enough, for a woman who always put business first, the very last thing on her mind at the moment was the Jamie Johnson trial.

Chapter Five

By the time Cal reappeared fresh from the shower exactly ten minutes later—looking fabulous in worn jeans that fit like a glove, a cotton shirt with the long sleeves rolled back to the elbows and his wet hair even darker than usual—the modicum of poise Amy had regained during his absence immediately evaporated.

"Right on time," she remarked breathlessly, glancing at her watch as she struggled to control the sudden staccato beat of her heart.

"My grandmother always told me never to keep a pretty lady waiting," Cal said with a wink, which did nothing to restore her equilibrium.

She was glad he wasn't privy to her elevated pulse rate—although there was nothing she could do to hide the telltale flush that suffused her face at the unexpected compliment. "I think I like your grandmother," she replied, struggling for a light tone.

He chuckled. "She's a hard lady not to like. Ready?"

Amy nodded, and Cal fell into step beside her as they headed for the exit.

"Is she still in Tennessee?" Amy asked.

"Yes. Always has been, always will be."

"By choice or circumstance?"

"Choice. She's perfectly content with her cabin in the mountains and her work at the local craft co-op."

When they reached the door, Cal pushed it open, one hand in the small of her back as he guided her out. It was an impersonal gesture, born of breeding and good manners, but it nevertheless sent a tingle up her spine. Get a grip, Amy admonished herself. It's okay to enjoy this impromptu date, but remember—there's no future here. You are two very different people.

"Where are you parked?" Cal asked as he surveyed the small lot.

Amy pointed toward a late-model BMW. "Over there."

Cal noted the car, but made no comment. Instead, he turned to her, his gaze moving swiftly over her attire, taking in the royal blue jacket with black buttons, wide gold choker, black slacks and heels. "Where would you like to go? You're dressed for the Ritz, but I don't think they'd even let me in the back door," he said with an engaging grin.

She smiled and shrugged. "Anywhere is fine. Fast food, if you like."

"Oh, I think we can do a little better than that. Have you ever eaten at Rick's?"

"No."

"It's a nice place—good food, comfortable atmosphere. And not too far from your apartment, so it will be convenient."

"For me, maybe. But what about you? I'm sure your day has been as long as mine. How about somewhere in between our places?" Amy countered. "Where do you live?"

He named the modest suburb—a far cry from her up-scale neighborhood. Considering his position, she was a bit surprised—but not too much. She was beginning to realize that Cal Richards was a man who preferred a simple life and didn't have a pretentious bone in his body.

"Frankly, unless you have some other preference, I'd enjoy going to Rick's. It would be a nice change of pace. By the time I get around to dinner most nights I'm too tired to go out, so I usually just nuke something."

Amy acquiesced. "That's fine with me, then. I'll just follow you."

He waited until she was in her car, with the doors locked, before he headed to his own. She watched in the rearview mirror, and wasn't the least bit surprised when he stopped beside an older-model compact. Despite his prestigious position, Cal Richards obviously saw no need for conspicuous displays of success. The man continued to amaze—and impress—her.

When they arrived at the restaurant, he was out of his car and beside her door almost before she turned off the motor. As she reached for her purse and stepped out, she smiled. "My compliments to your mother. She obviously raised a gentleman."

Though he smiled in response, a fleeting pain passed across his eyes. "Actually, my grandmother gets most of the credit. My mom died when I was twelve."

Amy's gaze softened in sympathy. "I'm sorry."

"Thanks. It was a hard time for everyone. Dad was

beside himself, so Gram suggested we move in with her until we got past the worst of the grief. It worked out so well, we never left. I always missed Mom, of course, but Gram was great. She did a terrific job as a surrogate mother. And Dad went above and beyond, trying to make up for the fact that I only had one parent. I don't think he ever missed a single event in my life, from spelling bees to camping trips with the Scouts.''

"I take it the three of you are still close.''

"Very.'' He ushered her inside the restaurant, and smiled at the hostess. "Hello, Steph.''

"Cal! It's good to see you. It's been too long.''

"Tell me about it,'' he said ruefully. "Life's too busy. But I'm overdue for a dose of Rick's cooking.''

She picked up two menus and led the way to a quiet corner table. "I'll let him know you're here. Enjoy.''

Once they were seated, he took one brief glance at the menu then laid it aside.

"A man of quick decision, I see,'' Amy remarked.

He flashed her a grin. "No, just in a rut. I always seem to get the same thing here.''

"Which is?''

"Seafood pasta and the house salad. It's a pretty tough combination to beat.''

Amy put her menu down. "You convinced me.''

A moment later the waiter arrived with a basket of crusty French bread still warm from the oven, and Amy helped herself while Cal gave their order. She closed her eyes and smiled as she took the first bite.

"Now *this* is the way to end a long day,'' she declared.

Cal chuckled and followed her example. "It sure beats a microwave dinner.''

"Amen to that," she replied fervently. "Unfortunately, that's my usual fare."

He smiled. "I take it the kitchen isn't your favorite room."

She tilted her head and considered the question. "Actually, I *like* to cook. But there's never any time."

"That commodity does seem to be in short supply these days," he agreed with a sigh.

"Yet you manage to find time to help out at Saint Vincent's."

He shrugged dismissively. "A lot of people do a lot more."

"Maybe they're not as busy as you are."

"Some are busier. And the basketball is only one night a week."

"Michael Sloan hinted that your support went way beyond that."

Cal shifted uncomfortably. "I help out here and there in different ways," he said vaguely. "I believe in the work they do. Those kids need all the help and encouragement they can get. I've been very blessed, and I feel the need to give something back, to demonstrate my gratitude in a concrete way. Saint Vincent's lets me do that."

He made it sound as if Saint Vincent's was doing *him* a favor, she thought, once again impressed by the way he downplayed his obviously significant contribution to the boys' center. "You certainly have a fan in Mark," she observed.

Cal smiled briefly, then grew more serious. "Mark's a great kid. He's smart, ambitious and willing to learn. Which is saying a lot, considering he comes from a single-parent home headed by an alcoholic mother, has no idea who his father is and lives in one of the poorest—and roughest—sections of the city. He and his brother are the kind of kids we're trying to help at Saint Vincent's. We want them to understand that they *do* have options and that there are people who care.''

"You seem to be doing a good job of it, to hear Mark talk. How did you get involved there, anyway?''

"Through my church. We sponsor an annual field trip for the kids, and I volunteered a few years ago. I've been helping out down there ever since.''

Amy tilted her head and studied him. "So you're a churchgoing man.''

He nodded. "All my life.''

Their salads arrived, giving her time to digest his comment. "I admire that,'' she said frankly when the waiter departed. "In fact, I envy it a little.''

"You don't go to church?''

"Not much anymore. We went every Sunday when I was growing up. But once I was out on my own—I don't know, other things somehow took precedence. Time was at more and more of a premium, and somehow religion dropped to the bottom of my priority list.''

"That can happen,'' Cal said without censure. "When I first came to Atlanta I was tempted to skip church. It was just one more obligation to fit into a schedule that was already too packed. But every time I missed a Sunday, I felt somehow out of sync for the rest of the week. I know going to church is just an outward sign of faith, but it reminds me to keep my priorities straight and helps keep me grounded.'' He paused and studied her for a moment. "Can I ask you something?''

"Sure.''

"Since you attended church most of your life, do you ever miss it now that you've stopped going?"

Amy propped her chin in her hand and considered the question. "Sometimes I feel guilty about not going. But I can't say I *miss* it, per se." She did, on occasion, however, sense that something was *missing* from her life. And she suspected it had to do with her lapsed faith. In some vague way she felt she had disappointed God, and the longer she stayed away from church, the harder it became to go back. But she wasn't about to reveal that to Cal. "I really don't think about it too often," she finished. "And I certainly don't live it the way you do."

"I don't know. Look at the story you were working on tonight. That will help a lot of people."

"I'd like to say I did it for purely selfless reasons. But my motives weren't really altruistic," she said frankly. "Yes, I hope the story benefits Saint Vincent's. But I also hope it gets me noticed."

Cal studied her for a moment. "Can I ask you something else?"

There was something in his tone that made her cautious. "Maybe."

"Are you ever off duty?"

"Of course. I'm not working right now."

"Are you sure?"

"What do you mean?"

He steepled his fingers and gave her a direct look. "I guess I'm wondering if you're still hoping to get something from me you can use in the Jamie Johnson coverage."

Amy stared at him, her fork frozen halfway to her

mouth. "You think I accepted your invitation just because of that?"

He shrugged. "I can't think of any other reason. Not that I'm complaining, you understand." He gave her a wry smile. "It beats eating alone."

Amy continued to stare at him as the waiter refilled their water glasses. He couldn't think of any other reason? Was he kidding? She could think of about a dozen without even trying. He was intelligent, handsome, articulate, generous, had a good sense of humor and, considering his comment, was obviously completely without ego—a refreshing attribute and a definite plus as far as she was concerned.

Amy laid her fork down carefully and cleared her throat. "Look, I know you think I'm a workaholic, and that everything I do has an ulterior motive, but will you believe me when I say that my only reason for accepting your invitation tonight was because I wanted to? Because I enjoyed our last evening together? And because, like you, I prefer not to always eat alone?"

He chose to focus on her last comment. "If you eat alone, it must be by choice. I can't believe you lack for male companionship."

She shrugged indifferently, pleased nonetheless by the backhanded compliment. "Relationships are demanding. And I don't have the time. So why start something I know will simply fizzle out as soon as the guy realizes he takes second place to my career?"

"Your job is that important to you? So important that you're willing to give up your personal life?"

She grimaced. "Now you sound like my mother."

"And what do you tell her when she makes those kinds of comments?"

"That of course I want a husband. And children. But marriage and kids aren't compatible with the demands of my career. I'll get around to those things eventually."

"After you do all the 'important stuff'?"

She gave him a startled look, then frowned. "I didn't say that. And besides, who are you to talk? You spend an inordinate amount of time at your job, too, and as far as I know you haven't made time for a wife or family, either."

He couldn't argue with her on that. And they were heading toward turf he preferred to avoid.

"Touché," he replied lightly. "How did we get on this subject, anyway?"

Amy shook her head. "I have no idea."

"How about we get off it?"

"Good idea. I don't want to end the evening with indigestion. So…tell me what you do for fun."

"I'm not sure I remember," he confessed, a smile playing at the corners of his mouth as he chased an elusive piece of lettuce around his plate.

She rolled her eyes. "See? You *are* as bad as I am. Well…what about vacations, then? Where do you go when you manage to get away?"

"Back to the mountains."

"Honestly?"

"Yes. I've been other places, but there isn't much that can rival a morning in the Smoky Mountains, with the mist floating over the valleys and the blue-hued mountains forming an ethereal backdrop. The majesty of it never fails to take my breath away. And the incredible peace there— it's a balm for the soul."

Amy hadn't expected such a poetic description from an assistant prosecuting attorney—nor one so heartfelt. "I can see now why you said you had to think long and hard about leaving," she said slowly. "I can hear in your voice how much you love it there."

He shrugged, suddenly self-conscious. He was rarely so open in expressing his feelings about the mountains, and he wasn't sure what had prompted him to be so candid tonight. "So where do you go?" he asked, turning the tables.

"Cancún. The Caribbean. Europe now and then."

"Ah…a world traveler. What's your favorite place?"

She considered his question as the waiter replaced their salad bowls with heaping plates of pasta. "You know, I don't think I've found it yet," she replied thoughtfully. "I guess I'm still searching for the ideal spot."

As the meal progressed, they hopscotched around a half-dozen topics, deliberately staying on safe subjects. When they finally left the restaurant, long after most of the other diners had departed, he walked her to her car.

"So when will the piece on Saint Vincent's air?"

"It's not 'when,' but 'if,'" she reminded him. "It was done on a purely speculative basis. But if they're going to use it, it will probably be in the next couple of weeks on a slow news night. Most likely the six o'clock program. I'd offer to alert you, but I probably won't know until right before it airs that it's going to run."

"Well, I'll just have to keep an eye out for it, then."

Amy tossed her purse onto the passenger seat and straightened up to look at Cal. He was leaning against her door, one arm draped over the top, the other hand in his pocket, and his brown eyes were friendly and warm. More than warm, actually. If she didn't know better, she'd almost think the man was *attracted* to her. Considering the cool treatment he'd given her during their first few encounters, it was quite a transition. In fact, it was hard to believe that this was the same unfriendly man she'd approached on the courthouse steps just a few weeks before.

"Thanks for joining me tonight," he said quietly, the unusually husky cadence in his voice playing havoc with her metabolism.

"Thanks for asking me. I just wish you had let me pay for my own dinner."

"I owed you this one, remember?"

"The debt was paid in full that night at my apartment," she said firmly. "The 'takeout' you produced was five-star. And then, to top it off, you sent flowers. We're more than even, Cal."

For a moment there was silence. Cal knew that it was time to say good-night. But as he gazed down into Amy's expressive green eyes, he was suddenly reluctant for the evening to end. It was the same feeling he'd experienced that night at her apartment when it came time to leave. He hadn't understood it then, and he didn't understand it now. He shouldn't feel this way about her. Each time their paths crossed, it became more evident that their priorities in life were completely different. She drove a late-model BMW, he drove an older compact. She lived in the high-rent district, he lived in a middle-class neighborhood. She went to exotic places on vacation, he went home to Appalachia. She thrived on the fast pace of life in the city, he yearned for the slower pace of the mountains. It was obvious that there was no way on earth they could ever get together.

And yet…as he stared down at her, his heart said differently. As illogical as it seemed, he intuitively sensed that, at their core, they were more alike than either realized. Given the opportunity to really get to know each other, they might find a surprising amount of common ground.

As a rule, he didn't put much stock in intuition. It didn't always reflect reality. But one thing *was* very real—the electric attraction between them. On a purely physical level, at least, they were compatible. He could see it in her eyes, in the pulse that beat in the hollow of her throat, in the white-knuckled grip she had on her keys.

Cal drew a shaky breath. Heaven help him, but he wanted to kiss her. To deny the impulse would be foolish. But to do anything about it would be even more foolish. The lady wasn't interested in romance—with anyone. She'd made that clear tonight. And neither was he. The time just wasn't right.

Calling on every ounce of his willpower, Cal resolutely stepped back, jammed his hands in his pockets and somehow summoned up a crooked smile. "Okay. If you say so. I just want to make sure you got your five hundred dollars' worth."

If you only knew! Amy thought fervently, her gaze locked on his. Even without the hoped-for angle for her coverage, she didn't regret one dime she'd spent. Cal Richards had given her two wonderful evenings that she knew would linger long in her memory. "Trust me, Cal. We're even." She tried for a nonchalant tone, but couldn't quite control the slight quaver in her voice.

Again there was silence, and Amy had the disconcerting feeling that Cal knew exactly what was going through her mind. But if he did, he made no comment. "I'll take your word for it. Drive safely."

"I will. And thanks again."

She slipped inside the car, and he shut the door firmly behind her. With one final wave, she put the engine in gear and drove away.

Cal watched her taillights disappear into the night, then turned and slowly walked to his car. He didn't understand the attraction he felt for Amy Winter. It defied all logic. But he did understand one thing. There was a lot more to her than he'd first thought. And the more he found out about her, the more he realized that she was one unforgettable woman.

For the first time in his life, Cal made it a point to watch the six o'clock news on Amy's station, even if he had to duck into the conference room at the office to do so. He told himself it was because he was hoping to see the Saint Vincent's story. But in his heart, he knew it was because he wanted to see *Amy*.

As one week passed, then two, Saint Vincent's never made the news. But other stories by Amy did, including several that related to the Jamie Johnson trial. She continued to attend at least part of the court session each day, and she had an uncanny knack for distilling the essence of what transpired and communicating it to viewers in a straightforward way. He had to admit that her professional and balanced coverage was impressive.

But what impressed him even more was how she used the trial story to delve more deeply into related issues. One day she supplemented her trial coverage by including an interview with alcohol-abuse experts. Another day she talked with families of drunk-driving victims about the devastating impact the tragedy had had on their lives. She interviewed a psychologist, who discussed the "sports star'' phenomenon and the sense of invulnerability many athletes had. And she spoke with the person who ran the homeless shelter where the victim had spent time, using it as an opportunity to create sympathetic awareness of a world with which few people ever had any direct contact.

So when the story on Saint Vincent's finally aired, he wasn't surprised to see that she had gone one step beyond on that coverage, too. Not only had she interviewed Michael and others at the center, but she'd fleshed out her coverage by talking with social workers, law-enforcement officials and educators about the plight of youngsters like Mark and the odds they had to overcome. Her coverage made it clear that these kids needed as much help and support as they could get to break free of the cycle of poverty, gangs and violence, and that Saint Vincent's was doing a stellar job providing just such support.

When the segment ended, Cal rose and slowly walked back to his office, pausing to stare out his window into the darkness. Over the past couple of weeks, two significant things had occurred. First, he'd developed a deep admiration for Amy's skill and sensitivity as a reporter. And second, he'd realized that she wasn't just good at what she did; she was exceptional. He thought back to the way he'd railed at her when they first met, how he'd made sweeping generalizations about the press, and his face grew warm. Although his overall opinion of the news media might be valid, based on personal experience, he hadn't allowed for exceptions. And Amy was clearly an exception.

Cal wanted to call and compliment her on the Saint Vincent's story. But he wasn't sure that was wise. Because even with no contact, he'd thought way too much about her over the past two weeks. For a man known to colleagues for his powers of concentration, he'd drawn more than a few curious looks at several meetings when he'd had to ask someone to repeat a question. Cynthia had begun asking him if he was feeling all right. Bill Jackson had good-naturedly speculated about why he was so distracted and come a little too close to the truth. Even his boss had commented that after this trial, maybe he should take a vacation.

He sighed and reached around to rub the tense muscles in his neck. Despite the fact that she was a newswoman, despite the fact that they seemed to be complete opposites, despite the fact that this *wasn't* the right time in his life for romantic involvements, he was attracted to Amy Winter. Though he'd dated plenty of women throughout the years, none had been memorable enough to disrupt his focus and his concentration. His analytical, logical mind had always been able to control his heart. But not this time. Bottom line, Amy had gotten under his skin, and he didn't have a clue what to do about it.

By the time Cal walked through the door of his apartment two hours later, he was wrestling with yet another problem. In the past, he had steadfastly followed one simple rule in dealing with the press: no contact and no comment. He'd already blown the "no contact" part with Amy. And now he was actually toying with the idea of waiving the "no comment" part, too. Tomorrow he would be questioning a newly discovered witness who had information the defense wasn't going to like. Thanks to the persistence of one dedicated detective who just wouldn't rest until every angle had been explored, an eyewitness to the "accident" had been found. And his story made it clear that the victim was blameless, that Jamie Johnson had run a stop sign at a high speed and hit the pedestrian just as he reached the middle of the crosswalk. Bringing the man forward was a calculated risk, because Cal knew the man's credibility was vulnerable if the defense dug deeply enough. He hoped they wouldn't. But either way, the witness was newsworthy.

Cal figured that Amy would be in court, anyway. She'd rarely missed a session. But on the off chance she might be pulled on to another story, Cal was tempted to suggest she stick close. After all, if anyone deserved to get this "scoop," it was her. The other reporters hadn't shown up in person since the opening day, relying on daily updates issued by Johnson's agent for their coverage. What could it hurt to suggest that she might want to be in court tomorrow?

With a sigh he reached for the phone. Maybe he should just call her and play it by ear. But instead of dialing Amy's number, he found himself punching the familiar Tennessee area code. He paused, then continued dialing. Not a bad idea, he mused. Gram might be a good sounding board.

She picked up on the second ring. "You must be sitting right by the phone," he said with a smile.

"Cal? Land, I didn't expect to hear from you tonight! How are you, son?"

"Good. How are things at home?"

"Couldn't be better. The craft co-op is going gangbusters, and your dad is busy as a beaver on the church picnic committee. He's at a meeting tonight, in fact."

"I'd like to make the picnic this year," Cal said wistfully as he switched the portable phone to the other hand

and slid a frozen dinner into the microwave. "Do they still put on that great spread, with homemade apple butter and Moira Sanders's biscuits?"

"Of course. And speaking of food, did I just hear you turn on the microwave for one of those processed dinners?"

Cal chuckled and straddled a stool at the eat-in counter in his galley kitchen. You couldn't put anything past Gram, even from two hundred and fifty miles away. "Guilty."

"Is that the way you eat every night?"

He thought of his last dinner with Amy. "No. Sometimes I go out. I had a good dinner two weeks ago, in fact."

"With good company, too, I hope?"

"Mmm-hmm."

For a moment there was silence, and then he heard her sigh. "Cal Richards, you are the most closemouthed man I ever met! Can't imagine where you get it from. Do I have to pry every piece of information out of you?" she complained good-naturedly.

He chuckled again. "If you're trying to find out whether my companion was female, the answer is yes."

"That newswoman you told me about?" she asked shrewdly.

"Yes. But don't get your hopes up, Gram. It was an impromptu thing. She was doing a story on Saint Vincent's, and I coincidentally happened to be there that night. We just grabbed a bite afterward. It was no big deal."

"She must be nice, though, or you wouldn't have suggested dinner."

"Yes, she is. Surprisingly so. When I first met her, I

thought she was the typical pushy, 'go-for-the-sensational' reporter, but I've been impressed by her coverage. She's gone above and beyond to present a balanced picture of all the issues surrounding the trial. Which, in one way, has created a bit of a dilemma for me.''

''How do you mean?''

''Well, there's something breaking tomorrow, and if anyone deserves a first shot at it, she does. None of the other reporters have even come close to providing the comprehensive coverage she has. Trouble is, there's a chance she might not be in court, and if she's not there she won't get the scoop.''

''So call her up and tell her to be there.''

He sighed. ''It's not quite that simple, Gram. I've always made it a rule to steer clear of reporters, and I never give tips. Ethically I'm not sure I should make an exception.''

''How is suggesting she be in court giving her a tip?''

''She'll put two and two together and figure out something is going to break. She's one sharp lady.''

''Well, remember the old saying about rules, Cal. And there are extenuating circumstances here. You said yourself she deserves this scoop.''

''Yeah. I'm just having a hard time being objective about this. I don't want to let personal feelings get in the way of good judgment.''

''So…you have personal feelings for this woman?''

Cal frowned. He should have chosen his words more carefully. Gram was one sharp lady herself. ''I hardly know her, Gram,'' he hedged.

''Hmm. Well, far as I can see, there's nothing wrong

with giving a deserving person a break. The news will get out either way. Might as well be from her."

She made it sound simple, Cal thought. And maybe it was. Maybe he was making way too much out of this. After all, he wasn't going to tell Amy anything. He just wanted to make sure she was in court to get the news when it did break. "Thanks, Gram."

"For what?"

"For helping me decide what to do."

"Well, it just seems like common sense to me. It's not like you're giving away a state secret."

Cal chuckled. "True. Listen, tell Dad I said hi, okay?"

"Will do. And, Cal? Do one thing for me, would you?"

"What?"

"Work on those personal feelings. You never know where they might lead."

"I'll give it some thought."

"Don't think too much, son. You have a fine mind. But some things are best left to the heart."

As Cal replaced the receiver a few moments later, he thought about his grandmother's advice. She might be right—but he wasn't sure he trusted his heart in this case. There were just too many odds stacked against a relationship between him and Amy. Yet, even as logic told him not to take the chance, his heart urged him to do otherwise.

Cal sighed. He didn't know which would triumph in the end, but he did know one thing. Ready or not, bad timing notwithstanding, incompatibilities aside, he had suddenly come face-to-face with an opportunity for romance. And he had a feeling that it was about to change his life forever.

Chapter Six

Amy glanced over at Cal. He'd only looked her way once since the afternoon court session began. But that one look, along with an undercurrent of tension in the courtroom, convinced her that something big was about to break.

As she studied his strong profile, she thought again about his unexpected call the night before. Though he'd complimented her on the Saint Vincent's story, it had been clear that his main purpose was to ensure that she would be in court today. Considering his impeccable integrity and "no comment" policy with the press, she suspected that he'd wrestled with the decision about whether to call her. The fact that he *had* made her feel...well, lots of things. And most of them didn't have a thing to do with the trial. Sure, her adrenaline was pumping, as it always did when she was covering a story that had potential for high drama. But the warm glow in her heart and the anticipatory tingle in her nerve endings had no connection to her job.

Knowing that Cal had come to respect and like her enough to stretch the limits of his ethics on her behalf made her feel very good—not to mention more than a little nervous. Although their relationship had started out rocky, and despite the fact that they were different in so many ways, she liked Cal Richards. A lot. Which wasn't wise, of course. Cal and she obviously weren't right for each other. And besides, she didn't have time for romance. She had a career to build, and that took every ounce of her energy and focus. She couldn't afford any distractions. And the assistant prosecuting attorney was a distraction with a capital *D*.

"The prosecution would like to call Eldon Lewis to the stand."

Amy refocused her attention on the courtroom proceedings. As she watched the older man make his way to the witness stand, she sensed that he was the reason Cal had called her. She leaned forward intently, watching as the man took the oath and sat down.

Cal walked over and smiled at the witness, who was clearly nervous.

"Mr. Lewis, would you please state your name and occupation for the court?" His stance was relaxed, his tone conversational, and Amy knew he was trying to put the man at ease.

"Eldon Lewis. I'm a janitor at the community college."

"And what do you enjoy doing in your free time, Mr. Lewis?"

"I'm a big sports fan."

"So you're familiar with the defendant in this case, Jamie Johnson?"

The man darted a quick glance at the sports star. "Yeah. He's a real good player."

"I want you to think back to last September. Can you

tell the court what you did on the night of September fourth?''

The man swallowed and nodded. ''Me and my friend Hal went to the game. Jamie was playing that night. After the game, we stopped at the Watering Hole by the stadium to get a burger.''

''What time did you leave?''

''About one in the morning.''

''Can you tell us what you saw when you were leaving?''

''Well, I waited in front while my friend went to get the car. I have a bum leg, and it was acting up that night. I was kind of back in the shadows, and next thing I know, Jamie Johnson pulls up at the bar next door. A girl got out of his car, and they were laughing.'' The man paused and shifted uncomfortably.

''Are you sure it was Jamie Johnson, Mr. Lewis?'' Cal asked, his tone still conversational.

The man nodded emphatically. ''Sure. He got out of the car to open her door, and the streetlight was shining right on his face. Then he kind of tripped on the curb, and he and the girl started laughing again. She called him 'Jamie' when she said good-night, and she told him to drive careful because the last thing he needed was a drunk-driving charge.''

A murmur swept the courtroom, and the judge banged his gavel until order was restored.

Cal waited until the room was completely quiet before he spoke again. ''Please continue, Mr. Lewis. What happened next?''

''After the girl went in, Jamie got back in the car and took off with his tires screeching. When he got to the corner there was a blinking red light, but he didn't stop. And that's when I saw the man in the middle of the crosswalk. Next thing I knew, Jamie hit him. Then he slammed into a streetlight.''

Once again, the courtroom erupted, and the judge banged more forcefully on his desk. ''Order, order,'' he barked.

When quiet was once more restored, Cal put his hands in his pockets and rested one foot on the elevated platform where Eldon Lewis sat. ''What happened then, Mr. Lewis?''

''I just kind of stood there in shock. Then Jamie got out of the car, so I knew he was okay. A couple of other cars came by a minute or two later and stopped.''

''Did you report this to anyone?''

The man looked down and shook his head. ''No. I—I didn't want to get involved, and other people had already stopped. So I knew someone would call the police.''

''Did you realize you were the only eyewitness?''

''No. Not until you folks told me.''

''Mr. Lewis, let me ask you one final question. Is there any doubt in your mind that the man you saw on the night of September fourth was Jamie Johnson?''

''No, sir. It was him, all right.''

''Thank you, Mr. Lewis. No further questions at this time, Your Honor, but I'd like to reserve the right to recall this witness.''

The judge nodded. ''Does the defense wish to question the witness?''

Jamie Johnson's lead attorney stood. It was obvious that the testimony of Cal's witness had taken the defense team off guard, and Johnson himself was clearly angry. ''The defense would like to request an adjournment until Monday so that we can process this new information over the weekend, Your Honor.''

''Very well. We will reconvene at ten o'clock Monday morning. Court dismissed.''

Amy instantly rose and headed toward the door, pushing through the crowd, her cell phone in hand. She needed to alert the station to get ready for a live feed. Steve was waiting in front of the courthouse, and she intended to catch Johnson on tape as he exited. She also needed to review the notes she'd taken and organize her thoughts for her on-camera report.

Steve was off to one side of the courthouse as she exited, and he quickly joined her.

''What gives?''

''The prosecution came up with an eyewitness.''

Steve gave a low whistle. ''Big news.''

''I think Johnson and his lawyers will come out the front. They aren't going to be expecting any of the TV stations to be here. I want to catch them off guard and see if we can get a comment.''

Steve hefted the camera to his shoulder. ''I'm with you.''

Amy stepped to one side of the main door, her heart banging against her rib cage. She forced herself to take several long, deep breaths. Her lips and throat felt dry, and she wished she had a drink of water. But she didn't dare leave her post. Johnson could be along any minute. And, thanks to Cal, she would at last have her scoop.

By the time the pandemonium in the courtroom quieted and Cal finished conferring with his own team, Amy had disappeared. A quick, sweeping glance of the room confirmed her absence—as well as the chaos in the opposing camp. His gaze lingered for a moment on Jamie Johnson, who was one angry jock. His defense team was huddled around him, and it was clear their plans were in disarray for the moment. But Cal expected a quick recovery. They would reappear Monday with both barrels loaded, and he fully expected that they would do everything they could to discredit Eldon Lewis's testimony. Unfortunately, they might very well succeed. But he hoped that the man's sincere recount would ring true with some of the jurors, or at least plant enough doubt to stave off an acquittal on the involuntary manslaughter charge.

As Cal gathered up his papers and stuffed them into his briefcase, Bill Jackson leaned over. "I sense wrath in the opposing camp."

Cal glanced again toward the defense team. "That's putting it mildly."

"We certainly took them by surprise. I expect those guys will be putting in some long hours this weekend."

Cal gave his colleague a brief, mirthless grin. "They'll be well compensated for it."

"Too true. Say, speaking of long hours, did you notice that our favorite reporter was in the courtroom again today? Talk about a coup! She'll definitely have the scoop on this news."

"Yeah." Cal picked up his briefcase. He didn't want to discuss Amy with Bill. "And as for those long hours…see you tomorrow."

Bill made a face. "I'll be glad when this is over, if for no other reason than I'll finally have my Saturdays back."

"Until the next case comes along," Cal reminded him with a wry grin as he turned to go.

As he strode out of the courtroom, he ignored the venomous looks hurled his way by Johnson. The man was clearly holding on to his control with great effort. In fact, in the absence of his lawyers, who were almost physically restraining him, Cal suspected Johnson would be punching someone out. Probably him. His seething anger was almost palpable.

As Cal stepped into the hall, he once again glanced around for Amy, but she was nowhere in sight. He supposed she was already on her way back to the station. The story would probably be in the top slot on the six o'clock news, and time would be of the essence in putting the piece together. Though he could understand her haste, he felt oddly disappointed by her absence. Which was not a good sign. Somehow, some way, he had to figure out a way to get over the attraction he felt for her. Problem was, he didn't have a clue how to go about it.

After detouring to drop some papers off in another part of the courthouse, Cal exited by a side door, glancing toward the main entrance as he stepped outside. The sight of Amy and the cameraman who had done the filming at Saint Vincent's brought him to an abrupt stop. She must be waiting for Johnson to come out, he realized with a frown. Considering the man's black mood, that might not be wise, he realized, suddenly switching directions. He needed to warn her to be prepared for the sports star's anger.

Amy was so focused on the door that she didn't even see him approach. But as he rapidly closed the distance between them, then paused a few feet away, Cal saw a great deal. He saw the slight tremor in her hand. He saw the pulse beating frantically in the hollow of her throat. He saw the way she nervously moistened her lips. He saw her swallow convulsively and take a deep breath. Most people would never notice those subtle signs of nervousness. But he did, which only caused his frown to deepen. Since when had he become something other than "most people," he wondered? Since when had he become so attuned to her nuances?

Cal didn't know the answer to those questions. All he knew was that right now, Amy was doing something she didn't enjoy. And he suddenly recalled what she had told him that night in her apartment—that there were some parts of her job she didn't particularly like. This kind of confrontational reporting was obviously one of them. A big one.

As Cal once again started forward, the main door suddenly opened and Johnson burst through, followed by his attorneys. Amy stepped forward and held the microphone out.

"Mr. Johnson, would you like to comment on the latest development in your case?"

Startled, he stopped and turned to her, his face growing even more thunderous when he saw the camera. "What the—?" He muttered an oath and roughly knocked the microphone aside. The violence of the action made Amy momentarily lose her balance, and Johnson reached over and gripped her arm as she teetered. He stepped close, towering over her. "You are asking for big trouble, lady," he said through clenched teeth, his face only inches from hers.

She stood her ground and stared up at him defiantly. "If

you don't let go of my arm, you're going to be in even bigger trouble than you already are,'' she said coldly.

It all happened so fast that Cal was momentarily stunned. He recovered at about the same time as Johnson's lawyers, who interceded before he could reach Amy.

''Come on, Jamie,'' one said placatingly as he put his hand on the man's shoulder. ''Let it go. Remember what we talked about inside.''

The sports star hesitated for a moment, then released Amy's arm, throwing in a shove for good measure. ''Yeah. But stay out of my face, you hear me?'' he called over his shoulder as his lawyers hurried him away.

Steve lowered the camera from his shoulder and shook his head. ''Man, that is one angry dude. You okay?''

Amy drew a deep breath and nodded. ''Did you get all that on tape?''

Steve grinned and patted the camera. ''It's recorded for posterity. Not to mention the six o'clock news.''

Amy managed a shaky smile. ''Great. Listen, give me two minutes to go over my notes. Then we'll do a live feed.''

''Sure thing. I'll wait over on the bench.''

As he ambled off, Cal watched as Amy ran the palms of her hands down her slacks and closed her eyes. Though she'd stood her ground calmly and coolly with Johnson, the encounter had clearly been traumatic for her. At least clear to him, Cal amended. Yet she'd displayed an amazing degree of calm and bravado.

Cal knew that Amy considered these kinds of assignments a proving ground, a step toward the kind of reporting she really wanted to do, but watching her now, he wasn't sure the prize was worth the price. And strangely enough, he suddenly wished he could just give her her dream so she wouldn't have to deal with people like Johnson. But he knew that the best he could do was simply let her know someone cared.

"Amy?"

His voice was gentle, but she gasped and instinctively stepped back, her body tensing into a defensive posture as her eyelids flew open.

"Cal!" Her shoulders sagged and she tried to smile. "You startled me."

"I'm sorry. I came out the side door just in time to witness your encounter with Johnson. Listen, I know you said you were okay, but are you sure?" he asked, his brow furrowed worriedly.

She drew a steadying breath. "Of course."

His gaze moved to her arm, red beneath the edge of her short-sleeved jacket, and his own anger began to simmer anew. "You have grounds for assault, you know."

She shook her head impatiently. "It's not the first time something like this has happened. If I pressed charges every time someone threw his weight around, I'd spend half my life in court. It just shakes me up for a few minutes." She frowned and glanced distractedly at her watch. "I need to get my report on tape. And I want to get back to the studio and do a little editing before airtime. It's going to be tight."

Cal nodded. "I'll let you get to work, then."

He started to turn away, but paused when she reached out and tentatively touched his arm. "Cal, I... Thanks."

He looked back at her, thrown by the electric jolt that shot through him at her simple touch. And he wasn't sure how to respond to her gratitude. He was glad she'd gotten her story. But the scene he'd just witnessed had upset him more than he cared to admit. The moment Johnson had touched her, he'd wanted to deck the guy. It wasn't an impulse he had often, and considering that she was a strong, independent woman, he wasn't sure she would appreciate the fact that he'd felt the need to "rescue" her.

But what disturbed him even more was the knowledge that this scenario wasn't a one-time occurrence. This time there'd been plenty of people around to intervene. But what about the times when she was in danger and there was no one to step in? Cal wasn't a man accustomed to fear. But the realization that Amy put herself in situations where she could get hurt—badly—made his gut twist painfully.

"Why do you do this to yourself?" he said abruptly. There was anger in his question, and bewilderment. The words—and tone surprised him as much as they did her, judging by the startled expression on her face.

"It's part of the job," she said after a moment.

"But do you *like* doing this? Do you *like* dealing with scum like Johnson?" he persisted.

"Do you?"

He shrugged dismissively. "It's part of my job."

She just looked at him, and her silence spoke more eloquently than words.

He sighed and conceded her point with a nod. "Okay, you win. But do me a favor, will you? Make it an early night."

Again she seemed momentarily taken aback. "Why?"

He frowned. Why, indeed? Because he thought she'd been through enough today? Because she worked too hard and needed a break? Because he didn't like the fine lines of strain around her eyes? Because he cared about her more than he should, more than was wise, more than he wanted to?

The furrows in Cal's brow deepened. There was no way he could verbalize any of that. Especially since he didn't understand how he had come to feel that way.

"Never mind," he said shortly, his fingers clenching the handle of his briefcase. "It's none of my business, anyway." And with that he turned and strode away.

Amy stared after him in confusion. Now what was that all about? First he was solicitous, then he was angry. Men! It was a good thing she *wasn't* romantically involved. She'd spend her life trying to figure the guy out instead of focusing on her career. But as she watched Cal's stiff, retreating back, she was startled to realize that maybe that wouldn't be such a bad use of her time—especially if the man was Cal Richards.

Amy took a soothing sip of tea and sighed contentedly. She had a lazy Saturday morning all to herself to bask in the glow of the coup she'd pulled off yesterday. As the other stations scrambled to piece together something for their ten o'clock news programs, Amy's coverage of yesterday's events had been picked up nationally by affiliated stations, giving both her—and the story—coast-to-coast exposure. She'd even received a call from the station vice president congratulating her for her diligence and for her comprehensive coverage of the case.

Amy took another sip of tea and stuck an English muffin in the toaster. She *was* diligent. She'd worked hard to stay one step ahead of the competition on this story, and she'd succeeded. Yesterday's piece had done exactly what she wanted it to do. It had gotten her noticed by the right people. Thanks to Cal's tip. While she might have been in court anyway yesterday, there were days when she spent less time at the trial because of other assignments. Yesterday could very well have been one of them.

As she buttered her English muffin, she suddenly recalled Cal's question yesterday about whether she liked dealing with scum like Johnson, and a shadow crossed her face. She hadn't answered him directly. Because up until now, she hadn't really answered it for herself. Mostly because it was irrelevant. Bottom line, it didn't matter what she liked or didn't like. The station chose her assignments, and she did what she was told. And did it well.

But as she munched on the muffin, she came face-to-face with something she'd been dancing around for the past couple of years. For some reason, she couldn't avoid the question anymore, couldn't chase it away to some dark corner of her consciousness. It demanded an answer. And the answer was simple. She *hated* dealing with people like Johnson. Hated it to the very depths of her being. And then came the inevitable follow-up question, the one she'd *really* been avoiding. If she hated it so much, was the end result worth all the stress and strain?

Amy stopped chewing. Up until now, she'd always kept her gaze firmly fixed on her goal—first an anchor slot, and ultimately a network position that would let her do in-depth issues reporting, such as the coverage she'd done around the Johnson case relating to alcohol abuse or with the Saint Vincent's story. Solid, feature reporting that had the potential to create awareness about problems and change lives for the better. Those were the kinds of stories that gave her the greatest satisfaction. Because they counted for something. They made a difference. And their impact was far longer lasting than anything she would ever report about the Jamie Johnson trial.

Amy frowned. Funny. In the past, whenever she'd thought about her career, she'd always listed "celebrity status" and money as her top reasons for wanting a high-profile feature job. When had they slipped to second place? What had brought her to the realization that it was the opportunity to make a positive difference in people's lives that was *most* important to her?

Amy's gaze fell on the card that had come with Cal's flowers. It was still lying on the counter, waiting for her to make what had been an oddly difficult decision—keep or pitch? Both choices seemed to symbolize something, and she wasn't ready to deal with that yet. So she'd uncharacteristically made no decision and done nothing. She reached over and fingered the card thoughtfully. Until a few weeks ago, she was content and in control, certain about what she wanted out of life. Then along came Cal Richards, with his steadfast values, solid faith and clear priorities, to disrupt her equilibrium—both emotionally and professionally.

And yet…Amy couldn't honestly say that she was sorry they'd met. Okay, so maybe it wasn't too comfortable to reexamine her carefully crafted career plan. Maybe it wasn't too comfortable to deal with her lapsed faith. Maybe it wasn't too comfortable to think about just how long she planned to defer creating the family she ultimately wanted to have. But maybe it was time.

Amy sighed. For the last few years she'd sailed along, single-mindedly focused on one thing—making it big in broadcast journalism. She was now well on her way to achieving that goal. But meeting Cal had not only made her question that journey, it had also made her realize just how lonely it had been. Even more, it made her yearn for someone special to share it with. And different though they were, she couldn't help but wistfully wonder for one brief moment what it would be like if that special someone was Cal.

Chapter Seven

"Eldon Lewis called. He was pretty upset."

Cal gave Cynthia a distracted look, then paused beside her desk and wearily raked his fingers through his hair. It had *not* been a good Monday. "I'm not surprised."

"Was it bad?"

"Brutal. I warned him they might get rough, but I didn't expect it to take such a vicious turn."

"One of those situations where he almost felt like *he* was on trial, right?"

"Right. And it certainly didn't help our case that the judge let it go on far too long, despite our objections." The weariness in his voice was now tinged with frustration.

Cynthia eyed him sympathetically. "Listen, how about I get you some coffee?"

Cal gave her a tired grin. "Since when do you offer to fetch coffee?"

"Since you look like you're about to cave in without some."

"I don't deserve you, you know."

"Yeah, I know," Cynthia said pertly as she rose and headed toward the coffeemaker. "Just remember that when you're deciding on next year's raises for your hardworking law clerks."

Cal smiled and continued toward his office. He dropped his briefcase on the desk, then went to stare pensively out the window, his hands thrust into his pockets.

"One cup of coffee," Cynthia announced a moment later.

He turned and took it from her. "Thanks. Now get out of here. Go home to that new husband of yours."

"When are *you* going home?"

He shrugged and took a sip of the coffee. "Later."

She gave an unladylike snort and planted her hands on her hips. "Maybe it's a good thing you *don't* have a wife," she declared. "The poor woman would need to keep a picture of you on hand just to remember what you look like."

"Good night, Cynthia," Cal said dryly.

She threw up her hands. "I give up!"

"Can I count on that?"

Her face grew thoughtful. "On the other hand, maybe if you *had* a wife, you'd keep more reasonable hours."

Cal groaned. "Go home, Cynthia, before you get any more ideas."

She grinned. "Oh, I'm full of ideas." Then her face grew more sober. "Seriously, Cal, try to get out of here before midnight."

"I'll see what I can do."

Cynthia shook her head. "You're hopeless. But even if

you won't take *my* advice, I intend to take yours. Good night."

When Cynthia left, Cal walked to his desk and sank into the overstuffed chair. He felt sick about the way the defense attorney had distorted the facts to discredit his witness. And there wasn't much he could say to comfort the man. Still, he had to try. So, with a weary sigh, he reached for the phone.

The man answered on the second ring.

"Mr. Lewis? Cal Richards."

"How could they do that?" the witness burst out, clearly distraught.

"I'm sorry you had to go through that," Cal said sympathetically. "In cases like this, where the stakes are very high, the defense can sometimes play pretty dirty, as I warned you. I was hoping they wouldn't this time, but I guess we gave them too much credit."

"But I know what I saw!" the man protested.

"And I'm sure it happened exactly the way you described to the court."

"But they made me sound like—like some kind of derelict! Like I made it all up. They kept dragging up all that stuff from the past, and they twisted everything I said. It wasn't fair!"

Cal drew a deep breath. No, it wasn't. But he'd seen it happen more times than he cared to remember. And though he'd done his best to keep the cross-examination focused on the Johnson incident, objecting whenever the defense attorney brought up Eldon Lewis's past, enough information had been imparted to instill doubt about the witness's credibility in the minds of the jurors. Which had been the precise intent of the defense, of course.

"I know, Mr. Lewis. But you did your best and told the truth. All we can do is hope that the jury sees that."

The man gave a bitter laugh. "I don't think that's going to happen."

After watching the jurors' faces today, Cal didn't, either. He had hoped for more from them. But the defense team had done a masterful job of planting doubt, and there was little he could do now to change that. "You did everything you could, Mr. Lewis. That's all any of us can do. And I appreciate your cooperation. I know this wasn't easy for you."

The man sighed, and suddenly his anger evaporated. "I guess I thought I'd put the past behind me, moved on as best I could with my life. This made me realize that my mistakes will always haunt me," he said resignedly.

"You *have* moved on with your life," Cal corrected him firmly. "From every standpoint—ethical, moral, legal— the defense team should never have brought all that up. It *is* history. Remember that."

"Yeah. Well, I'll be seeing you."

The line went dead, and Cal slowly replaced the receiver. The man was clearly unconvinced, and Cal felt a deep pang of regret for the need to involve him in the trial. But he'd been their only hope. It was a chance they'd had to take in the cause of justice. He'd known that the defense team might use Lewis's past against him. The man's struggle a dozen years earlier with serious depression and a temporary drinking problem shouldn't have had any bearing on the credibility of his testimony, given the exemplary life he had led for the past ten years. But Johnson's team had positioned the facts in a way that implied that the witness was still unstable and not to be fully trusted.

It was one of those days when the injustice of the justice system weighed heavily on Cal's heart. Wearily he reached for his briefcase. Despite Cynthia's advice, it was going to be a very long night. As he spread his papers out and prepared to draft an outline of his closing remarks, he wished there was someone he could talk with about his feelings, someone who would listen to his doubts and reassure him that he had done all he could, someone who could fill the empty place in his heart and offer him understanding and support.

Suddenly an image of Amy Winter flashed through his mind, and he frowned. She'd been cropping up in his thoughts more and more lately, but so far he'd been able to convince himself that it was only because she was an attractive, appealing woman, and that his reaction was simply a normal male response to a beautiful woman. But right now he wasn't thinking about her in terms of her good looks. He was thinking of her in the context of confidante/friend/comforter, he realized, his frown deepening. That was serious stuff. And it wasn't good. He wasn't in the market for romance—particularly with her, he reminded himself firmly.

Nevertheless, a surge of longing just to hear her voice swept over him, so strong that it made him catch his breath. So strong that it scared him. So strong that it made him wonder if perhaps he should give up the fight and simply let the attraction he felt for her play out, see if their differences were really as irreconcilable as they seemed.

And then logic kicked in. He had issues of his own to resolve before he even *considered* trying to deal with the issues between them. That had to be his top priority.

But first he had a closing argument to write.

* * *

"Not guilty."

A muscle twitched in Cal's jaw and his lips settled into a thin line as he stared at the judge, oblivious to the sudden pandemonium in the courtroom. It wasn't as if the verdict was a surprise. He'd known from the beginning that the odds were stacked against them. But as always, he'd held on to a sliver of hope that in the end justice would triumph. A hope that far too often was in vain.

He drew a slow, deep breath, then glanced toward Jamie Johnson. The defendant was beaming and shaking hands with his attorneys, his "golden boy" image restored. For a moment Cal actually felt sick. How could the man feel so little remorse for the life he'd carelessly destroyed? Cal hoped that at least Johnson had learned something from the experience. But he doubted it. The sports jock would probably emerge from the trial even cockier, more convinced than ever that he was invincible, he thought with a disheartened sigh.

Cal felt a hand on his shoulder and looked up.

"You did your best, you know," Bill Jackson said.

Cal gave a noncommittal shrug. "Too bad it wasn't good enough."

His colleague glanced at Johnson's legal team. "Considering the guns we were up against—not to mention the money, the sympathetic press and Johnson's boy-next-door image—don't be too hard on yourself."

Cal drew a deep breath and stood up. "Who said life was fair, right?"

"Right."

Cal held out his hand. "Well, I know one thing. I couldn't have done even half as well without you, Bill. I may have been the lead on this case, but you worked just as hard as I did. Thank you."

His colleague took his hand but brushed the comment aside. "You've done the same for me in the past. And will again, no doubt."

Cal smiled. "Count on it."

"See you back at the office?"

"Yeah. I'll be along in a few minutes."

By the time Cal packed up his papers and left, the courtroom was mostly empty. He strode down the hall toward the front entrance of the building, then suddenly changed his mind and veered off toward a side door. No doubt Johnson was triumphantly holding court for a gaggle of reporters, and that was one show he had no desire to see. He assumed Amy was among them. What had been her reaction to the outcome? he wondered. Surprise? Anger? Disappointment—in him?

The last question gnawed at him. He tried to tell himself that it didn't matter, but in his heart he knew it did. Because like it or not, he cared what she thought about him.

And he had his answer a few minutes later when he reached his office and discovered on his voice mail the slightly husky voice he found so appealing.

"Cal. Amy. I wanted to let you know how sorry I am about the verdict. You did everything humanly possible to convict Johnson, and I thought your entire prosecution—especially your closing argument—was masterful. How the jury could let that scumbag off is beyond me. I would have waited to talk with you, but I had to file the story and you were pretty tied up, so this is the best I could do." There was a moment of silence, and when she spoke again her voice had taken on a different, more personal—and slightly uncertain—tone. "Listen, I don't suppose our paths are likely to cross again anytime soon, so I just wanted to say that I... Well, it's been a privilege to get to know you. I really enjoyed the time we spent together. And I wanted to wish you all the best in the future."

The line went dead, and Cal slowly replaced the receiver. He knew she was working at warp speed to get the story ready for the evening news, and he was touched that she had taken time to place the call. He hadn't expected it. Or even let himself *hope* for it. Just as he hadn't allowed himself to dwell on the fact that she would no longer be a daily—albeit professional—presence in his life. Though they had rarely spoken, merely knowing she was in the courtroom had brightened his days. Now he had to face the fact that even that limited contact had come to an end. It left him feeling strangely empty—and more than a little melancholy.

"You've been summoned by the chief, Cal."

Cynthia's voice intruded on his thoughts and Cal glanced at her, forcing himself to shift gears. "Okay. I'm on my way."

As he strode down the hall to David Morgan's office, he wondered what the senior member of the department would say about the outcome of the case. He hoped Morgan wasn't disappointed in his performance. Cal, like all of the staff attorneys, had great respect for the older man's opinion. His incisive legal mind, combined with a great sense of fairness and humanitarianism, had made him almost a legend in the Atlanta legal community. His praise—or censure—was never taken lightly.

Morgan's secretary glanced up when he entered, then waved him inside. "He's expecting you."

The older man was engrossed in something on his computer screen, but he looked up immediately when Cal stepped to the door and knocked lightly.

"Come in, Cal. Have a seat. Would you like something to drink?"

"How about a gin and tonic?" Cal replied with a wry grin. At the older man's startled look, he added a quick disclaimer. "Just kidding," he assured him.

"For a minute I wondered if the trial might have been even more stressful than I thought," Morgan said with relief. "I've never known you to drink anything more than an occasional glass of wine."

"I still don't."

"Well, you probably *could* use something stronger after these last few months. I know how hard you worked on the Johnson case. And I know how hard it is to lose. I've been there. Feel like doing a little rehashing?"

Cal nodded. "Sure."

"Tell me about the approach the defense used."

By the time Cal talked the case through with the older man, recounting the defense's tactics and his strategy, he felt a lot better about the decisions he'd made in planning his prosecution. And he suspected that had been Morgan's intent.

"So I'm not happy with the verdict, but I honestly don't know what I would have done differently," Cal concluded, feeling more at peace with the outcome.

Morgan nodded. "Your approach was sound. By rights, you should have won. But a lot of factors that we have no control over often influence the outcome. That's what happened here, you know."

"I'm beginning to accept that."

"Good. I don't want you beating yourself up over this. You're a fine attorney, and you did as much as anyone could have in this case. More, I'd venture to say."

Cal felt a flush of pleasure at the older man's praise. "Thank you."

"So now I want you to take a few days off. Can't have our people working themselves into the ground."

Cal hesitated. "Actually, I was saving my vacation for later in the summer."

The older man waved his protest aside. "Who said anything about vacation? How many hours a week have you put in for this trial? How many weekends have you worked?"

"A few," Cal acknowledged.

Morgan snorted. "That's an understatement if I ever heard one. Just go, boy. Spend a few days in those mountains you love. Although why I send you there, I don't know. I have a feeling one of these days you won't come back." He eyed the younger man shrewdly.

Cal shifted uncomfortably. "I'll be back," he promised.

"This time," the older man amended. "But what about next time? None of my business, of course. But I want you to know that you have a bright future here."

"I appreciate that."

"Just stating the facts, son. Now go tie up the loose ends of this case and take off for a few days."

"Thank you, sir."

"No need to thank me. You earned it."

Yes, he had, Cal acknowledged as he made his way back to his office. It had been a grueling few months. All trials were stressful, but the high-profile nature of this case had increased the pressure exponentially. Though the trial itself had been relatively brief, the months of behind-the-scenes research and preparation had taken a toll, and he was tired. He needed a break. Except for brief visits home on major holidays, he hadn't had more than two consecutive days off in almost a year.

Home. The word itself was telling, he mused. That was how he thought of the mountains. And Morgan, with his keen insight, had picked up on that. Perhaps on this trip he would find a way to talk to his father about his growing desire to return, Cal reflected. He would find a way to make Jack Richards understand that his definition of success wasn't necessarily his son's. The last thing in the world Cal wanted to do was disappoint the man who had given so selflessly to him for so many years. But he had to live his own life. And he was growing more and more certain that he wanted to live it in the mountains.

Amy glanced at the phone for the tenth time in as many minutes. She hadn't heard from Cal since she left the message for him earlier in the week, but then, why should she? she told herself curtly. He had no reason to call her. Sure, they'd spent a couple of pleasant evenings together. But neither one had been a "real" date. The first night she'd *bought* his time. And the dinner at Rick's resulted from a chance meeting at Saint Vincent's. The few words they'd subsequently exchanged during the trial hardly counted as "social" interaction. There was certainly nothing in any of their encounters on which to base a relationship. Which she didn't want, anyway, of course—right?

Amy sat back in her desk chair and sighed. Six weeks ago—was it only six weeks?—she would have answered that question with a resounding "Right!" She'd been perfectly happy with her life. She'd known exactly what she wanted and exactly how she intended to go about getting it. Relationships weren't even *on* her list of priorities. She considered them a distraction, an impediment to her career goals. And career was everything.

But that was BC—before Cal. Somehow, her BC life now seemed shallow and empty. The goals she'd prized so highly—fame, power, prestige, money—no longer had quite the same luster or appeal. Instead, she'd come to discover that the work itself was just as important to her. Especially issue-oriented kinds of stories. But only since Cal entered her life had she begun to analyze *why*.

It was becoming more and more clear to her that despite her efforts to leave her farm roots behind, to live the life of big-city glitz and glamour, at heart she was still the same Amy Ann Winter who had been raised in a loving family with solid values and instilled with a belief that she should count among her priorities a commitment to doing good work that made life better for other people. She was still the same young girl who had been brought up to believe that the real satisfaction in life came from focusing on others, not on oneself. It was part of who she was. Period.

She'd pushed that upbringing aside for seven years as she devoted herself to making her mark in broadcast journalism. And she was succeeding. But at what price? Though she'd learned to play them, she didn't like the political games. She didn't like the jockeying for power. She didn't like the cutthroat nature of a business in which you had rivals, not friends. And she especially didn't like dealing with the Jamie Johnsons of the world.

At the same time, she was good at what she did. She

not only had a solid news sense, but even better, a knack for ferreting out the "story behind the story." That skill had brought her to the attention of the "right" people more than once. They had recognized that her coverage was more thorough, well-rounded and dimensional than that of her competitors, and that was gratifying. But she now knew that covering fast-breaking stories just didn't cut it for her, good as she was at it. She was ready to move on to pure feature work, work that had a lasting impact on people's lives. It was time.

There was only one little problem, she thought with a sigh. Because she *was* so good at what she currently did, more and more of these assignments were coming her way. While she'd worked hard to put some meat on her coverage of the Jamie Johnson case, for most of the stations the story had been more about entertainment than reporting. It certainly hadn't been about justice. No wonder Cal had such a poor opinion of the press.

Amy propped her chin in her hand. A few weeks ago, if someone had told her that she'd feel sympathetic toward Cal Richards she would have laughed in their face. And the notion that she would actually *like* him would have been ludicrous. Though they were different in many ways, she admired Cal. He had impeccable ethics built on a solid foundation of faith; he was generous and kind; and he radiated strength and trustworthiness. Bottom line, he was the kind of person she would like to have as a friend.

The phone rang, startling her out of her reverie. She wondered—as she had every time it had rung since she'd left her message—if Cal might be on the other end, and the thought sent her pulse into double time. Yet a phone call from someone toward whom she felt merely "friendly" would hardly produce such a visceral response, she realized with a startled frown before a second ring prompted her to pick up the receiver.

"Amy? We've got a hostage situation at a day-care center. We need you there pronto. Steve is already on the way."

Amy automatically switched gears and reached for a notepad. But even as she jotted down the information the news editor was relaying, she acknowledged that she'd been dodging her feelings about Cal for too long. It was time to face them and either put the relationship to rest— or do something about exploring it. Though she'd always considered relationships too much of a distraction, Cal Richards was proving to be a distraction with or without a relationship, she admitted. And until she figured out how—or if—he fit into her life, she didn't think that was going to change.

Cal folded his long frame into his favorite overstuffed chair, opened a can of soda, picked up the newspaper and punched the remote on the television. This was the first night in weeks that he'd been home in time to watch the evening news on his own TV, and he intended to savor every moment. Now that the burden of the trial was lifted from his shoulders, he felt more relaxed than he had in months.

He settled back and glanced at the screen. He wasn't particularly interested in the events of the day, but he *was* interested in seeing Amy. In the past couple of days he'd been tempted to call her more times than he cared to admit, but so far he'd resisted. He needed to get his life in order first, and he hoped the trip home would help him do that.

In fact, in forty-eight hours he'd be sitting down to some of Gram's homemade biscuits and gravy right about now. He could hardly wait, he thought with a grin.

Cal scanned the newspaper, giving only marginal attention to the TV until the news program began and he discovered that Amy was covering the lead story.

"The Child First Day-Care Center is the scene of a drama that began this afternoon at three when a gunman entered the facility and took the students and teachers in one of the classrooms hostage," announced the anchorman. "He has been tentatively identified as the father of a former student who died in a bus crash on one of the school's field trips. We go live now to reporter Amy Winter who is on the scene. Amy, can you give us an update on the situation?"

A shot of Amy standing across the street from the day-care facility filled the screen.

"It now appears that there may also be a bomb involved, Peter. A few moments ago the gunman issued a warning that if police try to enter the building he will, and I quote, 'blow the place up.' He has also been positively identified as Roger Wilson, whose son, Dennis, was killed about a year ago in the bus accident you mentioned. Following that incident, Mr. Wilson unsuccessfully sued the center for negligence. According to his ex-wife, whom I spoke with moments ago by phone, he has been under psychiatric care for some time and may have a drug problem."

"How many hostages are still inside?" the anchorman asked.

"Eight children, ages three and four, and two teachers. The gunman has yet to make any demands, so at this point the authorities are waiting to—"

An explosion suddenly ripped through the air, and the camera jerked, making the image of Amy tilt crazily. Cal jumped to his feet, nearly choking on the soda he'd just swallowed. Pandemonium broke out at the scene, and the camera showed media and bystanders ducking for cover before it refocused on the day-care center.

"Peter, as you can see, the bomb threat wasn't an idle one." Though Amy's voice was controlled, the slight quiver that ran through it told Cal she was badly shaken. But she was all right, thank God! "It appears that the explosion occurred at the rear of the building, which is relatively close to where the hostages are...."

Suddenly a toddler appeared at the front door of the day-care center, and Amy paused and turned as a murmur ran through the crowd. The little boy was clearly dazed, and there was blood on his face. A hush fell over the scene as he wobbled unsteadily into the open, then faltered, and Cal heard Amy whisper, "Dear God!"

The child stood there for several eternal seconds as the bystanders stared at him in shock. Just as Cal thought, Why doesn't someone do something? Amy suddenly appeared in front of the camera. Cal caught his breath sharply as she slipped through the police barricade, dashed toward the toddler and scooped him up, cradling him protectively against her chest. She turned and started to run back toward the camera, but she'd only gone a couple of steps when a second explosion ripped through the building. This one was much closer to the front and spewed debris in all directions. Amy staggered momentarily, then continued her flight. The camera stayed on her as she returned to the safety of the sidelines and gently placed the crying child in the waiting arms of a paramedic. Someone thrust a microphone into her hands, and she stared down at it in confusion.

Suddenly a paramedic touched her shoulder. "Ma'am, I think you're hurt. Why don't you let me take a look?"

Amy turned. The back of her hair was matted with blood, and Cal felt like someone had kicked him in the gut. Suddenly she swayed, and as he watched in horror, her face took on an ashen tone and she crumpled to the ground.

And then the live feed went dead.

Chapter Eight

∞

Cal's heart stopped, then lurched on, and his hand convulsively crushed the soda can. Every nerve in his body was taut and his lungs seem paralyzed as he stared at the screen.

The scene shifted back to the studio. "We'll keep you informed about the situation at First Child Day-Care Center just as soon as we have additional information," the anchorman promised.

The co-anchor started talking about some sort of labor contract that had been signed that day, and Cal stared at her incredulously. How in heaven's name could they go on with the news as if nothing had happened? *Didn't they realize that Amy could be seriously injured?*

Throughout his career, Cal had scrupulously avoided using his connections for personal reasons. But during the next five minutes he used every one he could muster. And after several terse calls, he had the information he wanted.

Amy stared up groggily at the nurse, trying vainly to focus on her face. From her curled-up fetal position, she was looking at the woman sideways, which didn't help in the least.

"There's someone here who would like to see you," the woman said in a voice that seemed to come from far away. "He's been waiting for quite some time. May I let him come in?"

Amy blinked, still trying to clear her vision. But the effort only made her head hurt worse. "Who is it?" she mumbled.

"He didn't give his name. He just said he was a close friend."

Amy frowned, trying to concentrate. It must be Steve, though she was surprised he hadn't stayed at the scene to continue his live coverage. After all, it was a hot story. But who else could it be?

"Okay," she agreed, closing her eyes against the bright lights. The nurse's shoes squeaked on the tile floor as she retreated, and Amy felt herself quickly drifting back into oblivion. She didn't fight the blackness. Maybe the next time she woke up, her head wouldn't hurt so much and—

"I hope you don't mind if I stretched the truth a bit to get in here."

The familiar, though slightly roughened, voice brought her abruptly back to reality, and her eyelids flew open. She squinted against the lights as she stared up at the tall, slightly out-of-focus figure towering above her. "Cal?"

"Yeah. It's me."

She made an attempt to sit up, but he restrained her with a gentle but firm hand on her shoulder. She heard the sound of a chair being pulled across the floor, and then he sat beside her, his face only inches from hers.

"I don't think you're supposed to move around too

much," he said gently. "I'll come down to your level, okay?"

Amy continued to stare at him incredulously. Never in a million years would she have expected Cal to show up at the hospital. But she had never been happier to see anyone in her life, she realized with a start. Suddenly her throat constricted and she found herself close to tears. Without even stopping to consider, she reached out a hand and drew a deep, shuddering breath. "Oh, Cal." It was all she could manage.

He enfolded her hand in a warm, firm clasp. "It's okay, Amy," he said with an odd catch in his voice. "It's over. You'll be fine."

The words were as much to reassure himself as her, he realized, as he studied her pale face and tried to swallow past the lump in his throat. He was still badly shaken by his first sight of her, huddled under the thin white blanket on the gurney, looking so fragile and vulnerable—the antithesis of the strong, gutsy woman he had come to know. And he didn't feel much more reassured up close. Her luminous green eyes were slightly dazed, and in her hand he could feel the tremors that still radiated throughout her body.

Cal watched as she closed her eyes and struggled to keep her tears in check, the spiky fan of her damp, dark lashes sweeping against her too-pale cheeks. He wanted to tell her not to bother, to go ahead and cry. But she was a woman accustomed to being in charge, and he understood her need to regain some semblance of control. So he waited quietly, simply stroking his thumb comfortingly over the back of her hand.

As Amy struggled to stem the tears that threatened to spill from her eyes, she tried to come to grips with Cal's presence. Why had he come? What did it mean? She hadn't heard from him since the trial ended, had come to the conclusion that any further contact between them would have to be initiated by her. She hadn't figured out just what she was going to do about that—if anything. But now fate had dramatically stepped in, taking the decision out of her hands. Cal was here, and she was happy.

Amy knew that those last two facts were significant, and that she'd have to think about them later. But right now her brain felt too fuzzy to process anything other than gratitude.

When she at last felt more in control of her emotions, she drew a long, shaky breath and opened her eyes. Cal's face was still only inches away, and at this proximity, she noticed things she'd never seen before. The irises of his troubled, deep brown eyes were flecked with gold, for example, and there was a fine sprinkling of gray at his temples. The two deeply etched lines in his brow made her yearn to reach over and smooth them away, but she resisted the impulse, letting her gaze drop to his lips instead. They were set in a grim, unsmiling line, and his jaw was rigid with tension. The strain of the last few hours was clearly evident in his haggard face—and all because of her, she marveled, deeply touched by his concern but also sorry to be the cause of it.

"Please don't worry," she murmured.

He squeezed her hand, and forced his lips into a smile. "Well, it's not every day I see someone I—" He paused and cleared his throat. "Someone I know practically get blown up on TV."

He tried for a light tone, but he was shaken by what he'd almost said to Amy. Fortunately, she didn't seem to notice.

The door opened, and they both glanced toward the white-coated figure who entered. The woman looked at Amy as she approached them, then held out her hand to Cal.

"I'm Dr. Whitney. And you're...?"

"Cal Richards. I'm a friend of Amy's."

The woman nodded, then turned her attention to Amy. "I've checked the X rays, Ms. Winter. You're one lucky lady. Everything looks fine. There isn't even any evidence of a concussion."

Amy managed a weak grin. "My mother always said I had a hard head."

"Not too hard," the doctor amended. "The flying debris put a nice gouge in the back. To the tune of twenty stitches, in fact. Fortunately, once your hair grows back, you'll never notice the scar."

"How about the little boy, doctor? And the others in the building?"

"A number were injured in the explosions, but there were no fatalities. Thanks to you, the boy has just minor cuts and abrasions. But it would be a different story if he'd still been standing by the building when the second explosion went off."

Amy shrugged dismissively. "Someone else would have gone to get him if I hadn't."

Cal's hand tightened around hers, and she was struck by the intensity in his eyes when she looked up at him. "But everyone else hesitated, Amy. You didn't."

"He's right," the doctor confirmed.

Amy tore her gaze away from Cal's. "I love kids. It was just instinctive."

The doctor glanced at Cal. "This is one special lady, you know."

Cal nodded. "Yeah. I know."

"Okay, here's the scoop," the doctor continued, turning her attention back to Amy. "We have no reason to keep you. You'll probably recover much faster at home, anyway. I'll give you a prescription for pain, but the best thing you can do for the next few days is rest. You may experience a bit of light-headedness for the next day or two, so move slowly. You can see your own doctor to have the stitches removed in a few days. Any questions?"

"No."

"Let's have you sit up, then."

The woman reached over to assist Amy, and Cal moved to her other side. She carefully swung her legs over the edge of the gurney and let them dangle for a moment, closing her eyes as a wave of dizziness and nausea swept over her.

"Oh, wow," Amy said faintly, gripping the edge of the gurney. She felt Cal move closer and put his arm around her shoulder.

"Dizzy?" the doctor asked.

She nodded.

"Nauseous?"

Again Amy nodded.

"Just sit there a moment and breathe steadily. It should pass quickly."

Amy kept her eyes closed and focused on following the doctor's instructions. When she finally felt more normal, she opened her eyes.

"Okay?" the doctor asked, studying her critically.

"I think so."

"Your blouse and jacket are on the chair," the woman said, nodding toward the items. "Can you manage, or should I send a nurse in?"

Amy's head was rapidly clearing, and she shook her head. "No. I can handle it."

The doctor glanced at Cal. "Will you see that she gets home? Or should we call someone else?"

"I'll take her."

"Good. All right, Ms. Winter. You should be fine. If you have any problems—extended dizziness, excessive bleeding from the cut—let us know. You'll need to change the dressing every day, maybe twice a day for the first couple of days. I'll have a nurse bring in some gauze and tape for you, along with the prescription."

"Thank you."

"My pleasure," the woman said with a smile. "We don't get too many heroes in here."

Amy flushed, then turned to Cal as the woman exited. He was looking at her with such tenderness that her breath caught in her throat. If she didn't know better... But no, that was ridiculous. That knock on the head was giving her all sorts of crazy ideas. Besides, his expression was gone so quickly that she wondered if she'd just imagined it.

"Ready to go home?"

She nodded. "Could you hand me my clothes?"

"Can you manage this?" he asked as he retrieved her blouse and jacket.

"I think so." She reached around, then frowned. "Except maybe for the ties on this gown. Would you undo them?"

"Sure." He stepped to her side and she angled her body away from him. The green hospital gown was tied in two places, and as his fingers worked the knots he tried to ignore the expanse of creamy skin visible between the edges of the gown. It wasn't easy. More than once his fingers inadvertently brushed against the curve of her slender back, and each time an electric shock seemed to ricochet through him, jolting him not only physically, but emotionally. No other woman had ever drawn such a powerful response from him with so little provocation. That response, coming on the heels of his unexpectedly gut-wrenching panic at her injury, left him floundering in an unfamiliar sea of emotions.

He fumbled through the second tie, drawing a ragged breath when at last it slipped open. "Should I leave while you change?" he asked unsteadily.

She shook her head. "Just turn around, please."

Cal gladly complied. He needed some time to compose himself and get off the emotional roller coaster he was on. Like a couple of weeks, maybe. Unfortunately, the two minutes it took Amy to change wasn't nearly enough.

"Okay. I'm decent."

He turned slowly, and though she smiled, he could see the weariness and pain in her face.

"I'd be happy to call a cab, Cal," she offered. "I hate to put you to all this trouble."

"Forget it."

From the tone of his voice, she figured the subject wasn't open to discussion. And she wasn't up to one, anyway. Instead, she gripped the edge of the gurney and started to stand.

Cal was beside her in an instant. "Whoa! Remember what the doctor said. Move slowly." He put an arm around her shoulders. "Okay, try it now."

Amy rose gingerly to her feet. She swayed for a moment, and he gave her a worried look as he tightened his grip.

"I'm okay," she assured him. "Just a little light-headed."

Before he could reply, a knock at the door drew their attention, and the nurse entered. "Dr. Whitney said to give you these." She held out a package of gauze and a prescription, and Cal took them. "Do you need any help getting to your car? Would you like a wheelchair?"

"Yes."

"No."

They spoke simultaneously, and Amy glanced up at Cal. "I can walk."

For a moment she thought he was going to argue, but instead he turned to the nurse. "Could you wait with her at the entrance while I pull up?"

"No problem."

"That's really not necessary," Amy protested.

"Humor me, okay?"

There was something intense but unreadable in his eyes that made Amy's protest die in her throat. "Okay."

By the time she was safely buckled into his car a few minutes later and they were on their way, a deep-seated weariness had settled over her. She answered his few questions in monosyllables, and was grateful when he lapsed into silence. Though the drive home was swift, with just one stop to get her prescription filled, the road seemed excessively bumpy, and the throbbing pain in her head intensified. When they at last pulled into her parking lot she let out an audible sigh of relief.

Cal parked the car and glanced over at her with a worried frown. He'd been stealing looks at her throughout the drive, and she seemed to have grown paler over the past half hour. He wasn't entirely convinced that the hospital should have released her, but he supposed the doctor was right. She would get more rest here.

"Wait there. I'll come around and help you out," he instructed.

Amy acquiesced with a nod. She'd planned to simply thank Cal in the parking lot and send him on his way, but she suddenly felt too shaky to make it into her apartment without help.

"Okay, nice and easy," he said as he pulled her door open and extended his hand.

With his help, she stood carefully—only to suddenly find herself in his arms.

"Just take a minute to get your sea legs," he said huskily as he held her protectively against his chest. He had planned to give her a moment to get her balance—but he lost his the second her soft curves pressed against the length of his body. She felt so good in his arms. So right. A powerful surge of yearning swept over him, and it took every ounce of his willpower to fight the temptation to lean down and taste the sweetness of her lips.

Cal swallowed convulsively. He didn't want to feel this way about Amy. And he especially didn't want to feel this way right now, when he was struggling with other choices and decisions that would affect the rest of his life. Cal didn't understand why the Lord had put this woman in his life at this particular time, but he also trusted that there must be a reason. And so he turned to the Master, as he often did in times of turmoil, for guidance.

Dear Lord, I'm confused, he prayed as he held Amy in his arms. *After today, I know that I care deeply about this woman. But we seem ill suited in so many ways. Our priorities—and our lifestyles—are completely different. Amy could never be happy in a cabin in the mountains. But I'm more and more convinced that I can't be happy anywhere else. Please, Lord, help me resolve this dilemma and give me the wisdom to discern Your will.*

As Amy leaned against Cal, savoring the haven of his strong, sure arms, she felt strangely content. She wasn't a woman who leaned on *anyone* very often, but at this moment it felt wonderful. In fact, oddly enough, it felt as if she'd somehow come home. She didn't understand the feeling, but neither did she fight it. It felt too good. So with a sigh, she closed her eyes and nestled her cheek against his chest, conscious of the rapid beat of his heart beneath her ear. Amy didn't think his elevated pulse was from the exertion of helping her out of the car, and a sudden tingle of excitement ran through her that had nothing to do with her recent trauma.

Cal felt her tremble and pulled back slightly to gaze down at her, his eyes troubled. "Are you okay?"

No, she wasn't. Her own pulse had gone haywire, and she was having trouble breathing as she grappled with her own conflicting emotions. It felt way too good in this man's arms. And though she tried desperately to stifle the thought, she couldn't stop wondering what it would be like to feel his lips on hers.

"Amy?"

Cal's worried voice brought her back to reality, and she forced her stiff lips into the semblance of a smile. "I'll be better once I'm inside."

If Cal noticed the unevenness in her voice, he made no comment. Instead, he closed the door and took her arm, matching his pace to hers as she made her way slowly to the door. She fumbled in her purse, all too conscious of his hand resting protectively in the small of her back.

When her fingers closed over the key, she turned to him and again summoned up a smile.

"Thank you for everything, Cal. I'm really sorry about tonight. I'm sure you had better plans for your evening then spending it at the hospital."

He tilted his head and gave her a crooked grin. "Are you telling me to get lost?"

She looked at him in surprise. "Of course not. You're welcome to come in. I just don't want to ruin the rest of your evening."

He reached over and took the key from her hand. "Trust me, Amy. This is where I want to be."

She didn't know how to respond to that, so she simply let him open the door and guide her inside.

"Why don't you sit down and I'll get you some water so you can take a pill?"

"You really don't have to wait on me, you know. I'm used to taking care of myself."

He turned toward her and placed both hands lightly on her shoulders. "I know. You're a very strong, independent woman. But you've had one tough day. And frankly, so have I. It's not a pretty thing to watch someone you—you care about get hurt right in front of your eyes. In fact, it's as close to hell as I ever want to get. So let me do this for you, okay? It will make me feel better."

Cal had a way of making it sound like *he* was the beneficiary of his own good deeds, Amy realized, remembering his comment about his work at Saint Vincent's. And positioned that way, she could hardly object.

"You win," she capitulated.

When he returned a few moments later, she was playing back the messages on her answering machine. "I need to call the news editor back. The rest can wait," she told him.

He handed her the water and a pill. "Would you like some dinner?"

She made a face. "No way. I'm still kind of queasy. What time is it, anyway?" She glanced at her watch and her eyes widened. "Ten o'clock! I must have been at the hospital for hours. What about you? Did you have dinner?"

"Not yet."

"Oh, Cal! You must be starving!"

"Only in the last few minutes."

"I've got some microwave stuff in the freezer. You're welcome to anything in there, but I think my supply is pretty depleted," she said apologetically.

He grinned. "A starving man isn't very picky. Go ahead and make your call while I scrounge something up."

The news editor wasn't available, but the station promised to have him get back to her shortly. She rose to go to the bathroom, pausing in the kitchen doorway to find Cal with a chocolate-chip cookie stuck in his mouth as he searched through her freezer.

"That's not very nutritious," she teased.

He turned to her and removed the cookie. "Maybe not. But it's very available."

"True," she conceded. "Listen, would you mind answering the phone while I change into something more casual? My station should be calling back any minute."

"Sure. Take your time."

Amy continued to the bathroom, where she washed her face and then used a hand mirror to gingerly examine the back of her head in the vanity mirror, cringing when she saw the large white bandage. Good thing they only showed her from the front on camera, she thought wryly. It was going to take a long time for all that hair to grow back.

Just as she finished dressing she heard the phone ring, and she padded barefoot toward the living room, tucking her T-shirt into her sweatpants as she walked.

"Yes, she's okay," she heard Cal say. "Shaken up, of course, and she has a nasty cut on the back of her head. But the doctor said she'll be fine."

There was a moment of silence, then he spoke again.

"No, don't worry. I'm going to stay tonight until she's settled. And I'll stop by to check on her again first thing in the morning…Mmm-hmm…I already asked, but she said no. Any suggestions on what might whet her appetite in the morning if she's still not hungry?"

Amy's brows rose in surprise and she paused in the doorway. Jarrod Blake, the night news editor, was good at his job, but it wasn't like him to ask about anyone's health—or eating habits—in any detail. And he certainly wouldn't know anything about Amy's favorite foods.

Cal listened for a moment, then turned and caught sight of her. "She just walked in. I'll put her on." He covered the mouthpiece with his hand. "Your sister," he said.

Amy frowned and walked toward him. "Kate?"

"She saw your clip on the national news a few minutes ago, and she sounded pretty frantic. I told her you were okay, but I don't think she'll believe it until she hears your voice."

Amy reached for the phone. "Kate?"

"Oh, Amy! I was so afraid you were—" Her voice broke on a strangled sob.

"Kate, really, it's okay," Amy reassured her. She gently lowered herself into the desk chair, her gaze on Cal's broad back as retreated to the kitchen. "I just needed a few stitches."

"I wish I could be there with you!"

"I love you for the thought, but really, I'm okay. Cal is here. And you've got that baby to think about. Please, don't worry."

"Have you heard from Mom?"

"No. Have you? Did she see it, too?" Amy asked in alarm.

"I guess not, or she would have called. But she'll hear about it in the morning from someone."

"I'll call her first thing," Amy promised.

"Okay." Kate was beginning to sound more like herself. "Listen, isn't this Cal the one you bought the date with at that auction?"

"Yeah."

"I didn't know you'd been seeing him."

"I haven't been."

"Then what's he doing there?"

Amy lowered her voice. "I don't know. He just showed up at the hospital, and then he brought me home."

"I thought you said there wasn't anything between you two?"

"I didn't think there was."

"Hmm. Sounds like you better revise your thinking, sister dear."

"What I think is that you're reading too much into this," Amy said firmly. "Besides, my head hurts too much to think about this tonight."

"You're right," Kate said, instantly contrite. "Go to bed and get some rest. Will you call me tomorrow and let me know how you are?"

"Of course."

"Say good-night to Cal for me. And, Amy…he sounds really nice."

As Amy rang off, she couldn't disagree with Kate's assessment. Especially when Cal walked in a moment later bearing a plate of toast and a cup of tea.

"I know you aren't hungry, but you should try to eat something," he said before she could protest. He set the plate and cup on the desk beside her.

Once more, Amy felt her throat constrict. It had been a long time since anyone had looked after her, and Cal's simple gesture made her realize just how alone she'd been for so many years. Amy blinked rapidly to clear the sudden film of moisture from her eyes and then looked up at him. "What about you? I hope you had more than that cookie."

He shrugged. "I nuked something while you changed. Go ahead, eat a few bites at least."

Amy nibbled on the toast and watched as Cal leaned against the back of the couch, hands thrust into his pockets, legs crossed at the ankles. He looked tired, she thought, her gaze softening in sympathy.

"I'm really sorry about dragging you into this, Cal. After all the stress and strain of the trial, this is the last thing you needed."

"You didn't drag me into this, Amy. I willingly got involved."

"Why?"

The question was out before she could stop it, and she felt hot color rise to her cheeks. "Listen. Forget I asked that, okay?"

There was silence for a moment, and when he spoke his voice was cautious. "Why don't you want me to answer that question?"

Because I'm afraid, she cried silently. Afraid of disrupting my carefully planned life. And even more afraid that your answer won't be the one my heart wants to hear.

"I don't think I'm up to dealing with heavy questions tonight," she replied instead, her voice quavering slightly.

"I think you're right." He stood up and walked slowly toward her, and she stared at him silently, her heart hammering in her chest. For a moment his intense gaze locked with hers, and then he glanced at her plate, now empty except for a few crumbs. "I guess you were hungrier than you thought," he said softly.

The husky cadence in his voice made the last swallow of toast stick in her throat. Did the man have even a remote clue how appealing he was? she wondered, trying to ignore her staccato pulse. "I—I guess so," she said inanely as she stared back up at him, mesmerized by the banked fire she saw in the depths of his eyes.

He took a deep breath, then cleared his throat. "Come on. You need to get to bed."

Amy didn't object when he took her arm as she stood. She suddenly felt off balance again.

"Do you need to change?" he asked.

She shook her head. "I'm too tired. This will do."

When she reached the bed, she sat down wearily. The physical and emotional upheavals of the past few hours had completely sapped her energy.

Cal waited for her to lie down, but when she continued to simply sit there, shoulders drooping, head bent, he lifted her legs onto the bed, then gently helped position her on her side. He reached for the blanket, pausing in surprise at the hand-stitched quilt that lay at the foot of her bed. The homespun touch seemed out of place in Amy's sophisticated lifestyle.

"Is something wrong?" Amy asked sleepily when he didn't move.

Cal quickly finished drawing up the quilt and tucked it around her shoulders. "I was just admiring your quilt. It reminds me of ones Gram has done. Did you mother make it?"

"No. I did."

He stared down at her in surprise. "You quilt?"

"I grew up on a farm, remember?" Her words were slightly slurred now.

"But I thought you left all that behind."

"Me, too." She sighed. When she spoke again, he had to lean close to hear her fading voice. "Life's funny, isn't it?"

Cal stared down at her. Yeah, life was funny, all right. And surprising. Not to mention confusing.

He reached down and gently brushed a stray strand of hair off her face, his fingers lingering on her soft skin a moment longer than necessary. Then he drew a ragged breath. He had no idea where this thing between them was leading. But he did know one thing. It was time to find out.

Chapter Nine

The delicious smell of fresh-baked cinnamon rolls slowly coaxed Amy out of her deep slumber, and she sighed contentedly, savoring the aroma. What a nice dream. Cinnamon rolls were one of her all-time favorite treats, and it had been a long time since she'd indulged in them. They were *way* too fattening. But at least she could enjoy them in her dreams, where they came calorie free and…

A sudden clatter brought her fully awake, and Amy sat bolt upright, a move she immediately regretted. A wave of dizziness and pain swept over her, and she dropped her head into her hands as yesterday's nightmare events came vividly back to her. And now it seemed she was plunged into yet another nightmare. Someone was in her kitchen! A shiver of alarm raced along her spine, and she groped in the drawer of her nightstand for the pepper spray she'd kept there ever since Cal's mugging. When the world at last stopped spinning, she rose slowly and silently crept to the kitchen, her heart hammering in her chest, pepper spray poised.

If she was inclined to jaw dropping, the sight that greeted her when she peeked around the doorway would have done the trick. Cal was at the stove, concentrating on making what looked like an omelet. His jacket hung over one of the kitchen chairs, and he'd rolled the sleeves of his white shirt up to the elbows. Her gaze lingered on his broad shoulders for a moment before she transferred it to the table, where a plate of cinnamon rolls dripping with icing sent her salivary glands into overdrive.

As Cal reached for a plate, he caught sight of her and, in one swift, discerning glance, assessed her condition. Though her clothes were in disarray, her makeup nonexistent and her hair unkempt, her color was more normal and her eyes looked clearer, he noted with relief. Then his gaze fell on the pepper spray, and he gave her a quizzical grin.

"Your sister told me you had a weakness for cinnamon rolls and anyone who tempted you was in trouble, but don't you think the pepper spray is a little extreme?"

Amy stared at him in confusion. "What are you doing here?"

"Fixing breakfast."

"I can see that. I mean…*why* are you here?"

"I told your sister I'd check on you this morning. And she made me promise to try and get you to eat something." He slid the omelet onto a plate and placed it on the table, then pulled out her chair with a flourish. "Can I tempt you?"

That was definitely a loaded question, Amy thought wryly as she tried to ignore the sudden flutter of her pulse. "Actually, I'm, uh, pretty hungry today," she stammered.

"A good sign," he pronounced, pushing in her chair as she sat down.

"Aren't you eating anything?" she asked as he walked back toward the counter.

"I might try one of those cinnamon rolls with a cup of coffee."

She reached for one herself as he rejoined her, and closed her eyes to savor the first bite. "Mmm! This is heaven!"

Cal chuckled and took a sip of his coffee. "I'll have to tell your sister that her strategy worked."

Amy wrinkled her nose. "She knows me too well. Not that I'm complaining, you understand." She took another big bite and chewed slowly. "Just out of curiosity, may I ask how you got in? Did you call on one of your police connections to jimmy the lock or something?"

"Nothing so dramatic. I left your key on the table by the door when I brought you home last night, so I just borrowed it."

"How late did you stay?"

He shrugged. "A couple of hours after you went to bed. I wanted to make sure you were sleeping okay before I left. By the way, your station called. Somebody named Jarrod. I told him you were asleep, and he said not to worry about coming in for a few days. How's the omelet?"

Amy speared another forkful. "Surprisingly good."

Cal pretended to look offended. "Well, thanks a lot. I do have *some* culinary talent."

She chuckled. "And I suppose you made the cinnamon rolls, too?"

"You've got me there," he admitted with a lopsided

grin. "I know a little mom-and-pop bakery that works magic with dough."

"They have my vote," Amy concurred as she helped herself to another roll.

Cal drained his coffee cup and glanced at his watch. "When you finish that, why don't I change your dressing before I head to the office?"

Amy looked at him in surprise. "Cal, you've done more than enough as it is. And you're probably already late for work. I can manage."

"Not easily. You won't even be able to see what you're doing without juggling a mirror in one hand, and I think it's a two-handed job."

She couldn't argue with his logic. "Don't tell me you're a medic, too."

He gave her a disarming grin. "Hardly. Believe it or not, the sight of blood makes me pretty squeamish."

Amy looked at him in surprise. "Honestly?"

"Yep. So much for my macho image."

She smiled, charmed yet again by his lack of pretense. "Then your offer is doubly appreciated. I don't think it's a pretty sight back there. You're not going to pass out on me or anything, are you?"

He chuckled. "I'll let you know if I feel dizzy."

He rose and retrieved the gauze and tape, as well as some antiseptic cream, then positioned himself behind her.

"Ready?"

"I guess so."

Cal carefully eased the tape off her scalp, and though she didn't say a word, he knew by the rigid lines of her body and her white-knuckled grip on her coffee mug that she was hurting. When at last the dressing came free and

Cal got his first look at the gouge on the back of her head, he sucked in his breath sharply.

"You okay?" Amy asked, her own voice strained.

"Yeah."

"Does it look bad?"

Cal gazed down at the jagged abrasion. It was nearly three inches long, caked with dried blood and framed by angry, inflamed skin. "Bad" was an understatement.

"Could be worse," he replied, striving to keep his voice light as he reached for the gauze. "I think I'll clean it up a little before I put the cream on, though." He walked over to the sink and dampened the gauze, giving himself a moment to recover from his first look at the cut. He hadn't been kidding when he told Amy he was no medic. He didn't like blood. Never had. Especially when it was on someone he cared about. And seeing her injury in living color only brought home to him again how close she had come to something more serious.

He took his time at the sink, and by the time he repositioned himself behind her, he felt calmer. "This will probably hurt," he said apologetically.

"I'm sure it will. But I can handle it," she said with more bravado than she felt.

Cal was sure she could. Amy Winter was one tough lady. But he didn't want to test her limits, so he cleaned off the dried blood as carefully as he could until at last the long row of stitches was revealed. He paused once when she winced, and let his hand drop to her shoulder.

"I'm okay," she said shakily.

He waited a moment, then carefully applied the cream and rebandaged the wound, using a much smaller piece of gauze than the one applied by the emergency room staff.

"I think they overdid it with the bandage at the hospital. In fact, you should be able to disguise that premature bald spot pretty well with your hair," he teased, hoping to distract her.

When she made no comment, he finished up quickly, then came around and squatted beside her. Her face looked strained, and slightly paler than when she had first come into the kitchen, and he reached over and touched her cheek gently, his gaze tender. "I'm sorry if I hurt you," he said softly.

She drew in a deep breath. "It's okay. There's no way around it for the next few days, I guess. I'll just try to get a lot of rest, and hopefully it will heal faster."

He hesitated for a moment, then cleared his throat. "I have a suggestion about the rest part."

He seemed suddenly...*nervous* was the word that came to mind, and she looked at him curiously. "What?"

He didn't answer her question immediately. Instead, he rose and returned to his seat, where he wrapped his hands around his empty coffee cup. Now he really had her attention. "What is it, Cal?"

He looked over at her. The idea had come to him late last night, and at the time it had seemed inspired. Now, in the light of day, he wasn't so sure. But he had already decided that he could no longer ignore the attraction between them, and this was an ideal opportunity to test the waters.

"After the trial ended, my boss suggested I take a few days off and go home to the mountains to recharge my batteries. I'm leaving tomorrow. Your boss told me last night that they want you to take a few days off to rest and recuperate, too. Since there's no better place for that than the Smokies, I was wondering if you—if you might like to join me. The mountains can do wonders for your mental and physical health.''

Amy stared at him, clearly stunned by the invitation. Cal had expected her to be surprised, had known it was a gamble. And the odds of her accepting seemed to be dropping rapidly with each second that ticked by. When the silence lengthened, he shifted uncomfortably.

"Listen, I know this is unexpected. Why don't you think about it today and give me your answer tonight?'' he suggested. "I'll stop by on my way home to change the dressing again.''

Amy hardly heard his addendum. She was still too busy trying to process the unexpected invitation. "Did you just ask me to go home with you?'' she said carefully.

"Yeah. There's plenty of room in Gram's cabin. I know it's not the Caribbean or the exotic resorts you like, but it's quiet and restful. And it might do you a lot of good.''

His voice was casual, but Amy could sense his tension as she considered the invitation. While she wanted to explore the possibilities of their relationship, this was a giant step. One she wasn't altogether sure she was ready to take. She'd figured on easing into this thing, not jumping in feetfirst. And a few days in the mountains, with Cal's family and on his turf, was definitely feetfirst. On the other hand, maybe that's exactly what she should do. She'd probably find out pretty quick whether there was any potential between them. As she tried to weigh the pros and cons of accepting, her head began to ache, and she reached up to rub her temples.

"How long will you be gone?'' she asked, stalling.

"Until Wednesday night.''

"Let me check with my station and find out just how much time I can take, okay?"

"Fair enough. I'll be here about six. And don't worry about food. I'll pick up a pizza."

She looked at him and shook her head. No matter what happened between them, one thing was clear. "You're an amazing man, Cal Richards," she said softly.

He felt his neck grow red, even as his heart grew warm. "I have to eat, anyway." He rose and reached for his coat. "Take it easy today, okay?"

She nodded. "I don't think I'm up to doing much else."

He laid a hand gently on her shoulder, and for a moment their gazes locked—and sizzled. Amy's mouth went dry; she moistened her lips with her tongue. Cal's gaze dropped, and she heard his sharply indrawn breath, saw his Adam's apple bob convulsively. Then, without another word, he turned and left.

"Amy! I've been praying for you ever since I woke up! If you hadn't called me in the next ten minutes, I was going to call *you!*"

Amy pulled her knees up and snuggled into the corner of the couch. "I didn't want to wake you. I know you've been sleeping later since you got pregnant."

"Not this morning. I hardly closed my eyes all night, thinking about you. Did you call Mom?"

"Yes. She hadn't heard anything about it, so I downplayed the whole incident as much as possible. I don't think she was too worried."

"Unlike your sister, who saw it all in living color."

"I'm sorry, Kate. I still can't believe it made national news."

"I can. It was a pretty heroic thing to do."

"Anyone would have done the same."

"But they didn't. You were the only one."

"You sound like Cal. And thanks a lot for telling him about the cinnamon rolls. I probably put on five pounds in the last two hours."

"He brought them!" Her sister sounded delighted.

"Yeah. Bright and early. Almost too early, in fact. I heard noises in the kitchen and thought it was an intruder. I almost zapped him with the pepper spray."

"Amy! You didn't!"

"I said 'almost.' Good thing I didn't. It would have ruined the cinnamon rolls. Not to mention the omelet."

"He made you an omelet?" her sister said reverently.

"Yes. And a very good one, I might add."

"This man sounds like a keeper, Amy."

Amy sighed. "Yeah, he does, doesn't he? The thing is, I'm not sure I have time for romance, Kate. And besides, we're so different. He's a country boy at heart, and I like the bright lights. I don't see how it could ever work."

"You'll never know if you don't give it a chance. What do you have to lose?"

My heart, Amy replied silently. But her spoken words were different. "You're assuming that he's interested."

"A man doesn't show up at a hospital emergency room if he's not interested, Amy. I bet if you gave him any encouragement, he'd pursue this."

Amy sighed. "It seems you're right again, dear sister. He does want to pursue it. The station gave me a few days off, and he invited me to go to the mountains with him."

There was a long beat of silence, and when Kate spoke, her tone was suddenly cautious. "Look, Amy, maybe this isn't such a good idea after all. Up till now, everything you've told me about this guy has led me to believe that he's got his head on straight and has pretty solid moral values. But if he's inviting you to shack up with him for the weekend, then—''

"Hold on, Kate," Amy interrupted with a laugh. "Trust me, that isn't his style. We'd be staying with his grand-mother.''

The relief in Kate's voice was obvious. "Well, thank goodness! You're going, aren't you?''

"I don't know.''

Again there was a moment of silence. "It wouldn't be because you're afraid, would it?" Kate finally asked, her voice gentle.

Amy frowned. "What do you mean?''

"I don't know if I can explain exactly," Kate said hes-itantly. "It's just that...well, all these years I've watched you single-mindedly go after what you want. I've admired you in many ways, even envied your drive and commit-ment at times, as well as your ability to stay focused. You just didn't let anything into your life that could deter you from capturing the golden ring. But I honestly can't say that you've ever seemed really happy or...or content. And I think maybe you've missed some good things along the way, all in the name of your career. I'm not saying career isn't important, Amy. You've worked hard and done well, and I know that means a lot to you. But it's not everything. And maybe it's not even the most important thing.'' She paused and took a deep breath. "I guess what it comes down to is this. I don't want you to pass up a chance at love just because the guy came along at the wrong time or is a little different than what you expected.''

Kate's comments mirrored her own recent thoughts so closely that for a moment Amy was too surprised to speak.

"Amy?" Kate's concerned voice came over the wire. "Listen, I didn't mean to offend you, but..."

"It's okay," Amy assured her sister. "You just hit a little too close to home. I guess maybe I am afraid. After investing so much of my life and myself in my career—pretty much to the exclusion of all else—it's pretty scary to think about changing course. Especially when I've been so sure about my destination."

"I know it's hard for you. You've always been the type to hang on tenaciously once you set your mind to something. Remember the violin?"

Amy chuckled. "Yeah."

"You drove us nuts at home. Even though the teacher kept telling you that it just wasn't your instrument, you were determined to be the next Itzhak Perlman. We all deserve a special place in heaven for putting up with that screeching for...how long? Four years? Five?"

"It was only two."

"Well, it seemed at least twice that long."

Amy laughed. "I must admit, you guys were pretty good sports. And you're right. I have a hard time letting go, once I make my mind up to go after something."

"Well, let me tell you, we all got down on our knees and thanked the Lord when you took up quilting. It was the answer to our prayers. And you would never have discovered you had a talent for it if you hadn't gone to that meeting for Mom. In fact, until then, whenever she brought it up you just laughed it off. You said it wouldn't be a good fit. But you found out differently once you tried it. I guess all I'm saying about Cal is that maybe it's the same kind of thing. It might not look like a good fit on the surface, but you might be surprised if you give it a chance.''

''You know something, Kate?''

''What?''

''You're one sharp lady.''

Kate chuckled. ''I wish you'd thought that when we were teenagers. It would have prevented quite a few squabbles. So you don't mind the advice, then?''

''No.''

''Then can I give you one more piece?''

''Sure.''

''I know you haven't kept up with your faith these past few years. But it wouldn't hurt to ask for a little guidance. The Lord always comes through, you know.''

''Frankly, Kate, I don't think He even remembers my name.''

''Of course He does. That's the nice thing about the Lord, Amy. Even if we ignore Him, He never ignores us. But enough preaching. You'll let me know what you decide about the trip, won't you?''

''Absolutely. Just as soon as I know myself.''

Amy sat there for a long time after she rang off, weighing the pros and cons of accepting Cal's invitation. When the minutes ticked by and she didn't seem to be any closer to a resolution, she decided to take Kate's advice and try asking for guidance from a higher power.

It had been a long time since she'd prayed, and at first she felt awkward. But as she closed her eyes and struggled to express her chaotic thoughts in the silence of her heart, the words suddenly came.

Dear Lord, I know You haven't heard from me in a

while. It's not that I stopped believing. I've just been too busy to take time for prayer. Or, I guess more truthfully, I just haven't made time for prayer, the way Cal has. Anyway, he's the reason I'm coming to You now. I like him, Lord. A lot. But I'm afraid if I let him get too close, it could change my life forever. On the other hand, Kate could be right. I might be letting something really good slip away if I don't pursue this. I'm confused, Lord. I need Your help. I know I've been a wayward soul for too long, but I'm going to try to find my way back to You. And in the meantime, please guide me to make the right decision about this.

When Amy opened her eyes, she had no magic solution to her dilemma. But somehow her burden seemed lighter. And she had a feeling that by the time Cal arrived that evening, she'd be ready to give him an answer.

As the first blue-hued mountains appeared on the distant horizon, Cal drew in a slow, deep, cleansing breath. The familiar and comforting sense of homecoming swept over him, and he turned to glance at Amy, anxious to share this moment with her. But she was still sleeping soundly.

His gaze softened as it lingered on her face, and only with great effort did he turn his attention back to the road. He was glad she was sleeping. She'd looked exhausted when he'd arrived to pick her up this morning. Though her wound seemed to be healing nicely, the skin around the abrasion was badly bruised from the trauma. Apparently she'd inadvertently turned on her back a few times during the night, and the pressure on her tender skin had rudely—and painfully—jolted her awake. Though she'd tried to keep up a breezy conversation during the first hour or so of the trip, the gentle lulling motion of the car had eventually made her drowsy, and she'd drifted off. That had been almost three hours ago.

Cal didn't mind. He was just glad she'd accepted his invitation. It had seemed touch-and-go for a while, and he'd been prepared to press her if she'd turned him down when he'd arrived with the pizza. But surprisingly she had said yes with no further discussion. She'd mentioned that she'd talked with her sister that day, and if Kate was responsible for Amy's decision, then he owed her. Big time. Because the more he'd thought about it, the more confident he was that his middle-of-the-night inspiration to invite her home was sound. Though they'd never discussed—or even acknowledged—the attraction between them, it was as real as the mountains looming ahead. And it was time to face it. Here, away from the distractions of their everyday lives, perhaps they could both come to grips with their feelings.

Amy made a soft sound, and he glanced toward her just as her eyelids flickered open.

"Hi, sleepyhead," he teased with a smile.

She blinked and rubbed her eyes in an endearing little-girl gesture that tugged at his heart.

"Hi." She peered at her watch, and then quickly straightened up, her eyes widening. "Have I been asleep for three hours?"

"Uh-huh."

"Oh, Cal, I'm sorry! I meant to keep you company during the drive."

"You needed the rest. And I've made this drive alone more times than I can count. It's only five or six hours. It gives me a chance to unwind and let the cares of the city slip away."

Amy gazed out the window and scanned the landscape appreciatively. "It's beautiful here."

"We're just in the foothills. It's even better closer to the park. We should be at Gram's cabin in less than an hour."

They chatted companionably during the remainder of the trip, and in what seemed only a few minutes, Cal turned into a gravel driveway that led toward a cabin.

"This is home," he said quietly, stopping the car for a moment to gaze at the scene.

The cabin was fairly rustic, separated from the road by a large meadow. Colorful flowers spilled from planters along the porch railing, and a grove of pine trees seemed to come right up to the back door. In an adjacent pasture a horse grazed contentedly against a serene backdrop of misty blue-hued mountains.

The peace of the scene stole over Amy, and for the first time in a long while she felt the always-present tension in her shoulders begin to ease. There was a calmness to this place that made the location seem far away from the hustle and bustle of her world—not only in miles, but in spirit. The quiet—broken only by an occasional birdcall—and the beauty of nature were like a balm for the soul, and Amy drew in a long, slow breath.

When she turned to Cal, he was watching her with an enigmatic expression on his face. She sensed that he was waiting for her to comment, and she struggled to find the words to capture her first reaction.

"I think I already understand why you love this place so much," she said softly. "It's like a world apart. There's so much beauty and calmness here, and a kind of…I don't know how to describe it exactly. It's like a special tranquillity that you just breathe in.''

His smile warmed her to her toes. ''I hoped you might see it that way.'' Their gazes held for a long moment, and then he turned and nodded toward the porch. ''I think the welcoming committee is waiting.''

Amy followed his gaze. Two people stood by the railing, waving.

''Gram and my dad,'' Cal explained as he put the car in gear.

As they closed the distance to the cabin, Amy studied the two people who were so special to Cal. Interestingly enough, neither was exactly what she'd expected. Though there was a resemblance between Cal and his father, the older man was much shorter than his son, and slightly stooped. His thinning hair was mostly gray, but there were enough sandy-colored strands left to provide a clue to its original color. He had a nice but careworn face and kind eyes. *Quiet* and *gentle* were the words that came to mind as Amy looked at him.

Cal's grandmother was also thin, but she radiated energy. She was dressed in jeans, her white hair closely cropped, and anticipation flashed in her eyes. Amy could almost imagine her hopping from one foot to the other in her excitement, an image so ''ungrandmotherly,'' it brought a smile to her lips. By the time Cal stopped the car and started to alight, the older woman was waiting at his door.

''My, it's good to see you, son!'' she said, hugging him fiercely. ''You've been way too scarce.''

Cal's father followed more slowly, a pipe in one hand, and patiently waited his turn to greet his son. When Cal at last stepped free of Gram's enthusiastic embrace, he reached out and pulled his father into a bear hug.

"Hello, Dad."

"Hello, son. It's good to have you home."

The two men stood like that for a long minute, and Amy could sense the bond of love between them. In fact, the three of them shared a circle of love that suddenly made her feel like an intruder. She didn't belong here. Cal should have used this rare break to spend time with his family, not entertain her. Maybe he was already regretting the invitation. Maybe she should...

As if sensing their visitor's sudden discomfort, Gram leaned in the open door of the driver's side and smiled warmly.

"You must be Amy." She held out her hand, and Amy's was engulfed in a firm clasp. "I'm Gram. Or Amanda. Whatever you prefer. I hope you'll excuse us. We're kind of a gushy bunch when we haven't seen each other for weeks. Usually we have a little more decorum when it comes to public displays of affection." She turned back to the two men and clapped Cal on the back. "Break it up, you two. Let's go inside so our guest can settle in and I can get dinner on the table."

Cal smiled and leaned in to look at Amy. "Sit tight. I'll get your door."

Before she could protest, he strode around to her side and pulled it open, Gram and his father close on his heels.

"Gram, Dad, this is Amy Winter. Amy, I'd like you to meet my family."

Cal's father stepped forward shyly and took her hand. "I'm very pleased to meet you, Amy. Cal has told us a lot of nice things about you."

She smiled at the older man's courtly manner. "I've heard good things about you, too. I'm glad we had this chance to meet."

Gram stepped forward next and enveloped her in a hug. She was small and wiry, but there was strength in her arms—and in her face. "We're mighty glad you came to visit, Amy. And honored. Cal told us all about how you got hurt saving that little boy. You feeling okay after that long ride?"

Before she could reply, Cal spoke up. "She's tired. And I'm sure she's hungry. We didn't stop to eat on the way up."

"Well, say no more. Dinner's on the stove. Some good food and rest will fix you up in no time, Amy. And the mountain air will do wonders for you. Clear your lungs of all that smog you breathe down in Atlanta."

Cal smiled. "It's good to be back, Gram."

She returned the smile, and when she spoke, her voice was warm and rang with a quiet sincerity. "Well, we're mighty glad to *have* you back. Welcome home—both of you."

Cal glanced at Amy. For a moment their gazes met and held. And as he wondered if Gram's words were somehow prophetic, Amy had the oddest feeling. She'd never been anywhere near the Smokies before. But for some inexplicable reason, it really did feel like coming home.

Chapter Ten

Two hours later, stuffed with fried chicken, mashed potatoes, homemade biscuits with honey and warm-from-the-oven apple pie with ice cream, Amy thought she was going to explode.

"I haven't eaten that much since…well, maybe never," she groaned as she and Cal rocked gently on the porch swing.

He smiled. "Gram's a great cook."

"Agreed. I feel guilty about not helping with the cleanup, though."

"Don't. Hospitality is Gram's middle name. We'll have more luck pitching in after we've been around for a few days."

The slowly-sinking sun cast a golden glow on the landscape, and Amy sighed contentedly as the swing moved rhythmically back and forth. "It's nice here," she murmured.

"I thought you'd be missing the city lights by now," Cal teased.

"I'm used to rural life, remember?"

"But you don't like it."

"I wouldn't want to go back to the farm," she conceded. "But this is different."

When he didn't respond, she turned to find him studying her, a cryptic expression on his face.

"What are you thinking?" she asked curiously.

He seemed momentarily taken aback by the question, but he recovered quickly. "Just wondering how you're feeling. How's the head?"

She glanced away. "Okay."

"Amy…"

She looked back at him, caught off guard by his gently chiding tone. "What?"

"The truth."

She tilted her head and studied his deep brown eyes, a frown creasing her brow. "How do you know I'm not telling the truth?"

He shrugged. "Your tone. Your body language. I don't know how I know. I just know."

She shook her head. "No wonder you're such a good attorney. You have amazing powers of perception."

"Only with certain people." Before she could ponder that remark, he distracted her by draping his arm around her shoulders and pulling her close. "Lean your head against me and relax."

Relax? With her cheek pressed against the soft cotton of his shirt, the steady beat of his heart beneath her ear? With the faint scent of his aftershave filling her nostrils? With the angle of his jaw brushing against her forehead, the faint end-of-day stubble creating a sensuous texture against her skin? He must be kidding!

But as they swung gently back and forth, and dusk slowly deepened, she did relax. Cal could feel the gradual easing of her tense muscles, knew exactly when she finally dropped her defenses and simply gave herself up to the moment. He also knew she was afraid, just as he was, and he understood her caution. But he also knew—in fact, was even beginning to hope—that perhaps their fears were groundless. And before they left the mountains, he intended to find out.

"Amanda, these are gorgeous!" Amy held up yet another intricate hand-stitched quilt, her eyes alight.

Gram looked pleased. "The ladies do a wonderful job," she agreed. "But all of our craftspeople are talented."

Amy carefully laid the quilt down and glanced around the attractive and bustling craft co-op. Cal had told her how Gram had started it years ago to give locals an outlet for their work—as well as a chance to supplement often meager incomes—and how she had worked tirelessly to build it into a thriving business that visitors now sought out. Amy could see why. The quality of the merchandise was excellent, as was the variety.

"I'm impressed, Amanda," she said honestly. "Cal told me about this, but I had no idea it was anything on this scale."

Gram waved the praise aside. "I like to keep busy. And if I can help my neighbors at the same time, all the better. I'm glad it worked out for everybody."

"Ready to go?" Cal came up beside Amy and draped an arm across her shoulders, something he'd been doing quite a lot of since they arrived.

She turned to look up at him, melting in the warmth of

his eyes. Her voice suddenly deserted her, and she simply nodded.

"We'll be home in a couple of hours, Gram," Cal said.

"Don't hurry. I'll be here awhile yet, and your dad's at a church committee meeting. You give Amy a good tour, show her some of our great scenery. But don't wear her out," she warned.

Cal smiled. "Don't worry. I'll take good care of her." He let his arm drop from her shoulders, but in the next instant captured her hand in a warm clasp as they headed for his car.

It was just another manifestation of the change that Amy had sensed in him almost from the moment he'd picked her up at her apartment. Until then, he'd held his feelings carefully in check. She figured that, like her, he'd probably overanalyzed the situation and arrived at the logical conclusion that nothing could develop between them. But neither had reckoned with the power of the heart or the strength of their mutual attraction, she admitted. She was still waging the fight between logic and emotion, but it appeared that Cal, at least for the duration of this trip, was letting his heart dictate his actions. Which suggested some interesting possibilities, Amy realized, as a delicious shiver of excitement swept over her.

Once they were on the road, Cal took on the role of tour guide as they drove along some of the many scenic roads in the park. Finally he pulled into a parking area and turned to her.

"Do you feel like a little walk?"

"Sure. I even dressed for outdoor activity."

"I noticed." Her cotton blouse softly hugged her curves, nipped in at her slender waist by a hemp belt that emphasized her trim figure. Her long legs were encased in formfitting jeans that highlighted her lean, athletic build. But despite the ruggedness of her attire, she looked incredibly feminine—and very, very appealing. Yes, he'd definitely noticed, he thought wryly.

"I'm not exactly up to mountain climbing, though," she cautioned, redirecting his train of thought.

"What I had in mind was a nice, easy walk along that stream." He nodded to a tumbling brook, just visible through the trees.

"Sounds just my speed."

As they set off, he once more took her hand, and Amy felt a lightness of heart that was at once strange and wonderful. Here, in this place, so far removed from the normal routine of her life, she suddenly felt free to let her feelings bubble to the surface—and to savor them instead of fear them. She liked being with Cal, liked the feel of his strong, sure fingers entwined with hers, liked the sense of being cared for that his presence invoked. They were good feelings, new feelings, feelings that at once both frightened and stirred her. And though she still didn't know where this was leading, she did know one thing with absolute certainty: her decision to accept his invitation had been the right one.

They walked quietly for some time, the silence broken only by the splashing water and the call of birds. When at last the stream widened into a small pool fed by a tiered waterfall, Cal paused and looked down at her.

"This is one of my favorite spots. The waterfall isn't as dramatic as others in the park, so it gets fewer visitors. Usually I have the place to myself. Would you like to sit for a while?"

"Yes. It's lovely here."

Cal led her to a large, flat rock dappled by the sun. She sat and drew her knees up, wrapped her arms around them and sighed contentedly.

He chuckled as he joined her. "My sentiments exactly."

She turned to look at him. He, too, was dressed in jeans that hugged his slim hips and outlined his muscular legs. The sleeves of his cotton shirt were rolled to the elbows, revealing an expanse of sun-browned forearm flecked with dark hair. As he leaned back, putting his palms on the rock behind him, his shirt stretched tautly across his broad chest. Amy swallowed and, with an effort, transferred her gaze to his face. He had closed his eyes and tilted his head back to the sun, and she was struck again by the change in him since they'd arrived in the mountains. All evidence of strain had vanished, and he seemed completely happy and at ease—like this was where he belonged, she realized, inexplicably troubled by the thought.

He turned at that moment, and his eyebrows rose quizzically. "Why the frown?"

She dismissed his question with a shrug, unsure of the answer herself. "This place is good for you, you know."

"Why do you say that?"

"You seem more…content here, I guess. And laid-back. In the city you always seem a little tense and on edge, like you never really relax."

"I have a demanding job."

"Yeah, I know all about demanding jobs," she replied wryly.

"Yours seems particularly demanding. Not to mention dangerous."

She shrugged. "Demanding, always. Dangerous, rarely."

"Forgive me if I can't quite accept that. Not after this." He leaned over and gently touched her head.

"That's the exception, Cal. I'm not in this work to get killed. Trust me."

"But you don't hold back, either. Do you ever do anything halfway?"

She tipped her head and considered the question. "I've never thought of it quite that way before, but no, I guess not. I'm the type who does everything full-out—you know, the old 'Anything worth doing is worth doing well' philosophy. And I can't just stand by when people are in trouble, either. That's always been one of my weaknesses."

"I'd hardly call it that."

"It is in my business. We're supposed to report stories—not become part of them."

"Then maybe you're in the wrong business."

His quiet remark hit too close to home, but she forced herself to smile. "Well, if I switched careers you'd have one less reporter to hate," she countered, striving for a light tone.

He looked at her, and the intensity of his gaze made her breath catch in her throat. "I was wrong to make such a sweeping generalization, Amy. And I was especially wrong about one particular reporter. In fact, *hate* is the last word that comes to mind when I think of you."

The husky cadence and intimate tone of his voice, along with the sudden warmth in his eyes, scared her, and she glanced away nervously.

"I liked your grandmother's shop," she said with forced brightness. "Some of the things are so..."

The touch of his hand on her arm made the words stick in her throat.

"Amy."

His voice was gentle but firm, and she drew a shaky breath. They'd been dodging this thing between them for too long, and Cal was finally facing it. But it took her several more moments to gather the courage to look at him. When she did, the tenderness in his eyes made her heart catch, then race on.

"Don't be afraid," he said quietly.

Her throat constricted, and she swallowed with difficulty. "You sound like Kate."

"How so?"

Amy broke eye contact and dropped her cheek to her knees. "She told me I was afraid, too. And you—you're both right."

Cal slid closer and took her cold hand, cradling it in the warmth of his clasp. "You know what? So am I. But there's something between us too powerful to ignore. I've seen it in your face. And I've spent too many sleepless nights grappling with it. We need to deal with this thing."

She looked at him again. "We're too different, Cal."

"I used to think so. I'm not as sure anymore."

"But we want different things out of life."

"Do we?"

She drew a ragged breath. "Even if we had the same priorities, this isn't a good time for me. I'm still trying to build my career."

"It's not the best time for me, either. I'm struggling with some pretty heavy decisions and, frankly, I don't need the distraction. But I've got it whether I want it or not. Because you, lovely lady, are one big distraction.''

He reached over then and touched her face, his gaze locked on hers. The feel of his fingertips against her skin sent her pulse off the scale, and she closed her eyes as he slowly traced the line of her jaw and the curve of her cheek. When he let his fingertips glide over her lips with a feather-light touch, she moaned softly.

''Oh, Amy, I've wanted to do this for so long,'' he said hoarsely. And then he pulled her gently into his arms, one hand in the small of her back, the other beneath her hair, cradling her neck. For several long moments, he just held her tenderly, taking time to simply relish the long-dreamed-of closeness. He could feel her trembling, but she didn't pull away, and he stroked her back reassuringly.

''It's okay, sweetheart,'' he murmured, his lips against her hair. ''I'm just as scared as you are. We'll take this slow and easy, okay?''

Amy wasn't at all sure it was okay. This whole thing was moving far faster than she'd anticipated. But she could no longer deny her feelings for this man. She cared about him—deeply. Okay, so maybe this wasn't the best time in her life for romance. Maybe Cal didn't exactly fit the profile she'd created of her ''ideal man.'' She'd always imagined that someday she'd be half of a ''power'' couple, living a glittering, jet-set type life. Yet Cal had no interest in that. He liked things simple and unpretentious, and his priorities clearly didn't include power or prestige or worldly success. Amy's did. Or had. Oddly enough, she wasn't so sure they did anymore.

But she put those thoughts aside for the moment. As she savored the feel of Cal's strong arms about her, she felt safe, protected, cherished—and free. Which was odd. Even in a perfect relationship, she'd always imagined that one was less free because the partner's needs always had to be considered and accommodated. But for the first time, she considered the possibility that maybe she'd had it all wrong. Because here, wrapped in his arms, she sensed a love so supportive, so unconditional, that it was liberating, freeing her to take risks she might otherwise not consider because she always knew she had the safety net of his arms—and his love—to catch her if she fell. It was an astounding revelation, one to be carefully thought through later, when her mind was behaving rationally. Certainly not now, when the feel of his hard chest against her soft curves was driving all lucid thoughts from her brain.

Cal felt the tension in her body slowly ease, and he pulled back slightly to gaze down at her, framing her face with his long, lean fingers as he brushed his thumbs over her cheeks. She looked up at him, her deep green eyes slightly dazed—but also trusting. It was a look that said, "I don't know where this is leading. I'm not even sure if it's a good idea. But I care for you. I trust you. And, at least for the moment, my heart is yours."

Cal's throat tightened. He'd dated any number of women through the years, but none had looked at him in quite this same way. And given how hard Amy was fighting this thing, he was even more deeply touched. He drew a long, unsteady breath, then combed his fingers through her hair, careful to avoid the back of her head. When he lifted her soft tresses aside to brush his lips against her nape, he heard her sigh softly. And as he slowly kissed her forehead, then each eyelid, making a slow, tantalizing journey toward his ultimate destination, he felt her hands clutch his back convulsively.

When at last he claimed her lips, her surprisingly ardent response almost snapped the tenuous hold he had on his emotions. She gave as she lived—fully, completely, no holding back, without pretense or reservation. His initial touch, gentle and exploratory, rapidly grew fierce and demanding as he gave way to the hunger that had consumed him for weeks.

Amy had been kissed before, but never with such a mix of tenderness and passion. It took her breath away and sent her world spinning out of orbit as a long, sweet shiver of delight swept over her. When Cal's hands moved over her back, molding her slender frame against the muscular contours of his body, she made no protest. The tension between them had been building for weeks, and it was pure joy to at last release her feelings. Strangely enough, Amy felt that she'd been waiting for this moment not just for the last few weeks, but all her life. Here, in this man's arms, she felt somehow as if she'd come home.

When at last Cal pulled reluctantly away, Amy shakily raised her fingers to her lips, which still throbbed from his touch. She stared at him dazedly, stunned by the storm of emotion that had swept over her.

Cal tried to draw a deep breath, only to discover that his lungs weren't working very well. Nor was his heart, which was thudding as hard as if he'd just run a thousand-yard dash. He ran unsteady fingers through his hair, then reached over and took her hand.

"Are you okay?" His voice was as uneven as his pulse.

"Just make the world stop spinning, okay?" she whispered.

Somehow he summoned up a crooked grin. "Sure. Just as soon as I come back to Earth."

Now it was Amy's turn to try for a smile. "Well, I guess we know now that on at least one level we're compatible."

"That's putting it mildly."

"Cal, I—I've never experienced anything quite like that before. It was like—like an earthquake and fireworks and Christmas morning all in one."

He smiled, and the warmth in his eyes made her tingle all over. "I couldn't have said it better myself."

"But…" Her look of wonder changed to a frown and she distractedly brushed her hair back from her face. "I mean, where do we go from here? I'm not sure I can handle this kind of…intensity…knowing that we may not have any kind of future together."

He studied her for a moment, a slight frown now marring his own brow. "You sound like you've already decided we don't."

"I didn't mean it that way. It's just that I've always been practical, and I see a lot of obstacles in our path."

"Obstacles can be overcome if two people are committed to finding a way around them."

"I'd like to believe that."

"Then do. Let me tell you something, Amy." He laced his fingers with hers and cupped the back of her neck with his other hand, massaging gently, his eyes only inches from hers. "I don't know why our paths crossed at this particular time in our lives. I don't know why we feel the way we do about each other, given our apparent differences. But I do know this. It happened for a reason. And I'm willing to put this in the Lord's hands and trust that He'll reveal that reason to us in His own time and in His own way. Until then, I'm inclined to let this develop. And to be perfectly honest, I'm not sure I could walk away now even if I wanted to.''

Amy gazed into his sincere, caring eyes, and knew she was lost. She couldn't walk away, either. And maybe he was right. Maybe the best way to deal with this was to simply trust in the Lord to give them guidance. She hadn't done that for a long time. But she was in over her head on this one, and she needed help from a higher power to resolve her dilemma. At last she drew a deep breath and nodded.

''Okay. I'm willing to give it a try.''

His relieved smile chased the tension from his face. ''Good. I was prepared to argue my case with some pretty convincing evidence, but I'm glad we were able to settle out of court.''

She smiled, a teasing light suddenly flitting through her eyes. ''Do you think maybe you might want to present some of that evidence, anyway, Counselor?''

For a moment he looked surprised, then a deep chuckle rumbled out of his chest. ''I think that could be arranged.''

And as his lips once more closed over hers, Amy prayed that they would somehow find a way to resolve their differences. Because one thing was becoming very clear to her. She was rapidly falling in love with Cal Richards. And it was getting harder and harder to imagine the rest of her life without him.

Cal glanced at Amy sitting beside him in the pew, still amazed that she'd agreed to go to Sunday services with his family. He'd told her last night that she didn't have to do it for him, that if they were going to make this thing between them work, neither should feel compelled to do something out of character just to please the other person. But she'd assured him that she was doing it for herself, that it was something she'd decided even before they'd acknowledged their feelings for each other.

Gazing at her now as she raptly listened to Reverend Mitchell's sermon, Cal couldn't doubt her sincerity. She seemed genuinely interested in what the kindly minister was saying—as *he* should be, he reminded himself sternly, refocusing his attention on the pastor.

"And so it is that the Lord gives us choices. Free will is truly a wonderful gift—but it can also be a hardship. Because sometimes we must make difficult decisions. Decisions those we love do not agree with. Decisions that will change our lives forever, in ways we cannot fathom at the time. Decisions that we know in our hearts we *must* make in order to be true to ourselves and to the Lord.

"But we never have to make those decisions alone, my friends. For as Matthew tells us, the Lord stands ready to help us if we simply make the request. 'Ask, and it shall be given to you; seek, and you shall find; knock, and it shall be opened to you.'

"As all of us know, today's world is not always compatible with the ways of the Lord. It's easy to lose sight of priorities in this material age. Temptations face us at every turn. But on your journey through this world, I encourage you to cling to the things that truly last—faith, hope and love. For these will sustain you into eternal life, long after the fleeting glories and gratifications of this world have faded away.

"So as you face the choices in your life, ask yourself if your decision is consistent with those three things—for yourself and for others. And when you answer that question honestly, your decision will be clear—though not always easy. But remember, my friends—the Lord never promised us an easy life in this world if we followed his teachings—only eternal life in the next. And His grace to help us along the way in this one.

"And now let us pray...."

As the minister led the congregation in prayer, Amy was struck by the odd coincidence that Reverend Mitchell would have chosen this weekend to speak on the subject of choices and priorities. Or *was* it a coincidence? she wondered, lost in thought.

Only when a beautiful, soaring solo voice began to sing did she return to her surroundings. She glanced over at the choir, her eyes widening when she realized that the voice belonged to Amanda. When she turned to Cal, she found him watching her with a smile.

"Why didn't you tell me your grandmother could sing like that?" she whispered in awe.

"I thought it would be more fun to surprise you," he murmured.

"*Surprise* is hardly the word. She could be a professional."

"Ask her about it sometime," Cal said quietly as the congregation joined in on the refrain.

Amy intended to do just that, but after the service they were kept busy as Cal greeted and introduced her to a number of old friends.

"Cal! I thought that was you!"

They turned to find a fortyish, slightly balding man approaching them. Cal grinned and held out his hand. "Tony Jackson! I don't believe it! What are you doing here?"

"I'm home for the weekend visiting my folks. Cindy took the kids to her parents' for a few days, but I couldn't get away from the station for more than a couple of days."

"Station?"

"Didn't you know? I operate a Christian cable station out of Knoxville now."

"No kidding! Last I heard you were a business tycoon jetting all over the world."

The man grinned. "Being an investment banker hardly qualifies me as a business tycoon. It had its exciting moments, though. But I found better work—not more profitable, you understand, but more worthwhile." He nodded to Amy. "Are you going to introduce your friend, or do I have to take the initiative?"

Cal put his arm around Amy and drew her forward with an apologetic grin. "Sorry about that. I was just so surprised to see you. Amy, this is Tony Jackson. We grew up together. Tony, Amy Winter. You two have something in common, it seems. Amy is a broadcast journalist in Atlanta." When he named the station, Tony's eyebrows rose.

"I'm impressed," he said.

Amy smiled and shook her head dismissively. "Don't be. I'm still working my way up the proverbial ladder."

"You have to be pretty exceptional to even *get* on that ladder, from what I hear."

"'Exceptional' is a good word for Amy," Cal said, his warm gaze connecting with hers briefly. She felt a flush spread over her face as she turned back to Tony.

"He's being kind," she demurred.

"Honest is more likely. Cal always had great judgment. Listen, I don't suppose you'd consider it, but if you ever have any interest in exploring a different kind of reporting,

I'd love to talk to you. Of course, we can't compete with the glamour or salaries the big guys offer. We're in the early stages, and building a station from the ground up is a gradual process. Still, slowly but surely we're finding talented people who believe in our message enough to make a commitment to our work and sacrifice some of the worldly gain.''

Amy smiled. "I'm flattered. But I'm pretty happy right now where I am.''

Tony grinned engagingly. "Well, it was worth a try.'' He held out his hand, and shook hers, then Cal's. "Good to see you, pal. Keep in touch.''

"I will. And good luck with your new venture.''

Tony's grin widened. "We can't miss, you know. Remember—if God is with you, who can be against you?'' With a wave he sauntered off.

Cal turned to Amy, but was interrupted by Reverend Mitchell before he could speak.

"Cal. Good to see you. And you must be Amy.'' The minister turned and extended his hand. At Amy's quizzical look, he smiled. "News of strangers travels fast in this part of the country. Though I hope you won't be a stranger for long.''

She returned his smile. "Thank you.''

He squeezed her hand, then turned back to Cal. "Are you staying long?''

"Just a couple more days.''

"Too bad. I was hoping you'd have time to stop in and see Walter Thompson.''

Cal frowned. Walter was one of the hardest-working, most well-respected men in the community. He'd run a local trout farm for as long as Cal could remember and was always the first to offer a hand when his neighbors needed help. "Something wrong?"

"I think he could use some good legal advice. Or at least someone to point him to some good legal advice. There's a big developer planning a mall of some sort next to his property and they're putting a lot of pressure on him to sell a section of his land. He hasn't budged so far, but now they're getting pretty nasty from what I hear, digging up all sorts of obscure laws that he's supposedly violated and threatening to put him out of business. He's pretty worried. And none of the local attorneys he's contacted seems able to cope with the legal eagles at this big conglomerate."

Cal's frown deepened. "I'll put him in touch with someone who has experience dealing with corporate law firms."

"He can't afford big-city prices, you know."

"Yeah, I figured. I'll work it out."

The minister smiled. "I'm sure anything will be appreciated, Cal. Sorry to bother you with this, but I know Walter's at his wits' end." He turned back to Amy. "It was very nice to meet you. Take care, both of you. And don't be strangers."

As Reverend Mitchell walked over to talk to another couple, Amy turned to Cal. "Do you know *everybody* here?"

He gave her a troubled glance. "Pretty much."

Amy tilted her head and gazed up at him. "You're upset."

He drew a deep breath and nodded. "I don't like to see the little guy get trampled on."

"Can you do anything?"

He sighed. "Not much. Except contact someone who

can deal with the big guns of a corporate law firm. But it will come at a price.''

''Which Mr. Thompson can't pay.''

Cal shrugged. ''I might be able to call in a few favors. I'll work something out.''

As they walked toward his car, Amy considered Cal's response. He probably did have connections, probably *could* hook the man up with a good attorney who might discount his fees as a favor. But they would most likely still be more than the man could afford. And Amy suddenly had a feeling she knew who would pay the difference. The evidence was clear. Cal lived simply, and well below his means. The director at Saint Vincent's had implied that Cal contributed more than time to the boys' center. Amanda had said that he took good care of her and his father. It wasn't too hard to figure out who would come to Walter Thompson's aid, though the man would probably never realize it. Because Cal's generosity would be quiet, unobtrusive and anonymous.

Amy shook her head. She might still be puzzling over why the Lord had brought the two of them together, but one thing was clear. She'd never met anyone like Cal before. And she suddenly had a feeling that she never would again.

Chapter Eleven

"So when are you going to put that forestry degree to use?"

Leave it to Doug Howell to ask the tough questions, Cal thought ruefully as the two men walked through the field next to Gram's cabin. Though Doug was several years older than Cal, they'd been fast friends since childhood, and he was one of the few people Cal had confided in about his extracurricular study. A head ranger for the National Parks Service, Doug shared Cal's love of the outdoors. So Cal had known Doug would understand his desire to study forestry. He'd also known that his friend would eventually raise this question.

The two men paused at the edge of the field, and Cal rested his forearms on the split-rail fence as he gazed out over the meadow. The midafternoon sun felt pleasantly warm on his back, easing the sudden tension in his shoulders. But it didn't make Doug's question any easier to answer.

"I never said I was."

''You didn't have to.''

Cal turned to him, his mouth lifting wryly at one corner. ''You know me too well.''

Doug shrugged. ''We've been friends a long time. I know how you feel about this place. What I *don't* know is how you've survived in that concrete jungle all these years.''

Cal sighed and stared into the distance. ''Neither do I. But I've built a life there now, and a career. It gets harder and harder to walk away.''

''I'm sure it does. Success can be addictive.''

Cal frowned and turned to his friend. ''You know better than that.''

Doug studied him shrewdly. ''Then tell me what holds you to the city.''

Cal considered the question, then carefully formed his answer, putting into words what, until now, had only been in his heart. ''Dad, for one,'' he said slowly. ''He takes such pride in my success, and he'd be tremendously disappointed if I threw my career away. Then there's the guilt. I'm not always successful in my work, but I win often enough to feel that I'm contributing *something* to the cause of justice. After all my years of training and experience, it seems wrong somehow not to put that to good use. And frankly, I'm not sure I want to give up law. Despite the frustration, I get a lot of satisfaction out of helping people who really need someone on their side, who might otherwise get lost in the legal system. And yet...'' He sighed and raked his fingers through his hair. ''I want to come home, Doug. I don't like the city. I never have, and it hasn't grown on me over the years. This is where I belong.''

"Then come home."

"You make it sound so simple."

"It can be. It's your life, Cal. And if this is where you want to spend it, come back."

"And do what?"

Doug rested one elbow on the fence and angled toward Cal. "I'll have a part-time ranger slot opening up in about three months."

Cal shot him a surprised look. "Are you offering me the job?"

Doug shrugged. "There'd be a lot of paperwork to fill out, of course. But you certainly have the credentials."

"What about my law career?"

"Why can't you do both? We could use an attorney with your skills and experience around here."

Cal frowned, jolted by Doug's suggestion. His friend was right about the need for good legal counsel in the area. Walter Thompson's situation was clear evidence of that. But the idea of splitting his time between two careers— he'd never even considered that before. Yet it was like a beam of light breaking through the clouds after a storm, illuminating a dreary world and filling it with the promise of brighter days ahead.

"You might be on to something, Doug," he acknowledged as the idea took hold, sending a surge of excitement through him.

"Seems like a logical solution to me. You'd still be using those legal skills you spent so many years honing, only you'd be helping your own people. And you'd have the chance to share your knowledge and love of nature with those poor city folks who have to squeeze their visits to God's country into a week or two of vacation."

Cal shook his head. ''I should have talked to you a long time ago. I've been wrestling with this for months.''

''Us mountain folk have a few good ideas now and then,'' Doug teased.

Cal grinned. ''More than a few. I don't know why this option never occurred to me before. It was always either/or in my mind. But this is definitely worth some thought.''

''It's still a big decision, though,'' Doug pointed out. ''You'd be giving up a lot.''

''A lot of things that don't matter to me, anyway,'' Cal countered.

''And how would your friend feel about it?'' Doug nodded toward the distant porch where Amy and Gram sat.

Cal frowned. ''That's part of what I have to think about.''

It was funny, Cal reflected, as he turned once more to stare out over the meadow. He'd been praying for guidance on this decision. And the Lord had come through. But He'd thrown in a complication. Namely, Amy. A few weeks ago, the thought that she might even *consider* leaving the city or her present job to live in the mountains would have seemed ludicrous. And yet, as he'd come to know her, he'd begun to believe that at heart they weren't quite as different as they'd first seemed. Though their lifestyles were poles apart, their values were compatible. And she *had* expressed some dissatisfaction with her present job. So maybe, given time, she would consider rethinking her priorities. Especially if she happened to fall in love with him.

Cal prayed that she would do exactly that. Because one thing had become very clear to him on this trip. He was in love with her. And he couldn't imagine spending the rest of his life without her.

Amy watched the two men at the far end of the field with a vague and troubling sense of unease. When Cal had introduced Doug Howell to her as a childhood friend, it was her suggestion that the two men take a walk through the field. Now, for some strange reason, she wasn't so sure that had been wise.

"I remember those two boys as youngsters," Gram said from her rocking chair on the porch, reclaiming Amy's attention. "They sure were pals. Couldn't find one without the other. I think they've hiked every inch of the national park. I really can't say which one loved the mountains more."

Gram's comments did nothing to ease Amy's odd sense of trepidation, so she changed the subject.

"I enjoyed your solo in church this morning, Amanda. You have a beautiful voice."

The older woman brushed aside the comment, though she was clearly flattered. "Can't claim any credit for that. The Lord blessed me with it. So I return the favor by using it to honor Him. I've been singing in the church choir since I was fourteen—more than sixty years now, believe it or not."

"When I commented to Cal that you could have been a professional singer, he told me to ask you about it. Sounds like there's an interesting story there."

Amanda smiled. "My, that's a long time ago. Are you sure you want to hear ancient history?"

"Absolutely."

Amanda gazed out at the meadow, her eyes focused not

on the misty mountains, but on the past. "Let's see, I was about twenty-five, I guess. We had a visitor at church one Sunday, a record producer from Nashville on vacation in the mountains. I did a solo that day, and he came up to me after the service and handed me his card, said he'd like me to come to Nashville and make a test record. 'Course I had a husband and baby to think about. Cal's father was just five or six at the time. But I must say I was flattered."

"Did you go?"

"I turned him down at first. But Warren—my husband—could tell it was eating at me. So finally he said to call the man and go do the test. Told me I needed to see it through, check out the opportunity, or I'd always wonder where it might have led. So I did."

She paused for a moment, and Amy leaned forward. "What happened?"

"Well, I went on down to Nashville and made the record. I guess I was there four or five days. It surely was an exciting time, I remember that, what with seeing the studio and hobnobbing with musicians and staying in a fancy hotel. Then I came home and waited. And about two weeks later the man called me, said he'd played the record for a number of people, and they thought I had great potential. Offered me a recording contract."

"No kidding! What did you do?"

"I turned it down."

Amy stared at her. "But why? You could have been a star!"

"It was a funny thing," Amanda reflected. "After I went to Nashville and had a little exposure to the music world, I sort of got it out of my system. The contract offer gave me a lot of satisfaction, told me that someone who knew music thought I was good enough to make it, and that was enough. Because during those two weeks while I waited to hear back, I had a chance to look around here and evaluate what I really wanted out of my life. If I signed that contract, I'd be on the road a lot, away from my family and my mountains, for weeks and months on end. I didn't want that.''

"But you could have been rich and famous," Amy protested.

Amanda shrugged. "I was already rich in all the ways that counted. I had people to love, and who loved me. I lived in one of the most beautiful places in God's creation. And I had my faith. As for fame—that's fleeting. I preferred to put my energies into things that last."

Amy digested that for a moment. "And you never had any regrets?" she pressed.

"Not a one," the older woman declared.

"I envy you," Amy said quietly.

"Why is that?"

"You seem so…content with your life. And happy with your choices."

"You sound as if you aren't."

Amy sighed. "I'm beginning to wonder."

"Nothing wrong with wondering. And you're too young for regrets. So if there's anything you want to change in your life, you still have plenty of time."

As Amy glanced toward the field where Cal and Doug stood, she pondered Amanda's words. She supposed she did still have the time to make changes. But did she have the courage?

"Amy?" Cal leaned back in his chair and smiled. "It's good to hear your voice."

"You just heard it last night," she teased, even as a

flush of pleasure tinged her cheeks at the warmth in his tone. Though they'd spent every possible free minute together since their return from the mountains, it never seemed enough.

"That was ten hours ago. And besides, good-night calls aren't cutting it anymore. I need more than a voice at the end of the day, sweetheart."

The husky, intimate cadence in his voice sent a sweet shiver of delight up her spine. "I agree. This work thing is starting to get old. Either you're tied up late or I am. We've got to do something about this."

"Any suggestions?"

"How about a trip back to the mountains?"

Cal's eyebrows rose in surprise. "We were just there six weeks ago."

"Can't you get away?"

"Probably. For a couple of days, anyway. What brought this up?"

"Honestly? Work. I'd like to do a piece on Amanda's craft co-op. I think it has great human-interest potential. And it would give me a chance to focus some attention on the economic problems in Appalachia. Not to mention focusing some attention on us. Do you think she'd go along with the idea?"

Cal fought down his disappointment. For a moment he'd thought her suggestion for the trip had been motivated not only by a desire for the two of them to have some time together, but by a growing love for the mountains. She'd talked glowingly about the Smokies in the weeks since their return, but clearly he'd read too much into those comments.

"Cal? Are you still there?"

"Yeah. I think we could convince Gram. When would you like to go?"

"Well, once she says okay, I have to sell the idea to the station. But the Saint Vincent's piece went over really well, so I don't think I'll have any trouble. Probably in a couple of weeks."

"Okay. I'll give her a call. Any chance of getting together for dinner tonight?"

Amy glanced at her calendar and noted the late-afternoon meeting she'd scheduled with one of the producers for an upcoming series. It was sure to run into the early evening. She bit her lip and considered her options: Sit through a long meeting, or share dinner—and hopefully some kisses—with Cal. Put that way, it was no contest. She reached over and crossed out the meeting.

"That's the best offer I've had all day," she replied with a smile. "Just pick the time and place."

Cal propped one shoulder against the door frame of the co-op, shoved his hands into his pockets and crossed one ankle over the other as he watched Amy wrap up the last bit of filming for the story. Though the trip had turned out to be far more work than play, he had nevertheless been impressed once again by her professionalism, intensity and thoroughness. She was extraordinarily talented, and he had no doubt that, given time, she would reach all of her career goals. The network slot she craved was a very real possibility in her future.

Cal fingered the ring box in his pocket and frowned. Was he wrong to ask her to give up her dreams? Or at the very least, dramatically modify them? Because that's what

being his wife would entail. And yet, during the two
months since their first visit to the mountains, it had become clear to him that Amy's priorities were shifting. He
wasn't sure if she was even aware of it yet, but he'd seen
enough evidence to validate his theory. She'd begun to
work more normal hours. She'd traded in her car, as she
said she did every three years, but she'd exchanged her
sporty model for a practical four-door compact sedan. She
now seemed perfectly content to spend quiet evenings with
him, cuddled up on the couch eating popcorn and watching
old movies, instead of hitting the hot nightspots. Okay, so
it was all circumstantial evidence. But it was also compelling. She was already altering her lifestyle, and he'd
begun to hope that maybe, just maybe, she'd consider
other career options, as well, such as freelancing, which
would allow her to use her exceptional reporting talents
and still live in the mountains. That was what he was praying for, anyway.

He transferred his gaze to his father, who had come to
watch the filming and was now sitting quietly off to one
side. That was the next hurdle, Cal thought, his stomach
churning. But Cal had taken Reverend Mitchell's sermon
about decisions, as well as Doug Howell's suggestion, to
heart and had made the only choice that would allow him
to be true to himself. He was going to return to the mountains. Doug already knew, and Cal had spent the last couple of weeks looking into office space in nearby Maryville
in anticipation of setting up a local practice. On this trip,
while Amy had been busy working, he'd also found the
land he wanted to buy and build on—assuming Amy liked
it, as well. He planned to show it to her later in the day—
then ask her to be his wife on the very spot he planned to

build the cabin they would share. But first, he wanted to break the news of his career change to his father. Though he knew the older man would be disappointed, he also knew in his heart it was the right thing for him to do.

"Okay, Steve, that should do it."

The cameraman turned off his lights and hefted the camera from his shoulder. "Looks like another good piece, Amy."

"Thanks. Are you heading back this afternoon?"

"Yep. What about you?"

"Tomorrow. I have a few things here to attend to first." She glanced toward Cal, whose lazy smile brought a flush to her cheeks.

As Steve put away his equipment, Cal pushed away from the door frame and strolled toward her. She watched him approach, her pulse accelerating at the banked fire in his eyes.

"So am I finally going to get you to myself for a while?" he asked huskily when he came up beside her.

She gave him a guilty look. "I'm sorry, Cal. I didn't expect it to take quite this long."

"I'm not complaining. Yet."

She smiled. "Message received. My evening is yours."

"Good. Because there's something I want to show you."

She tilted her head and gazed at him curiously. "What?"

He reached over and touched the tip of her nose with his finger. "Take off your reporter hat. No more questions for now. It's a surprise. Didn't you tell me once you liked surprises?"

"I believe I did."

"I rest my case."

"Okay, Amy, I'm taking off." Steve came up beside them. "See you back at the studio."

"Right. Have a safe trip."

As the cameraman left, Amanda appeared from the back room, her eyes sparkling with excitement. "My, wasn't that fun! I hope everything went the way you wanted," she said to Amy.

"Perfect. I think it will be a great story."

"Are we ready to head home?" Cal asked.

Amanda nodded. "Soon as we find your dad."

Cal glanced toward the empty chair where his father had been sitting. "He was over there a few minutes ago. I'll round him up and meet you ladies outside."

"I expect you're tired," Amanda commented as she and Amy exited. "All that running around doing interviews, not to mention all the research you did before you came here. Even I learned something about the economy of Appalachia, and I've lived here all my life."

Amy grinned. "Cal says I never do anything halfway. I guess he's right."

"There's a lot to be said for... Cal, what is it?"

At the alarm in Amanda's voice, Amy turned back toward the door. Cal stood on the threshold, his face pale and tight with tension. There was fear in his eyes, and Amy's stomach plummeted to her toes.

"I think dad's having a heart attack. Call 911." Without giving either woman time to respond, he turned on his heel and disappeared back inside.

"Dear Lord," Amanda whispered, automatically moving toward the door. Amy followed, dumping her shoulder tote on a chair before going in search of Cal and his father.

She found them in the back hall. The older man was sitting on the floor clutching his left arm, his back against the wall. His face was gray and creased with pain, and he was sweating profusely. Cal was down on his haunches beside him, holding his father's hand.

"Everything will be okay, Dad. Just try to relax."

Amy knelt beside them and put her hand on Cal's shoulder. "Can I do anything?" she asked quietly.

"Just pray," he said tightly, his gaze never leaving his father's face.

Amanda joined them a few moments later, and the three of them kept a silent, agonizing vigil. It seemed to take hours before the distant sound of sirens signaled the approach of help. Though Amy knew the wait had been less than fifteen minutes, she also knew every second counted with a heart attack. And so she did as Cal asked—she prayed that the emergency crew would arrive in time to keep the damage to a minimum.

The paramedics went into action immediately, quickly confirming Cal's diagnosis. When they whisked the older man off in an ambulance a few minutes later, Cal accompanied them while Amy and Amanda followed in his car. The older woman was clearly distraught, and Amy wished she could think of something comforting to say. But until they knew more, any hope she offered would be just that— hope, with no basis in fact. And so she remained silent, continuing her prayers—as she knew Amanda was doing.

Cal was in the hospital waiting room when they arrived, and he answered their question before they could ask.

"No word yet. The nurse said they'd let us know something as soon as they can." His gaze rested on Gram, and he frowned. For the first time in his memory, she actually looked her age. Deep lines were etched in her face, and she seemed old and frail. He put his arm around her shoulders and guided her to a chair. "Sit down, Gram," he said gently. "I'll get you some tea."

"I'm fine," she protested shakily. "Don't bother with me."

"I saw a snack shop down the hall," Amy said quietly to Cal. "I'll get the tea. Do you want coffee?"

He nodded, but as she turned to go, he restrained her with a hand on her arm. She glanced back, and for a moment their gazes connected—as did their hearts. "I'm glad you're here," he said softly. And she knew he meant not just here, in this hospital waiting room, but here, in his life.

Her throat constricted with emotion and she laid her hand over his. "So am I."

When she returned a few minutes later, the questioning look she directed at him was met with a shake of his head, and she slipped into the seat beside him and reached for his hand. He gripped it fiercely, like a lifeline, as they kept their silent, tense vigil.

It was almost an hour later—an hour that seemed like an eternity—before a doctor finally stepped into the waiting room and looked in their direction.

"Are you the family of Mr. Richards?"

They were on their feet instantly. "Yes," Cal replied, his grip tightening on Amy's hand.

The man walked toward them. "I'm Dr. Douglas. Let me put your minds at ease right away. I think Mr. Richards will make a good recovery."

"Thank God!" murmured Amanda fervently. Though

Cal made no comment, Amy could feel the sudden release of tension in his muscles, and she squeezed his hand.

"Let's sit down for a moment, shall we?" the doctor suggested.

When they complied, the doctor opened a folder and withdrew several pieces of film. He walked them through the images, explaining the extent of the heart damage and the good prognosis for recovery.

"Your father is in excellent physical condition, and fortunately the damage is minimal. With therapy and common sense, he should do very well," he concluded as he slipped the film back inside the folder. "We'll watch him closely for a few days just to be sure, but I don't expect any complications."

"Can we see him?" Amanda asked.

"We're moving him to intensive care right now. I'll have the nurse come get you as soon as he's settled." At their looks of alarm, he raised his hand reassuringly. "Cardiac intensive care is standard procedure for at least twenty-four hours after a heart attack. And don't be alarmed by all the equipment and monitors. We just want to play it safe. Please trust me on this. I believe in being honest, and I often have to deliver a prognosis that's much more grim. In this case, I'm very hopeful about recovery."

He stood, and they followed suit.

"Thank you, Doctor," Cal said.

"Glad we could help."

As they watched him leave, Amy's vibrating pager went off, and she removed it from her belt to glance at the message.

"Work?"

She responded to Cal's question with a distracted nod.

"I need to call in. There are some phones by the coffee shop. I'll be back in a couple of minutes."

"Take your time."

Only when Amy reached up to punch the numbers in the phone did she realize how badly shaken she was by the events that had transpired over the past couple of hours. Her fingers were trembling, her legs suddenly felt unsteady and a tension headache pulsated in her temples. She was *not* in the mood to talk about work.

"Newsroom."

"Jarrod? Amy Winter. I got your message. What's up?" Though she tried for a businesslike tone, she couldn't control the tremor that ran through her voice.

"Where are you?"

The news editor was certainly living up to his reputation for not mincing words, Amy thought in irritation. "I'm still in the Smokies."

"How quickly can you get back?"

She frowned. "Why?"

"Remember those rumors that were going around a few months ago about one certain very influential and powerful alderman with national political aspirations who supposedly had mob connections? Looks like it was more than rumor. We've got a hot tip that a major scandal is about to break, possibly as early as first thing in the morning. Could result in criminal charges. We want you here to cover the story."

Amy knew she should be flattered to be singled out for such a high-profile story. She knew that it could move her up another rung or two on the career ladder. She knew that she would be the envy of her colleagues for being handed such a plum assignment.

She also knew she didn't want to go back. She wanted—needed—to be here with Cal. *For* Cal.

It was decision time. And she knew the choice she was about to make wasn't going to sit well with the news editor. She drew a deep breath and willed the pounding of her heart to subside.

"There's a complication here, Jarrod," she said as evenly as she could.

The silence on the other end of the line communicated his reaction more eloquently than words. It was the first time in her career that she hadn't responded by dropping everything when the station said "Jump," and Jarrod was clearly shocked.

When he finally spoke, his voice was cautious. "What do you mean?"

Amy played with the phone cord. "A friend's father just had a heart attack. I'm at the hospital now, in fact. I need to stay a couple more days. I have plenty of vacation saved up."

"Is this friend the guy who answered the phone at your apartment after you got hurt covering the hostage story?"

She hesitated, surprised by the question. "As a matter of fact, yes."

"Look, Amy, romances come and go," Jarrod said impatiently. "You're building a career here. I think you need to get your priorities straight."

She took a deep breath. "So do I."

"So are you coming back?"

"No."

She cringed at his crude expletive. "Fine. Stay in the mountains. But don't expect us to call you first the next time a great story comes along."

The bang on the other end abruptly ended their conversation, and she slowly replaced the receiver. Jarrod might be a good news editor, but his interpersonal skills could definitely use some polishing, she concluded as she took a deep, steadying breath. Yet he'd put into words what she'd always known instinctively. If she wanted to get ahead in this business, the job had to come first. That was the expectation. And until now she'd always accepted it. Somehow, though, in the face of what had transpired in the past few hours, the "job first" philosophy had a hollow ring.

As she made her way back to the waiting room, she reflected again on Reverend Mitchell's sermon about choices. She'd made a career choice once, a long time ago, when she'd set her sights on a network feature slot. She'd made a choice just now, one that could cost her dearly. And yet, it felt right. Because over the past few months she had learned something. Success was important to her. But so was love. And if making the two compatible meant revising her definition of success, maybe that was okay. Maybe a job that didn't allow her to put the people she loved first wasn't worth having. After all, Atlanta was a big city. There had to be other options.

For the first time in a long while, Amy didn't have a clear vision of what her future held. It was an unsettling—and unwelcome—feeling. And yet, in her heart she knew that it was time to face some of the questions that Cal's presence in her life had raised. The choices ahead of her weren't necessarily going to be easy, she realized. But supported by Cal's love, and guided by her renewed faith, she had the courage to hope for a tomorrow that was even better than the one she'd so carefully planned.

Chapter Twelve

Cal watched Amy's Atlanta-bound plane disappear into the clouds, then turned and walked wearily back to his car. The last two days were a blur of images in his sleep-starved brain—his father's face, pale against the stark white of the hospital sheets; the impersonal beeping and blinking of high-tech health care, a sharp contrast to the folksy print of a country doctor that he'd stared at for hours on end in the waiting room between visits to the cardiac intensive-care unit; and Amy, always close by, her quiet presence a balm on his tattered nerves.

A wave of tenderness swept over him as he recalled her concerned eyes, soft with sympathy and shared pain, which had made him feel less alone and afraid; her delicate hand entwined with his, the touch of her slender fingers giving him strength; her tired face, relaxed in sleep when she'd drifted off during their middle-of-the-night vigils, the shadows under her eyes offering a mute testament to her empathy and worry. He'd tried to convince her to go home with Gram and get some rest, but she had categorically refused. Her steadfast presence had meant more to him than he could ever say—and reaffirmed for him how much he wanted her to be a permanent part of his life.

Unfortunately, he'd had no opportunity to tell her that, he thought ruefully, fingering the small, square box in his pocket. The ring that he had hoped she would now be wearing still lay nestled on its velvet cushion. But not for long, he resolved. His first priority when he returned to Atlanta was to put the ring where it belonged—on the third finger of her left hand.

The timing on his other piece of unfinished business—breaking the news about his career shift to his father—was less clear. As he parked in the hospital lot and made his way to the older man's room—a regular room now, not cardiac intensive care, thank God—he prayed for guidance on how and when to broach the subject.

When he reached the doorway, he paused to study his father, whose gaze was fixed on something outside the window. The lines of pain in his face had eased, and his color was much better, Cal noted with relief. He seemed to be resting comfortably, though it was odd to see him in a prone position. While his father had always moved at a slower, more methodical pace than Gram, he was always busy doing something—usually for other people. Only in recent years had he allowed himself the luxury of time for himself, to read or go for walks or take in an occasional movie or sports event. Through all of Cal's growing-up years, his father had always been a quiet, dependable figure who put his family above all else. Only as an adult had Cal come to fully appreciate the extent of the sacrifices his father had made to give his only son a good education and a better life.

As if sensing his presence, the older man turned and smiled. "Hello, Cal."

Cal swallowed past the lump in this throat. "Hi, Dad."

"Amy get off okay?"

"She's almost back to Atlanta by now." Cal moved toward the bed and dropped into the chair beside it, stretching his long legs out in front of him.

"Nice girl."

"Yeah."

"You look tired, son."

"It's been a tough few days."

"I'm sure sorry to put you and your grandmother through all this."

"It's not your fault, Dad."

The older man sighed. "I suppose not. But I don't like just lying around. I have things to do."

"They'll wait. The most important thing you can do right now is rest."

"Can't say that's ever appealed to me much. I like to keep busy. But I guess the Lord has His reasons for things." He hesitated and glanced down, picking at the white blanket that covered his slight form, a frown creasing his brow. When he spoke again, he seemed to be choosing his words carefully. "Fact is, I've had a lot of time to think during the past few days. About things I've put off coming to terms with for too long. I'm grateful that I came through this so well, but it sure was a wake-up call. Reminded me I had some unfinished business."

Cal looked at him curiously. "What do you mean?"

The older man sighed. "I realized something, lying here in this hospital, Cal. I'm a selfish man."

Cal frowned and straightened up. "That's ridiculous,

Dad. You're one of the most *unselfish* people I know. All those years you sacrificed for me, put my future above everything… How can you say that?''

''Because it's true. I *am* selfish, and it's been weighing heavily on my mind. I should have said something to you years ago, but I just couldn't get the words out. Took a heart attack for me to realize how wrong I've been, and to be grateful for having a second chance to make things right.''

''What are you talking about?''

The older man fixed his gaze on Cal and took a deep breath. ''Here it is in a nutshell, son. I always knew you loved the mountains. Loved them in a way I never did. You're like your grandmother, born with the mountain mist in your veins. I could see the joy in your eyes when you came back, and the pain every time you had to leave. But I ignored it. I wanted you to have a better life, and in my mind that meant a good job in the city. And you've done me proud on that score, son. So proud that I didn't want to give up bragging rights. And too proud to do the right thing. Which is to tell you that I love you, and that if your idea of success is different than mine, you need to follow your heart and do what's right for you without worrying about disappointing me. I don't want you to look back at the end of your life and discover that you've lived someone else's dream. You're a fine man, Cal, and you deserve to follow your own dream, whatever that is. Because more than anything else, I want you to be happy.''

Cal stared at his father, his vision blurring as his eyes slowly misted with tears. He'd always loved and admired the man who'd given him life, but now his father had given him the most precious gift of all. Freedom. Freedom to pursue his own vision of happiness without worrying about disappointing the man who meant so much to him. He felt as if a great burden had been lifted from his shoulders.

"I stand by what I said earlier, Dad," Cal said in a choked voice. "You're still the most unselfish man I've ever met."

His father's own eyes looked suspiciously moist as he reached over and clasped Cal's hand. "I'm glad you still feel that way, son. But I should have done this years ago."

"I've had a good career in Atlanta, Dad. I've learned a lot. The time wasn't wasted."

"But you're coming home now, aren't you?" It was more statement than question.

Cal nodded slowly. "Yes. As a matter of fact, I'd already made that decision. I was just waiting for the right time to tell you."

His father smiled gently. "I guess my timing was pretty good, then. Can I ask you something else?"

"Of course."

"I don't mean to pry, but Amy sure is a nice girl, and I wondered... Will you be coming back alone?"

A hopeful smile touched the corners of Cal's mouth and his eyes grew tender. "Not if I can help it, Dad."

As the doorbell rang, Amy glanced at the clock and smiled. Seven o'clock on the dot. Punctuality was just one of Cal's many admirable qualities, as well as a reflection of the solid dependability she had come to count on in him.

She glanced in the mirror and adjusted a stray strand of hair, smoothed down her pencil-slim black skirt and took a deep breath. Though Cal had returned from the mountains two days ago and they'd spoken frequently by phone, there'd been no opportunity to get together. And for her, like Cal, phone conversations just weren't cutting it anymore.

She opened the door eagerly, but before she could say a word she found herself pulled into his arms as his lips hungrily claimed hers. Though momentarily surprised by his ardent greeting, she didn't object. She felt need in his kiss, as well as fire, and she returned it fully. When he at last lifted his head, he kept his arms looped around her waist and gave her a smoky, intimate smile.

"Hi," he said huskily.

"Hi, yourself," she replied breathlessly. "I think I like this greeting much better than a mere 'hello.'"

He chuckled. "Sorry. I got a little carried away. In case you haven't figured it out, I missed you."

Her gaze softened. "I missed you, too, Cal. How's your dad?"

"Improving every day. But it will take time."

She reached up and caressed his weary face. "You look exhausted."

He passed off her comment with a shrug. "I've been more tired. Like when I was cramming for the bar exam. But I was younger then, too," he added, his lips tipping up into a rueful grin.

Amy stepped out of his arms and took his hand. "Come on in. I have some wine chilling, and you look like you could use some. I thought we might have a glass before we went to dinner."

"That sounds great."

By the time Amy returned with two glasses, Cal was settled comfortably on the couch. A white envelope lay on the glass-topped coffee table, and she looked at him curiously as she handed him a glass and sat beside him.

"What's that?"

He didn't answer immediately. Instead, he took a slow sip of his wine, willing his pulse and respiration to behave. Now that the moment was upon him, he was filled with doubts. So much of his future depended on what transpired in this room in the next few minutes, and he was suddenly afraid. Afraid to ask the question. Afraid to hear the answer. Afraid that all along he'd been reading more into Amy's feelings than was actually there. But he'd come too far now to let fear stop him, so he took a deep breath, placed his wineglass carefully on the table and picked up the envelope.

"Pictures. I wanted to show you this place in person, but the best-laid plans and all that…"

As he opened the envelope, Amy suddenly found her own pulse skyrocketing. Cal was not a man who got rattled easily, but he was definitely nervous now—and doing his best to hide it. She could sense it in the almost imperceptible tremor that ran through his hand, in the way his Adam's apple bobbed convulsively when he swallowed, in the tense line of his jaw. Something big was in the wind.

Cal withdrew several photos from the envelope and handed them to her. "I found this spot while you were filming the story with Gram. Take a look."

Amy slowly examined the four photos, her own hands none too steady. They were all shots of the same beautiful, serene spot, taken from different angles. She paused on the last one, a meadow backed by misty mountains, then glanced up at Cal.

"This is a lovely place, Cal. Is there something special about it, other than its beauty?"

Cal took a deep breath and nodded slowly. "I'd like to buy it. Build a cabin that looks out directly on that view." He nodded toward the photograph in her hand.

Amy glanced back down at the picture. "It would make a great weekend getaway."

He cleared his throat. "Actually, Amy, I'm thinking of making it a permanent getaway."

She sent him a startled gaze. "What do you mean?"

Cal reached into the pocket of his jacket and withdrew a small jeweler's box. Amy's gaze dropped to the square package, then returned to his as her heart stopped, then raced on.

"I wanted to do this right there," he said, again nodding toward the photo, "on the spot where I'd like to build a cabin. I wanted to stand with you under the setting sun, in the midst of God's beautiful creation, and ask you to spend the rest of your life with me. But this will have to do, because I can't wait any longer."

He reached over and took her hand, his intense gaze locked on hers. "If someone had told me the day we met that someday I'd ask you to marry me, I would have thought they were crazy," he admitted, his voice slightly unsteady. "But I think we've both discovered over the past few months that we have a lot more in common than either of us expected. And somewhere along the way I fell in love with you. With your energy and compassion and commitment and sense of humor—all the things that make you who you are. I want to spend the rest of my life listening to your laughter, waking up next to you, watching your eyes glow with passion and enthusiasm and joy and all the other emotions that have enriched my life so much these past few months. I want to build a future with you, Amy. A future that counts for more than dollars or prestige or power, and that will leave a lasting legacy of love for our children and their children.''

He paused and drew a deep breath. "I love you, Amy. And I want to share the rest of my life with you. Would you do me the honor of becoming my wife?''

Amy stared at him in shock. Not because of the proposal. She'd known for some time that they were heading in this direction. Cal had made his feelings for her clear, and she had reciprocated. Over the past several months she had come to accept—and love—him for who he was: a man who had the opportunity for power and wealth, but who found no inherent value in those things. A man who gave generously, and without recognition, to others. A man of both strength and gentleness, who had an infinite capacity to love.

Amy had also learned much from Cal. Thanks to him, she had begun to realign her own priorities, had begun to set some limits on the sacrifices she was willing to make to advance her career. And she had come to realize that she could be content to share a simple life with this very special man, who made her rich in ways that couldn't be measured in dollars and cents. She was more than willing to change her lifestyle.

But Cal wasn't asking her to change her lifestyle. He was asking her to change her *life*. Dramatically. It was one thing to put career in second place and live a simpler life in the city, but to give up her career entirely and move to the mountains—it was too much. Though she was prepared to modify her dreams to accommodate him, she couldn't give them up entirely. Not after all the years she'd spent honing her skills. She'd worked too hard and come too far to just walk away.

Cal saw the emotions sweep over Amy's face—first shock, followed in succession by confusion, disbelief, hurt and, finally, resistance. His gut clenched, and he suddenly found it difficult to breathe. Apparently his closing argument had been unconvincing, though he'd labored over it far longer than any he'd ever prepared for the courtroom. As he watched, her eyes slowly filled with tears, and his throat tightened painfully. He sensed her closing down, slipping away, and he felt powerless to stop it.

Slowly he reached over and gently touched her cheek. "I can't say this is the reaction I was praying for," he admitted, his voice catching. "I always hoped, whenever I finally proposed to the woman I loved, that she'd be happy, not sad."

"Oh, Cal." Amy's voice was choked, as well. "I—I am happy. And honored. But I had no idea you were thinking about making such a radical change in your life. Why didn't you say something about this sooner? At least give me a clue about what you were considering?"

It was a valid question. And she deserved an honest answer. "For one thing, I wasn't sure myself," he said slowly. "I've been struggling with this for a long time. Years, actually. I've never felt at home in the city, Amy. I've tried to make it work, but the only place I'm really happy is in the mountains. I put off this decision longer than I should have, because I didn't want to disappoint Dad. And then, just when I finally got to the point of deciding that I had to follow my heart, you came along. I know I should have shared this with you sooner, but I was afraid of what it would mean to us. I guess I hoped that if I waited long enough, if we fell in love, we'd find a way to make this work.''

"But how?" she asked helplessly. "What would I do? And what about *your* career?"

"I'll still practice law part-time. And I've been offered a job with the National Parks Service as a ranger. I know it doesn't have the prestige of law, but it's what I've always wanted to do. And you've said more than once that you're not altogether happy with your job, that you'd like to find a way to do more feature and issues reporting. I thought you might be open to exploring that."

Amy stared at him incredulously. "In the mountains? My contacts are all here, Cal. In this business, the 'out of sight, out of mind' adage really holds true."

"I'm sure we can find a way to make this work, Amy." There was a pleading tone in his voice, but he didn't care. "I'd stay in the city if I could, but I feel like I'm dying a little more each day in this concrete jungle. And I can't live someone else's dream any longer."

"Yet you want me to live yours."

Her blunt comment jolted him, and he frowned. "That's not true."

"Yes, it is. You're asking me to give up everything and follow *your* dream."

"No, I'm not. You're too good at what you do to stop doing it. I'm just asking for some compromises."

"It sounds to me like all the compromises are on my side." The hurt in her eyes had given way to anger, and her voice was taut. She rose and walked across the room, clearly agitated. When she turned to him, two bright spots of color burned in her cheeks and she wrapped her arms around herself in an almost protective gesture. "I thought I knew you pretty well, Cal. But I was wrong. You let me fall in love with you, knowing all along how I felt about my work, knowing that you were thinking of leaving the city, knowing how difficult it would be for me to continue in my profession—in any capacity—in the middle of nowhere. You weren't honest with me, and that was wrong."

He couldn't dispute her accusation. He'd always known that withholding that vital piece of information from Amy was a calculated risk, and now he realized just how serious a mistake he had made. Slowly he rose and walked toward her. Her body language clearly said "Back off," and so he stopped a couple of feet away from her.

"I'm sorry," he said quietly. "You're right. I should have shared this with you sooner. I was just so afraid of losing you."

Amy turned away, fighting to keep her tears at bay. She didn't want to cry in front of Cal, didn't want to feel his comforting arms around her. That would make it too easy to give in, to offer to make sacrifices she'd later regret.

"What if I said I'd stay here?"

His quiet voice, touched with desperation, tore at her heart, and she choked back a sob. "After telling me you're dying a little bit more in the city every day, do you really think I could live with myself if I let you do that?"

Amy walked to the window and stared out, oblivious to the city lights twinkling below. Her world was falling apart, and she saw no way to hold it together. Even if they found a way to accommodate each other's needs, the pain would remain. She felt betrayed and used and disillusioned. Love was built on trust, and Cal hadn't trusted her with the greatest secret of his heart. He hadn't shared his dreams. Amy wasn't sure if the outcome would have been any different if he'd opened up to her sooner, but at least they could have talked it through, maybe come to some understanding. As it was, he'd thrown the proposal and announcement on her all at once, linking them inexorably. The implication was clear: If you accept one, you must accept the other. And she couldn't do that.

Slowly she turned back to him. The pain in his eyes almost did her in, but she steeled herself to it, and when she spoke, her voice was surprisingly steady.

"You've made your decision, Cal. Without consulting me. You have your life set up exactly the way you want it, and I'm happy for you. But it's not the life I want. You're asking me to give up my dreams, just like your father did with you. I thought you understood how important my work is to me. You may be able to be a part-time lawyer in the mountains, but I can't be a part-time journalist, at least not doing the kind of stories I want to do. Sure, maybe I could get hired to read the news on a local station. But that's not good enough, Cal. I have more to offer than that."

Cal wanted to pull her into his arms, into a world where only they existed, unencumbered by conflicts and complications. But love didn't happen in a vacuum. And the real world wasn't going to go away. He'd hoped their love would be strong enough to overcome their differences. But he'd been wrong. Wrong to think love could solve all problems, and wrong to expect Amy to so easily accommodate his dreams. Somehow, somewhere along the way, he realized he'd discounted her dreams. He hadn't meant to do that, and her resentment was valid. But one of them had to give, and much as he loved her, he couldn't give any more. He needed to go back to the mountains as badly as he needed air to breathe. The trouble was, he needed Amy, too.

Cal raked his fingers through his hair, silently berating himself for how badly he'd handled the whole situation. When his gaze met hers once again, it was filled with love and apology. "I know I've hurt you, Amy. I should have brought all this up a long time ago. But I was so afraid of losing you. Can we at least talk about it?"

She shook her head. "I don't think we have anything to talk about. There's no way to make this work, Cal."

He looked at her for a moment in silence, and when he spoke, his voice rang with quiet sincerity and an intensity that came right from the soul. "I love you, Amy."

At the simple, heartfelt statement, she drew a ragged breath and turned away, blinking back her tears. "Trust is part of love, Cal. So is understanding. And respect."

Cal looked at Amy's rigid back, realized just how deeply he'd hurt her and knew that there was nothing else he could do at the moment. He walked back to the coffee table and picked up the ring box, weighing it in his hand before slipping it into his pocket.

"I'll call you," he said.

"It might be better if you don't."

The finality in her tone made his stomach clench painfully. He didn't want to leave, not like this, but she was giving him no choice. Slowly he walked toward the door, hoping that she would stop him. But when he looked back, she was still turned away, her posture stiff and unyielding. It was clear to him that this was one problem he couldn't solve by himself. And so, as he let himself out, he turned to a greater power.

Lord, please help me, he prayed silently. *I love Amy. I thought her priorities were changing, that she could be happy in the mountains, but obviously I was wrong. Maybe she can only be happy here, in the city, working in that dog-eat-dog business. But I can't. And I've sacrificed my own needs for so long. Do I have to continue to do that in order to have the woman I love? And wouldn't I eventually resent her if I did? Lord, I don't want to be selfish. Please help us find a way to make this work that doesn't require either of us to give up our dreams. I know that's a large order, but I also believe that nothing is impossible with You. So please, Lord, help me find a solution. Because I don't want to lose this once-in-a-lifetime woman.*

Chapter Thirteen

Amy stared at the photo of the mountain meadow, as she did most mornings while she sipped her tea. It would be pretty there this time of year, she reflected wistfully, with the leaves touched by the russet tones of autumn and the sky most likely a clear, cobalt blue. Almost three months had elapsed since she'd last seen Cal. Three long, lonely months filled with questions and doubts. Over and over she had asked herself if she'd been wrong to turn down his proposal. And always her heart said yes. Called her a fool. Berated her for throwing away the gift of such a special man's love. But the yearnings of her heart were overridden by the strident voice of pride, which wouldn't let her forget his seemingly cavalier dismissal of her dreams. And by logic, which told her that after investing so much time and energy in her career, she couldn't change course midstream. And by hurt. Cal's unwillingness to trust her with his own dreams still stung. And finally by fear. Fear that kept her clinging tightly to the lifeline of her job, which, as she knew, played far too large a role in helping define her life and give it value.

Amy fingered the photo, then picked up the only other physical evidence of Cal's presence in her life—the card that had been attached to the flowers he'd sent after their first date. Four photos and a tiny florist card. That was it. There were no other lingering reminders of Cal in her life.

Except for the memories.

Ah, the memories. Of their initial, unfriendly meeting on the courthouse steps. Of their first "date," strained in the beginning, then cordial. Of their warm and friendly encounter at Saint Vincent's. Of her emergency room visit, and Cal's touching care and concern. Of their trip to the mountains, when they had at last acknowledged their growing feelings for each other. Of the subsequent development of their romance and the glow it had added to her life. And finally, of their painful and heart-wrenching breakup.

Amy sighed and glanced at the phone, knowing that she had only to pick up the receiver and dial Cal's number to bridge the impasse between them. He'd told her that on one of the many messages he'd left, his mellow voice playing havoc with her tattered emotions. "I'm here if you ever change your mind, Amy," he'd said. "I still love you. I always will. But I won't force the issue. I only want you to come if it's what you want."

His calls had tapered off lately, and she couldn't blame him for cutting back, especially given her total lack of response. He'd made his position clear, laid his feelings on the table for her to accept or reject, and now the ball was in her court.

Trouble was, she didn't know what to do with it.

What she *did* know was that she'd changed over the past few months. She'd begun to find the hustle and noise and impersonal nature of the city less and less appealing. She'd begun to look at her job with an increasingly jaded eye, her earlier disillusionment fed by several less-than-plum assignments that made her realize what a fickle business the daily news game was. More than a few times, she'd found herself wishing for the quiet, serene beauty of the mountains. And always she found herself longing for Cal—for his gentle touch, his caring ways, his ability to make her laugh one moment and send her pulse skyrocketing the next.

Amy had always known that a proposal from Cal would require her to modify her lifestyle. And she'd been prepared to do that. Had, in fact, found that idea more and more appealing. She'd also been more than willing to cut back on work, even if that meant it would take her a little longer to reach her goals. What she *hadn't* been prepared to do was pack up her entire life, move to the mountains and strike out in an entirely new career direction. That kind of change seemed far too abrupt and permanent—and it scared her.

And yet…she missed Cal. Desperately. It was as if the sun had dimmed since he'd left, casting a dark shadow on her world. She'd tried praying about the situation, but so far, no guidance had been offered. She felt in limbo, alone and confused. Even Kate hadn't been much help. Her sister had been sympathetic, of course, and supportive, but Amy knew that Kate didn't really understand. For her, love always came first, no matter the sacrifice. And maybe she was right. Maybe if love didn't come first, it wasn't strong enough to survive the test of time.

Yet she *did* love Cal, Amy cried silently. With all her heart. But couldn't she also love her work? Why did it have to be either/or? She didn't want to give up doing broadcast work that made a difference, that touched and improved people's lives. Like the Appalachia piece. Good, solid reporting that combined feature and issues work in a seamless way that increased awareness about a serious economic problem under the guise of an entertaining personality profile. In fact, that piece had been nominated for a local Emmy. It was a career coup, one she'd always yearned for, and yet she hadn't been able to work up much enthusiasm about it, even with the awards dinner now only hours away. Somehow, without Cal to share it with, the honor lost some of its luster.

With a sigh, Amy rose and emptied the dregs of her tea into the sink. Unfortunately, her doubts and confusion couldn't be so easily washed away, she thought resignedly. Why did life always present such difficult choices? Cal had suggested that the choice didn't have to be that difficult, that she could have both, but she'd denied it. Told him that a move to the mountains would require tremendous compromises on her part. But was that really true? she suddenly wondered. Certainly, it would require *changes*. But a change was only a compromise if it was done to make someone else happy. If freely chosen, it was no longer a compromise.

Amy frowned as she considered that new insight, which put a different slant on the whole situation. Maybe, if she approached it from that perspective, she might be able to find a way to work things out.

It was certainly worth some deliberation, she resolved, as she slung her purse over her shoulder and headed out the door. Because the thought of spending the rest of her life without Cal was even more scary than making a major career change.

"And the winner is...Amy Winters, for 'Appalachia: A World Apart.'"

The ballroom erupted in applause, and Amy let her breath out slowly. She'd done it! She'd actually done it! The coveted Emmy was hers. Okay, so the presenter had said her name wrong, adding an *s* to Winter. What did he know? She was just one more name on a long list to him. As she was to most of the people in the room, she thought, as she rose and made her way to the front.

Amy took the statuette, stepped to the microphone and looked out on the sea of mostly unfamiliar faces. The room was filled with strangers who didn't really care about how much this honor meant to her, she realized, who wouldn't care, in fact, if she got hit by a car while going home tonight. The people who did and would care, and the one face that meant the most to her, were absent. And without those people to share this moment with, the victory was less sweet, she acknowledged with a poignant pang.

As these realizations swept over her, she took a deep breath and forced herself to concentrate on remembering the short speech she'd prepared in case she won.

"As all of you know, the Emmy is one of the highest honors in our profession. So I'm deeply grateful to have been chosen for this award. At the same time, I'm also grateful to have the opportunity to work on stories like this, which have the potential to make life better for so many people. That's the real reward in this business. I think we often get so involved in the day-to-day reporting that we lose sight of the bigger picture, of the tremendous potential for good that our medium offers. And I think it's our responsibility to exploit that potential whenever possible.''

Amy paused. The presenter was fidgeting with a piece of paper, clearly eager to move on to the next award. The audience members looked slightly bored, their eyes glazed by too many speeches and too much wine. At least the bigwigs from her station were smiling at her politely from their table in front. But only because the Emmy would generate more viewers for their station and thereby increase commercial revenues, she concluded cynically.

Suddenly Amy thought of Tony Jackson in Knoxville. There was a man she could admire. His Christian station was in business for the message, not the money. He was committed to doing good work that made a difference in people's lives. The kind of work she liked to do. To him, the money was secondary.

As Amy quickly wrapped up her comments and returned to her table, she felt as if a burden had been lifted from her shoulders. In an instant her doubts and confusion were resolved, and the solution to her dilemma had become clear.

She looked at the statuette in her hand. It was a career milestone, certainly. But more importantly, it was a turning point. Because now she knew exactly what she was going to do.

Cal propped one shoulder against the porch railing and took a sip of his coffee. Autumn was one of his favorite times in the mountains, and he breathed deeply of the fresh, clean scent. There was a nip in the early-November air, and the morning mist still hung over the field in front of the cabin, giving the scene an ethereal beauty. The leaves were a blaze of color on the hillsides, scarlets and oranges and yellows intermingled on a green background, creating a colorful tapestry.

He turned his gaze to the cabin and let it move slowly over the golden logs, still fresh and raw. He'd only moved in a few days ago, but already it felt like home. His part-time law practice was going well, and his job as a ranger was everything he'd hoped it would be. Best of all, he had plenty of opportunity to enjoy the mountains he loved.

Cal knew he was blessed. True, he'd spent a lot of years away from this place, but he'd done good, worthwhile work and, in the end, his time in the city had bought him his dream. He'd invested just about every penny he'd saved in this land and the cabin, but it had been worth it. His needs were simple. And he already had everything he wanted.

Almost.

Cal sighed. His separation from Amy hadn't dimmed his love for her, nor had it eased the ache in his heart. He longed for her with an intensity that produced an almost physical pain. He'd replayed their last conversation over and over in his mind, and each time he felt a renewed pang of regret. She had been right to be deeply hurt by his error of omission. He *should* have told her about his dreams much sooner, just as she'd pointed out. And he *had* discounted *her* dreams. He'd placed her in a position of choosing him or her career, assuming that if she loved him enough, she'd be willing to follow him to the mountains. But he now realized just what a sacrifice he'd asked of her. He didn't doubt her love. She'd demonstrated it to him on every level. And she'd been honest in her feelings and about her priorities. He'd simply chosen to overlook a few key things.

Such as her talent. And her independence. And all the hard work she'd put into her career. And just how difficult it would be for her to continue doing the work she loved in such a remote location.

Bottom line, he'd made some bad mistakes.

He'd also realized something else during these past three months. Much as he loved the mountains, much as they filled a real need in his soul, they couldn't take the place of Amy's love. And so he'd reached a decision. It wasn't the ideal solution from his standpoint, but at least it might be a way around the impasse they seemed to have reached.

Cal took another sip of coffee as he listened to the sound of the nearby stream. It always reminded him of the day he and Amy had hiked to the waterfall, when they'd first acknowledged their feelings for one another. In his mind he could see her just as she'd looked on that day, her eyes tender and filled with longing. He recalled the breathless excitement of their first kiss and remembered the feel of her soft, yielding body in his arms. A surge of desire shot through him, and he steadied his cup with both hands as he drew a deep breath. He'd thought by now that the intensity of his feelings would subside, that the attraction would wane, but just the opposite had occurred. She filled every waking thought, not to mention his dreams, and his need for her grew day by day.

Cal stared out over the meadow, and for just a moment he could almost see her walking up the gravel road to his house, out of the mist, her hair caressed by the gentle breeze, striding with that long, loose-limbed grace that was so much a part of her. It was a scene he imagined every day. Except...

Cal frowned and straightened up. He *wasn't* imagining it! Amy *was* walking up his drive! His heart stopped, then raced on, and he reached out to the support beam, grasping it with a white-knuckled grip. Dear Lord, was he going crazy? Or could this be real?

She didn't seem to be aware of his presence, half-hidden as he was by the morning shadows under the porch, until she was less than twenty feet away. When their gazes did connect, her step faltered and she stopped.

"Amy?" The word came out hoarsely, half question, half incredulous statement.

Slowly she moved forward again, until she was only a few feet away. "Hello, Cal. I hope you don't mind an early-morning visitor." Her words were choppy, and there was a touch of uncertainty in her voice.

His first instinct was to reach out and pull her into his arms, but he hadn't heard from her in three months and he wasn't about to make another mistake by jumping to conclusions. So, with great effort, he restrained himself. "What are you doing here?" he asked cautiously.

Amy tried to smile, but couldn't quite pull it off. "Applying for a job."

He gave her blank look. "What?"

Amy hadn't been sure what reaction to expect from Cal after all this time, but she'd hoped at least for warmth. Maybe more. Instead, he seemed distant. But she wasn't turning around now, even if her stomach was tied in knots and her legs were shaking so badly she was afraid they wouldn't support her weight.

"Is there somewhere we can sit?"

"Sit?" he repeated, still trying to decipher her last statement.

"You know—that thing you do with chairs." Maybe if she tried to lighten the atmosphere a bit he'd loosen up, she thought in desperation.

"Oh…sure. I've only been in here a few days, but I do have a kitchen set." He pushed the door open, and nodded her inside.

Amy had only a fleeting impression of golden log walls, hardwood floors and vast windows as Cal led her to the back of the cabin. "Would you like some tea?" His tone was polite, but still cautious.

"Yes. If you don't mind."

Cal turned away to fill the kettle, willing his erratic pulse to stabilize. He needed a moment to compose himself, plan his course of action now that the woman he loved was actually in his home. Because he didn't want to lose her again. *Couldn't* lose her again.

Amy stared at Cal's broad back as he made her tea, and once more her courage threatened to desert her. What right did she have to barge in here after three months and expect to be greeted with open arms when she hadn't even returned any of his countless calls? What right did she have to think he still felt the same way about her? And what if he *didn't?* Her stomach plummeted to her toes, and she suddenly felt dizzy. She probably should have taken time to eat breakfast, she realized. Especially since she'd skipped lunch yesterday and barely picked at her dinner. But she'd been so anxious to get here. Now she was paying the price. She closed her eyes and willed the world to stop tilting.

"Amy?"

At the sound of Cal's concerned voice, her eyelids flickered open. He was bending down toward her, only inches away, and she wanted to reach out and touch his dear face, smooth away the twin furrows of worry in his brow. But she forced her hands to remain motionless on the table.

"Are you all right? What's the matter?"

"I'm fine." Her voice seemed to come from a distance and sounded faint even to her ears.

"You're not fine. You're pale as a ghost. Are you sick?"

"No." With a triumph of will over body, she forced the world to right itself. But she couldn't do anything about the tremors that ran through her hands.

He hesitated a moment, then sat down across from her, his own hands tightly gripping his mug. He was clearly waiting for her to speak, so she took a deep breath and plunged in.

"Gram told me where to find you. I parked down on the road and walked up because I needed time to gather my courage."

He eyed her warily. "For what?"

She reached into her purse, withdrew a long white envelope with his name on it and laid it on the table. "For this." She took a deep breath a pushed it toward him. "Go ahead and open it."

He gazed at her for a moment, then reached for the envelope and withdrew the contents. The cover letter was addressed formally, and seemed to be a standard job application. He frowned and flipped to the second page. The word *position* was in bold letters, followed by the word *wife*. The next line read, ''Top ten reasons why candidate would excel at this job.''

Cal scanned the list, a tender smile quirking his lips as he perused it.

10. Good sense of humor
9. Excellent conversationalist
8. Willing to learn how to bake Gram's fabulous biscuits and apple pie—if she is available for lessons
7. Loves children
6. Likes the way you kiss
5. Considers you her hero
4. Is tired of city life
3. Looks forward to living in the mountains
2. Loves you with all her heart
1. Never does anything halfway

The words blurred in front of his eyes when he reached the end of the list, and he blinked a few times before he looked at her. He wanted to accept what she offered at face value, forget about her dreams, but he couldn't. He'd made that mistake once, and he wasn't going to do it again.

''What about your career?''

''I'm resigning from the station in Atlanta.''

He shook his head. ''I can't ask you to do that. I was wrong to suggest it in the first place.''

She reached over and laid her hand on his, her gaze intense and compelling, her voice firm. ''I'm resigning, Cal. No matter what happens between us today, I'm moving on. I spent the past couple of days with Tony Jackson in Knoxville, and he's offered me a job. I believe in what he's doing, and he's willing to let me work on the kinds of stories I like best. It's an ideal arrangement.''

Cal couldn't doubt the sincerity in her eyes, knew he shouldn't press his luck, but he had to be sure. "And what about your dreams of a network feature spot?"

Amy shrugged. "It's funny. I worked toward that goal for a lot of years. Pretty much to the exclusion of all else. In fact, at some point the quest became more important than the goal. And then you came along, and suddenly I began to question a lot of things. It wasn't easy to admit that maybe my priorities were out of whack, that somewhere along the way I'd gotten so caught up in the glamour and prestige and power and money part of the business that I'd lost sight of what really counts—doing good work that can help others. I'm not saying you can't do that in a network spot, but I can do it a lot more easily with far fewer personal and ethical sacrifices at Tony's station. And the icing on the cake is that it gives me you, too. Assuming, that is, that you—that you still want me," she finished, her voice faltering.

He studied her in silence for a moment. Then, instead of responding, he rose and retrieved a small envelope from the counter. It was stamped and addressed to her, she noted, as he placed it in front of her. "I was going to mail this today. Open it."

She hesitated, then did as he asked. With her heart pounding, she quickly scanned the single sheet of paper.

My dearest Amy,
Over the past few weeks, as I've settled into the life I always dreamed of, I've discovered one very important thing. Much as I love living in the mountains, my life feels incomplete. I know now that I can never be truly happy and content here without you by my

side. Your love added so much joy and light to my days. Without you, I feel only half-alive.

I know that I hurt you deeply by not sharing my dreams with you. I was wrong to hold them back. Whatever the consequences, I should have told you from the beginning what was in my heart. I only hope you can find it in your own heart to forgive me.

I also know I hurt you by discounting your dreams. Again, I was wrong. You have every right—perhaps even an obligation—to fully develop and use your exceptional talent. But I placed the burden on you to figure out how to do that here in the mountains.

You were right when you said that all the compromises in my original proposal would be on your side. And that's not fair. So I have an idea that may allow us both to pursue our dreams. What if we divided our time between the city and the mountains? Could we find a way to make that work?

What it comes down to, Amy, is this. I love you. And I don't want to spend the rest of my life without you. I'll work with you to find a solution that is acceptable to both of us. Please…forgive me for hurting you, and say that you'll try. Because I count your presence in my life among my greatest blessings, and I love you with all my heart.

As Amy finished the note, her throat grew tight. Cal did still love her! So much that he was willing to compromise his own dream to accommodate hers. He could have given her no greater gift, or demonstrated his love in no more credible or touching way.

"That offer is still open, Amy," he said quietly.

She looked at him, the love shining in her eyes. "And I'll treasure it always. But this is where I want to stay."

Suddenly he took her hand in a warm clasp, then stood and pulled her to her feet. "Come with me," he said huskily.

They retraced their steps through the house to the porch, which was now bathed in golden morning light. He could feel her trembling as he reached over to frame her delicate face with his powerful hands, his thumbs gently brushing her cheeks. He was none too steady himself as he gazed into her beautiful, deep green eyes, misty now, but filled with unmistakable love and tenderness. As his heart overflowed with joy, he suddenly knew that this would always stand apart in his memory as one of the shining, defining moments of his life. A moment he would look back on, in the twilight of their lives, as representative of the dawn of a new day for both of them.

For several seconds they simply gazed at each other, savoring the wonder of their love, filled with hope and joy and the promise of a bright tomorrow. When Cal finally spoke, the catch in his voice tugged at Amy's heart and sent a rush of tenderness through her.

"Three months ago, I planned to bring you to this meadow and propose on the spot where I wanted to build my home—our home," he said. "I can't promise you that our life here will always be easy, Amy. It certainly won't be glitzy or glamorous. But I can promise you that while our home won't be filled with silver and gold, it *will* be filled with something far more precious—love and friendship and laughter. And I promise you this, too. From this day forward, I will always share with you the secrets of my heart and my dreams. And I'll do everything I can do to help make yours come true. Because I love you with all my heart. Will you marry me?''

Amy's eyes filled with tears, and when she spoke her voice was choked with emotion. ''Oh, Cal! You've already made my greatest dream come true. You've given me your love. And you've also helped me find a new life grounded in faith, with a clear sense of what truly matters. For that gift alone, I'll be forever grateful.''

His heart soared with joy and his lips curved into a smile as he reached over to gently wipe away a wayward tear that had slipped down her cheek. ''Is that a yes?''

A tremulous smile, filled with wonder and anticipation and unbridled joy, lit her face. ''That is most definitely a yes,'' she confirmed.

And as he pulled her into his arms to seal their engagement in the most traditional of ways, Amy said a silent prayer of thanks. For this wonderful man. For this wonderful place. And for a future that she now knew, with absolute certainty, was going to be even more wonderful than the one she had planned.

* * * * *

Dear Reader,

As I write this letter, summer is drawing to a close. Soon I'll put away my gardening tools while the world takes time to rest and renew itself beneath a blanket of snow. I will miss my garden and my woodland retreat, but always I am comforted by the hope and promise of spring.

The hours I spend in my garden are among my most joyous—and most contemplative. And I have learned much—about flowers and about life. Sometimes plants need space so they can grow and fully develop. Sometimes they become weak or vulnerable and do best when close together so that they can prop each other up. Water must be dispensed in just the right proportion— too much, they drown; not enough, they shrivel and die.

Like a garden, love is a balancing act. We must learn when to get close—and when to back off. We must learn how much affection is enough—and how much is smothering. And while we sometimes make mistakes, true love, like a flower, is tenacious. It struggles to survive, even under difficult conditions. Because real love never ends.

In this book, Cal and Amy learn the balancing act of love. They also learn that love sometimes involves difficult choices. But as they ultimately discover, those choices aren't really compromises when willingly made. In fact, love often spurs a healthy realignment of priorities and offers new hope for a better tomorrow, even in times of trouble.

Through all your winter days, may the promise of spring remain in your heart.

Irene Hannon

REQUEST YOUR FREE BOOKS!

2 FREE INSPIRATIONAL NOVELS
PLUS 2
FREE
MYSTERY GIFTS

Love Inspired.

YES! Please send me 2 FREE Love Inspired® novels and my 2 FREE mystery gifts. After receiving them, if I don't wish to receive any more books, I can return the shipping statement marked "cancel." If I don't cancel, I will receive 4 brand-new novels every month and be billed just $3.99 per book in the U.S., or $4.74 per book in Canada, plus 25¢ shipping and handling per book and applicable taxes, if any*. That's a savings of at least 20% off the cover price! I understand that accepting the 2 free books and gifts places me under no obligation to buy anything. I can always return a shipment and cancel at any time. Even if I never buy another book from Steeple Hill, the two free books and gifts are mine to keep forever.

113 IDN EF26 313 IDN EF27

Name _____ (PLEASE PRINT) _____

Address _____ Apt. _____

City _____ State/Prov. _____ Zip/Postal Code _____

Signature (if under 18, a parent or guardian must sign) _____

Order online at www.LoveInspiredBooks.com

Or mail to Steeple Hill Reader Service™:

IN U.S.A.
P.O. Box 1867
Buffalo, NY
14240-1867

IN CANADA
P.O. Box 609
Fort Erie, Ontario
L2A 5X3

Not valid to current Love Inspired subscribers.

Want to try two free books from another series?
Call 1-800-873-8635 or visit www.morefreebooks.com

* Terms and prices subject to change without notice. NY residents add applicable sales tax. Canadian residents will be charged applicable provincial taxes and GST. This offer is limited to one order per household. All orders subject to approval. Credit or debit balances in a customer's account(s) may be offset by any other outstanding balance owed by or to the customer. Please allow 4 to 6 weeks for delivery.

LIREG06

Love Inspired.

CLASSICS

TITLES AVAILABLE NEXT MONTH

Don't miss these stories in November

THE BEST CHRISTMAS EVER
AND
A MOTHER'S LOVE
by Cheryl Wolverton

Single parents learn that it's never too late for
love in these memorable stories.

FAITHFULLY YOURS
AND
SWEET CHARITY
by Lois Richer

Love conquers all in two classic romances
set in the American heartland.